THE
ECHO
MAN

THE ECHO MAN

A NOVEL

SAM HOLLAND

CROOKED
LANE

NEW YORK

Copyright © 2022 by Sam Holland

Published in the United States by Crooked Lane Books, an imprint of The Quick Brown Fox & Company LLC.

Crooked Lane Books and its logo are trademarks of The Quick Brown Fox & Company LLC.

Library of Congress Catalog-in-Publication data available upon request.

ISBN (hardcover): 978-1-64385-991-0
ISBN (ebook): 978-1-64385-992-7

Cover design by Russell Cobb

Printed in the United States.

www.crookedlanebooks.com

Crooked Lane Books
34 West 27th St., 10th Floor
New York, NY 10001

First Edition: April 2022

10 9 8 7 6 5 4 3 2 1

For Ed

THE ECHO MAN

HAVING ALWAYS BEEN fascinated with the dark and macabre, Sam Holland has a love of reading that was forged in the library through Stephen King, Dean Koontz, and James Herbert. A self-confessed serial killer nerd, Holland studied psychology at university, then spent the next few years working in Human Resources, before quitting for a full-time career in writing. *The Echo Man* is the result.

Sam can be found on Twitter and Instagram at @samhollandbooks.

He who fights with monsters might take care lest he thereby become a monster. And when you gaze long into an abyss, the abyss also gazes into you.

Nietzsche, *Beyond Good and Evil*, 1886

PROLOGUE

LEAVES CRUNCH UNDERFOOT. The black closes around him; he exists only in the narrow tunnel of light from the car's headlights. He takes a deep breath in. The forest smells of wet foliage; mud; clear, crisp air. So far it has been as good as he imagined it would be. It's all coming together perfectly.

He's holding a woman, one arm hooked under her knees, the other around her back. She's still fresh, and blood runs out of the stab wounds, down his white plastic trousers. He savors the warmth on his cold hands.

He looks at her fondly for a moment, then heaves her into the trunk. She lands with a heavy thud against the second body, her leg lolling out over the bumper. He pushes it inside.

Everything has to be just right.

He looks at them both, then leans down and undoes the handcuffs. Even in the darkness he can see faint red and black marks on her wrist, made while she had a body responsive enough to bruise. He's pleased: it'll show what he did.

He walks back to the front of the car, opening the passenger side door. He picks up the two implements left in the footwell, taking the cover off one of them. The stainless steel blade of the knife shines, clean and newly sharpened. It's his favorite; he knows it works best for instances like this. Smaller and more precise than the one he used to kill.

He takes both instruments back to the bodies. Stops. Looks at the girls. He's never done this out in the open before, in the dark. He doesn't like to be rushed. But needs must.

He grabs an arm and tugs her half out of the car trunk. He straddles her body, taking a good handful of hair. Blood flows, but he knows what he's doing, it doesn't interfere with his process.

He changes position, pulling the body around so he can get access to the other side. Then he puts the knife down and picks up the other tool. It's bigger, heavier. The weight is reassuring. He does what he needs to do, and then, with a final twist and pull, it's finished.

He stands up, rearranges the bodies, then repeats the action on the second girl. This one is quicker, his technique is better second time round, and after, he pauses, standing back from the car and appraising the scene in the trunk.

It's not perfect. He sighs. It bothers him that he can't complete the tableau properly this time, that none of this is in the correct order, but he wants these to be found.

He shuts the trunk. With the heel of his shoe, he smashes out the right taillight. He walks over to the second vehicle, pulling off the plastic clothing, placing it in another bag to burn later. He climbs in and puts his hand on the ignition key, willing the old car to work. As it splutters into life and he drives away, he looks back at the car. From the outside, nobody can tell what lies within.

Nobody can imagine what horrors are still to come.

PART 1

1

Day 1
Monday

I AM SO FUCKING bored.

The thought darts into her head, intrusive and distracting. She looks in the mirror above the sink. The expression on her face isn't lust or desire—it's boredom. Pure unmitigated boredom.

She's bent over the taps: the soap dispenser in front of her, the hand dryer to the left. She can see the man behind her. The man that's doing a below average job of fucking her in the disabled toilets of the community center, barely fifteen minutes after dropping their children off at school.

Her underwear is around her ankles; her skirt, pulled up to her waist. He has his hand shoved under her bra, kneading her breast like unproofed dough, the other gripping her hip as he thrusts into her.

Ethan? Evan? Whatever, she thinks. She remembers his kid's name is Hayden. He'd said he was in the same class as Alice, pointing toward the throng of indistinguishable children running into the school as the bell rang.

He stood out among the throng of yummy mommies in tight gym gear and hurried career women on their way to work. Short brown hair, a little skinny for her liking, but decent enough. No wedding ring. That was the only sign she needed before making the suggestion. He ignored hers, the platinum band now reflecting in the stark fluorescent lighting.

She cringes as he spasms, coming with a suppressed cry, then slumping against her back. She wriggles out from underneath him and stands, pulling her skirt down, trying to preserve some sort of modesty.

He has his back to her, cleaning himself up. He drops the piece of toilet paper and the condom into the loo, then flushes it.

He refastens his belt before opening the door and peering out nervously.

"Jessica, right? Do you want to . . .?" he asks.

"Just go," she says. He leans over to give her a kiss, but she pulls back.

"Thanks," he mutters awkwardly, closing the door.

She locks it behind him and sits on the toilet. She shakes her head with disbelief, pulling her tights back on.

I'm so fucking bored, she thinks again.

*   *   *

Jess has a shower when she gets home, washing away all traces of Ethan/Evan. She makes a cup of coffee and takes it out to the garden.

It has stopped raining, and the winter's air is cold and biting. She sits on the edge of one of the concrete steps, dressed only in a sweatshirt and jeans, her feet bare, her hair still wet from the shower. She knows she can't stay out here long, but she enjoys the feeling of the cold on her body.

Their garden is large and rambling. Overgrown grass, weeds pushing their way through the gaps in the paving slabs, shrubs no more than twigs. Her husband occasionally makes comments about the mess, but she tells him she likes it this way—nature forging its own path, ignoring regulation or order.

She finishes her coffee and looks down at her feet. The flesh has turned white, her toenails blue. She's started to shiver slightly. It's time to go inside, and she turns her attention to what needs to be done before she picks Alice up from school.

She used to work, but the balance with the school run was a nightmare. She doesn't miss it—she was just as bored then as she is now—but she liked the distraction it gave. Now, there is nothing for her to focus on. Nothing to do.

*   *   *

At school pickup she nervously scours the crowd, but Ethan/Evan is mercifully absent. She hovers at the edge of the playground, ignoring the other moms as they chat, their banalities an anathema to Jess. The door opens and the children bound out, one by one, directed by the teacher toward their mothers.

And then, there's Alice. Her curls are escaping from her hairband as she skips toward Jess, a huge grin on her face, her school bag still massive in comparison to her tiny body. Jess pulls her into a hug, then ushers her toward the car, listening to her chatter about her day.

As she drives, she looks at her daughter in the rearview mirror. It astonishes her how she managed to create this beautiful, confident creature: unselfconscious, lithe, full of energy. The only good thing to come from her, she thinks ruefully. Alice talks about Georgia, about Isabelle, about Ned. Faceless kids Jess has never met.

"What about Hayden?" she throws back to her daughter.

Alice shakes her head. "I don't know him," she replies, and Jess is relieved. The last thing she needs is a forced playdate with the guy.

They get home. Alice rushes off to her toys and Jess gets on with dinner. She's making beef in a red wine sauce tonight, chopping vegetables carefully, sautéing the meat. She hears her husband come in the front door, and Alice runs to greet him. Jess barely looks up until she feels him behind her, kissing the back of her neck.

"Smells good," Patrick murmurs into her hair.

"Me, or dinner?" she asks, and he laughs.

She turns and watches him as he goes into the hallway. He's taking his suit jacket off as he walks, pulling the tie from around his neck. She takes him in objectively.

Patrick's never been slim, but lately his metabolism seems to have been getting the better of him. His shirt strains at the neck, a belly pushes over the waistband of his trousers.

She turns back to the hob. She's not being fair, she knows. He's devoted, compassionate, hard-working. All the Good Husband adjectives. She should be making the most of him, she thinks, pouring a glass of red from the bottle, then transferring the rest into the pan. She should be screwing *him* in public toilets, rather than nameless strangers. Maybe then he wouldn't be so keen to get it elsewhere.

She goes to take a swig from the glass of wine, but her hand is slippery from the cooking and it slips, smashing on the floor.

"Mommy?" she hears Alice shout from the living room.

"It's okay—just dropped something. Don't come in here."

She looks down, scowling, at the spikes of glass on the tiles, the red from the wine flowing slowly outward. One shard is curving from the floor, the sharp tip pointing toward the ceiling. Her feet are bare, shoes and socks unnecessary with their expensive underfloor heating, and she picks up her right foot, placing it down on the fragment. She slowly transfers her weight across. She hears a crack as the piece splinters, then senses the slight pop as her skin breaks and the glass enters the soft tissue.

It feels good.

She watches a slow trickle of blood ebb away from her foot, the bright red mixing with the lighter hue of the wine.

"Jess! What the hell are you doing?"

She feels Patrick's hands on her upper arms. He pulls her away from the mess, pushing her toward a chair. She sits down with a thump. He looks at her, his hands on his hips. She can tell he's angry, but he doesn't want to shout.

"You know better than this," he says, bending down and looking at the wound. "Shit," he mutters under his breath, wincing as he pulls the slice of glass from the fleshy part of her forefoot. "You're going to need stitches."

"I'll sort it," she says. "I'll get Nav to come over."

Patrick stands up and looks at her. He goes to say something, then stops himself. "I'll get dinner finished," he says instead.

She pulls her foot around so she can look. The edges of the cut are straight and precise, but they gape apart, blood flooding from the incision. Patrick passes her a roll of paper towels, and she roughly wraps several around her foot, then hobbles off to the bathroom.

Inside, she locks the door and sits on the closed lid of the toilet. She takes the first aid kit out of the cupboard and opens it up, resting it on the edge of the bath. It's more than your usual household plasters—a collection of bandages, gauzes, tape: everything she might need for situations like this.

She looks at the bottom of her foot again, then sets to work, pushing the sides of the cut together, drying the area around the wound and sticking it as best she can with surgical tape. But it's still oozing blood. Patrick's right: it's going to need stitches, and she picks up her phone, sending a text. A response comes back immediately.

I'm at work, Jess. I'm on nights. Go to the urgent care clinic like a normal person.

She replies: *I'm not a normal person, Nav. You know that. It can wait. When's the earliest you can come round?*

Three small dots appear—he's typing. Then a pause. She knows she pushes their friendship to the limit, but she can't bear to go to another drop-in center. The same questions, over and over again. The same looks, the same suspicion.

Her phone beeps.

Fine. Tomorrow morning. I finish at the hospital at 8.

Then a follow-up: *I can't keep doing this.*

She sighs and puts her phone down, bandaging her foot as best she can. She puts socks on: she needs to hide the injury from Alice.

When she goes back into the kitchen, Patrick and Alice are sitting at the dining table, Patrick starting to serve dinner. She ruffles Alice's hair as she sits down, and her daughter looks up, beaming at her.

"Everything okay?" Patrick asks.

She gives him the response he wants: a smile and a nod. She wonders, not for the first time, what's wrong with her.

* * *

They eat dinner, and Alice tells them about her day at school. It's a ramble of words, an incoherent telling of a story, but they listen, the indulgent parents of a five-year-old only child. Patrick asks her questions at the right points as she babbles away; she doesn't notice any hostility between her parents.

Jess runs her bath and puts her daughter to bed. She reads her a story. Everything is calm. Alice snuggles down under her duvet, and Jess gives her a kiss and a cuddle. Her daughter smells of shampoo and warmth and innocence, and she feels a swell of love in her chest. She is thankful—for the hundredth time—that her daughter is normal.

Patrick comes in after her and says goodnight, turning off the light. Jess waits in the hallway as he closes the door, but he walks past her without a word, going downstairs. She follows him into the kitchen, hovering in the doorway as he takes a beer from the fridge.

"I'm sorry, Patrick," she says, and he nods slowly without looking at her.

He opens the bottle and puts it to his lips, downing a long swig.

"I'm going to London in the morning," he replies. "It's an early start. I'll sleep in the spare room so I don't wake you." He pauses. "I'll set up an appointment with Dr. Crawford."

Without another word, he turns and goes into the living room. She can't stand the thought of another insufferable hour with Dr. Crawford, a woman who doesn't care or understand. She asks Jess questions she can't answer. *"What makes you want to hurt yourself? What do you think will happen if you continue to be this self-destructive?"* Jess recognizes the threat implicit in the seemingly innocent question.

She hears the television turn on and the sound of football. Patrick knows she hates football. He's telling her: Stay away. I don't want to be near you right now.

She doesn't blame him. She doesn't want to be near herself right now, either.

*   *   *

She goes to bed. She watches television in their bedroom, some true-crime documentary, but the overblown drama doesn't provide the distraction from her own life that she hoped it would. After a while she hears Patrick clean his teeth, then close the door to the front bedroom. She wonders if she should go and say goodnight, apologize again, then decides against it. An apology means "Sorry, and I'll try not to do it again." Useless words, when she knows they're not true.

She turns the television off, plunging the room into darkness.

She lies in the black, counting slowly as she breathes in and out. Her daughter is silent next door, and she can't hear any movement from Patrick in the spare bedroom. Slowly she drops off to sleep.

*   *   *

As night takes over, a hand slowly pushes the mail slot open. Liquid is poured through the door into the hallway; it runs across the tiles, soaking the mat. Then something else follows: a lit match.

It falls to the floor, and with a whoosh the fire ignites.

Hampshire Chronicle

July 15, 1994

ANIMAL KILLER STILL AT LARGE—12 CATS KNIFED

A sadistic pet killer is on the rampage, estimated to have killed eight cats and injured a further four in the last two months. Other animals may have also been targeted, the RSPCA claim, citing two dogs and four rabbits that have gone missing in the same time period.

Mother of two, Michelle Smith, says her kids are "traumatized" after they returned home on Friday to find their pet cat, Stimpy, dead and disemboweled on their front porch. Anonymous sources from the police have also shared instances where pets have been found skinned, possibly while they were alive, although this has yet to be confirmed.

The RSPCA and Hampshire Constabulary are working together to find the killer, and ask any members of the public noticing suspicious behavior to call 101.

They advise any pet owners in the area to keep all animals indoors until the offender has been apprehended.

CHAPTER

2

THE GLASS GLOWS red and orange, flames lighting up the windows, turning the inside to black. Smoke claws up the walls, gray fingers reaching skyward.

With an almost silent surge across the carpet, the fire grasps at curtains, furniture—anything in its wake. Glass cracks with the heat, dark wisps creep up the stairs, skulking under doors.

It steals into her nose. The coughing wakes her, the lack of oxygen forcing her to take sharp breaths. Jess opens her eyes. It is nearly pitch black, but she can see a fog lurking at the edges of the ceiling. It hovers, a malingering specter, thick and intimidating. She coughs again, feeling her lungs starting to clog.

Suddenly, through her daze, her consciousness clicks into action. She jumps out of bed, dressed only in her oversized T-shirt, and goes to the door. The handle is cold, and she slowly opens it into the hallway.

The entire first-floor landing is filled with smoke. Instinctively, she drops to her knees, her heart racing as she crawls across the carpet. She glances down the stairs, recoiling from what she sees.

The front door is obscured; the whole of the hallway is filled with flames. A lake of fire licks at the edge of the stairwell. The crackling terrifies her, eclipsing every other sound. And then she realizes. The smoke alarms. She looks upward through the gray, staring at the redundant white discs on the ceiling. Why aren't they going off? Why haven't they woken Patrick or Alice?

The thought of her family boosts her into action. She screams her husband's name over and over, choking, coughing, as she crawls across the hallway floor, feeling the heat of the flames behind her. She pulls the door open to her daughter's room, rushing over and trying to shake Alice awake. The smoke is thicker in here, almost filling the room to the floor. She knows they don't have much time. But Alice doesn't move, her eyes staying closed, her breathing labored.

The porch is below the window in the spare bedroom, where Patrick is sleeping. She looks back, praying her husband has already made his escape. There is no way they can get there. The hallway floor is now a blanket of flames, red and yellow arching to the ceiling. She can feel the heat, the carpet starting to melt under her knees.

Jess kicks the door closed, frantically trying to think of an alternative way out as she pulls her unconscious daughter into her arms. She drops as low as she can to the floor and edges to the window.

It's a two-story drop to the garden. She knows the minute she opens the window, the gust of oxygen will add fuel to the flames, and she peers through the blackening glass. The lawn is below them, but still. With a freezing frost it could be as hard as concrete.

But stay here, and both of them will almost certainly die.

Coughing uncontrollably now, she pushes the window open. The fresh air is soothing to her lungs, but instantly she hears the roar of the fire gain strength behind her.

Awkwardly, Alice still in her arms, she pulls herself up onto the windowsill. Her legs dangle out into nothing. She looks at her daughter's face. She can't tell if Alice is breathing, and panic takes over.

She looks down into the dark.

And jumps.

Her body crumples as she hits the ground, and she collapses onto the cold grass, Alice on top of her. She feels her head hit something hard: the edge of the concrete patio. The adrenaline makes her shake, and she looks up at her house. Every window is lit up, bright red and yellow dancing behind. The living-room bay next to them has smashed, blown outward by the ferocity of the blaze.

She tries to move, but her head spins. She's dizzy, nauseous, and she lies back on the grass, taking deep gulps of air.

She hears sirens, sees flashing blue lights in the road. People arrive. A man dressed in reflective yellow stands next to her, calling for medical assistance on his radio. She sees ladders, her house swarming with motion.

Her daughter is pulled out of her arms. She grabs at air.

"Where are you taking her?" she gasps as she watches Alice being carried away. A paramedic appears at her side.

"Your daughter's safe now. We'll get her to the General—you won't be far behind." Jess feels his hands all over her, checking for injuries. "I'll give you something to take away the pain," he says.

"I don't . . ." she starts, but she's too tired to argue as the needle is thrust into her arm.

A fireman stands over her.

"Who else is in the house?" he shouts.

"Patrick," she mutters. "My husband. Front bedroom."

The message is relayed, and she lies back on the grass. The paramedic is trying to talk to her, but she can't hear him. She thinks of nothing but her daughter.

A mask is put over her face, a rigid collar fastened around her neck.

She feels the grass in her hair, the damp seeping into her T-shirt. The heat from the fire is replaced by a cold wind as they roll her one way, then the other, onto a stretcher.

Her brain can't catch up with what just happened: the fire, the speed with which it spread, the flames destroying her house. She wants Patrick. Every part of her wills Alice to be okay. Take me, she thinks. Take everything from me, except my daughter.

The emotion overwhelms her, and she starts sobbing, her tears making clean lines in the black soot on her face. She is carried into an ambulance. A paramedic stays next to her as they head toward the hospital, sirens blaring, and he takes one of her hands in his.

"We'll be there soon," he says. His face is kind. Understanding. "Do you need anything else for the pain?"

"No," she whispers. Everything is numb, she thinks. Her whole world is numb.

3

Day 2
Tuesday

THE POLICE OFFICER standing at the edge of the cordon looks pale. The day is freezing: the grass crisp with cold, puddles frozen solid. She climbs out of the car. Her breath blows out in smoky plumes; she stamps her feet, trying to keep warm.

Behind her, DS Noah Deakin finishes his cigarette and discards it, stubbing it out with the toe of his shoe.

"Ready?" she asks him, and he nods, his mouth already set in a grim line.

A crime scene guard presents them with the head-to-toe white suits, and they pull them on, wobbling awkwardly on one leg and then the other, putting plastic covers over their shoes and a double layer of gloves on their hands.

They push under the tape and walk down the path, negotiating their way across the stepping plates put there by the scene of crime officers already flooding the woods. In the dim light they seem otherworldly, ghostly figures moving between the trees. She sees the occasional flash of a camera, documenting the scene.

The car was found at five AM. A man walking his dog noticed bloody lines on the bodywork and a puddle of something red by the trunk. The call woke her soon after that, jerking her rudely out of the darkness. She'd dressed quickly, picking up Noah on the way.

She sees the car. She recognizes the make—a Ford Galaxy, beloved by many a mother on the school run. It's pale blue, old, and slightly grubby. The back light is smashed, small fragments of red plastic on the ground. The trunk is open, a tall figure peering inside.

Large floodlights on metal frames have been put up around the car, the sudden brightness making her squint.

The man notices them and stands up, stretching out his back.

"Detectives," he says. She recognizes his voice and posture—straight, tall, middle class.

"Dr. Ross," she replies. "I'm DCI Cara Elliott; this is DS Deakin."

"Detective Chief Inspector. They've sent the big guns in." He sighs, turning back to the car. "What a fucking mess this is."

He stands back, allowing them to see inside. They both recoil, Cara's hand going to her mouth. She knew what was coming, but seeing it in person is still shocking. It's inhuman.

"Fuck," she hears Noah mutter next to her, his voice guttural and hoarse.

She looks back to the trunk, trying to stay dispassionate. A blanket has been pulled aside, revealing two dead bodies. She assumes them to be women. Their clothes are torn, tights ripped, bare legs.

There is blood everywhere. Smudges and smears across the skin, clothes soaked, dyed red.

"Any idea about cause of death?" she asks.

"Clear evidence of penetrating wounds on both girls," the pathologist says. "Although I'll have to get them back to the mortuary to ascertain definitive COD. Time of death, between three to eight hours, but don't quote me on it. Rigor has set in; bodies are still fairly warm."

"And when will we get the post back?"

Dr. Ross surveys the car. "Probably not before tomorrow. Give us twenty-four hours before you start nagging."

He passes Cara an evidence bag, and she holds it up to the light. Two driving licenses are inside. She looks at their faces in the photos. They're young, around twenty years old, with long brown hair, innocent smiles. Unrecognizable from what's in front of her now. "Found in their pockets along with quite a bit of cash," Dr. Ross adds.

"Not a robbery, then."

"Not for me to say, Detective Chief Inspector."

Deakin takes the evidence bag from her and makes a note of the two names on the driving licenses.

Cara forces herself to look back to the trunk. The bodies are heaped on top of one another, abandoned with no thought for the victims. Plus the—

She shakes her head, trying to get what she's seeing out of her mind. Who would do such a thing? Whoever it was had no boundaries, no hesitation. He—and she assumes it was a he—was devoid of compassion.

Blood has run out of the car, pooling in the mud below. She notices two deep ridges running across the width of the bumper.

"What do you make of these?" Cara asks Ross, pointing toward them. They are straight, about six inches long.

"My guess?" Ross makes a downward chopping motion with his arm, and Cara shudders. "Forceful enough to break through the black plastic. SOCO will take impressions when I'm done."

Cara's had enough. She moves away from the trunk and opens the door to look in the back. There's blood pooled on the seats, splatters and drips up the sides of the car's interior and across the roof. She can see what she assumes to be vomit in the footwell, and even through her mask, the car smells of urine and sweat. Of fear.

She clears her throat. She has a job to do. "Killed in here?" she directs backward at Deakin, who looks over her shoulder.

"Maybe. Did you see the marks on their wrists? Obviously restrained. He came prepared."

They look in the front, opening the glovebox, peering under the seats. She wants to see for herself, although Cara knows the crime scene techs will do a full sweep, check for anything left behind: biologicals, fingerprints, trace evidence. But there's nothing obvious here.

Cara nods a goodbye toward Ross, and they walk back down the track. Deakin holds the tape as Cara ducks under it. They pull off their suits, and she bleeps the car open. They climb inside, relieved to get some respite from the freezing cold.

Deakin lights a cigarette almost immediately and takes a long drag. He opens a window and blows smoke out into the cold air. She presses her fingers against her mouth, thinking, watching the SOCOs move around the scene.

Two women dead—no more than girls. She remembers their clothes: glittery tops, tights, and short skirts.

"On a night out?" she says.

"On a Monday?" He takes another drag, and she looks at him. Noah Deakin is the sort of person that smokes as if he's been doing so since birth. And it fits with his overall look. Today he's wearing a slim-fitting shirt, tie loosely done up, dark jeans. On anyone else it would look scruffy; on Deakin it's effortlessly cool.

"Students?" Cara suggests.

"But what are they doing out here?"

They're in the middle of nowhere, more than ten miles from the closest town.

"They're walking home, he picks them up, abducts them?" she replies.

She eyes his cigarette enviously. She's seen dead bodies before, sure, but nothing like this. What must have been going through their minds as he drove them here? As he handcuffed them? They must have been terrified.

Cara's phone rings, interrupting her chain of thought. She puts it on speaker.

"Boss? Are you at the scene?" The voice of their DC—a diligent, quiet guy by the name of Toby Shenton—fills the car.

"We're here. Anything back on the plates?" Cara asks him.

"Reported stolen last night," he says, and Cara sighs. "They're bringing the owner in for questioning."

"Good. Noah's sending you the names of the victims now. I want to know everything about them by the time we get to the station."

"You don't want me to—" he stutters, and Cara interrupts him.

"No, don't worry, Toby. I don't want you to notify the families. Leave that to us." Next to her Noah is rolling his eyes. She smiles indulgently. "Just do the background."

"Boss . . ." Shenton hesitates again. "Is it true, what they're saying?"

Cara frowns. It was bound to get out. Details about a double murder like this, so unique, so graphic, would find their way around the Major Crimes team in minutes, as much as they might try to suppress it.

"Yes, it's true."

"That the victims were . . ."

Cara glances to Noah. He takes another drag of his cigarette, staring out the window.

She remembers the inside of the car. Two bodies, crumpled, broken. Two bloody necks: white bone, flesh, tendons visible. And two heads lying alongside. Casually discarded, wet hair trailing in blood, glassy eyes wide open.

"Yes," she says. "Decapitated."

TIME PASSES IN a blur. Jess remembers the ambulance, asking about Alice, about Patrick, being wheeled into the hospital, bright lights overhead. She remembers the doctors, different faces in her line of sight.

When she wakes, she instantly knows where she is. She recognizes the noises: the beeping, the chattering in corridors, the squeak of comfortable shoes on a linoleum floor. She recognizes the feel of rough sheets against her skin.

She's in a hospital ward; the blue curtain has been pulled around, isolating her from the rest of the patients.

She hears a creak of someone shifting in the chair next to her, and she turns. There's a man there, a big guy, wearing a black jacket and scuffed jeans, with large heavy boots.

"Who are you?" she asks. Her voice is croaky, her throat sore.

"How are you feeling, Mrs. Ambrose?"

"A bit wobbly," she replies. But then she remembers, fear taking hold. "Where's Alice? Where's my daughter?"

"She's in the ICU, with your parents," the man says. "She inhaled a lot of smoke from the fire and was in respiratory distress from the carbon monoxide poisoning. But she's over the worst of it. She's going to be fine."

Jess tries to sit up but her head swims. "I have to see her," she mutters, but the man shakes his head.

"Not yet, Mrs. Ambrose. I need to speak to you about how your husband died before we can let you see your daughter."

"My husband . . ." Jess repeats. "Patrick's dead?"

The man has the decency to look ashamed. "I'm sorry, I thought you knew. They found a body in the spare bedroom. We're assuming that was your husband?"

Jess nods slowly. She starts to cry. What the hell had happened? How could Patrick be dead? He was there, he was just there, with her at home. He was going to London today. Has anyone called his work to tell them? Has anyone spoken to his parents? Should she . . .?

"Could you tell me about last night?" the man asks calmly.

"You're police." She recoils, her jaw clenching, heart beating. A familiar twitch of alarm. "I don't want to speak to you."

He sits up straight in his seat. He levels her with a stare. "This isn't going to go away, Jessica," he says. "The sooner you tell me, the sooner we can get this cleared up and you can see your daughter."

"Cleared up? What do you mean?" But then she realizes. She glares at him through her tears. "You think I did it?"

"It was arson. Someone started that fire deliberately."

"It wasn't me!"

"So tell me what happened." He pauses, and she feels him studying her face for a reaction. "Don't you want to see Alice, Mrs. Ambrose?" he adds.

She nods. Yes, she wants that more than anything.

He hands her a tissue from the box on the bedside table and she wipes her eyes and blows her nose. The snot on the tissue is black from soot.

Jess shakes her head. "I don't remember much. Honestly, I don't. I woke, I smelled smoke. I left my bedroom. The fire was everywhere. I grabbed my daughter and got out the only way I could see."

"Did you call the fire brigade?"

"No, no, I didn't."

"Why not?"

"I . . . I don't know." Why hadn't she called 999? It just hadn't occurred to her. In her panic the only person she'd thought about was her daughter.

"Why were you sleeping in a different room from your husband?"

"He had to get up early for work. He doesn't like to disturb me."

The man nods, thinking. He isn't what she expects from a police officer. He's dark, solemn, with messy hair, and at least a week's worth of stubble. He has a smell about him: not unpleasant, but slightly musty, with diesel oil. It reminds her of a garage.

"What's your name," she asks. "Detective . . .?"

"Griffin," he says. "And had you noticed anyone strange lately?"

"Strange?"

"Anyone you didn't recognize in your neighborhood. Watching you, or your house? Had your husband mentioned anything odd?"

She thinks back. "No, nothing I can think of."

"Does your house have CCTV or an alarm?" She shakes her head. "Pity."

Jess notices his gaze shift to her left forearm, to the straight silvery lines, stark on her skin. She hurriedly pulls the bed sheet up to cover them.

"The smoke alarms," she remembers suddenly. "They didn't go off."

He nods again. He's not taking notes, just listening, the frown still on his face. "When did you last check them?" he asks.

She can't remember. She opens her mouth and closes it again. She doesn't know what else to tell him, to make him believe her.

But then the curtain is pulled aside, and a man appears in front of them. Griffin stands up and backs away as he takes in the lanyard and ID, the stethoscope around the man's neck.

"Jess! I'm sorry, I came as soon as I heard. Are you okay?"

Jess feels herself relax at the welcome sight of her friend. The doctor turns, acknowledging the other man standing at Jess's bedside.

"Nav Sharma," he says, going to offer his hand, but Griffin is already walking away, his head bowed, back hunched.

Nav turns back to Jess, sitting down in the chair the detective has just vacated. He takes her hands in his.

"Nav, have you seen Alice?" she asks.

"Yes. She's awake but still on oxygen, confused, with a nasty head-ache." He smiles, but she can see the lost night's sleep and the worry on his face. "They're a great team on the ICU. She's in the best possible hands. And I know my goddaughter—she's strong. She's a fighter."

"And Mom and Dad?"

"They're looking after her." Jess feels marginally better, knowing her parents are there with her daughter. She imagines her mom, gently stroking Alice's hair. Her dad bustling around, ensuring everything is taken care of.

"And how are you?" Nav repeats softly.

His kindness starts her crying again, and he reaches forward, hugging her in a tight embrace. She leans into him. He smells of antiseptic and a long night on the wards. He slowly lets her go.

"I'm sorry about Patrick," he says. "He was . . . he . . ." And he stops talking, his mouth turned down, eyes closed. She smiles weakly at her friend, squeezing his hand. He takes a long breath in, pulling himself together before turning his attention back to her. She knows Nav is more upset than he'll let on now, but his professionalism takes over.

"Do they know—" Nav asks, but Jess cuts him off.

"Of course they know, Nav. It's written all over my medical records." She snaps more than she intends, and instantly feels guilty. There's a pause, and she knows Nav is looking at her. She doesn't like being the person he is seeing. Weak, sick. Pathetic.

Jess looks down, the soggy tissue still clutched in her fingers. She notices the black under her nails, lines of dirt from the fire etched into her skin.

"And who was that?" he says eventually.

"Police."

He turns and looks in the direction Griffin has gone, but the corridors are empty.

"They won't let me see Alice. They think I . . ." Jess's voice fades as Nav nods, his expression grave.

"I know. Your mom said."

"You'll look after her, won't you?" Jess asks, feeling her eyelids start to droop. Her body is weary, needing the energy to recover.

She takes comfort in Nav being next to her. He's her oldest friend, since they met at their local dive bar at university. Nav had been part of a group of testosterone-fueled, ritual-drinking medical students. Jess had been on a quiet night out with friends. He'd slurred an apology before puking on her shoes.

The next day—somehow—he'd tracked her down, presenting her with a brand new pair of sneakers. It was an unexpected gesture, but something fully in keeping with the way Nav was. Polite, posh, preppy. She's always trusted him with her life. And now, she trusts him with her daughter's.

She closes her eyes.

"I promise," she hears Nav say as her mind slips away into nothingness.

CHAPTER

5

Cara notices the whispers from her colleagues as soon as she and Deakin walk into the police station. Two young women. Murdered. Heads removed. Cara knows her every step will be watched to see how she handles the case; she's guessing there's already a pot going for time before first arrest. Not that anyone will admit publicly to something so callous.

"Elliott!" Cara hears a bellow from the other side of the room, and turns to see her detective chief superintendent heading toward her.

DCS Marsh is a man under pressure, surviving off a surfeit of nicotine and caffeine, with the pallor to match. His face is gray, hollows under his cheekbones, with a grubby mug in one hand. He takes a swig from it now, winces, then instructs the nearest DC to fetch him a fresh cup.

He gestures for Cara to follow him into her office, then rests his nonexistent bum on her desk, crossing his arms.

"I hear the owner of the car is a dead end," he says, getting straight to the point.

Cara takes her coat off and sits down on her chair.

"Has an alibi for last night," she confirms, repeating what Shenton had told them on the drive back from the crime scene. "But the families have been notified, and the boyfriend of one of the girls is waiting downstairs."

Their DC had been working hard, and sure enough, the two victims were students. Clever, hard-working, diligent women with bright futures. And families in different parts of the country.

She doesn't like to admit it, but Cara is glad it wasn't her that had to deliver the terrible news. She's done it too many times. Ashen-faced parents, distraught husbands, crying wives. There is no good way to tell someone their loved one has been brutally murdered.

"Good. See what you can get out of him." Marsh frowns, looking through the open door at the whiteboard in the incident room. Shenton has stuck photos of the victims along the top, their names written in black marker pen. Marisa Perez. Ann Lees. They smile out, oblivious of their futures, snapshots taken from their student IDs.

"Anything on CCTV?"

Cara points to the computer at which Shenton's now sitting, Deakin leaning over his shoulder. "On it."

Marsh nods. "Keep me updated," he says.

Cara follows him into the incident room, then watches him walk back to his own office. As he goes, he takes the new mug of coffee, almost downing the scalding hot liquid in one gulp on his way out.

"Deaks," she calls, and he turns. She tilts her head toward the door. Follow me, she's saying. Interview time.

* * *

Rick Baker is young and fashionable and nervous. Boyfriend of a few months, and clearly a fan of the gym. They've placed him in an interview room, where he's been waiting for the last half hour, sweating through his shirt.

Cara and Deakin sit down in front of him. They start the video and give the standard warnings for a voluntary interview, at which point he looks as though he might cry. Deakin leads. Time is of the essence, and Cara knows Noah has a way about him that men instantly bond with. He starts gently, expressing sorrow for his loss. The boyfriend nods, his lips clamped together.

"Could you tell us when you last saw Marisa?" Noah asks.

"Yesterday. Lunchtime. We agreed we'd do something today. She wanted a girlie night out with Ann." Cara watches as the boy tries admirably to hold it together; then his face crumples and he starts to cry.

Deakin looks to Cara and raises an eyebrow a fraction. With that one expression Cara knows what Noah's saying: the guy's either a traumatized boyfriend, or he's trying his hardest to look that way.

Deakin hands him a tissue. "And where were they planning on going?" he says.

Rick wipes his eyes. He blows his nose loudly. "Reflex. Their usual. It's an eighties club in town. I should have gone with them. I should have insisted they got a taxi home for a change."

Cara sits up in her seat. "How did they normally get home?"

"They'd walk. But it was cold last night, they might have . . ." His voice trails off. He shakes his head. "They would sometimes hitchhike. Someone would always pick them up. Marisa laughed at me when I said I was worried about it—she'd say there's two of them, they'll be fine." He looks up. His eyes are bloodshot. "But they weren't, were they?"

Deakin leans forward, looking the poor kid in the eye.

"You weren't to know," he says quietly. "And what were you doing last night?"

Rick talks them through his evening. Working on an essay in his room. Went to bed about eleven.

"Did anyone see you?" Noah asks.

Apparently not.

*   *   *

They wrap up the interview. Rick leaves. Cara and Noah watch him as he pushes the double doors open, stepping out into the crisp January afternoon.

Cara glances at Noah. He's deep in thought, then he runs his hand across his hair.

"Not our guy, is he?" he says.

"He's short but he's strong. He could have easily done it. But stolen a car, driven an hour out of town, murdered them like that? What would be the motive?" Cara screws up her face. "We've taken his samples—who knows what forensics might show. But no. I don't think it was him."

"So we're saying it's a random?" Deakin asks. They turn and walk back up the stairs to the office.

Cara doesn't answer his question. She knows what he's thinking. The majority of murders are committed by someone close to the victim. An attack in a pique of rage, obvious motives. Easy to find. Something like this, out of nowhere—it's tricky.

They open the door to the incident room. There's nothing for it, but good solid police work. CCTV. Forensics. Door-to-door. The boring stuff. Following up on witness statements until something pops out.

She glances at the clock on the wall: it's four already. She knows she won't be home for dinner.

Because below the clock are new photos, taken that morning from the crime scene. Shenton has obviously received them from the lab, and they demand her attention. She tears her eyes away from the dead women, the disembodied heads, to the rest of the car.

The bloodied back seats, handprints across the doors, smears on the roof. She frowns. Deakin catches her expression.

"What are you thinking?" he asks.

"It's just . . ." She taps one finger on the crime scene photo. "Everything about this scene screams frenzied attack. The stabbing. The blood. Up close and personal."

"Yes. And?"

"But the location—in the middle of nowhere—and the removal of their heads." She looks at Noah. "That seems planned. He'd have needed tools, the right sort of knives. And why decapitate them, Deaks? When would we expect to see that normally?"

"For easy disposal of the body?"

"Right. But there's none of that here."

"Perhaps he changed his mind?" They stand side by side, facing the board. Their postures mirror each other's: arms crossed, identical frowns.

"Rape gone wrong?" Noah suggests. "They did something to piss him off, he lost control?"

"Escalated pretty badly, then," Cara mutters. "This was overkill."

Cara doesn't want to add her last thought. Deakin knows what will be going through her head, but to say it out loud feels like tempting fate.

If this guy lost control, she thinks grimly, it won't be just once. There's a high chance he'll do it again. And soon.

CHAPTER

6

WHEN JESS WAKES, the room is darker. She feels muddled, struggling to get a grip on how much time has passed.

She looks to the chair by her side. Nav is slumped, his head at an uncomfortable angle, dark hair falling over his face, fast asleep. He's obviously been away and come back: a bag is by his feet, his coat draped over the chair.

Even with Nav here she feels sick and alone. She thinks about Patrick, about how they argued last night. About how they left things, without even a goodnight kiss.

She starts to cry, huge wracking sobs. All she wants to do is see her husband, hold her daughter. Alice has lost her father. She should be with her. How can they possibly think she had anything to do with this?

But then she hears voices outside the curtain. She stops and strains to listen. Hushed, urgent tones. Something important.

"Just because the smoke alarms didn't have batteries doesn't mean she murdered her husband." She recognizes the voice: the male detective again, gruff and annoyed.

"No, but her fingerprints were on the watering can that held the paraffin. What does that say to you?" A woman this time, obviously not happy. "And she has a record—have you even read her file? No, of course you haven't."

Jess's mind is reeling. Somehow she still believed that the fire had been an accident. That some faulty wiring or damaged plug had caused a spark. But this? And they *know*. About what happened two years ago. About—

"I don't agree."

"Griffin, with all due respect, I don't give a shit. You are not work-ing for the police. This is not your case. You shouldn't even be here." Jess lifts her head, and through a tiny gap in the curtain, she can see the woman's face. Mouth pinched, eyes cast down. She looks as if there's a hundred things she's holding back from saying.

"Have you asked her about the earring?"

"Seriously, Griffin, this theory of yours . . ."

"Have you?"

"The fucking earring has nothing to do with the other cases. This is a separate investigation. *My* investigation. Not everything is con-nected." A pause. An intake of breath, then a long sigh. "Fine. As soon as the doctor clears her, we'll arrest her and we can ask."

"And when will that be?"

"Right now, if it were up to me. But she had a nasty fall, and I don't want her keeling over in a cell." The man goes to say something, but she cuts him off. "Seriously, Griffin. Enough. Stay away from my suspect, I'm warning you."

Jess listens to footsteps as the woman stomps away, then closes her eyes quickly as a hand pulls back the curtain. She imagines the man standing there—the man who's apparently *not* a detective, who seems to be on her side—then hears an exhale as the curtain is replaced and his heavy boots fade into the distance.

She opens her eyes again and feels tears prickle behind them. She puts her hand up, tentatively feeling the bandage. She looks at the drip going into her arm. She's stuck in a hospital bed with a detective, poised to arrest her, who believes she killed her husband and tried to kill her daughter. A daughter whom she's not allowed to see, whom she can't hold in her arms and comfort and tell her that everything will be okay. What sort of mother is she?

She can explain her fingerprints—it was probably her watering can, that she'd used a hundred times before in the garden. But the paraffin? That she doesn't know. And she's seen the shows on Netflix; she knows that once the police have a theory, that's all they'll go after. They're blinkered, blind to any other possibilities.

She's met police like this woman before. Cold, unfeeling eyes, see-ing her as one thing, and one thing alone, and never changing their mind. She remembers the pull of her arms behind her. The cold metal on her wrists, sharp gravel against her cheek. She remembers the feeling of complete helplessness and the certain knowledge that she was never going to let that happen again.

Her mouth feels dry and fuzzy, so she reaches over and takes a drink from the glass of water on the table. It's warm.

She looks at Nav. He's fast asleep, leaning to one side. Jess knows what she has to do. And she has to do it now.

She sits up. Her head spins and she feels slightly sick, making it hard to get out of bed. Hard, but not impossible.

She looks at the IV in her arm and removes the dressing, then pulls the needle slowly out. Red blooms at the injection site, and she picks up a tissue from the box next to her, pushing it hard against it.

She shuffles around, both feet now on the floor. She stands up slowly and glances at Nav. But he hasn't stirred. She feels the cold waft around her. She's wearing no more than a backless hospital gown.

She can't see her T-shirt anywhere and realizes with a jolt that the detectives probably have it as evidence. She opens the cabinet next to her bed and says a silent thank-you to her mother—a few basic toiletries and a pile of brand new clothes have been left. Underwear, tracksuit bottoms, a pullover. She puts them on, along with socks and a pair of sneakers. With the brush and elastic tie, she pulls her hair back into a high ponytail, doing her best with her disheveled appearance. She forces a smile onto her face. This will work. It has to.

She goes over to Nav and gently pulls his bag away from his feet. Jess rests it on the bed, scrabbling inside.

Her fingers come in contact with cold metal, and she pulls the car keys out. As an afterthought she takes whatever cash is in his wallet.

"Sorry, Nav," she whispers.

She knows this is a bad idea. She knows that when she is injured, the worst thing she can do is ignore a doctor's advice, but this is different. This is an emergency.

But to leave her daughter?

On wobbly legs, she pushes the curtain aside. The ward seems empty, so she walks out.

She follows the signs to the ICU. Doors open automatically as she goes. It's late, and the corridors are deserted; her progress goes unchallenged.

But then she stops. A man stands in the doorway in his recognizable black uniform, waiting, guarding, hands behind his back. He nods, smiling, as a doctor goes past him into the ICU, and Jess knows there's no way she's going to see her daughter tonight.

She ducks back around the corner, breathing heavily, on the edge of tears. She'd just wanted to check on Alice, hold her warm hand, kiss her, tell her that everything was going to be okay. But Mom and Dad are there, she tells herself. She remembers the hundreds of times in her past that her parents had commanded the doctors, sitting patiently by her bedside, for however long it took. She may not be able to see Alice, but they are the next best thing.

She turns. She could go back to her ward. Put her faith in the police, that they will find out the truth. But the unease that follows that thought quickly pushes it out of her head.

She starts to walk again. She passes two nurses chatting in the corridor and smiles at them confidently. "Cigarette," she mutters. They scowl but let her go without question, and she breathes a sigh of relief when she's clear.

She looks for signs for the main entrance. Her heart is thumping in her chest the whole time, convinced that at any minute someone is going to see her and pull her back to her ward, this time in handcuffs. But perhaps it's too late, or people are too weary. Either way, nobody stops her.

She sees the double doors of the main entrance in front of her. There are more people here—nurses getting coffees at Starbucks, the bored receptionist checking her computer. All it would take would be for one person to recognize her. And it would be game over.

"Hey." A voice speaks next to her, a hand grabbing at her sleeve. She turns, her breath caught in her throat. "You dropped this," the man says, holding out a five-pound note.

She takes it, her hand shaking. "Thank you," she croaks.

"Can I help you with anything?" he asks.

"No, no, I'm fine. Just going out for a cigarette." She smiles, the expression feels strained.

"In this weather?" he asks. She looks at the doorway. The rain is coming down in sheets, puddles flooding the concrete. She doesn't have a coat. He seems dubious; he's looking at her as though she's a mental patient, escaped from the wards on level three.

She smiles again. "I won't be long." She forces a laugh. "They've cut me off from my methadone, so nicotine's the only drug I'm allowed."

The tactic works and the man backs away from her. "Well, look after yourself," he says, and hurries away.

The rain is worse than she anticipated. She's soaked in seconds, clothes sticking to her body, water dripping over her face. She moves as quickly as she can toward the staff parking lot, freezing, head dizzy, guessing at the location of Nav's black Renault Clio.

She walks down the rows of the top floor of the multistory garage, pressing the button on the car keys over and over again. The wind is whipping through the soaking pullover, and she starts to shiver. And then, at last, a flash of orange. She says a silent prayer, thanking Nav for being a man of routine, and heads toward the car, throwing herself inside, shutting the door against the wind and the rain.

But go where?

There's Nav. She could go to his house. Hide until he comes home.

Her parents too. But they're still at the hospital. With Alice.

She realizes with a jolt she doesn't have any other friends. At least, not close ones where she could knock on their door in the dead of night and say, "Hey? Would you like to harbor a suspected murderer?"

But she knows there's only one place to go.

She wants to go home.

7

THE HOUSE BARELY stands. The blue and white crime scene tape flaps, bedraggled ribbons in the wind.

Jess parks the car behind a white panel van and turns the engine off. She stares through the open window. She can hear cars passing a few roads over, but otherwise the street is quiet. It's 5:34 PM.

The sight of her ruined home is horrifying, but she can't look away. A broken mess of black and gray, the roof on the left-hand side gone, collapsed into where she knows the front bedroom would have been. Where Patrick had been sleeping. A sob bursts out of her, and she starts to shake as she cradles her head in her hands. If they hadn't had the argument, he would have been sleeping in the same bed as her. He would be alive.

Meeting Patrick all those years ago had been unexpected, and even more surprising to Jess when he asked her to marry him. She'd thought herself unlovable. Too much of a mess, too broken. He'd been warm, funny, loving—and tolerant of her problems. He'd just wanted her to feel better. To be normal.

But now he's gone. And her home has been destroyed.

Jess opens the car door and stands in the freezing cold. She knows there can't be anything left, but part of her wants to go inside. Most of the windows on the front are shattered, and there are teetering piles of debris in the front garden, more littered around the house, obviously placed there by the people investigating the arson. She can see a large yellow and white sticker plastered to the front door, telling people to keep away. "Active Crime Scene," it says.

Is this what it's reduced to? The first house she bought with Patrick, the horrendous seventies decor disaster lovingly renovated into their home. The place they brought their newborn daughter to, where she cried through the night, where she took her first steps.

Jess angrily wipes away the tears blurring her vision. There's no use standing here now. She climbs back into the car, preparing to drive away, when she sees another car pull up, directly outside her house.

It's an old-style gray Land Rover, and the driver gets out and leans against the door. A sudden flame casts his face in a flickering glow as he bends down to light a cigarette. Jess can just make out dark hair, stubble. It's the man from the hospital: Griffin. First there, now here. It's no coincidence, he's definitely interested in what happened to her. But why?

She remembers his conversation behind the curtain. He didn't think she was responsible. She wonders what makes him so sure, when the other detective was ready to arrest her.

He finishes the cigarette and drops it on the road. He climbs back into the Land Rover, and Jess starts the engine of Nav's car.

She hears the roar of the old truck, then follows him as he pulls away. He drives slowly at first through the residential streets, then speeds up, as if realizing she's behind him.

His car is quicker than Nav's shitty 1.2 Clio, but she knows the streets around here well. After about twenty minutes of quick lefts and rights, he pulls into an industrial estate, and she follows him in. She doesn't want to let him go. The back of her mind registers the potential danger, but this is the only thing she can think to do right now. This man knows something.

His car slows. There are few street lights here; the buildings are large and intimidating. The Land Rover turns into an alleyway behind a huge unit and stops, and she pulls up behind him.

The car door opens and he climbs out, looking at her. Her heart jumps, but he walks past, then heaves a large recycling bin behind the Clio. She turns in her seat, frantically realizing the enormity of the situation she's got herself in. She's trapped. The car is pinned between the bin and his Land Rover. She thinks about getting out and running, but she knows she won't get far. Not feeling like this. Her hand hovers over the gear lever. She could reverse quickly, put all the power of this little car into the bin and hopefully it would move. She could try, at least.

But something stops her. He casually walks up to her driver's side window, and knocks on it, twice. The Clio's doors are locked—he can't get in—and she stares at him for a second, her wide eyes meeting his.

He gestures for her to lower the window. She presses it down a fraction.

"What the hell are you doing out of the hospital?" he growls.

"What the hell were you doing at my house?" she replies, forcing her voice to sound more confident than she is feeling.

It starts to rain again. Large droplets fall in the glow of the head-lights, scattering across the windscreen. He squints upward as it settles in his hair. He gestures to the passenger side, pulling the collar of his coat up.

"Let me in," he says. He sees her reluctance. "For fuck's sake, I'm not going to do anything to you—just open the door. I'm getting cold."

Jess takes a deep breath in. She knows this isn't a good idea, but what has she got to lose? Her husband and her home are gone. The police are almost certainly now looking for her. She's not allowed to see her daughter. In terms of risky behavior, this is no more than the next in a long line of shitty decisions.

She clicks the lock, and he walks around to the passenger side, pulling the door open. He gets in. He smells of wet dog and cigarette smoke.

He shakes his head. "They can't possibly have let you out."

"They were going to arrest me—"

"So you're running from the police?" He snorts with derision. "Sensible," he adds sarcastically.

"I don't trust them. And who are you?" she demands. "Don't say you're a cop, because I know you're not."

"I am a detective, just not for the time being," he says. She sees his jaw clench. He goes to say something to her, but his phone rings in his pocket, interrupting him. He pulls it out and glares at her before answering.

Griffin talks in grunts and single syllables; Jess can't hear the other side of the call.

"I'll be there," he says finally, then turns to her. "You need to stop following me."

"Tell me why you're so interested in what happened, and I'll leave you alone."

"I have to go."

"So I'll come with you," she replies. He stays silent, so she carries on. "You seem to be the only person who doesn't think I killed my husband, and I want to know why."

Even though he's police, or was, something about him feels different from the cops she's encountered in the past. Back at the hospital he listened; he believed her, stood up for her against the woman detective. And he doesn't look like a cop. That helps, somehow.

He pulls a pack of cigarettes out of his jacket pocket and lights one. He doesn't ask permission. Jess worries about Nav's car and the smell, then dismisses it. He's going to be angrier about a lot more, after all.

Griffin's eyes stay downward, his brow furrowed as he smokes. Then he swears under his breath and sighs. "Fine. But you need to leave this car. They'll be looking for you, and it won't take them long to work out what you're driving." He notices her hesitation. "Look, that's my offer, take it or leave it. If I was going to do something to you, I would have done it by now." He gestures around the alleyway. "There are no cameras here, and it's not like you could have defended yourself. Look at the size of you. I could have strangled you within seconds."

He's right. He's a huge bloke, with meaty hands and muscular shoulders. She wouldn't stand a chance. She's not sure whether to feel reassured or scared by the fact he'd already worked out the method for her murder, but she turns off the engine.

He climbs out, discarding his cigarette butt on the concrete and walking back to his car. She follows him, and he leans across and pushes the passenger door open.

"Get in."

She climbs inside and fastens her seat belt.

"Where are we going?" she asks.

He shakes his head. "Stop asking so many questions. You'll see soon enough."

The Land Rover splutters into life, and he pulls out of the alleyway.

CHAPTER

8

HE'D WANTED TO see it for himself; there's no substitution for being at the scene of a crime. Griffin had stood, looking at the burned-down house, at the crumbling walls, at the smashed glass, and thought: Were you here?

If he'd been there twenty-four hours earlier, would he have seen him? Would he now know?

But a fire is different. He'd scowled, smoking his cigarette down to the butt, then discarding it on the ground. Even after all this time, his thoughts feel scrambled. He needs to get some rest. To stop thinking about this every moment of the day.

And now she's here.

Somehow, she's got out of the hospital. Somehow, despite a head lac and a possible concussion, she's driving around as night falls and is now sitting in the passenger seat of his Land Rover. He should call Taylor. He should take her back to the hospital, at the very least. But fuck, he can't stand DS Taylor, never could. She hangs onto investigations like a fetid limpet, never fluctuating from the obvious suspect. She's so far in the box, she's almost six feet under.

And this woman, Jessica Ambrose? He recognizes the look in her eyes. That confusion, grief, fear—mixed with dogged determination. He remembers how that felt and how much in the beginning he'd needed someone just to stay with him. A quiet presence to stave away the sinking loneliness.

The isolation he still feels.

He's been by himself for so long.

But as desperate as he is to talk—to her, to someone, to anyone who will listen—he says nothing. Just lights another cigarette and focuses on the road ahead.

Children's Services Report—Home Visit

Name of Child: Robert Daniel Keane (DOB 03/31/1986, age 9)
Siblings: none
Date: January 25, 1996
Reason for Referral: Continual absence from school, concerns about well-being of child, flagged by class teacher.

On arrival at the family home on Millmoor Way, I was introduced to Gary Keane (father) and Marcus Keane (uncle, living with the family). The house presented as poorly maintained and dirty. There was evidence of alcohol consumption (empty bottles) and suspected drug use (smell of marijuana) throughout the property.

I asked after Robert's mother: father said she left in February 1990, when Robert was three; neither Robert nor Gary Keane have seen her since. Robert stayed outside in the hallway while we spoke. We discussed the reason for my visit and Robert's continued absence from school: father stated that Robert has been bullied by other children and suffers anxiety as a result. He mentioned home schooling, although was unable to expand on this or provide any evidence to this effect.

His father described Robert as generally healthy, sleeping and eating well, although previous health checks at school confirm Robert is underweight, in the second centile for his age and height. He has a scar on his left forehead, in his hairline. Father refused permission for access to Robert's medical records.

On viewing Robert's bedroom, I asked about the lack of sheets on Robert's bed. Father explained they were in the wash because of some problems with bedwetting.

I asked for time alone with Robert, which was granted with initial hesitation from his father. Robert has few toys, with the exception of two large, battered hardback books, which he showed me after encouragement. One is *James and the Giant Peach*, the other a complicated medical dictionary. I believe these to be library books, although I was unable to confirm. I asked if he could understand the dictionary, and he said he didn't, but he liked the pictures.

School have stated that Robert is an intelligent child with a reading age beyond his years. He is quiet and shy, but started to open up as our conversation progressed. He refused to answer when I asked if he had any friends, and doesn't seem to have any other adults or female influences in his life. Throughout our discussion he was holding a notebook bound with an elastic band. He refused to let me see inside, and when I pushed, he shouted, "No," and said, "It's mine—you're not allowed to look at my stuff."

At the end of the allotted hour for the visit, the father interrupted our conversation, stating, "You need to leave now. We have to go out."

Recommendations: The home environment is clearly below standards of cleanliness and hygiene, and both caregivers smoke, with regular use of expletives in their language. Because of this, and Robert's low body weight, I believe he is unlikely to achieve a reasonable standard of health without provision of services from the Local Authority. I would therefore like to refer Robert's case for an interagency review, with the potential of further specialist assessments from representatives from the Hampshire Constabulary and the Early Help team. In addition, an application for a court order for access to Robert's medical records is recommended and may shed further light. Referral to an educational psychologist, to be made. Conversation needed with headteacher to explore allegations of bullying, with main priority to get Robert back to school as soon as possible.

Child to remain with family while investigations continue.

THEY DRIVE IN the rusty Land Rover in silence. Every now and again, Jess glances Griffin's way, willing him to speak, but she doesn't dare open her mouth. After about a quarter of an hour of driving, he meets her eye.

"Stop staring at me," he growls.

"Tell me why you believe me. The detective at the hospital said you think something's connected."

He looks her way sharply. "You heard that?"

"Tell me."

Griffin hesitates, then takes a turn off the road. He pulls down a darkened track, stops the car, and switches off the engine. Jess looks out the window, and in the silence she suddenly realizes how isolated she is, how stupid she's been. Griffin leans toward her and her hand flies to the door handle to escape, but he reaches down into the footwell and pulls up a black rucksack. She's breathing heavily, and he notices what she was about to do. He gives her a disparaging look.

"For fuck's sake," he mutters. He pauses. "You squeamish?"

Jess glances at the bag. What could he have in there? A dead animal? Chopped off fingers? "I don't know," she says nervously.

He scowls at her for a moment, then opens the top of the rucksack. "This all started about two years ago," he says. He pulls a scrappy cardboard file out of the bag, resting it on his lap and opening it. With his other hand he turns on the overhead light.

"I was called out to a crime scene of a woman, strangled and raped, obviously been tied up and tortured before she was killed." He shifts through a pile of what Jess recognizes as crime scene photographs, and hands her one. She gasps. In the harsh light, she can see pale skin, dark bruises. A face, eyes closed. "She was twenty-one, a waitress at a local café. Her name was Lisa Kershaw."

Jess looks again. The body is naked, ligature marks clear on her neck, wrists, and ankles.

"So you *are* a detective?" she asks.

"I was," he says gruffly. He quickly moves on. "Then two more bodies were found." He hands her the photos. Two more women. Naked. Dead. Jess cringes at the images. "Daria Capshaw and Sarah Jackman. Strangled, tortured, and raped." He talks with the manner of a man getting something off his chest: words that haven't been spoken for a long time, released in a flurry. He turns and looks at her. "So that's three. We have a serial killer."

"I didn't hear about any of this on the news," Jess says, stunned. "How come?"

"My chief was worried about the publicity encouraging the killer. So we kept it quiet. But then more major crimes came in. Two rapes—home invasions, lengthy and brutal. At first we didn't think there was a connection."

"And there was?"

Griffin nods. "The victims had heard someone on their property before the attacks. Footprints were found in the flower beds, a star-shaped pattern traced back to an old-style Adidas running shoe, also found near the body of Sarah Jackman. But it was odd. Killers don't usually devolve. They start with rape, then move on to murder as they get confident. They don't go backward. So we wondered whether there had been more murders we hadn't noticed."

Jess sits forward in her seat. It seems dreamlike, Griffin's recounting of death and violence. But how could these possibly be linked to her?

He turns to the next photograph and Griffin points, his face grim. "Two more, same MO as the first—raped and strangled." Grainy, dark photos, bodies hard to make out. "Happened a few years before. But in two different counties, so nobody joined the dots. Unsolved."

"And then what?"

"We linked up, started a task force. But we found nothing. And it went quiet. Until these two."

He points again. "Emily Johnson and Isabelle Richards," he says. "Both sex workers. Hit over the head with what the pathologist believed to be a hammer, then stabbed to death."

"It's different," she says.

"It is. But that's a lot of violent unsolved murders for England. Especially when you consider most homicides are committed by someone known to the victim." He looks at her, thinking. She's started to shiver in the cold car, and wraps her arms around herself, but he doesn't seem to notice. "Then a year ago, there's another home invasion," he continues slowly. "A couple. They're threatened with a handgun, flashlight shined in their faces. They're separated, tied up. The woman, raped repeatedly. For hours." Griffin's voice is low; he's talking slowly, his words measured. "The husband is beaten severely and knocked out with a log from the woodpile. When he wakes up, his wife is dead. Bludgeoned to death in the same way, her hands bound with cord from the curtains."

Griffin goes silent for a second, and Jess can see his jaw muscles working, obviously trying hard to get a grip on himself. She can tell these unsolved murders have taken a toll on him. "If we'd caught the guy before . . ." Griffin stops again, and Jess can only imagine the guilt he must have felt, knowing someone else had died on his watch.

Griffin takes a deep breath, then looks over at her. "But then the trail goes cold."

"Nothing since then?" Jess asks in disbelief. "Nothing for a year?"

Griffin shakes his head. "Nothing until I got a call last night—one dead in a house fire. Suspected arson. Suspected murder."

A knot forms in her stomach. That's her house. Her husband. She starts to feel sick. Jess knows she didn't start the fire, but she'd assumed it was something random. A teenager on a dare that went wrong. A revenge attack in a case of mistaken identity. She didn't think the attack could be connected to something as widespread as this.

"It can't possibly be linked," she stutters.

He pulls his phone from his jacket pocket, thumb scrolling, then shows her an image. She shies away, but this time it's innocuous—an earring, a crescent moon, flashes of green and blue in the silver.

"That yours?"

She shakes her head.

"You sure?"

Jess looks again. "Yes." She pauses. She hardly dares to ask.

"It was found just inside your front door." Jess opens and closes her mouth. Griffin looks at her. "It belonged to the last rape victim. I believe it was placed there deliberately."

"But why?"

"That I don't know."

He reaches forward and starts the engine again. And she realizes what the phone call was about.

"There's been another one?" she asks. "We're going to a murder scene?"

"Me, not you. You're staying in the car."

And without waiting for agreement, he guns the engine and they're back on the road.

* * *

The road turns into a divided highway, then leads into a town. Jess still has the photographs in her hands, and she goes through them again as they drive. Flickering images in the street lights. Death. Destruction. Murder. What could this possibly have to do with her?

Fear takes hold, and she quietly starts to cry again. Who wanted her family dead? There's nothing exceptional about the three of them that might mark them out as a target. Patrick's job is dull and desk bound, and she's no more than a housewife.

She feels disoriented. She's read more books, watched more TV about this stuff than she can count: documentaries, forensic psychology, the strange and macabre, but right now it's not helping. Everything she's heard from Griffin could be torn straight out of the pages of one of those true crime accounts.

And her head is a problem; if she moves too quickly, she still feels dizzy. It's obvious there's something not right in there. But she can't worry about that now.

Less than twenty-four hours ago she was at home with her daughter and her husband. And now she's cold and wet in a grubby Land Rover with someone she knows nothing about, driving toward another murder.

She's never seen a dead body—not in real life. But she's doggedly hanging on to this man as if he holds the solution to the hell that has become her existence.

* * *

They drive for about an hour, until Griffin pulls up in a suburban street. It's a nice area: big faux art deco houses with gates, and Discoveries and Evokes in their sprawling driveways. Jess looks at him: he's squinting out the windscreen, obviously searching for someone. He opens his car door as a man walks down the road toward them. He's older, with a bald head, a round tummy, and a hangdog expression.

Griffin glances back to Jess. "You stay here." He sees her about to reply. "No argument. Stay here."

He climbs out of the car and stands with the man, who glares at Griffin. They're close enough that Jess can still hear their conversation.

"This has got to stop," the man says. "You can't hold one mistake over me forever."

"When this is over, Alan, I'll stop."

The man looks at Jess through the windscreen of the Land Rover.

"She's staying here," Griffin reiterates, as much for her benefit as for the man's.

They start walking quickly down the road. Jess briefly watches them go, then opens the door and follows them. Screw Griffin. She needs to see this, to know it's all for real. This is *her* life, *her* nightmare.

She pauses behind a parked car as Griffin and the man stop by a large white van. In the distance she can see blue and white tape fluttering in the darkness.

"What do we have?" she hears Griffin ask.

Alan reaches into the back of the van and hands him something white. Jess watches Griffin as he puts on the crime scene suit; then the two men move away. She waits until they're a good distance, then grabs one herself: it's huge, soft and plasticky, and she does her best, pulling the white overshoes on over her sneakers, blue gloves on her hands.

"It's a massacre," she hears Alan say as she creeps behind them. "Blood everywhere."

"You think it's him?" Griffin asks, and Alan nods.

"Not seen anything like this for a long time. We're still waiting for the pathologist, but it's definitely murder. Major Crimes have been and gone. Didn't say much."

Jess watches as they put on the face masks, then the hoods over their heads. She does the same. With this outfit on, Jess suddenly feels safe—indistinguishable from the other people teeming around in the road.

They shuffle toward the house and stop at the police cordon. The scene guard watches as Alan bends down and writes in a turquoise logbook, then gestures behind to Griffin.

"He's already signed in," Jess hears him mutter as they both pass through.

Jess waits. She's debating trying a false name, hoping the guard won't check ID, when a large crowd of scene of crime investigators comes up behind her, talking loudly in their identical white suits. She integrates herself into the middle of the homogenous group as they joke with the scene guard, taking turns to sign the book.

And then he waves them through and she's in.

It's a mansion with a long drive leading up to a grand entrance. Jess can see the glow from the open front door, and scene of crime officers move in and out of the area. The ground is littered with small yellow triangles; every now and again she sees the flash from a camera. In the darkness it's eerie, and Jess feels a shiver run down her back. To their left, a car is parked, driver's side door open, people leaning inside. She catches up quickly to Griffin, just as Alan points to the car.

"The first one's in there. Eighteen-year-old boy. Shot. Quite a few times at what seems to be point-blank range. And slashed with a knife. We're not sure of the specifics yet."

Jess can't look away, imagining what might be inside. But then she feels a tight hand on her arm. She looks up into Griffin's furious glare.

"What the fuck? I told you to stay in the car."

"I'm coming. I'm a part of this."

"You know what—"

"I know."

He stares at her. Takes in her defiant expression behind the mask. "Fine," he snaps, even though it's obvious to Jess it's not. But she knows he can't afford for her to make a scene, to draw attention to the fact that neither of them is supposed to be there.

They've stopped at the entrance to a large white tent to the right of the house. Alan's been watching their exchange and now glowers at them both.

"She wasn't part of the deal," he hisses to Griffin.

"The deal is exactly what I say it is." Griffin stands over him, clearly the bigger and stronger man. "You fucked up, and if it wasn't for that . . ." He shakes his head. "Just do what I ask, and once this is over you'll never have to see me again."

Alan meets Griffin's stare for a moment, then drops his gaze, backing down. He wearily holds the tent flap open, and Griffin ducks inside. As Jess goes past Alan, Griffin grabs her arm again.

"Are you sure you want to see this?" Griffin asks, and she nods.

But nothing could have prepared her for what's inside.

A body—a woman, Jess realizes—is lying on the ground. Floodlights have been set up and light the woman's face in a grimace. Everywhere Jess looks, there's blood. The woman's white nightgown is ripped and soaked in it. The grass around is stained red. Jess feels dizzy and realizes she hasn't been breathing. She forces herself to take in small gulps of air.

"We haven't touched the body, obviously," Alan whispers. "But it's a good guess cause of death is from penetration wounds, probably from a knife. At first look I would estimate she's been stabbed at least thirty times."

"That's a pretty chaotic attack," Griffin mutters, and Alan nods. "And that's not all."

There's a second body behind. His face is mutilated beyond recognition, but from his hair and clothes Jess assumes it's a man.

"Multiple blunt force trauma to the head, plus what we think are more stab wounds but could be a shooting—we had reports of gunfire," he mutters. "Looks like he was trying to run. Poor guy."

They don't stop.

Alan leads them back out into the darkness. He points toward the house.

They walk up the large stone steps and go inside. It's an incredible place. Jess's eyes slowly adapt to the brightness, and she takes in the sweeping staircase, the stone floors, photographs of a smiling couple on the wall.

The stepping plates slide on the marble as they walk across them; the floor is covered with smears and smudges of blood and mud. Alan points to it as they walk.

"Mess from first responders," he mutters. "We won't get any useable footwear marks from that."

The hallway leads to double wooden doors, left ajar. Alan pushes them open with a gloved finger, and Jess stops in her tracks.

The living room is a double-height extension, rain starting to tap on the skylights in the roof. Jess can see it would have been tasteful, understated, minimally decorated in beiges and creams, but right now, the room is utter chaos. The coffee table has been tipped over, the sofa pushed to one side, every other item of furniture in disarray.

And every surface is covered in blood. Spatter runs down the walls. The cream chairs are smeared and streaked. A large pool has settled in the middle of the room, where the bodies slump.

The smell is alien and disturbing. Ferrous and metal, it sticks to the inside of Jess's nose. Even with the mask, she can almost taste it, and she gags, putting her hand over her mouth.

There are two bodies. A space has been cleared in the center of the room, and they rest against each other, wet and bloody. Jess can see a white rope has been slung over one of the ceiling beams above them, then wrapped around their necks. The man's hands are tied.

"Have they . . . Were they . . ." Jess begins, pointing to the rope, but Alan shakes his head.

"We found them like this. And there are none of the obvious ligature marks around their necks that you'd expect if they'd been hung."

It looks like a woman and a man. It looks like—Jess takes a step forward to look more closely. Griffin puts his arm out to stop her.

"Is she . . ." she starts. She can barely bring herself to say it.

He nods slowly, his eyes narrow.

The woman's hands are tied behind her back, her body coated in blood. She's slumped forward awkwardly, but Jess can just make out the curve of her stomach.

She had been pregnant.

Jess feels nauseous. She feels her hot breath inside the crime scene mask. The blood, the frenzied nature of the attack is one thing, but to tie up and murder a pregnant woman? It was barbaric. Insane. She remembers how she felt when she was pregnant with Alice. She would have done anything to protect her unborn child. She wonders what went through this woman's mind. Whether she begged, whether she pleaded for her baby's life. Jess chokes back tears and starts to back away from the bodies.

"Could have been worse," Alan says, and Jess looks to him quickly. How? she thinks. How exactly could this be worse? Alan carries on: "There were supposed to be two others here yesterday evening, but they changed their minds at the last minute. They came around to apologize this afternoon and found the bodies on the lawn. And a kid, about nineteen, staying in their granny annex at the back."

"A witness?" Griffin asks, but Alan shakes his head.

"High as a kite. Slept in. Says he didn't hear a thing."

"What's with the flag?"

A large American flag has been draped over the sofa just behind the dead woman. It's bright and gaudy. To Jess it seems deliberately placed—its edges are straight and precise. It's the only thing in the room not covered in blood.

Alan looks at it. "We don't know for sure. We have a few theories."

But before they can ask, they hear a commotion behind them. People move aside as another figure enters the room. He looks the same as everyone else, but he obviously has authority over the scene. Griffin pulls Jess backward.

"Has anyone touched them?" the man shouts.

"No one, no," Alan replies.

The man nods with satisfaction and crouches next to the corpses. His shoulders slump when he sees the woman. Jess hears him mutter a string of profanities.

Griffin taps her on the shoulder and gestures for them to move away. She follows him back through the house. Once they are outside the living room, she feels a pull on her hand, and Alan stops her.

He watches Griffin as he walks out of the house, then turns to Jess.

"Listen," he says. "I don't know who you are or what you're doing here. But I'm telling you now, don't let him drag you into this mission of his. Nate's so deep he doesn't know where the surface is anymore. I'm going down with him—and that's as much my fault as it is his—but you seem new to this. Don't let him take away everything you have."

Jess frowns. "It's pretty much gone already," she replies, and walks away.

She sees nothing but blood as she leaves the house. Handprints. Smears and smudges. A photographer is capturing evidence on the wall outside the front door, and it catches her eye. Something is written there. Bright red daubs in what she can only assume is blood.

Jess stops and stares at the word.

PIG, it says.

10

JESS CATCHES UP with Griffin at the Land Rover. He angrily pulls off the crime scene clothes, ripping them in the process and rolling them into a ball. He throws them into the back of the car, then climbs into the driver's side. She does the same and sits next to him, sighing with relief as she closes her eyes for a second. She's feeling dizzy again. The added exercise will not have done her head any good.

Griffin starts the engine and they drive in silence. He doesn't look her way. His displeasure toward her is clear.

Her head is spinning with everything she has seen. The murders seem insane; the sheer amount of blood, the stabbings, the flag. She doesn't understand how this could possibly be linked to her, to setting fire to her house. Patrick's murder is nothing like what she saw today.

Thoughts buzz in her head. She sees the blood. The pregnant woman. She thought murderers had a type, one way of killing. Why would someone set fire to a house one day, then kill five people in their home, with knives and rope and guns?

Griffin's revving the engine hard, charging into every corner. She glances across at the speedometer: it says sixty, then seventy miles an hour. She hangs on to the car as she's thrown this way and that. He's taking out his anger on the road, and she can't blame him.

She has no idea where they're going until they stop outside a secondhand car garage. It's one of those locally owned places, with crappy Ford Fiestas and ten-year-old Vauxhalls on the lot. Griffin doesn't wait for her as he slams out of the car, opening a large side door to the garage and stomping down steep metal stairs to the apartment below.

She hurries behind him, but before she gets inside the door, she can hear the noise.

It's the bang of something thrown, then a crash.

She tentatively opens the door.

The place is no more than one large room and what she assumes to be a bathroom behind the door on the left. It has bare brick walls and wooden floors, but there are rugs and a sofa. A basic kitchen takes up the space on the far wall, with a double bed to the right of it. A large set of dumbbells are stacked in a corner.

Griffin has overturned one of the chairs; a beer bottle is smashed against the wall next to her, splinters of glass across the floor, liquid running down the bricks. He roars and pummels his fists against the wall, then thumps one into the brickwork. He shouts, and she runs up to him, hanging onto his arm to stop him from doing it again.

He turns suddenly, his fist raised, directly in line with her head. She feels the tension in his muscles, the strength in his arms. It's all she can do not to be thrown to the floor as she hangs on. His face is twisted with anger.

He looks at her. There's nothing in his eyes. No recognition, no humanity. Just rage. He moves, forcing her against the wall, backed into a corner.

With his other hand he grabs her wrist; she feels his fingers dig into her flesh, and she lets go of his arm. Her body floods with adrenaline, but it's not fear this time. It's something else. A wave of energy. She's angry, like him. He snatches her other wrist and holds her arms either side of her head. She feels the rough brickwork against her skin. She pushes against him as hard as she can to get away, but he holds her still, his face barely inches from hers.

She's breathing heavily, she can feel her heart racing. She looks into his eyes, but all she can see in her head is the blood. The holes in their bodies, the flood of red. That unborn baby, *the unborn baby*—

And then her mouth is hard against his. There's no elegance here, just bumped teeth, his stubble against her chin, her tongue in his mouth. He returns the kiss, pushing his hands into her clothes. They're cold against her warm skin, and she does the same to him, reaching under his shirt. His body is solid, rough, and she wants him—to help her feel something, anything, to take the thoughts out of her head.

She kicks her shoes off, she feels his hands push down into her trousers. His teeth knock against her lip, and for a second she tastes blood. It reminds her of the bodies . . . the red . . . but she pushes her eyes tightly closed and focuses on what he's doing. One hand down the back of her trousers, the other—

She takes a quick breath in. Oh God. She pushes herself up against him, and she can feel his mouth on her neck, on her collarbone. She pulls his shirt off, then struggles with his belt and his jeans, his fingers still inside her, playing, distracting.

But then, abruptly, he stops. He pulls away, his eyes meeting hers.

Something's changed. He shakes his head, still out of breath, taking a step backward.

"No. No, we can't do this," he mutters, almost to the floor. He turns away, pulling his jeans up, then picks up his shirt and the pack of cigarettes from the table and walks out of the apartment.

She watches the door close. She stands there, against the wall, stunned. She liked it, she wanted it. To feel something other than the bottomless detachment.

But something stopped him. She pulls her trousers up again before collapsing on the bed. She stares at the ceiling. She thinks she should feel guilty, anything, for what she tried to do so soon after Patrick's death, but she feels nothing except the sting of his rejection. I'm that much of a shitty person, she thinks. That's why he wouldn't fuck me. Not even a man like Griffin wants me.

The door opens and Griffin comes back into the room with a sweep of cold air. He looks at her.

"Jessica—" he begins, but she cuts him off.

"It's Jess. And I don't want to talk about it," she says, and he nods.

"Suits me."

He joins her on the bed, taking his shirt off over his head and lying on his front, facing away from her. He pulls the duvet over himself. A flash of light reflects on his left hand, and for the first time, Jess notices the wedding ring. So was that why he stopped them? But then why is he living here?

She can't think about that now. Exhaustion hits her and she rests her head on the pillow. Despite his rebuff, he doesn't seem to mind her being in the bed next to him, and she's glad.

"Griffin?" she asks, and he grunts. "What's your name?"

He turns to face her, frowning. "What do you mean?"

"That man called you Nate."

He turns away again. "Nate. Nathanial Griffin," he says, his voice muffled by the pillow. "Not many people call me that anymore. Just stick with Griffin."

Jess listens to his breathing. It's slowed now to a soft in and out. She closes her eyes. Images flash in her mind. The blood. The dead pregnant woman. Her ruined house.

Think of something else, she tells herself, screwing her eyes tightly shut. Something good.

Alice.

The ache of being apart from her daughter makes it almost hard for her to breathe. But Alice is alive. She's safe, Jess thinks, with my mom and dad and Nav.

And with thoughts of her daughter in her head, lying next to a strange man in a strange apartment, she slowly falls into a deep, dreamless sleep.

CHAPTER

11

H E LIKES THE *thump thump* of the bass line, so loud it reverberates on his diaphragm. The flash of the lights, the haze from the shots hastily downed at the bar. He dances, his hands above his head, the smell of sweat—from him and the other men in the club. He closes his eyes for a moment, feeling their bodies against his. Smooth skin, hard muscles.

He feels a hand on his arm. Gentle, caressing.

"Not seen you here before," the man shouts over the music. He meets his eyes; he sees his interest.

"My first time," he replies.

"Really?" The man smiles suggestively. "You wanna do something about that?"

He looks at him. He looks young, barely out of his teens. But his confidence is attractive; this club is clearly somewhere he feels at home in his tight white T-shirt, ass-hugging jeans.

He nods and the man smiles, then grabs his hand and starts pulling him from the dance floor toward the toilets. He pulls back and the man turns, looking at him curiously.

"Not here," he shouts. "Let's get a taxi, go back to my place."

The man tilts his head to one side in a mock sulk. Then he grins. "You better have something to make it worth my while."

"I'm sure I can knock up a rum and Coke," he replies with a small smile. "What's your name?"

"Steve," he replies. "What's yours?"

But he's already turned, the man following obediently after him, the name fixed in his head.

Steven, he thinks. Perfect.

Perfect.

12

Day 3
Wednesday

J ESS WAKES AS daylight pushes its way into the room. For few minutes she's disorientated, but then she realizes where she is and turns
toward him.

Griffin's still lying on his front, facing away from her. The duvet
has been pushed off in the night, and she looks at him in the dim glow,
taking in the muscles of his shoulders, the dips in his back. She can just
see a collection of silvery-pinkish lines running across the bottom of his
spine, disappearing into his jeans. They seem to be newish scars, and
she wonders how he got them.

She thinks of her own arms and legs. Of the white puckered lines,
crisscrossing her skin. Some parallel to each other, some old, some new.
They're a mess. She knows Griffin must have seen them by now, but he
hasn't commented.

And what on earth is this place? She frowns and gets out of bed. It's
colder this morning, and she grabs the first thing close to her and puts
on Griffin's sweatshirt. It smells of cigarettes and his skin. It conjures up
a memory of last night, and something stirs in her. But she knows what
happened—or rather, what didn't happen—wasn't an act of romance.
Just a release of stress and anger, no more than that. She pushes it out
of her mind.

There's a long wooden table in the center of the room, and she
wraps her arms around herself and walks over. Papers litter the surface,

and she reads a few of the newspaper articles. They all report homicides. Some have lines highlighted, others with comments scribbled in the margins. Some of the documentation seems to be printouts from a computer system or some sort of database. Dates, names, descriptions.

But it's the wall to the left of the door that demands her attention the most. It's huge, every inch of it covered in photographs and articles, seemingly pinned up randomly. A whiteboard is in the center, with a scrawl in almost illegible black marker pen. She stands in front of it.

Jess looks more closely at the photos. Some of them are of places and people—smiling faces—but the others are photos of the dead. Some she saw last night, some new. Broken bodies, distorted and gray. Parts missing, eyes open, staring blindly into nothing. Blood, torn flesh, ripped skin. Jess's stomach turns over, but she can't look away, gripped by the horror on display.

Then she remembers. The bodies. The pregnant belly. The child now motionless inside. The blood.

Before she can stop herself, images flicker through her mind. So much blood. Everywhere, splattering the floor, the walls. She remembers the writing by the front door, crudely daubed in red: *PIG*. She stops. It's strangely specific. Was it a message to the police or a note to someone else? An estranged lover maybe?

She frowns and stares at the whiteboard. Something about the nature of the recent murders niggles in her brain. Something she's seen before. Five people dead, one of them heavily pregnant. And *PIG* daubed next to the wall in blood.

She takes a quick breath in.

"Griffin," she shouts without looking away from the board. He stirs in the bed, squinting at her with bleary eyes.

She starts moving the photos about on the wall, pulling some off and dropping them to the floor. Her destruction moves him out of bed, and he stands up, putting a T-shirt on and joining her.

He watches as she continues, her movements quick.

"What are you doing?" he asks.

She gestures to a photo on the table. "Pass me that one and those two there."

He does, and she sticks them back on the wall, together.

After a moment she stops and takes a pace backward, looking at it from afar.

She points at the wall, then turns to Griffin. His face is still wrinkled from sleep, and she notices that every time he moves, he winces.

"What are you seeing?" he asks.

She points to the group at the top, their names scrawled in black marker. "Lisa Kershaw, Daria Capshaw, and Sarah Jackman. All strangled, tortured, and raped."

Griffin nods. He pulls a pack of capsules from his bag and pushes one out of the foil, then stops and takes out a second. She watches as he throws the pills into his mouth and swallows them dry, then points to the next group of photographs.

"Hit over the head with a hammer, then stabbed."

"What are you saying?" Griffin asks slowly.

"Two very specific ways of killing," Jess says. "Give me your phone."

Griffin unlocks it and hands it over. He looks over Jess's shoulder as she enters words into the search engine. Then he stands up straight, looking from the board back to the phone, still in Jess's hand.

Jess points to one of the groupings. "Where did these murders take place?" she asks.

"Both Leeds," Griffin starts. "Isabelle Richards was Roundhay Park."

"Yorkshire," Jess says. She looks at Griffin. "Both prostitutes."

Griffin's mouth drops open. "Sutcliffe," he says slowly. "So this group . . ." he starts, pointing to the first murders.

"The Hillside Strangler," Jess replies.

Griffin shakes his head. "It must be coincidence," he says, almost to himself. "And what about yesterday?" he asks. "That was completely different again."

Jess's face is grim. "A pregnant woman? Five violent murders in a house?"

"Fuck me," Griffin mutters.

"Manson," Jess finishes for him.

The revelation makes Griffin take a step back. His face is gray. He looks stunned, almost in shock.

"They're all MOs of different serial killers," Griffin says, articulating out loud what Jess is thinking.

She nods slowly. "The sick fucker is copying serial killers," she whispers.

08/23/90 1330hrs A&E SpR (Dr. Evans)

Trauma Call: 4-year-old male (Robert Daniel Keane, DOB 3/31/86)

HPC: Father reports fall down stairs earlier today, approximately 14 steps onto tiled floor.

No preceding symptoms, reported brief loss of consciousness, vomit x2, subjective confusion.

Denies seizures, no post-ictal state.

Subsequent deformity of right wrist, ongoing pain of right lower limb.

PMHx: Reported car accident at 36 months, no prior attendances.

DHx: Nil of note, father unsure re: immunizations, NKDA.

Imp:
    (i) Fall down stairs
    (ii) ?Traumatic Brain Injury
    (iii) ?Right distal radial fracture 2° to FOOSH
    (iv) ??Soft tissue injury of right lower limb
    (v) ?? Nonaccidental Injury

Plan:
    1. CT head in view of ?TBI
    2. Observation in Ped CDU until CT reported
    3. Plain X-ray right upper limb and right lower limb
    4. D/w Trust Child Protection lead given ?NAI
    5. Refer to Peds

1500hrs A&E SpR (Dr. Evans)

Imaging Update

CT Report: Frontal extradural hematoma and overlying linear skull fracture

Right Arm Radiograph: Nondisplaced distal radius fracture

Right Lower Limb Radiograph: No acute bony injury, evidence of previous tibial mid-shaft fracture

D/w Pediatric Cons on call: father attributes old fracture to car accident as toddler.

Plan:
1. Admit under Pediatrics
2. Ongoing observation, for review mane
3. Pediatrics to complete Child Protection proforma

13

Today the crime scene is quieter. One lone officer guards the woods; only a few figures in white remain. This time Cara's alone, Deakin declining to join her. She didn't argue—she knew why.

As Cara drives up, she sees Libby waiting. Dressed in full white crime scene overalls, Libby Roberts smiles broadly at Cara as she climbs out of the car. Her hood is down, and her long, bright pink hair shines incongruously against the trees.

Known as one of the best in her field in blood pattern analysis, Cara was pleased to hear Libby was going to be assessing the crime scene. Getting her view firsthand was invaluable. Cara knew she'd make sense of the chaos.

"Coffee?" she asks, and Cara hands her a tiny paper cup of espresso, exchanging it for the white suit in her other hand. Libby drinks as Cara puts the outfit on, discarding the empty cup back into Cara's car.

Cara hates these suits. They never fit properly; the gloves are always sweaty, even in this cold, and the mask's constrictive, making her feel breathless and suffocated. But also because of what she's come to associate them with: the death, the blood, the horror of what's to come.

They don their gloves, shoe covers, and masks, pulling the hoods up. Cara follows her under the cordon.

"Those poor girls," Libby mutters. They stand next to the car, and Libby points out dark brown patches on the grass. "Blood and apparent drag marks. What I'd expect to see from moving a body from the back seat to the trunk."

"Body?" Cara asks. "Just one?"

Libby takes her around to the back. "Impossible to say for sure, but we've taken swabs throughout so we'll be able to confirm whose blood is whose. However, if you're forcing me," she says, and Cara nods, "from the pattern, I'd say victim number one was killed in the back seat, then dragged around; number two in situ in the trunk. See this pooling here and this void?" She points to a gap in the dark red stain. "That's where her body was lying. It's neat, with undisturbed edges, so I'm assuming she wasn't repositioned after the head was removed. And speaking of the decapitations . . ."

Libby points to the two deep ridges in the bumper and the pool of blood on the ground. "My assumption is they were done here." She mimes a chopping motion with her arm. "One final strong strike on each, going straight through the vertebrae of the spine, into the car."

"Any idea with what?" Cara asks, and Libby frowns.

"Something like a meat cleaver? Find us a weapon and we can compare. Moving on," Libby continues, "we have some impact spatter on the top of the trunk, indicating at least one contact into wet blood. See?" Cara grimaces. "This could have originated from repeated stabbing into an already injured area."

They move around to the back seat, Cara following Libby without comment. It's a lot, almost too much for her to take in.

"Same pooling, same spatter, but more of a mess as the victim tried to get away." She points to smears on the car window, thick lines of red, smudges around the door handle. Cara can't help but imagine her last moments, desperately trying to escape. And the girl inside the trunk, listening to her friend being murdered, knowing what must be coming for her.

Libby points to another arc of dark red. "And this here," she says, "is suggestive of arterial blood, which I'm guessing would tie up with a peri-mortem wound on the victim's neck or similar. Postmortem report back yet?"

Cara shakes her head. "Today, I hope."

Libby walks around to the other back door and opens it. She directs Cara's attention to a speckled pattern of blood on the back of the driver's seat, some drops dribbled downward, some hollow and round. "This looks like expired blood. See the air bubbles within the spots? And the stringing where it's mixed with saliva? I'd guess this is the victim coughing after being stabbed in the chest."

Libby's eyes narrow.

"Those poor girls," she repeats. She takes a deep breath in. "We have fingerprints in blood all around the car, some smudges, some patterns from material."

"From gloves?"

"Could be. Let's hope that at some point he nicked himself on the knife and we get something from him."

Cara looks at the position of the driver's seat. It's a big car, but there's little leg room behind: it's been pushed right back, the rearview mirror tilted up to a high angle.

"What're your thoughts about that?" Cara asks, showing Libby.

"We noticed it. Definitely not moved postmortem. You see the linear pattern of drips?" She moves out of the way so Cara can see. "Where the victim's blood ran down to the floor from the back of the seat?"

Cara nods. "So could be our guy's natural driving position?"

"Could be. We took a few measurements. Estimated a height between five ten and six four."

They walk away from the car. Outside the cordon they pull their suits off, balling them up.

Out of her usual crime scene outfit, Libby cuts an impressive figure in tight black jeans and a black sweater, thick eyeliner and long lashes highlighting her light blue eyes. She takes the white gloves off, revealing shiny, silver-painted nails.

"You'll have my formal report within forty-eight hours," she finishes. Then she peers closely at Cara. "How are you doing?"

"I'm fine."

"Fine? You're the senior investigating officer for a violent double homicide, one of the worst I've seen for a while, and you're fine?"

Cara shrugs. "You know. Still on for drinks tonight?"

"Of course. And Deaks? Is he coming?"

"No, he's busy." Cara grins. "Hoping for a repeat performance?"

"Would never hurt." Libby smiles in reply. "He's not seeing anyone then?"

"Free and easy."

"I wouldn't go that far," Libby says, reaching over and giving Cara a hug goodbye. "Nothing about Noah is easy."

*　*　*

Cara appreciates the quiet on the drive back, but any sanity she's managed to preserve is ruined as soon as she steps in the building. DS Taylor is waiting for her at the door. Cara forces a smile.

"Griffin's been hanging around again," Taylor says, eschewing any sort of friendly greeting. "I thought you should know."

Cara beckons her over to the side of the corridor, out of earshot of other coppers.

"What do you mean, 'hanging around'?"

"Interviewing my arson suspect, for a start," Taylor snaps. "Somehow got in there first, made me look like a right idiot."

But you make it so easy, Cara thinks, but doesn't say out loud.

She's worked with DS Taylor before. She's quick to judge, too quick in Cara's opinion, and the two of them have exchanged words more than once to that effect. But this isn't the time to make enemies.

"Did he do any harm to your investigation?" she says instead.

"No, but . . ." Taylor scowls. Cara has the feeling there's something she's not telling her. "This is my case, and we know who did it. We have forensics tying the wife to the murder weapon, plus a history of previous violence. Just keep Griffin away from me."

"Thank you for letting me know," Cara says sweetly. "If you could leave it here—"

"I've spoken to the DCS already," Taylor interrupts, then turns and walks off down the corridor.

"Shit," Cara mutters under her breath. She could do without Griffin making things complicated. Then a thought occurs to her.

She goes into her office and clicks into the system. Sure enough, the time stamp of her last log in reads eleven forty-five PM last night. She chews on a nail, staring at it. She should change her password, she knows, but at least this way she can keep an eye on what he's doing.

She looks out to the incident room, where the detectives are all working hard. They've spent the last twenty-four hours flat out, knowing the golden hour of opportunity is closing.

Deakin sticks his head around the door.

"How did it go with Libby?" he asks. He stands in the doorway, leaning against the frame as she tells him Libby's analysis.

"So it's not Rick Baker. He can't have been more than five eight," he says as Cara tells him about the position of the driver's seat of the Ford Galaxy.

"That's what I thought. And Libby asked about you," Cara concludes. "Sure you don't want to come tonight?"

He gives her a sarcastic look. "That's all over with. As you well know."

"I live in hope."

"The PM report's back," he says, changing the subject. He comes in and sits next to her at her desk, leaning forward and pulling the report off the Record Management System. They read it in silence, taking in the complicated medical jargon, knowing exactly what it meant for these girls' last moments.

Dr. Ross talks about the incisions on the neck. A transverse cut, splitting the trapezius muscle and any number of nerves and veins Cara couldn't even start to pronounce. Severing of the spine between the C3 and C4 vertebrae.

He mentions the positive sign of petechial hemorrhages in the eyes and face on examination, damage to the larynx, to the superior horns of the thyroid cartilage. Bruising on the anterior and lateral aspects of the neck. No linear abrasions from fingernails, consistent with the hands being tied.

Cara knows he's referring to the common scratches caused by victims trying to pry away choking fingers. She looks at Noah.

"What's he saying? That they were strangled as well?"

"Looks that way," he mutters.

She turns back. There are photos: dark bruising on her wrist, broken fingernails. Cara imagines the poor girl rubbing her skin raw, scrabbling at the inside of the trunk, trying to get free as she listened to her friend being murdered in the back.

She forces herself to read on.

Antemortem stab wounds. Four in total, from the same weapon. Estimated to be from a single-sided blade about the size of a small kitchen knife.

Cause of death: strangulation compounded by blood loss from multiple penetrating injuries, likely resulting from knife wounds. Head removed postmortem.

Cara takes a deep breath in and lets it out slowly.

"Nothing back from the lab yet?" she says, at last.

Noah shakes his head. "Blood samples taken," he says, continuing to read. "Along with fingernail scrapings and EEK."

Early evidence kit. The standard swabs for rape.

"But Ross didn't see any signs of sexual assault?"

"Not on either victim, no."

Cara leans back in her chair. With any investigation, the responsibility lies with her to decide the focus for the team: what have they found, what does it mean, and what do they do next? She's used to it, but with these two girls, with this level of violence, she feels the accountability lie heavy on her shoulders.

The phone rings. Cara answers it, then puts it on speaker.

"DS Deakin is also here," she says as Dr. Ross's voice booms from the handset.

"Have you read it?" he asks.

"Yes," Cara replies. "Strangled and stabbed." She's surprised he's phoning. Pathologists, and Ross in particular, don't normally relish the opportunity of being questioned further by detectives.

"Not that," he says, sharply. "The bit about the decapitation."

Cara glances to Deakin, then back to the report. She's not sure what he's referring to. At the other end of the phone, they hear Ross grunt in exasperation.

"The cuts," Ross carries on. "They were sharp, precise. There were none of the hesitation marks that you would expect to see on a dead body with this sort of postmortem damage. Taking a head off isn't easy. Even if you get past the mental aspect, there's the practicalities. The muscles of the neck are strong. Vertebrae are connected by ligaments. They're tough."

Ross stops, and the hiss from the phone line fills the room.

"Do you get what I'm saying?"

Cara looks at Noah. His eyes are puzzled, waiting.

"Detectives," Ross continues. "These heads were taken off by someone who knew what he was doing." He pauses. "As much as I don't like to say so, your killer has done this before."

14

G RIFFIN FIDGETS ON a park bench while he waits. He smokes a cigarette, considers lighting another, then stops himself. He doesn't
know if she will even show up. He looks at the hastily gathered docu-
ments in his hand. What they're suggesting is insane, but . . . He knows
that Jess is right.

He's left her back at his apartment. It feels strange, this woman suddenly intruding in his life. But something's different about her: she has
none of the wariness, the distance he normally gets from other people.
He doesn't feel judged by Jess, and it's freeing.

At last he spots Cara, hurriedly walking along the path, her head
down, her coat pulled around her. She sees him and a look flashes across
her face before she hides it again. He knows what she's thinking. She'd
rather be anywhere than here.

She reaches the bench and stands in front of him, blocking out the
light. He can't see her face; her body is no more than a silhouette in
shadow.

"What do you want?" she asks.

"Sit down," he says.

After a moment of resistance, she does as he asks. He passes her the
folder.

"What's this?"

"Just hear me out."

She sighs. "Griffin, I don't know what you're doing, but this has
to stop. I've got detectives telling me you're interfering with suspects,

hanging around the hospital. And you're still using my log in. You'll get me in trouble as well at this rate."

"Cara." He turns to face her. "Listen for a minute. This file contains information about a series of murders occurring across the country. They've been across numerous constabularies, all with different MOs, so nobody's noticed the link."

"What link?" She opens the folder, flicking through the pages.

"The killer is copying the MOs of different serial killers."

Cara pauses. Then she looks at him. "Pardon?"

"Look at the details. These murders here all take after Sutcliffe. These ones are all the Hillside Strangler. And the multiple homicide in Dorset on Monday night? What does that remind you of?"

He's looking at her face, studying the features he knows so well, trying to see if he's getting through to her. She looks at the photos, at the writing daubed on the wall in blood, at the pregnant woman.

"Griffin, I have seen enough murdered women for one week, thank you very much."

He stares at her.

"What murdered women?" he asks.

"Two students, stabbed and strangled, their decapitated bodies left in a car just outside Cranbourne Woods."

"Decapitated? Why haven't I heard about these? You know that's not normal."

"We've deliberately kept it away from the news. They've only just updated the system." She says this quietly, almost under her breath. Then she shakes her head. "This is ridiculous. Please stop, Griffin. I can't protect you forever. You're under suspension as it is." She looks at him. He knows she's upset. "Please, Nate?"

He nods. But then he points to the folder again. "You'll see that we're right. And have a look at your double homicide. I bet you that fits the pattern."

"But that was Monday night too. What are you saying? That this guy spent an evening driving around on a killing spree, and nobody noticed?"

Griffin stops and thinks. She's right. It's a lot. But yet—

She taps a finger on the file. "And if this pattern is so obvious, why is it only coming to light now? Why haven't you spotted it before?"

It's a good question, and one Griffin's asked himself multiple times since Jess made the connection. But he's never been a fan of true crime—when your job is so full of death and destruction, why seek it out in your spare time?—and his brain has been so addled for the last year, some days he's barely remembered to eat.

He remembers Alan's comments at the crime scene. Perhaps they had joined the dots, and Manson had been one of their theories? But he and Jess hadn't stayed around long enough to find out.

He keeps this to himself. Instead, he says, "Multiple constabularies, different MOs, cops not working together. You know what it's like. Everyone's so overstretched, so focused on the detail, nobody has time to step back and think." He looks at her. "Just promise me you'll have a read."

"Okay, fine. But if I don't agree with you, you'll stop?"

He presses his lips together. Then nods.

She moves forward, sitting on the edge of the park bench.

"And go see Mom, please?"

"Cara . . ."

"Please? I'll do this for you on the one condition you go and see her. She worries about you. She misses you."

He takes a deep breath, feeling the tension in his body. "She always forgets," he says quietly. "She always asks about Mia."

She turns and takes his hands gently. She stares at them, her fingers rubbing on his. "I'm sorry about what . . . happened," she says at last. "It's bad for me too. She forgets the kids, she forgets Roo. She thinks I'm this silly twenty-year-old getting dumped by unsuitable boyfriends. But I go see her, week after week." She looks up at him. "You need to get help. Let me help you."

Griffin pulls his hands away and reaches into his pocket for a cigarette. He lights it with shaking fingers.

"You don't look well, Nate," Cara continues. "I miss you. I miss my little brother."

Griffin stands up. "I'll go see her. Just read it, please."

He turns away from her, taking a long drag on the cigarette as he walks away. He knew seeing Cara was going to be hard, but she is his best chance of being heard. And he misses her too. He misses seeing her every day at work. He misses arguing about their cases over the dinner table, her husband rolling his eyes as they'd banter to and fro. He misses his niece and nephew.

But he knows that he's in no fit state to see people now.

He strides quickly away, knowing she'll still be staring after him. But he refuses to turn around.

15

H E'S EXCITED. THE man lies in front of him on his back, motionless, on the sofa. His shirt is off and he can just see the slight rise and fall of his chest. His eyes are closed: he's asleep, drugged with sleeping pills.

This is the time he enjoys more than any other. The anticipation, knowing what he's about to do. In this second, he's in control. He owns them, these people, and once they're dead, they will become his possessions. They will be a part of him.

He felt that thrill at age nine, young and inexperienced. He feels it the same way now. He lies down slowly, placing his cheek against the man's warm, bare chest. He hears the man's heart beating slowly, feels his lungs taking in air. Steven, he thinks. He smiles.

This is different, this calm. He remembers the women from Monday night screaming. He remembers the pregnant whore, pleading for her life as he stabbed her over and over, the men crying like little bitches as they tried to escape. The feeling of sticky blood on his face, soaking his clothes, warming his skin.

He likes that too. More so, usually. But this? This is nice. Pleasant, even.

But it's time.

He sits up, then moves until he's straddling the man's chest. He carefully places his hands around the man's neck, his thumbs interlocking. Then he leans forward, all his weight on his arms. He starts to squeeze.

He feels cartilage give way, a snap as a bone breaks in the neck. The man's face changes color, turning red. Minutes pass. He watches for the telltale purply-blue tinge as hypoxia kicks in. A line of pink drool runs down from the man's open mouth—blood mixed with saliva.

He holds his hands there longer than he knows is necessary, feeling his arms starting to shake from the exertion. Just enjoying the moment.

Then he sits back. He places his cheek against the chest again. There is no heartbeat anymore, no rise and fall. He knows before long the body will start to grow cold, and he'd like to stick around a bit longer, but he has to go.

He stands up, leaving the corpse on the sofa. It'll be fine there for a while. He knows there is more he needs to do before it's ready.

CHAPTER

16

GRIFFIN PUSHES THE door open to his apartment. He starts to call out, then stops himself as he realizes nobody's there. Jess has gone.

He feels odd. Seeing Cara today has stirred up something in him. Memories of his past life. He's spent the last year resolutely by himself, but with the simple act of one night in someone's company, he suddenly can't bear to be alone.

He glances at his watch: he's been gone two hours. He wonders where Jess is. Before he left, he gave her his number on a scrap of paper, but she has no phone, and he has no way of contacting her.

He remembers last night. It wasn't a great thing to do, he knows that. To kiss her, then push her aside. In that moment he'd wanted her, and he knew she'd wanted it too, but something had felt amiss. Sex, for all the wrong reasons.

Her husband had just died. But who decides the best way forward after a death is quiet, dignified grieving? Maybe all she needed at that time was him. Maybe they were just two lonely people connecting the only way they knew how.

Is that what I am? he thinks to himself. Lonely? Since she's been here, he's certainly felt differently. Someone to share the burden, maybe. Because suddenly someone listened and believed him and made the connection he hadn't been able to reach.

He goes to the kitchen counter and puts the kettle on. He feels the familiar pain and tentatively bends from side to side, wincing slightly. It's not good. Griffin reaches into the drawer next to him, pulling out the box, the last box of drugs, pushing two free of their foil and putting them in his mouth, swallowing them. He feels them move slowly down his throat, and reaches for a glass. He runs the water and downs it. It would have been quicker to bend and put his mouth under the tap, but that movement is impossible, not before the capsules do their job.

The lack of drugs concerns him. He mentally counts up how long he has. Four days, maybe five if he holds back.

He makes a mug of coffee and sits at the table.

He could see Cara hadn't taken him seriously. His sister has had to put up with more than the usual level of shit from a sibling over the past year.

At first she was understanding. The grief, it seemed, she could deal with, but the obsessive searching, going off the book at work. She could only defend him for so long, and when he'd been suspended, she'd agreed.

"You need some time off," she'd said. Then, as an afterthought: "Try and get some help."

Griffin knows she'll be angry with him today. But he also hopes that maybe her detective instincts will kick in, and she'll stop for a second. She's a good cop, she's curious.

But so is he. He wonders about the murders she referred to. He goes online, using her log in, mentally swearing it will be for the last time. He looks at the details of the case—the forensic reports, the make of the car, the victims, the MO. He goes on Wikipedia, pulling up a basic entry on serial killers, his eyes scanning the pages.

He clicks and reads, time passing without him noticing. At last he finds something that makes him stop. He sends Cara a text, then glances up at the clock. Jess has been gone for four hours now.

He logs on to the system again, searching for Jess's name. Her record is still there, stating the live BOLO. But that doesn't mean anything; she could have been arrested. It often takes hours for these things to be updated.

He sighs, annoyed with himself. Worrying about some woman he's just met. What's got into him? He's not going to sit here and stress. He has to do something.

But he knows where he's going to go. He made a promise. After all, it can't make him feel any worse.

*   *   *

Griffin looks up at the house in front of him. It seems normal. Boring, even. It's square and evenly proportioned, encased in pebble dash and surrounded by a concrete parking lot. A few token trees are planted around, early daffodils poking through the measly patches of soil.

He rings the doorbell and a loud answering buzz comes almost instantly.

A man in a horrible mustard cardigan greets him by name as he approaches. He reads his name badge.

"How is she, Miles?" Griffin asks.

The man smiles. "She's good today, she'll be pleased to see you. It's been a while."

Griffin nods, then pushes through a set of double doors into the main part of the house. He takes in the tired decoration, the bland watercolors on the walls, door after door, all closed to whoever might be behind. There is a strong smell of disinfectant.

He stops at the end of the corridor. He knocks once on the door, takes a deep breath, then pushes it open without waiting for a response.

'Mom?" he calls as he goes in. "It's me. It's Nate."

It's one room, with a small bathroom off to the right. In the center is a hospital bed with rails on either side, decorated with a colorful throw. A stuffed brown bear leans drunkenly against the pillow. A woman sits next to the window in a large green chair. She has a blanket over her lap and a cup of tea on the table next to her. Her eyes are closed and her head is bent; she seems to be asleep.

Griffin walks up to her and kneels down next to the chair. He places one hand gently on her arm. "Mom," he repeats, "it's Nate."

She stirs and looks at him, smiling.

"Oh, how lovely to see you."

Griffin gives her a kiss on her papery cheek; she smells of lavender talcum powder. He pulls a chair around to sit next to her.

"How are you, Mom?" he asks.

"Can't complain." She squints through her glasses at him. "You look a mess, Nathanial. Have a shave. When was the last time you had your hair cut?"

He runs a hand through his hair. He smiles. Some things never change, after all. Mothers always like neat hair.

"Do you remember, I used to cut it for you when you were little? I once cut the bangs so lopsided we had to shave it all off. Like that friend of Cara's, you know. The skinny one."

"Noah comes to see you?" Griffin asks. He feels a flash of guilt. When even crappy Noah Deakin goes to see his mom, he knows he's been a shitty son.

"Yes. Such a pity that poor boy doesn't have a family of his own." Her voice tails off and she smiles, looking out the window. "The primroses are coming through in the garden. Spring must be around the corner."

Griffin's concentration fades out as his mom continues to chatter away. He looks at his mother, feeling sad. Her hair is completely gray now, tied back away from her face in a neat bun, and she is thin, her cheekbones protruding from her face, skin hanging loose without anything to fill it. She is wearing a thick pair of plastic glasses, and every now and again lowers them to look out the window.

The dementia has all but taken every fragment of the mother he remembers. He's surprised she recalled Noah visiting. Obviously, something about him stuck in her mind.

He looks at the photos around the room. Cara made all the arrangements for their mom to live here, now more than five years ago. And she's taken the time to make the room feel like home. There are pictures on the walls, prints of well-known paintings mostly, as well as a few framed photos decorating the shelves. Nate sees a family photo of Cara, Andrew, and the kids, and picks it up.

His niece and nephew are older here than he remembers. He smiles at the gaps in Tilly's teeth, her front two obviously having fallen out. He knows he hasn't sent either of them a present or birthday card this year. There's no excuse. More people he's let down.

His mother sees the photo in his hand and peers over at it.

"Is Cara still with that awful boyfriend?" his mother asks. "The one with the silly name?"

Griffin assumes she's referring to Andrew. Everyone's always called him Roo. "Er, yes. Very much so."

His mother beams. "And how is Mia?"

The tragedy of dementia, Griffin thinks, is how random the memories are. Cara and Roo were married a long time before him and Mia, yet Mia is the name she remembers.

"She's fine, Mom."

"Bring her with you next time you come," she says.

Griffin notices her eyelids drooping. He sits quietly for a while, listening to her slow, rasping breathing. He remembers his childhood, growing up with Cara. Carefree days, not a worry in the world except for reaching the next level on *Lemmings*, racing his sister on *Super Mario Cart*. Cara was smarter than him but hadn't rubbed his face in it, his grades trailing hers by miles. Even though he was younger, he'd always been bigger, protecting her on the playground when she needed it, a steady arm around her shoulder at their father's funeral at the age of sixteen. He'd joined the force first; then, after university, to his surprise, she'd done the same, quickly overtaking him. She was the better result of their upbringing.

He stands up to go but then catches a glimpse of a photo, hidden behind the others. It's an old one. In it he's clean-shaven; short, neat hair; in a suit. Must have been a wedding, maybe Tilly's christening. And she's next to him, smiling broadly, her arm around his waist.

His wife was beautiful. Sometimes he wonders if he's built her up in his mind, but no, this photo proves it. Long, curly black hair, sharp green eyes, a delicate chin. She had been too good for him, and he'd known it, but he would have done anything for Mia. She'd softened him, she made him palatable for the first time to the outside world. She had been his everything.

He feels his jaw clench, something stick in his throat. The familiar tension returns. He puts the frame down, but before he does so, he takes the photo out of the back and puts it in his pocket.

He bends down slowly and gives his mother a gentle kiss on the cheek, picking up her blanket from where it has fallen on the floor, tucking it carefully around her.

"Bye, Mom," he whispers.

17

CARA THROWS GRIFFIN'S file on to the passenger seat with disgust and starts the engine. She's got too much going on of her own without Griffin's delusions to worry about, and his latest obsession seems more surreal than usual. Serial killers? For Christ's sake! He's going to get himself fired, and then what? He'll end up living in that basement forever.

She starts the engine and goes to put the car into gear, then stops. He'd said "we," hadn't he? *"You'll see that we're right."* Who was he referring to? She frowns. She can't think about this now.

Deakin's waiting for her as she arrives back at the station.

"What did he want?" he asks. She knows who he's talking about.

She pushes past him and stands in front of the massive board. Information and photographs now cover it, headlines from the postmortems scribbled up. Two girls murdered. Griffin's right. It's not a common occurrence.

"What do we have from CCTV?" she asks, ignoring Deakin's question.

He opens his eyes wide at her obvious bad mood, then points to Toby Shenton, where he has footage up on his screen.

Shenton glances up at Cara, and his face colors. She feels a flash of irritation, then checks herself. The last thing this kid's self-confidence needs is a bashing from his superior officer; it's not her DC's fault her brother's a nightmare.

"So, we've finished tracking the whole of the victims' journey," Noah begins. They both sit down at the desk, watching as Shenton expertly flicks from screen to screen. "The quality of the CCTV varies, but here we have them arriving at the club"—Shenton changes the view—"then leaving at twelve minutes past one."

Noah nods at Shenton, and he takes over the narrative.

"They walk together down the road here," he says. "Then they stop at this junction for about five minutes. Until this car arrives."

Cara watches as the blue Ford Galaxy pulls up next to them. Only the rear of the car is in the shot, and the two girls go out of sight. Talking to him at the front window, Cara assumes.

"No other camera views?" she asks.

"None."

"Witnesses?"

"A few bystanders and other students earlier on, as they're walking down the road, but it's quieter here. There's no one else in shot."

Cara watches as one of the girls returns into view, opening the back door and getting into the car. It drives away and Shenton looks up at her.

"And that's it."

"Nothing on traffic cams? No other footage?" Cara sighs. "City's smothered in CCTV and that's it?"

Noah steps in as Shenton stutters in the face of Cara's disappointment. "That's what I said, but it's all we have. Either the guy was lucky, or he knew precisely where to drive to avoid the cameras."

She hears what Noah's saying. This is a man who knows what he's doing.

She places a reassuring hand on Shenton's shoulder.

"Thank you, Toby," she finishes, and gets up quickly, walking away from the desk, suppressing her annoyance.

Noah appears in the doorway.

"What did Griffin want?" he asks again.

Cara slaps the file on to the desk. "Nothing good," she says. Her phone beeps and she picks it up, then puts it back down roughly. "Go away, Nate," she mutters. Deakin's flipping through the file next to her.

"Don't bother, Deaks. It's just another one of his crazy theories."

But Noah's still looking and slowly sits down at her computer. He does a search on the system and Cara looks over his shoulder as he pulls up the details.

"Had you heard about this?" he asks. She pulls a chair over and sits down next to him, reading the screen.

Five dead, including one pregnant woman. Noah hands her the file and she pulls out one of the printouts Griffin has included. It's a color photograph of a wall—the word *PIG* written in red. She looks back at the screen, where Noah is staring between the two pictures.

"Yeah, I have that same photo here," she says, but Noah shakes his head.

"This isn't the photo you have in your hand," he says quietly. "This is a photo from a true crime website." He looks at her. "This is from the Manson murders."

Cara looks between the screen and the photo in her hand. There is no doubt about it. They are identical.

"What did Griffin just text you?" he asks.

Cara leans forward and Deakin moves out of the way of the computer. She types in a few search terms, and information appears on the screen. Two students, women, eighteen. Kidnapped when hitchhiking. Handcuffed, strangled, stabbed. Heads severed. Put in the trunk of a Ford Galaxy, one with a broken taillight.

Cara can barely breathe. She tears her eyes away and looks at Noah. His face is white.

"What did Griffin's text say?" he asks again.

Cara looks at her phone, then back to the screen.

"Kemper," she says.

18

Cara sees the whole range of emotions in her detective chief super-intendent's eyes. Quietly, she and Noah had gathered up the file and taken it to Marsh's office. They hadn't spoken—they'd barely dared look at each other. To acknowledge what they both knew as true seemed bonkers. And yet, they couldn't deny what they were seeing.

They go into the office and sit in front of their boss. They start with their own case, showing the similarities one by one to Marsh. At first, he seems to be humoring them. Then a look of confusion crosses his face.

"You're telling me that someone went to the trouble of reconstruct-ing a double murder from nearly fifty years ago in our back garden?" Cara recognizes the skepticism. She'd heard it in her own voice.

"We know it sounds crazy, boss. But all the details are the same. From the make of the car, to the way they were killed."

He frowns, picks up the file, then puts it down again.

"So, what? We're looking for someone obsessed with a serial killer from California?"

Cara looks at Noah and their boss sees the glance. "What?" he says.

"We think there's more."

Noah pulls out the second file, the one that Griffin had given Cara. He puts the pieces of paper on the desk.

"These are murders from the last few years. Prostitutes, killed in a way similar to Sutcliffe, the Yorkshire Ripper. And women strangled and raped, consistent with the Hillside Strangler."

Their DCS looks at them, his mouth gaping.

"Then this one, from yesterday. Five dead. Similar to Manson."

"Manson?" he repeats. "Charles Manson?" He looks at Cara and she nods. He runs his finger across the other photographs. "What about these?" He moves them around on his desk, and one comes into view.

"Is this . . .?" he asks, looking at Cara, and she nods. "How is this linked?"

"We don't know yet."

Their boss sits back in his seat and runs both hands through his hair. "Fuck," he mutters. "Why the hell are we only spotting this now?"

But Cara and Noah stay silent. There's no excuse. They both feel the failure. And Cara knows what her boss is thinking. At first it's pure disbelief, followed by a hollowing realization that they have a serial killer on their hands. And a very dangerous one at that.

Marsh taps his fingers on the desk, a quick, nervous movement. He fiddles with the photographs again.

"How did you come by this?" he says at last. "What made you look at other cases?"

Noah looks at Cara again.

"Griffin," Marsh says, frowning. He lets out an infuriated grunt. "Typical. Takes a fucked-up cop to make a fucked-up connection." He glances up quickly, realizing he's insulted Cara's brother, then continues without apology. "I heard he'd been sniffing around, getting in the way of our detectives." He stops. "Who did he interview in the hospital?"

"I believe it was this case," Cara says. "The death of Patrick Ambrose in an arson on Monday night."

"Arson? That doesn't sound like it's linked." Marsh sits forward decisively in his chair. "Here's what we're going to do. I want to be a hundred percent sure before we go talking about this elsewhere. Look into everything you have. Get a team on it, but for God's sake, keep it quiet. We don't want a panic on our hands. I'll alert the chief constable." He looks at Cara. "And what about Griffin? How unstable is he?"

Cara knows the incident he's referring to. "He seems okay, boss," she says, "but completely obsessed with this. We might need to bring him back in. Just to keep him on the straight and narrow, if nothing else."

"Fine." Cara can see he's not pleased about the idea, and to be honest, neither is she. Her brother had been suspended for a reason. His behavior had become unpredictable, with random outbursts of anger, culminating in him punching another detective, breaking his nose. He's not safe to have around, and her boss knows it.

But he also knows that once Griffin gets his teeth into something, he can't be stopped, and it's better to have him here, closely watched, than out doing something impulsive.

"But he's your responsibility, Elliott, you hear me?"

Before Cara can say anything in return, a hurried banging on the door diverts their attention. Noah pulls it open, and Shenton stands there. He's out of breath, his face red, obviously having run up the stairs.

"You weren't answering your phone, boss," he pants. "It's the blood results—they're back." He thrusts a piece of paper toward them, and Cara snatches it from his hands.

"Most of the samples come back to the victims, but one . . . One wasn't," he garbles. "We ran it through the system."

"And?"

"We have a match."

Cara and Deakin both stand up, ready to leave.

"DCI Elliott?" Marsh says, and she turns. "Get this wrapped up. And quick."

Cara nods. She feels the excitement churn in her stomach. They have a suspect. It's time to catch this guy.

19

"MICHAEL SHARP, HIGH-LEVEL shit, arrests for sexual assault, possession, intent to supply, assault and battery, multiple stints inside . . ."

Deakin's reading from a printout as they're rocked back and forth in the back of the van. Cara pulls on the black stab vest, passing another to Noah, who puts it over his head, fastening it around his body.

The energy is palpable. A team has been assembled, the armed response vehicle in front of them, ready to go. They're taking no risks with this guy. Knowing what they know now, they're going in hard and fast.

They have two possible addresses for Michael Sharp: his mother's house and his own apartment, which Cara and Noah are heading to now. Plan is to hit both at the same time. Two separate teams, two hyped up groups of guns and coppers, ready to search and seize, and—more importantly—arrest this bastard.

They bundle out on to the pavement, then go at speed toward the front door of the building. They know what they're there to do, armed response heading in first, Cara and Deakin behind.

They climb the stairs to the second floor, then hear a shout from the lead cop, followed by a thump as the battering ram knocks down the door. Heavy footsteps and noise fills the corridor as the officers storm apartment 213.

But as Cara approaches, she knows something's not right. At first it's the quiet. After the initial banging and shouting, there are usually yells from the apprehended suspect or disappointed mutterings from the cops, but today there is only silence. Then she notices the smell. It catches in her nostrils, unconsciously making her pause. She pushes herself forward into the apartment. The smell is stronger. She notices a buzz, and a fly goes past her ear.

An officer—a large, burly, six-foot-tall cop—pushes past Cara into the corridor. She watches him bending over, vomiting in the stairwell. She looks at Noah. He's frowning, staring inside.

The place is warm, too much so, and Cara puts a hand out to the scorching radiator. It's on full blast. But despite the heat, Cara feels the hairs on her arm stand up on end, a cold chill run down her back.

Deakin's radio buzzes and voices come down the airwaves.

"House two, clear. Mother brought in for questioning. No sign of Sharp." They can hear screeching in the background. "Mother being arrested for possession and intent to supply class A's."

Deakin swears under his breath, then looks back at Cara. He starts walking further inside, and she follows him into the kitchen.

The police officers are all standing facing one end of the tiny room. None of them speaks. Two more officers turn around and walk past her quickly, their faces showing pure disgust.

She pushes through the crowd. Then she stops.

In front of them is an open fridge. A cardboard box sits on the bottom shelf. Cara's hand flies to her mouth. Inside is a severed head, facing upward.

"Well," Deakin whispers behind her. "That answers that question."

"Detective Chief Inspector?"

A voice behind her pulls her attention away. She turns and another cop is standing next to a freestanding freezer. She doesn't want to, but she forces herself to peer inside.

There are three more human heads.

She feels her stomach turn, and she takes a step backward.

She leaves the kitchen, going into the bedroom. But if anything, it's worse. There's a single bed in the middle of the room, its mattress stained with what she assumes to be blood, as well as spatter up the walls and on the pillowcase. There's a metal filing cabinet next to the bed, then a chest of drawers and a box with a polystyrene lid.

Throughout is the indescribable smell of death and decay.

"What the fuck is that?" Deakin asks, pointing. In the corner sits a large blue plastic drum with a black cover.

Cara stares for a moment. She has a bad feeling about it.

"Don't open it," she says. "We need to get out of here," she shouts to the team. "Get SOCO as soon as possible. Someone call the pathologist."

The cops don't wait to be told twice. Cara hears quick footsteps, the apartment emptying. Deakin stays, then walks across to the filing cabinet. He pulls open the top drawer, then recoils.

"Fuck," he says again.

She goes over and looks in. There, staring up at her, lying on a black towel, are three human skulls. Stripped of their skin and flesh, they look almost surreal, like displays stolen from a science class. And they're painted—green with black flecks.

Cara can't stand the smell any longer. Combined with the sight of the skulls, her body rebels, pushing her out of the room and into the corridor. She makes it down the stairs and into the garden before she throws up, bent double, her stomach purging out whatever was left of her lunch.

She crouches on the grass, wiping her mouth with the back of her hand. She closes her eyes, but the image stays.

Decapitated heads. Decayed, brown skin, straggly hair. Skulls, grinning, eye sockets empty.

She throws up again, then stays there, collapsed on all fours on the grass, weak and gasping.

What else? she thinks, as she retches. What else is in that apartment?

decapitate dismember deflesh ?rubbish Place in acid to liquify—what
acid? Muriatic
smash bones with sledgehammer, scatter in woods
Three-eighth-inch drill one-sixteenth-inch drill bit claw hammer
handsaw
Fish food African cichlid tiger barbs trigger fish
Bicep—fry in skillet, tenderize, sprinkle with sauce
Boil skull—Soilex and bleach—BUT too brittle to keep? Dilute bleach
Strip flesh, cut off genitals, smash bones. Use acetone—soak
Head—cut off scalp, peel flesh off bone, keep skull and scalp
Dissect legs from pelvis at joints, boil in water and Soilex—1 hour. Pour
off, rinse in sink, removing remaining flesh. Place bones in acid 2 weeks
pour black slush down toilet OR oven skull? No—explodes.
separate the joints, the arm joints, the leg joints, two boilings.
Four boxes Soilex, each one boil 2 hours Turns flesh to jelly like sub-
stance just washes off
clean bones in light bleach, leave for day spread out on newspaper and
let dry
spray-paint skull coat with enamel
keep entire skin? Small sharp paring knife, incision at back of neck,
slice up to crown, then pull down skin (like chicken?) Outer layer peels
back from muscle with care. Pulls right off skull, might have to cut round
nose, lips, mouth (2 hours) Preserve in cold water and salt?
lift torso to drain blood. Slice liver smaller pieces, cut off flesh in leg or
arm area work down
head in saucepan of water eyeballs boil away flesh takes longer dessert
spoon to scoop out brain
but . . .?smell Febreze Incense sticks

CHAPTER

20

JESS WAKES TO the smell of food. She can hear a radio, someone moving around downstairs. She's comfortably warm under the duvet.

She thinks back. She remembers Griffin leaving the apartment. And then a sudden blank. She'd woken on the floor of Griffin's bathroom, vision blurry, another wave of dizziness making her wobble. She had stood and looked in the mirror. Someone she hadn't recognized had stared back, eyes red-rimmed, face gray and drawn. Her hand had gone up to the bump on the back of her head, the bit of shaved hair where she was stitched back up. She'd known then who she had to call.

Nav.

She contacted him on Messenger, logging on to Griffin's laptop with the password she'd seen him use that morning. Nav's reply was curt and immediate:

Jess! Where are you? The police are looking for you. You took my car!

She replied, *I know. I'm sorry. How is Alice?*

She watched the three gray dots rotate at the bottom.

Much better. She'll be out in a few days, I think. Your mom and dad are with her. They're going crazy with worry.

Knowing Alice was okay was a massive relief. She kept typing: *I need your help.*

She held her breath.

Your head.

Jess sensed his disapproval from the brevity of his message.

Yes. I'm sorry. I need you to check I'm okay.

The dots again. Then: *I'm not a damn mechanic. The brain is tricky, and I can't see what's going on in there. Come to the hospital.*

I can't. I'll be arrested, she replied. Then she typed back the words she knew would get him there. *Fine. Don't worry.*

He arrived at the apartment, pissed off and scowling. Nav had come to her aid more times than she could count over the years, patching her up, checking her over, but it had always been on the edge of what was acceptable for a doctor to do. Never something this bad. And never when there had been this much risk.

He pushed past her into the room.

"Sit down," he barked. "And where the hell am I?"

Jess didn't answer the question, just did what she was told. He grabbed another chair and sat in front of her, pulling a penlight out of his bag and shining it in her eyes.

"Watch me," Nav said. He shone the light into each eye in turn as she looked at his face. He seemed stern, concentrating. He moved it left and right, then up and down. He placed a warm hand gently on her forehead. "Look at my finger."

She watched as he'd moved it in an H shape in front of her eyes. She knew the neuro exam back to front, she'd done it so many times. He carried on and she followed his instructions, sticking her tongue out, shrugging her shoulders, holding her arms out and closing her eyes. She resisted his pressure on her arms, then her legs when he asked her to. She touched her finger to her nose, then to his finger, doing it over and over again.

"Have you had any problems with your vision?" he asked, gruffly.

"Just some blurriness. Felt dizzy a few times."

"No loss of consciousness? No slurred speech?"

"I fainted briefly."

"Been sick?"

"No."

He sighed. "You seem fine," Nav muttered. "I downloaded your CT scan from when you first arrived in the hospital, and it was clear. But there could be anything going on since then. Expanding hematoma, increasing intracranial pressure? And without knowing how much pain you're in . . ." His voice tailed off.

"Come back with me," Nav continued. "We won't go to the police, I promise. I need to know . . ." He'd stopped. "I need to be sure this is okay," he said, pointing to her head. "It's important you're okay."

She knew Nav was right. He didn't have to go through the list of medical complications; she was worried enough already. Overwhelming tiredness overtook her. Sitting in that apartment, her body felt gritty; the clothes she was wearing, the ones from the hospital, were uncomfortable. She looked at the pile of photos of dead women on the table, wondering what insanity she'd gotten herself into.

She looked around the room, seeing it with fresh eyes. Griffin was a grown man, living in a one-room studio apartment, if it could even be described as that. The furniture was old, worn out. And where was his wife? What did she know about him, really?

She knew it was the right thing to do.

So now, here she is. She's had a sleep and instantly feels better. Being with Nav, at his house, is everything she wants.

She sits up, her mouth furry, her head groggy. She glances at the clock: 4:35 PM. It's been seven hours. The whole day has passed without her noticing.

Jess pulls herself to her feet. She slowly walks down the stairs and into the kitchen. Nav smiles when he sees her.

"Feel any better?" he asks.

"Not much." Jess feels grubby, a layer of dirt under her clothes. "Can I have a bath?"

Nav goes toward the bathroom, but she waves him back. "I know where it is," she says. "I'll figure everything out."

He nods. "Dinner will be about an hour. And I got you these."

He passes her a Tesco carrier bag, and she looks inside. There's a pair of jeans, a T-shirt, a sweater, some socks, and underwear.

"They're not great, and I had to guess at your size—" he says, but she cuts him off.

"They're perfect, thank you."

She runs a bath and lowers herself into it. It's refreshingly hot. The water sears her skin, washing away the events of the days before.

She thinks back to the apartment with Griffin, and it feels surreal now she's here. She feels bad for just walking out, but he doesn't care about her, he won't mind, she tells herself. Griffin will be glad to get his space back.

She can hear Nav downstairs. He's singing along to the radio, out of tune. She smiles. It's reassuring, being somewhere familiar.

The water's tepid now and she's getting cold. Jess stands up out of the bath and wraps a towel around herself. She hears the doorbell ring and stops. She doesn't dare move.

The hallway is just below the bathroom, and Jess can hear a voice filter up the stairs. She opens the door a crack and listens.

"DS Taylor. Police." A woman, businesslike and formal. "Dr. Sharma?"

"How can I help?" she hears Nav say.

"I'm looking for Jessica Ambrose. And I'm hoping you know where she is."

"I haven't seen her since she stole my car on Tuesday," Nav replies.

"Tuesday?" the detective repeats. "And you say she took it without your permission?"

"Yes. As I told your colleagues at the time."

Jess glances around the room. There is no way she can get out of the bathroom without the detective seeing her. She holds her breath, shivering, still in just the towel.

"Can I come in?" Taylor asks.

"Look, I've just come off nights at the hospital." Nav's voice is calm, measured, but unmistakably frosty. "I work as a junior doctor in oncology. I'm exhausted, about to have something to eat, and, as you have reminded me, annoyed because you've seized my car. If you have more questions, could you come by later or arrange to meet me? I'm back there tomorrow." He's used to being under pressure. But not used to lying to the police, Jess thinks, feeling another surge of guilt.

There's a pause. Jess imagines the detective craning her neck into his house, looking for a sign she's been there. She glances across the bathroom to where her pile of clothes lie on the floor. She wonders what she might have left in the woman's view.

"Fine. I'll do that, Doctor."

She breathes out as she hears the front door close. She pokes her head out of the bathroom. She can just see Nav. He's standing next to the door, resting against the wall, his head in his hands.

* * *

Jess gets dressed as quickly as she can in the new clothes, then goes downstairs. Nav has gone back into the kitchen, and she can hear him rattling around with saucepans and plates. She stands in the doorway, watching him, and he jumps when he sees her.

"There you are! You hungry?" he says. His voice seems unnaturally cheerful. He turns quickly away from her.

"The police were here," Jess says, and he turns back. "I heard them. Thank you."

"You'd do the same for me," Nav replies, dismissing it.

"And I'm sorry about your car."

He looks at her for just a little too long. "Yes, well. That little problem I could have done without. You owe me." Jess nods. Another one to add to the collection, she realizes with a sting.

"Now come and eat."

It's the first proper meal since the fire, and Jess is starving. Nav has always been a good cook, but this evening the simple risotto is the best thing she's ever tasted. She eats it ravenously, barely pausing until it's gone.

When they've finished, Nav clears the plates away and they sit next to each other on the sofa. It's a place she's been a thousand times before: civilized dinners with Patrick, Alice asleep upstairs. New Year's Eve parties, surrounded by enthusiastically drinking medics. She knows Nav has a box of toys, Alice's favorites, squirrelled away for when he babysits. More than once she's dozed off on this very couch after a night out.

But today isn't the easy conversation she's had before with Nav. He looks at her and she refuses to make eye contact. She imagines the concern on his face. She can't stand it: the pity, the obvious sympathy.

"Stop looking at me," she mutters.

He frowns and sits back in the chair. "I just want to help, Jess."

She feels bad. He's risking everything by having her here. And all she can do is be a bitch to him.

"I know, I'm sorry," she says.

He nods in reply. "So what are you going to do?"

Jess shakes her head. "I don't know. I really don't." She notices him going to say something, but cuts him off. "I can't go back to the hospital, Nav. They'll arrest me, and then where will I be?"

"But at least they'll let you see Alice," he says quietly.

The mention of her name makes Jess want to cry. Alice has been at the forefront of her mind since she left the hospital: a constant worry, the separation from her daughter causing an almost physical pain. But she can't be arrested, to be in the hands of the police.

"I don't want supervised visits," she replies. "With a fucking social worker present. Don't you think I've had enough of those in my life already?"

"It's better than nothing. And I'll help you find a lawyer. They'll sort it all out before you know it." He pauses. "It won't be like last time. I promise," he adds softly.

Jess shakes her head, looking down at the floor. Big round tears start to fall. "I can't risk it," she says.

Nav puts his arm around her. He feels warm and familiar. It's all she can do not to sob in his arms, and she rests her head on his chest, closing her eyes. She can smell Nav—the unique mix of him—and it's comforting. Not for the first time, she wonders what life would have been like if she and Nav had gotten together.

They'd never even had a drunken kiss. For a while at university Jess wondered if he was gay, but the two-year live-in girlfriend put a stop to that pondering. She was long gone now, though. Jess couldn't remember why, something to do with the demands of medical training.

Nav was everything Jess wasn't. Grammar-school educated, ridiculously smart, cultured. He was fit: running marathons for children with leukemia. And he was a cancer doctor, for God's sake. A good bloke, through and though. Jess thought maybe that was why they'd never got together. They were too different.

She pulls away and wipes her eyes. She looks at him. The light is fading, and Jess can see how drained Nav is.

"We need to talk about this, Jess," he tries again. "You heard what the police said. They're looking for you."

Jess looks at her hands. Her nails are split and broken, she assumes from escaping the fire, and there is a scratch running across her wrist that she hasn't noticed before.

"And I don't want you going back to that apartment," Nav continues seriously. "Who lives there?"

"Griffin. He's a . . ." She's not sure how to answer the question. "He's helping me," she finishes.

"Helping you do what?"

Jess detects a trace of something in his voice. Jealousy? Surely not.

"Find out what happened. Someone started that fire deliberately. Griffin knows something . . ." She stops. She barely believes it herself. To repeat it seems ridiculous. "You heard the police," Jess says. "They have their minds set. It was me. They're not looking for anyone else."

"You can hardly blame them," Nav blurts out.

His words hang in the room.

"If you don't believe me, then why didn't you tell the police where I was?" Jess growls.

"I do believe you! I know you're not capable of doing something like that—"

"So act like it!"

"But, Jess, you have to see it from their perspective," Nav pleads. "Innocent people don't run."

"I don't trust the police. I'll end up in prison."

"But you trust me, right?"

Jess stays quiet. She does. But Nav's never been on the wrong side of the law. He doesn't understand.

"So that's how it is?" Nav replies, his voice bitter, taking her silence as a negative. "You trust some guy you barely know—"

"Why do you assume I barely know him?" Jess shouts, on the defensive even though he's right.

"You've never mentioned him to me before!"

"I don't tell you everything, Nav."

"Clearly not." She sees his eyes narrow, his temper flare. He lets out a loud yell of frustration, making her jump. "Christ, Jess," he snaps. "Why do you have to be so blind!" he exclaims. "So . . . so . . ."

"So . . .? So—what?" Jess barks.

"So fucking stupid!" She can see his body is tense, and he stands up, starting to pace the room. "You get yourself in these situations, and then you expect everyone—no, not everyone—me," Nav shouts, "to get you out of them."

Jess feels the bitterness of his words. His betrayal. She thought he was her friend. "I didn't start that fire," she protests, feeling her throat tighten.

"No, but you've walked out of the hospital even though you're ill. You're on the run from the police. And I have to lie . . . I have to hide you . . ."

"I'm sorry. I'll go." Jess stands up. She can't stay here. Knowing his true feelings, what she's driven him to. She starts to leave the room, but a sudden hand on her wrist stops her. She turns, looking up into Nav's eyes.

He blinks, his face distraught. "That's not what I meant, Jess," he says, quieter now. "I'm not kicking you out. I just . . ." He lets go of her wrist, then bows his head, pushing his fingers in his eyes and rubbing them hard. "I'm sorry," he adds. "I need some sleep, Jess. Stay here tonight. We'll talk again in the morning."

She hesitates. His words still sting.

"Please?"

Slowly, Jess nods. He reaches down and tries to give her another hug. But her body stays rigid, resisting his comfort.

She follows him up the stairs and watches as he closes the door to his bedroom. She lies back down on the single spare bed. Normally in this bed, she'd be drunk. Normally her mind would be full of laughter after an evening of fun and frivolity.

Tonight is different. The blackness closes in on her. She feels the loneliness claw at her insides. She doesn't know when she can hug her daughter again. Alice must be so confused, wondering where her mom and dad are, why she's not allowed to see them, and tears run down Jess's face, drenching the pillow. Jess thinks of Patrick, lying dead on a slab somewhere. She wonders if she would be allowed to see him one last time, then realizes there'd be nothing left to see. The shock tears through her. His body would be burned, the fire turning him into something devoid of recognition.

She'd done that. She hadn't lit the match, but the reason he'd been in the spare room? That was her. She wonders if he'd understood what was happening. She hopes he'd been overcome by the smoke in his sleep and hadn't woken up.

She feels familiar frustration swell, making her muscles tense. She turns over, pushing her face into the pillow, screaming, her whole body strained as she directs all her anger downward, the feathers muffling the sound.

She stays facedown, counting slowly, willing her breathing to return to normal.

Jess suddenly can't bear to be alone. She stands up and opens the door to the hallway, then slowly pushes down the handle to Nav's room. She can make out his shape, a lump under the duvet, and stands in the doorway for a second, listening to his steady breathing in and out.

She knows she's pushed him too far this time. But he's right. She's stupid. She makes bad, terrible decisions. But she thought that he saw past that; saw a woman that was more than the chaos she makes of her life.

But no. Nav sees her the same way that everyone else does: fucked-up. A mess. Unworthy.

She's asked him to do so much. He's had to lie to the police, risk his medical license. All for her.

She's pushed him too far. And the fact that he's reached his tipping point scares her. Without Nav, her best friend, the most loyal person in her life, who does she have?

She has to get out of there. She has to leave.

She goes down the stairs and picks up Nav's phone, charging in the kitchen. She looks at the keypad. The police would be here in minutes. She wouldn't have to run anymore. She could see Alice. Do the right thing for once in her life.

She makes a call, then sits in the living room to wait, nervously peering out the window.

After fifteen minutes, a car draws up outside. She goes out, pulling the front door quietly shut behind her.

This is her only option. She is sure now.

She climbs into the car. Griffin looks across at her.

"What happened?" he asks.

Jess shakes her head in response.

"Did he throw you out?"

"I didn't want to put him at risk," she mutters. "He doesn't deserve to be a part of this mess." She keeps quiet about the real reason, the shame of Nav's words still hot inside her.

Griffin starts the Land Rover and puts it into gear.

"Last of the good guys, eh?" he says to himself.

"You wouldn't understand. You're not like Nav." Jess turns away and looks out the window into the darkened streets. She realizes what she's implied, that the risk to Griffin doesn't matter.

But Griffin shakes his head. "No. No, I'm not," he mutters in reply.

21

THERE'S NO WAY the investigation is quiet anymore. It's exploded into a full-scale manhunt. Other constabularies are being drafted in; multiple investigations have to be combined. Cara knows the chief constable is having a coronary, shouting at anyone within contact.

Cara's taken control, allocating actions and tasks to the new detectives in the operation. She now stands outside the block of apartments, watching the flood of scene of crime officers begin their work. Libby has arrived with a flash of pink hair and a smile to Noah; Dr. Ross is already inside. Despite the late hour, journalists and TV crews hover around, desperate for a crumb of a quote. One shouts for her attention from the outer cordon. She knows him—Steve Gray from the *Chronicle*—but she responds with a "no comment" and leaves him disappointed.

They've only shared the theory with a handful of people so far—Libby, Ross, a few other detectives; the press have no idea just how bad things are. Cara knows a statement needs to be made, but what would it say? We have a serial murderer on our hands. One who has killed more than ten people. And no, sorry, we have no idea where he is.

She watches Deakin in the doorway. He's talking animatedly on the phone to the team back in the station, reiterating her orders, a cigarette burning down to the butt between his fingers. He'd handled the sight in the apartment better than she had, but he'd been shaken. And angry—she knows the signs. The furrowed brow, the twitchy hands.

Her phone rings and she looks at the number. She answers it.

"So we have a Dahmer," Griffin says.

"News travels fast."

"How many victims?"

"At least ten. But all in pieces, all in varying states of decomp, so who knows for sure."

"And the neighbors didn't notice anything?"

"They're taking their statements down at the station now," Cara says. "So far, they've just said they noticed a smell and complained, but there was a note through their door that said there was a rat problem."

"Pretty big fucking rats. Did they keep the note?" Griffin doesn't wait for an answer. "I'm coming down there."

"You'll do no such thing. I'm serious, Griffin. Come to the station first thing in the morning, but I don't want you here. Not now." She pauses. "The place is crawling with journalists, Nate. They'll have a field day if they see you."

She hears him pause. He knows she's right. She sees Deakin gesture to her from the door of the block of apartment buildings.

"Listen, Nate. I have to go. I'll see you tomorrow. Okay?"

There's another pause. "Okay."

Cara hangs up and takes a deep breath. She follows Deakin back inside.

*   *   *

"I don't know what you need me for," Dr. Ross is saying as Deakin and Cara approach the main living room. "There's fuck all I can do here."

His voice is strained. Cara's not surprised. It's not how she wants to be spending her evening either.

"We've found body parts in the freezer, both the one in the fridge and the freestanding one next to it. There's more in the closet in the hallway and what we think is a complete skeleton in the bedroom. Most have been dead for quite some time; he's been killing for at least a few years. Although there's a recent one in the bath, looks strangled, probably within the last twelve hours. And no, we won't know exactly how many bodies there are until we start piecing it all together." He turns away from them. "Literally."

Deakin leans forward, looking at the DVDs under the television. *Return of the Jedi* and the *Exorcist 2*.

"It hardly seems real, does it?" he mutters to Cara. "I mean, what does this guy do? Dismember people in his kitchen, then sit back and watch *Star Wars*?"

Cara shakes her head and looks around the room. In the corner is a black table, and on the top, a fish tank. In all the squalor, it stands out: it's spotlessly clean, a variety of tropical fish swimming around inside.

"If only you could talk," she whispers to them.

She follows Deakin out and they go into the bedroom again. The metal cabinet has been emptied, and a paper bag rests in a box, ready to be taken away as evidence. Deakin picks it up and pulls something out with his gloved hand. It's dark skin in a long roll.

"We think that's a penis," a voice says from behind them.

Deakin swears and drops it back into the bag.

They turn. Libby is there, recognizable from her black eyeliner.

"I kind of liked the idea," she says, her eyes creasing in a smile behind the mask. "I think I'm warming to this guy."

"What else can you show us, Libs?" Cara asks.

Libby points to the blue plastic drum. "We haven't opened that yet," she starts. "We'll take it away as is. Along with the freezer. But if this guy *is* copying Dahmer, we'd expect to find some human torsos in there."

Deakin trails behind them as they walk into the kitchen.

"He didn't use much in here for preparing food. Formaldehyde, ether, and chloroform found in the hallway cupboard. Acid and bleach in here." She holds up evidence bags, showing them each one in turn. "Large hypodermic needle. Drill and one-sixteenth-inch drill bits."

Cara doesn't like to think about what they might have been used for.

Libby continues: "We've emptied the trash—some scraps, fragments of paper. Not sure if anything's useful, but we'll go through it. Blood evidence across all surfaces—we'll take samples—fingerprints, some blood spatter up the walls. I don't know what else to tell you, Detectives, except this is one fucked-up puppy."

"And one that's good with knives." Dr. Ross joins them in the kitchen. "To dismember this many bodies in this way, we're looking at someone with a decent knowledge of human anatomy."

"The same guy as Monday night?" Cara asks.

"Possibly. We'll compare the tool marks used on both. I'll send you my report when I know more," Ross concludes. Cara and Libby enviously watch him leave, desperately wanting to do the same.

Deakin has wandered off to another part of the apartment. "Are you still on for drinks?" Libby asks her.

Cara looks at her doubtfully. "At this time of night?" She points to the busy scene. "With all of this going on?"

"I know a place. And night shift takes over in half an hour," Libby says. "What more can you do here? Really?" Cara shrugs. "Don't you think you could do with a bit of downtime?"

Libby's got a point. Cara's phone starts ringing. "Fine. Thirty minutes," she whispers to Libby as she answers it.

It's Shenton. "Anything from the mother?" Cara asks.

"No. She says she hasn't seen Michael Sharp in about a year. But we'll follow up; she might be holding out on us."

"That's great. Good work, Toby," she adds, trying her best to be encouraging. They need the boost. It's nearly eleven, she hasn't eaten since lunch—she could do with someone giving *her* a good pep talk now.

*   *   *

Outside, Deakin has changed out of his crime scene suit and is smoking around the corner of the block of apartments, out of sight of the reporters. Cara joins him and reaches out to take his cigarette, but he holds it away from her.

"Roo will kill me if I let you smoke."

"Just give me the damn cigarette, let me worry about my husband," Cara says. "I think I'm allowed one after the day we've had."

He raises his eyebrow but hands it to her; she takes a long drag before passing it back.

"You ever known anything like this before?" he asks her.

She shakes her head. "Thankfully, no. You?"

He blows out a cloud of smoke. "Some with the drug squad. A few with SO10," he says, giving her the cigarette again.

She knows what he's referring to. SO10: the old covert operations unit within the Met Police. One of Noah's early postings.

She goes to hand the cigarette back to him, but he waves it away.

"Finish it," Deakin says.

He leans back against the pebbledash wall of the apartments, closing his eyes for a second. They stand together in silence, and Cara realizes how much she appreciates him being here with her. In these moments, when something truly horrible like this happens, nobody outside the police force could ever understand.

On his first day in Major Crimes, Noah had arrived with a severe grade-one haircut, tight shirt, skinny jeans, and a battered pair of blue All Stars on his feet. He had the build of a greyhound on speed, and the metabolism to match. And he'd called her Cara. Not boss, not DCI Elliott, like the other detectives in her team. Certainly not "ma'am," a term she hates for making her feel about fifty. Noah had requested a transfer, and she'd read his file. Undercover until 2014. Drug squad since, with accompanying plaudits, and she'd agreed without hesitation.

But this man? she'd thought on first sight. He'd had a detachment about him that Cara had mistaken for arrogance, and she'd wondered if she'd made a mistake.

But she soon learned, none of her other detectives were like Deaks—and that was a good thing. Unconsciously, she'd found herself gravitating to his side. They'd go on callouts together, and she'd single him out to ask his opinion. He was serious, quiet, and worked harder than anyone else there, herself included. Their partnership became the norm: where DCI Cara Elliott went, DS Noah Deakin went too.

*   *   *

Deakin pushes himself up from the wall. He puts a hand on Cara's arm, then leans forward and gives her a hug. She's surprised by the sudden contact but realizes that it was just what she needed, and briefly she rests her head on his shoulder. He smells of some sort of soap or washing powder, an aftershave she's always liked, and Polo mints. He pulls away from the hug and offers her one of the mints now. She takes the candy out of the tube and pops it in her mouth.

"I'm going to head off," she says, breaking the silence. "Do you want a lift?"

He shakes his head. "I'll stay and keep an eye on things," he mutters.

Cara knows any attempt at persuasion will be useless. And she knows how Noah is feeling. That restlessness, coupled with despair at their lack of progress. But Libby's right: there's nothing more she can do here, she needs to let SOCO do their job. To log and take samples and process—and hope and pray that this guy has made a mistake.

Because God knows, she thinks, as she looks up at the bland block of apartments, knowing the horrors behind its pebble-dashed walls, this bloodbath is enough.

CHAPTER

22

J ESS HEARS THE phone beep, then senses Griffin get out of bed. She opens her eyes and watches him in the darkness, his head bent, talking on the phone in hushed tones. He is in just his boxer shorts, and she appreciates the sight, then wonders, who is this guy and what is she doing here?

When they got back earlier, they hadn't talked. Griffin hadn't offered her food or drink, just taken his clothes off and climbed into bed. She'd paused for a second, then done the same, her presence in this apartment seemingly now implicitly accepted.

Nav had been worried about her being here, and she knows he had been right to be. Griffin could be anyone.

But she feels like she knows him. Deep in her psyche, she recognizes something. The damage. The desperate search for the intangible. He is pretty much twice her size, but since that first night he's never done anything that has made her worry. But perhaps her bar is just low, she thinks. Perhaps she wouldn't know danger until it hit her square in the face.

Griffin finishes his call and gets back into bed. She can sense he's still awake. He's twitchy, fidgeting.

"Another one?" she says and he turns to her. He nods, she sees his face through the darkness.

"Does this mean Patrick's murder is definitely linked?" Jess asks quietly.

"Nothing's definite, Jess," he says. "But maybe."

He rolls away from her, and she shuffles down under the duvet, lying on her back, staring at the ceiling. She needs to do something to forget about this. The anxiety, the impatience. Waiting for the bomb to drop. She can feel the warmth of his body next to her; she wants to touch him. She wants to—

But she can't. She balls her hands into fists. She knows that sex with Griffin would make her feel better, if only for a moment, but after the rejection last time, she couldn't cope if he did the same again.

She needs to gain some control. Even if it's just over her own body.

Jess takes a long breath in, then gets up and goes to the bathroom, closing the door behind her. She blinks as she turns the light on, then sits on the cold linoleum floor, leaning forward and opening the cupboard below the sink. She finds what she's looking for and puts it next to her. A new razor blade, still in its packet. She's only wearing a T-shirt and briefs, and she pushes her bare legs out in front of her.

Inside she feels like a collection of tiny pieces, fractured and broken. So why shouldn't the outside look the same? She picks up the razor and breaks it in half, freeing the blades from the protective plastic shell. She drops the rubbish on the floor, then holds one blade between two fingers. She can feel her hands shaking.

Slowly, she puts the sharp edge against the top of her upper thigh. She sees the scars from previous times. Some no more than silver lines, others still red, barely healed. She pushes and draws the razor across her leg. She feels the blade puncture the skin, slice into her flesh. Blood blooms, runs down her leg. She does it again. She knows how hard she should push—enough to make it bleed, but not so much that she needs the hospital. After all, she hasn't got Nav anymore.

She feels tears running down her face, dropping onto her leg, mixing with the blood. She knows what she's doing is destroying her, piece by piece. But it's punishment for being such a fuck-up. Punishment for not being normal.

She counts. Seven, eight. She knows she'll stop at ten. Ten is always enough to release the tension, to open the safety valve of the pressure cooker. That, or finding some random man to do what they do so well.

But, like the razor, the sex never appeases for long. The initial excitement of attraction, the endorphins of a quick fuck—they're a rush, a distraction from the squalling in her head. But once it's over and the man has gone, she's back to the same screwed-up mess that she was before.

She'd always wondered if Patrick knew. If he had, he'd never said anything. And she'd dismissed his indiscretions too. The woman whispering in his ear with a smile and a glance her way at the Christmas party. The calls late at night that Patrick took from another room. She didn't blame him. She wasn't a good wife. She wasn't a good anything.

The door opens, pulling her away from her thoughts. She looks up. Griffin's standing there, squinting in the light. He swears, dropping down to his knees next to her.

"Fuck, Jess, what are you doing?"

He leans forward, taking the toilet paper roll and bundling up tissue, pushing it against her leg, trying to stem the bleeding. Then he stops, and Jess watches him take a long breath in, staring at the floor.

He looks up and slowly holds out his hand. She drops the razor blade into the ball of bloodied toilet paper.

She's expecting anger, disappointment, judgment, fear. All reactions she's seen before, from her parents, from medical professionals, from her husband. But Griffin seems different.

"Do you want to tell me what's going on?" he says. His voice is serious but calm.

Jess shakes her head. Griffin opens the cupboard again and takes out an old box of Band-Aids. Silently he does what he can to stop the bleeding, covering up the cuts one by one, balking at the mess. He glances up at her every now and again as he works, as if expecting some sort of complaint about the pain, but she just watches him impassively.

When he's finished, he sits back on the floor, cross-legged. She's still leaning against the wall, her legs in front of her.

"Do you want to talk to someone about it?" he asks.

She shakes her head again. "No."

"Have you? In the past?"

"It didn't help."

"Okay."

She sees Griffin looking at her, his gaze moves to the bandage on her head, then back to her leg. He knows something's up, she thinks. I should just tell him. But she's aware that once people find out, their perception of her shifts. They treat her differently. And after what she's just done with the razor, there's enough going on right now.

Griffin looks away, and he sighs, thinking. Then he stands up, holding out his hand. She takes it and he pulls her to her feet. Her legs feel wobbly. "Well," he says, almost more to himself, guiding her back into bed, turning the light off. "What a fucking state we're both in."

He lies down next to her in the darkness, pulling the duvet across. She listens to his breathing, to the cars outside on the road. Every time she thinks she's got the measure of Griffin, he proves her wrong, yet again.

*　*　*

She must have fallen asleep, because when she wakes, she's curled up next to him, skin touching skin. She moves away, embarrassed at what might have seemed like affection.

He's asleep and Jess looks at him in the dim light. All his features are relaxed, his usual frown gone. She pauses.

She wants to know more about Griffin. Her curiosity digs at her.

She pads across to the table, where Griffin has left his bag. She scrabbles around in the pockets, glancing back to the bed to make sure Griffin is still sleeping. There's his laptop, printouts, a few photos, all in the main compartment. Wrappers from some sort of energy bar, screwed up receipts. She turns her attention to the side pocket and pulls out what's in there. She looks at it—it's a small white box, with "OxyNorm" written on the front, "oxycodone hydrochloride" below. She pulls out the blister pack—small orange capsules that she has seen Griffin take on more than one occasion.

Jess doesn't know anything about pain relief, but she's heard of oxycodone. They're strong, addictive. She looks at the box: there are eight left.

She frowns but replaces it in his rucksack. Her attention turns to his jeans, discarded across the sofa, and she picks them up, feeling the pockets. There's a wallet in one side, and she pulls it out, looking at the cards. Nathanial Griffin. So that's something: it's his actual name at least.

She puts it back, then something in the pocket attracts her attention. It's a photograph, slightly crumpled, of Griffin and a woman. He has his arm around her and he's smiling. Jess realizes that in the time she's known him, she's never seen him smile like this, and she looks more closely. His hair is shorter; he's clean-shaven, handsome. He looks happy. Her gaze drifts to the woman next to him. She has long, dark hair, falling softly over her shoulders. His arm is tightly around her, and she's leaning into him.

And then Jess realizes. She goes to the table and scrabbles through the crime scene photos until she finds it. She looks at the photo that was pinned on the board, then back to the snapshot in her hand.

She stops, her hands shaking. No wonder it's personal for Griffin. No wonder he's a man on a mission.

The woman that was raped and murdered—this is her. And the husband left for dead? It was Griffin.

CHAPTER

23

THE BAR IS packed; Cara can't believe how busy it is at this time on a Wednesday night. She hovers in the doorway, looking through the throng. She can't spot Libby. She should be going home—she's so exhausted even her eyelids ache—but just as she is about to text her excuses and leave, she sees Libby push her way toward her.

"Come on," Libby says, seeing her expression. "Let's get you a drink."

*   *   *

Two glasses of wine down, and Cara has spilled her guts about the Kemper postmortems, the Manson murders, all the details about Griffin's theory. Cara knows her expression echoes Libby's: lowered brow, downturned mouth. There is nothing good here.

"But I can't help thinking," Cara adds, downing the last dregs in her glass, "why do it? Why go to all the effort of copying serial killers?"

"Adoration? Infamy? Recognition?" Libby replies. With one hand she signals the barman, who replenishes their glasses. "Why does any multiple murderer kill? You can't apply normal logic. Have you thought about getting a profiler in?"

"Marsh would never approve the budget."

"Worth an ask?" Libby stops, thinking for a minute. "And what does Noah say?"

Cara pauses, a smile creeping onto her face. "Why is it, with you, Libs, the conversation always finds its way around to Deakin?"

Libby pushes her long pink hair out of her face. "Just interested, that's all. And anyway, I don't need Noah," she says with a grin. "I have a date on Friday night." Libby opens up her phone and shows Cara the profile on the dating app. Cara nods in approval.

"But why *did* you two split up?" Cara asks.

Libby sighs. She puts her phone back in her pocket. "Ask Noah. Not my choice. He didn't tell you?" Cara shakes her head. "I thought you two talked about everything."

"We talk about murders and rapes and bad guys. We don't talk about his love life, and mine's too dull to mention."

Libby looks at her, then tilts her head to one side.

"What?" Cara asks.

"You know, I always thought there was something going on between the two of you."

"Between me and Noah?" Cara laughs. "Why?"

"You spend all day, every day together. You're always whispering in dark corners, laughing. Like a little impenetrable club." Cara snorts and Libby takes a swig from her glass. "You're saying you've never thought about it?"

"No!"

"Not even once?"

"No!" Cara repeats. "Well, maybe. Once."

"Ha!" Libby throws her head back, gleeful. "I knew it. You should, you know." She raises an immaculately arched eyebrow. "You'd like it."

"Really?"

"Oh, yeah." Libby stretches the word out into one long syllable. "Man's dirtier than an ex-nun at a *Fleabag* convention." She waves over Cara's shoulder. "In a good way," she adds, then stands up to say goodbye as one of her friends goes to leave.

Cara watches her, chatting and laughing on the other side of the bar. They were well suited, Cara had always thought, Libby and Noah. Both unconventional, but both unmistakably attractive. They'd looked good together. But he'd called an end to their relationship, and Cara wonders why.

And why is she so interested? She sips at her wine, already feeling woozy as the alcohol goes to her head. But it's nice, this fug. Helping her forget the violence and the death in the time-honored manner.

Libby swings back onto her bar stool, crossing one elegant leg over the other. She flashes a mischievous grin.

"So," she asks Cara, "shots?" And then, without waiting for an answer, beckons the barman over.

* * *

An hour later, Cara finds herself rolling out of the taxi at her front door. None of the lights are on. She knows her husband will be in bed, needing to be up early in the morning for the breakfast service.

She opens the front door, putting her keys on the hook as quietly as she can in her alcoholic haze. She takes her coat off, her shoes, and puts them away. She'd have liked someone to talk to about other things than murder and dead girls and dismembered body parts, but settles for making herself a bowl of cornflakes and eating them in front of an old episode of *Friends*.

She leaves the bowl in the sink and turns the light off again, going upstairs. She pauses outside the door to her daughter's room, then pushes down the handle, opening it quietly.

Inside, the stars on the ceiling highlight her face in a hazy glow. Tilly's sleeping, her hands tightly clasped around a small white owl, now grubby and worn from years of love. Cara rearranges the duvet back over her, then crouches by the side of her bed.

It's a parent's worst nightmare to hear the news that too many families had received that week. Your child is dead, and not only that, but their last hours would have been scary and painful. They would have most likely begged for mercy, prayed for their mothers, and their last thoughts would have been for the ones they loved. Cara looks at the sleeping face of her daughter and feels the anger eating away in her stomach. Losing a child from illness or an accident is tragic, but this senseless taking of a life, of so many lives, was unconscionable. It was inhuman. For the first time that week, she feels tears rolling down her face, then swallows them away, wiping them dry with her sleeve.

Cara leans forward and kisses her daughter on the cheek, and she stirs. She opens her eyes and looks at her.

"Go back to sleep, pickle," she whispers.

"Did you catch the monsters?" she asks. "Daddy said you weren't home because you were catching the monsters."

"Always, my love."

"What do they look like?" Tilly's eyes shine in the darkness. "Daddy says they look like you and me."

Cara silently curses her husband. "Yes, but I'm trained, so I can always tell the difference."

"Is Josh a monster?"

Cara smiles, tucking the duvet around her. "No, as much as you think so, your brother isn't a monster."

"Is Daddy? Is Noah? Is Uncle Nate?"

"No. We don't have any monsters here, Tils. I got rid of those long ago. Now go back to sleep."

She nods, satisfied with her answer, and closes her eyes, rolling over in bed, taking her owl with her.

Cara gets up and goes into her own room, cleaning her teeth in the en suite in the dark. She doesn't want to look at herself. To see the effects of the day on her face. She takes her clothes off and climbs into bed, pushing up against the back of her husband. He mumbles something incomprehensible.

"Roo?" she whispers. "Are you awake?"

She knows he's not, feeling guilty for wanting to wake him up. But he stays resolutely in slumber, and she envies her husband's ability to sleep.

Cara rolls away from him, and lies on her back looking at the ceiling. She waits for the tiredness to overtake her, for a blissful oblivion she knows will never come.

24

It's early morning, still dark, when the pain wakes him. Griffin shifts in the bed, testing out the extent of the problem, then slowly sits up. It's nothing he's not used to by now, and he stands tentatively, making his way toward the kitchen.

The apartment has cooled, and he feels the chill on his skin. He gropes his way toward his bag, pulling out the box of pills, swallowing two down quickly.

He's not a good guy—Griffin's always known that. He took no offense at Jess's earlier words; it's just how he is. Even when he was new to the police force, he wasn't one of the shiny fresh recruits, turning up eagerly, their shirts ironed, their boots clean. He'd be out the back, cigarette in hand, when he should have been reporting for duty.

But he was the one they called when a douchebag didn't want to go into his cell. The person they sent single-crewed to a dangerous area. He got into fights, broken bones and black eyes littering his record. He got the job done, and if that meant a few more pounds spent by the NHS, so be it.

He'd barely scraped through the written exams, but he made it to DC and then to detective sergeant. He forged alliances with both the good guys and the bad, traded favors, commanded respect.

And then it all went wrong.

He walks back to the bed and sits down, the mattress moving with his weight. Jess shifts slightly in her sleep, and he looks at her. He's glad she's back. He doesn't like to think about why, but when he heard her voice at the end of the phone, he didn't hesitate. Just got in the car and drove her back here.

He feels protective toward her, a connection, especially after what she had just done to herself. Her husband, his wife—both killed by the same man, but it's not only that. He knows how Jess is feeling. The propensity to self-destruction, the constant sense of failure.

He knows how it is to be different, to not live in the same world as everyone else.

Even before it all happened, he'd looked at people going about their normal lives. Men in the supermarket, with their kids, driving to work. And the majority of them looked happy. How was that even possible? Were they just not aware of the shit in the world? The injustices, the problems, the worries? Griffin came to accept that maybe they weren't the ones with something wrong with them. Maybe it was him.

But it means that he can look at these crime scene photographs, these dead bodies, and not blink. It doesn't keep him awake at night—not *that* anyway. He accepts that death and destruction are what he's there for.

He lies back down next to Jess and pulls the duvet across. He gets a waft of warm body, slightly stale, slightly sticky, but somehow reassuring. He's still not sure why she came back. In his darker periods, he used to question Mia's love, ask why she was with him despite everything he did wrong. "I am safe with you," she'd say, curling up like a cat next to him. "I'm yours, you're mine. I know you'll always look after me."

But he hadn't, had he? Not when it mattered.

He stares at the ceiling in the darkness, waiting for the edges of dawn to start to take hold; for the day to properly begin, all vestiges of sleep gone. With what they have discovered, his resolution burns brighter than ever.

He sees what this psychopath is doing. He knows he will catch him. And he knows he will make him pay.

Whatever it takes.

25

Day 4
Thursday

"JEFFREY DAHMER, CONVICTED of killing seventeen men and boys between 1978 and 1991. Particularly fond of dismembering bodies, with a little bit of rape and necrophilia on the side."

Griffin is standing in front of a screen, images projected onto the white, a group of nearly twenty detectives listening to him. This is the side of him Cara knows so well—confident, unflinching.

"Known for drilling holes in people's skulls while they were drugged and pouring acid or boiling water inside, supposedly to create walking zombies." He points to the crime scene photos as they flash across the screen. "We believe we have found eleven bodies in various states of decay. All echoing Dahmer."

Noah whispers next to her, "How did that many people go missing unnoticed?"

"Probably the same way that the victims of Dahmer did," Cara replies. "People on the edge of society. The homeless, the unemployed. Men estranged from their families." Cara silently resolves to find out their names. Every last one.

Griffin moves along the whiteboard.

"Peter William Sutcliffe, otherwise known as the Yorkshire Ripper. Convicted of murdering thirteen women. Our killer managed two." He clicks the button in his hand, and a gory image is displayed on the screen. Cara has seen it before in the crime scene photos, but projected up in front of them, so huge, it is guaranteed to make even the hardest detective flinch.

She rubs her eyes. She's hungover, exhausted, and the day has only just begun. Damn Libby and her tequila.

She barely remembers being asleep last night, knowing she saw three AM roll around on the digital clock, still awake. But she must have drifted off, as her husband woke her, his alarm bursting into life, ready to do the breakfast service at the restaurant where he is head chef.

He'd kissed her on the cheek as he got out of bed. "Back for dinner tonight?"

"I hope so," she'd mumbled back.

After trying to catch a few more hours of sleep, she'd heard the front door go as their nanny arrived. Lauren, a woman barely into her twenties, seemed to have her life together in a way Cara could only watch and envy. Cara could hear her laughing with the kids as she got them ready for school. Perhaps if she had a different job, she'd be like that too. Endless patience, boundless energy. A lithe body that hummed with vitality and warmth, rather than feeling worn out at the age of thirty-nine.

Cara had crawled out of bed into the shower, roughly drying her hair and tying it back from her face in a scruffy bun. Her daughter had leapt into the room and bounced on the bed, watching her.

"Lauren says do you want porridge?"

Cara had glanced at the clock, about to say no, then saw the hopeful look on her daughter's face.

"Yes, please," she'd replied, and went to join her family in the kitchen, grabbing a few minutes of normality and innocence before the horror of her day began.

*   *   *

She pulls her attention back to the incident room, where Griffin has clicked the button again.

"Manson," he says, then pauses. "The stabbing and shooting of five people on Monday night." Cara hears gasps from the room. "Including one pregnant woman."

"But Manson wasn't a serial killer," Shenton whispers next to her. "It was Tex Watson, Susan Atkins, and Pat Krenwinkel who carried out the Tate murders."

Cara glances across to him. "Let's not get caught up in semantics now, Toby," she replies. "Five people were killed. I'm not sure how much rational thought can be applied to what's going on."

Deakin leans forward. "I think you should tell him," he mutters, nodding toward Griffin.

But Cara stops Shenton just as he's going to speak. She glares at Noah.

"Don't wind him up, Deaks," she hisses. "This is hard enough as it is."

Cara knows there is no love lost between her brother and her partner. Both are passionate, stubborn individuals, but while Griffin does what he wants and to hell with the consequences, Deakin likes rules, procedures, and processes. And she knows Noah is pissed off with Griffin taking the lead on this briefing. At the heart of it, she thinks Noah is probably annoyed for not noticing the connections himself.

To add insult to injury, Griffin has moved on and is talking about Ed Kemper.

"In 1972, he picked up female hitchhikers, taking them to isolated areas where he would stab and strangle them, then dismember and dispose of the bodies. He was caught after killing his mother and fucking her head in 1973."

Cara winces at his language. She's going to have to have another word with him.

"Like Kemper, our killer used a Ford Galaxy. Like the word *pig* written on the wall and the American flag for the Manson murders, even down to the fish tank and the DVDs in the Dahmer apartment, he uses details similar to the real murders."

"So he's taunting us?" one detective asks. "Showing off?"

Griffin looks back at the projector. "He's certainly trying to say something."

Cara sees Griffin turn away from the room and take a deep breath. She knows what's coming next. He clicks the button and an image appears on the screen. She feels her muscles tense.

The room is silent.

Griffin clears his throat. "Other victims. Other murders we believe are connected."

It's a photo of Mia. Her sister-in-law. But here she's barely recognizable. Her body, half naked, is lying on the floor, her hands tied. Her long brown hair is over her face, and there is blood—blood everywhere.

It's a crime scene photo from just over a year ago. Cara remembers the day.

She'd been deployed to a knifing at a shopping center, staring at the CCTV when the call came over the radio. She hadn't seen Nate that morning, but that wasn't unusual; they were on different teams. Deakin had put his hand on her shoulder.

"It's Griffin," he'd said, his face dark.

They'd raced to the hospital, stood at the window to the ICU, looking at his unconscious, beaten body. Doctors spoke to her, but she hadn't taken it in. Until she'd turned to them and said, "Where's Mia?"

She'd liked Mia from the moment she'd met her. The first time: a weekend away at their lodge with Roo and the kids. Their retreat in the countryside, away from the bustle of Roo's kitchen and the grim nature of her police work. Griffin had arrived, late as usual, and he'd seemed jumpy. Her cocky younger brother, nervous? But all was explained when he introduced the beautiful woman at his side. Cara had realized that this one was different for Griffin. This one was going to stay.

Mia was dark, with a smile that lit up her bottle-green eyes. She'd held Tilly, a baby at the time, and talked about children in her future, giving a quiet smile to Griffin. Mia brought out a side of Griffin that Cara adored. He was calmer around her. Happier. He was in love. For once in her life, Cara didn't need to worry about her brother.

Until that day.

And now, here he was a year later. Standing in front of a brutal image of the body of his wife.

Griffin pauses. Everyone is quiet. Cara knows the majority of the detectives will make the connection between the bloody image on the screen and the man standing in front of it. He clicks the button again, and an image of Griffin's old living room appears, the room trashed, blood on the walls and floor. "This was the attack on a married couple last year, raping the wife and bludgeoning her to death. The husband was beaten but survived."

"Could the husband identify the killer?"

Heads swivel to face the guy speaking. He's new, over from West Yorkshire, so probably isn't aware. Cara sees the woman next to him nudge him and frown.

Griffin's jaw clenches. Then: "No," he says at last. "There was no useful information from the husband."

Cara stands up. She gestures to the man next to the door, and he flicks the lights on. Everybody winces at the sudden illumination.

She stands in front of the group. Griffin moves away to the back of the room.

"Right. So now we know what we're all dealing with," she says, taking charge. There are a huge number of detectives now, following multiple lines of inquiry, not to mention the army of PCs and PCSOs asking questions out on the streets. "We know this guy has killed over twenty people so far. To avoid doubt, we can assume he will kill again, and he will do so brutally and without remorse." She points to the photo of Michael Sharp on the board. "For the time being, unless evidence tells us otherwise, this is our prime suspect. His blood was found at the Kemper crime scene, and the Dahmer murders were staged at his apartment." She starts allocating jobs to the various groups around the room. "Those of you here from constabularies across the country, I want you to swap cases. Get the teams up to speed with what you know, then leave them to it." She sees the glances between detectives. "This is not about assigning blame. This is about putting fresh eyes on a murder case. Shenton," she says, pointing toward her DC. "You seem to know a lot about serial killers. Research everything about our murders so far— and put together a list of the most notorious serial killers out there. Something might pop up that links to another case. And Campbell,"— one of the new DCs nods in acknowledgment—"follow up with Missing Persons. I want these victims identified."

She finishes the briefing, and the room is filled with noise. Energy, conversation, people eager to get on and catch this guy.

She gestures to Griffin.

"You okay?" she says, and he nods. He's not, but she knows he won't want to be asked about it again.

"Fine. Listen, Nate." She turns to her brother. "If you're going to be here, on this investigation, I need you to keep in line. Don't ruffle any feathers, don't piss anyone off."

He tilts his head to one side, smiling slightly. "I'll do my best."

"Do better than that. Because this is my job on the line too. No one else will take you. Marsh has made it clear, you're my responsibility. So if you get fired, I get in trouble. Clear?"

He nods, raising one hand in a mock salute. "Crystal, boss."

"Good. Deaks?" she shouts across the room, and Noah comes over. Griffin scowls.

"And you need to apologize to Noah."

The two men glare at each other.

"I'm serious, Nate. Apologize. Because I can't have you two working together like this."

And there it was: the reason for his suspension. Tensions running high, late at night, no progress made on Mia's murder. Griffin barely out of the hospital. And an observation from Noah toward Griffin: "Maybe you shouldn't be here."

"Maybe, if you were a better cop, I wouldn't need to be."

And then the final comment: "Maybe, if you'd been a better husband—"

Noah had regretted it immediately after he'd said it, he'd later confessed to Cara, but by then Griffin had punched him full in the face, breaking his nose.

Griffin frowns at Cara, then sighs. "I'm sorry for punching you," he growls. "But you were a prick."

"And you, Noah. Let it go."

"Only if I can return the favor."

"For crying out loud," Cara mutters under her breath. Men. "Fine. If Griffin behaves like a prick, you have my permission to break his nose. But don't do it where anyone can see."

"Deal." Deakin holds out his hand, and Griffin reluctantly shakes it. "And I am sorry for what I said."

Griffin nods briefly in acknowledgment. Cara rolls her eyes. "Now go and do something useful."

Griffin heads off and Cara looks at Deakin. She shakes her head. "Tell me it was a good idea to get Griffin in on this, please?"

Noah gives her a withering look. His hand subconsciously goes up to his nose. "It wasn't. But we might as well make the most of it. As much as I hate the arrogant wanker, he's good at what he does." She sees his gaze shift to the whiteboard. "So, what's next for us?"

Cara closes her eyes for a few seconds, then opens them and looks at him. "Let's keep going with Kemper and Dahmer," she says. She shakes her head. "I can't believe we're calling them that."

Even with everything she knows, this case still seems surreal. But the reality can't be denied. The facts are there, on the board, in black and white.

And blood red.

26

Jess heard the alarm sound that morning. She'd feigned sleep, watching Griffin get up and go into the bathroom from under half-opened eyes.

She hadn't wanted a conversation after what she'd done last night; in the cold light of day, she'd felt the shame, the prickle of her foolishness. She'd shifted under the duvet and put her hand down to her thigh, feeling the bandages, the scabs, the sticky blood where the cuts hadn't healed.

She'd heard the shower stop and the bathroom door open. Griffin had come out, a towel wrapped around his waist. He'd seen her watching, a flash of self-consciousness passing his face before he'd continued getting dressed: boxers, jeans, sitting on the bed to do socks, then his heavy black boots. He'd pulled on a T-shirt, then a hoodie over his head. He hadn't looked much like a police officer. She liked that about him.

"You going to be here when I get back?"

He'd been standing facing the mirror, trying to smooth his hair down, and had said it without turning her way.

"If that's okay?" she'd said.

He'd smiled very briefly, and Jess had noticed him trying to suppress it.

"No problem," he'd replied.

* * *

But now the apartment is silent, and Jess feels unsure. The worry is back, the uncertainty about what her future might hold. When Griffin's there, his presence is reassuring. His quiet confidence, the solid mass of him has been grounding her. But now he's gone, she feels the jitters return.

She should be at home with Alice right now, watching cartoons, eating breakfast. Patrick would have been telling them off for getting crumbs on the sofa. A lump builds in her throat, and she swallows it down. She has to think about something else. Focus on working out who started the fire, who did these other murders.

She gets up, puts clothes on, and makes a mug of coffee. She cradles it in her hands, sitting down at the table. Photographs are still scattered across: notes, newspapers, Griffin's laptop.

She picks up a newspaper in front of her, buried under a pile of crime scene photos. It's from Wednesday, yesterday, pages turned inward, an article clear on the top page. *"ARSON MURDER SUSPECT RUNS,"* she reads, fingers trembling.

> *Jessica Ambrose, 29, under suspicion for the murder of her husband, Patrick Ambrose, who died as their house caught alight on Monday night, has fled the General Hospital, against doctor's orders. Patrick's parents, Cynthia and David Ambrose, plead to the public to be on the lookout for their son's alleged killer, saying that their daughter-in-law was "a little strange. There was always something not quite right about her."*
>
> *Jessica is not believed to be dangerous, but members of the public are asked to call 999 if they know of her whereabouts.*

She swears under her breath. She wants to tear it into tiny pieces but settles for throwing it on the floor instead. It flutters down, pages falling in a satisfying mess.

Her eyes shift to one of the photos on the table. She picks it up, staring at the face of the dark-haired woman: Griffin's wife. This photo shows her smiling, in happier times, and Jess recognizes the green and silver crescent earrings dangling from her ears.

The one found on her doormat.

Jess pulls the laptop closer and logs on, opening up Google. It's basic research. The cops must have done at least this already, she thinks as she types in *woman rape serial killer*, but she does it anyway. An insane number of results appear on the screen, each as brutal and graphic as the last.

She frowns and tries again, this time: *arson serial killer*, and a name pops up at the top of the search engine.

Bruce George Peter Lee. She clicks on the Wikipedia link, reading the page. Then, with one line, her breath catches in her throat.

. . . *pouring paraffin through the mail slot* . . .

She needs to tell Griffin. This is it—the connection between the other murders and Patrick. She frantically looks around for a phone, a landline, and eventually finds one, buried under a pile of clothes.

Jess pulls the scrap of paper from her pocket and dials.

He answers, his voice gruff, and she gets straight to the point.

"It's Lee," she says. "Look it up. This proves it. This proves it wasn't me. They have to let me see Alice."

There's a pause.

"I'd worked that out already," Griffin says. "But it doesn't prove anything."

"Have you told your sister? What does she say?" Jess pushes.

Silence again. "I'll mention it," he mutters.

"And the link to . . ." Jess stops herself. "The earring," she continues.

"I'll mention it," he repeats, and hangs up.

Jess listens to the empty handset for a second, then slowly lowers it from her ear. After the excitement of her discovery, Griffin's response feels like a massive anticlimax. She stands there, alone in the cold, empty apartment, bare feet, dirty clothes. She feels the void. She misses her family, her daughter, her husband; and, the dead phone still clutched in her hand, she starts to cry.

27

"Ten minutes," the voice on the end of the phone says; then the person hangs up. But Cara doesn't need to know any more. She sighs, pulls her hair away from her face, then lets it down again, wondering what to do with it.

"You know what Mom would say?" Griffin says, standing in the doorway to her office.

Cara smiles. "Don't rake it back?"

"Exactly—'*and put some lipstick on, you look a state,*'" he mocks, then smiles, coming in and sitting on the chair in front of her desk. "Listen, Cara—"

"Enough of this shit between you and Deakin, seriously," Cara interrupts.

"No, it's not that." He hesitates. "We need to talk about the fire from Monday. I think this is Lee—an arsonist from the late seventies."

He hands her the file. Cara knows what he's referring to. "But Taylor said this is different. Don't they have a suspect?" she asks. "Didn't the wife do it, then abscond? And how do you know about it?"

"I have an alert on the system. It flags up when there's a suspected murder," he says, and Cara rolls her eyes. "And you know what Taylor's like. Couldn't arrest the right person if the offender shat in her lap. And besides, I don't think it was the wife. Look at the points of the case. You have paraffin poured through the letter box. Mia's earring found on the doormat—another sign of the killer messing with us. And the evidence against the wife is circumstantial at best. Fingerprints on a watering can that even Taylor admits was probably taken from the garden shed."

"So why has she run?"

"She doesn't trust the police. She was scared, terrified they wouldn't let her see her daughter again."

"This is just conjecture, Griffin. How can you be so sure?" Then Cara realizes. "Oh, shit. Oh, Nate, you know where she is?"

"She didn't do it, okay?" he whispers. "Please keep it between us."

"Nate, you can't be hiding a suspected murderer!" Cara glances out into the incident room. "Especially not with you back here. Where is she? Is she at your apartment?"

"No! How stupid do you think I am?" he says, but Cara sees a look pass across his face. Exactly that stupid, she knows. "Just include the case. And if it doesn't fit, I'll bring her in."

"Haven't we got enough to do? We have few enough resources as it is." But Cara gives an exasperated sigh. "Fine. Just between us, look into it. But leave Taylor on it, too, for now. I don't want to assume that everything's linked." Griffin goes to leave, but Cara leans forward and catches him by the arm. "Nate, keep me up to speed, okay?"

He nods and leaves. She groans quietly under her breath. She hasn't got the energy for this, for her brother harboring a potential criminal. She decides that for now, she'll let it go. She'll pretend she doesn't know.

She stands up and leaves her office, watching the rest of the detectives hard at work. This is the part of her job she loves, the buzz in the room—a shared purpose, everyone working together to bring in a result. For a brief moment, she allows herself to feel confident. They will catch him. Then another thought: they have to.

Deakin comes up next to her.

"What was that all about?" he says, watching Griffin.

"Just another case he thinks will fit."

His gaze shifts to the far side of the room. "Roo's here for you," he says.

Cara turns, and sure enough her husband is standing in the doorway of the incident room, a uniform by his side. He's in jeans and a sweater; she guesses he's on his way back to the restaurant.

She goes over to them, greeting her husband with a surprised kiss. "Lauren said you left your phone this morning," he explains, handing it to her. She takes it gratefully. "So this is you?" he asks, gesturing through the door to the whiteboard.

"'Fraid so, yes," Cara replies. "You saw it on TV?"

"It's all anyone is talking about." He pauses. "And I've just had a call from the school. Tilly's been sick."

"Shit," Cara mutters under her breath. There's a pause. She doesn't know what to say. There's no way she's leaving right now, and her husband knows it. "Can Lauren get her?" she asks.

"She's got the afternoon off," Roo says, then sighs. "I'll call her. I'm sure it'll be fine."

"I'll be back for dinner," Cara says, trying to appease her husband. "I promise."

"That'll be good. I'll bring back something from the restaurant. Noah coming too?" he asks.

Cara looks into the incident room, where Deakin is now talking to Shenton. "I'll make sure he does," she replies. "And Roo?"

"Hmm?"

"When this is over, let's go away. Take the kids. To the lodge, somewhere quiet. I don't mind." All Cara wants right now is some peace. Sleep, good food. Spend some time with her husband.

He smiles. "That would be good."

Then she sees Marsh gesture to her from down the corridor. Two fingers, pointing away. It's time.

* * *

She quickly follows Marsh through the station, and as she goes, she feels the usual guilt. The burden to be all things: mother, wife, detective, partner, sister. Her daughter isn't well, and here she is, facing potentially the most shocking multiple murder case this country has ever known. She sighs. If she will do only one thing tonight, she will be home in time for dinner.

But she can't think about that now. She knows where they're going, and it's not something she's looking forward to.

"Just keep quiet. I'll let you know if I need you to talk." Marsh pauses at a set of wooden double doors. "And if in doubt, say, 'No comment.'"

He pushes them open. The noise hits them immediately. Conversation, shouting, jostling for attention as they walk through the throng of journalists to where the chief constable is waiting. Flashes from the cameras make her blink.

"Fucking vultures," Marsh mutters to Cara as they both take their seats at the front. Cara does what she is told and stays silent as Marsh raises his hands above his head.

"Quiet!" he shouts. "Shall we get started?"

The room is bland and boring—scuffed white walls, dirty blue patterned carpet. They've shifted from their usual, nicer public relations setting to this one, but even so, it's standing room only. Cara has never seen anything like it. Every seat is taken, the press pushing forward, desperate for even small snippets of information.

Slowly the hubbub dies down and the press conference starts.

"As I'm sure you're all aware, at approximately four fifteen yesterday afternoon, police raided an apartment on the west side of town, where detectives discovered the remains of what we now believe to be eleven adult males in various states of decay."

"Is it a serial killer?" one journalist shouts, followed by a barrage of questions from the others.

Marsh raises his arm again, frowning.

"We believe these murders were all committed by one perpetrator, yes." Marsh is visibly sweating, a reflective sheen across his forehead.

"And is that perpetrator a guy called Michael Sharp?"

Marsh glares at the woman. "No comment."

"Were the bodies found at Michael Sharp's apartment?"

"No comment."

Eyes drop as journalists scribble. Cara knows that to these guys Marsh's response is as good as saying yes.

"Have you managed to identify the victims?"

"Not yet. We have contacted all the next of kin that we can, but inquiries are ongoing. Any concerned relatives should contact the helpline number on the press release you have been given."

"DCI Elliott! Can you confirm the rumors that these murders are linked to others across the country?"

Cara glances to Marsh, but before she can answer, another journalist shouts from the crowd.

"Can you confirm the Echo Man is copying murders from notorious serial killers?"

The room falls silent. Cara recognizes Steve Gray from the *Chronicle* as all eyes swivel his way.

"What did you say?" Marsh hisses.

"That's what they're calling him," Gray continues. "Because he's echoing murderers from the past."

Breath stops in Cara's chest. The wall of noise and cameras bursts into life again. She swears under her breath.

This isn't good. The one thing they didn't want to happen.

He has a name now.

The Echo Man.

PART 2

Hampshire Chronicle

February 20, 1996

SHOCKING STABBING AS BROTHERS MURDERED

A murder investigation is underway after Hampshire Constabulary were called to a house on Millmoor Way at seven AM on Monday. Neighbors raised the alarm after seeing a child emerge from the house, covered in blood. On entering the property, they discovered local brothers, Gary and Marcus Keane, stabbed to death in the upstairs bedrooms.

The child, age 9, who cannot be named for legal reasons, was unharmed and is now in the care of Social Services.

Police have yet to issue a full press release, but sources state both brothers were confirmed dead at the scene. It is also rumored the bodies were mutilated, with their genitalia removed.

Both brothers, unemployed, were notorious in the community, with alleged links to drug and pedophile gangs.

No arrests have been made, and police are not currently looking for anyone else in connection with the deaths. However, an unnamed source within the force was keen to add that there is no cause for alarm and no risk to the general public.

28

GRIFFIN'S WATCHING THE press conference on the screen in the incident room. He sees Cara's reaction as the moniker is spoken: The Echo Man. He knows as much as they try to contain it, that's it, out in the world.

He doesn't like this new development, and Griffin can see neither Cara nor Marsh like it either. Naming a serial killer gives the perpetrator a sense of importance. A level of infamy shared by other murderers of the past—the Son of Sam, BTK, the Green River Killer.

He sees the other detectives glance his way.

"I don't want to hear that name uttered by anyone here," he says to the room. "You hear me?" And the detectives nod. But he knows his warning will be useless. Police love a nickname as much as the press.

"DS Griffin?" A voice distracts him.

He just wants to be left alone for a while. He's worried about Jess, about what happened last night, and he needs to gather his thoughts. Try to stop thinking about Mia. But the DC has sidled up, hovering behind his chair.

"Just Griffin," he replies. "What?"

"DC Toby Shenton, Sarge." He sits down. "I had a thought about something, about your case, actually, and I wanted to . . . I just . . ."

"Get on with it," Griffin growls.

Shenton puts three photos on the desk. Griffin glances at them.

"I know what they look like, Shenton. I was there."

"Yes, but . . . I think it's the GSK."

Griffin looks at him. Shenton has his full attention for the first time. "GSK?"

"Golden State Killer. Convicted for thirteen counts of first-degree murder and thirteen counts of kidnapping, but was believed to have committed more than fifty rapes and over a hundred burglaries in California between 1974 and 1986." Shenton looks more confident now. "The facts of your . . . your attack, match up to the murders of Lyman and Charlene Smith. The killer entered through the bathroom window and tied them up with cord from the curtains. He . . ." Shenton pauses. "He raped her, then beat them both to death with a log from the wood-pile." Shenton hesitates, then looks at Griffin. "I don't think you were supposed to survive, Sarge."

Griffin swallows hard. He looks at the information Shenton has put in front of him. He remembers the light dazzling him, the gun shoved in his face. He remembers the utter helplessness of being tied up as he listened to the screams from his wife in the other room.

"But there's one thing that's different."

Griffin manages to clear his throat. "Go on?"

"The shoes. For the other home invasion rapes, the shoe marks found at the scene match an old-style Adidas sneaker, hexagon print, same as the GSK. But the ones found outside your bathroom window? They're different."

Griffin tenses. "Have you found a match?"

"Not yet. But do you think it's deliberate? Or did the killer make a mistake?"

"Follow it up, find out. And tell Elliott," he says. Shenton gets up to leave. "How do you know so much about this stuff anyway?"

He notices Shenton's face color. "I studied it at university." Griffin raises an eyebrow. "I have a master's degree in criminology and another in behavioral psychology. I did my dissertation on the effects of child sexual abuse resulting in serial murder."

Griffin takes a deep breath in. "Tell Elliott that too," he says at last.

29

CARA PUTS HER key in the front door and listens. Inside she can hear screaming, high-pitched wails, followed by shouting. She pushes the door open. The house is in chaos. Toys litter the floor of the living room, the TV still on, the *Lego Ninjago* movie playing out on the screen. Noah follows her, closing the front door behind him.

The noise is coming from upstairs, and she follows it. The bathroom is flooded, towels scattered across the floor. She picks up her daughter's sweater, then gathers up the rest of the clothing.

"Mommy!" Her daughter pokes her head out of the room, then runs to Cara. She bends down as her daughter charges against her, wrapping her arms around.

"You're home!" she says into her chest. "Will you read us a story?"

Her daughter looks over her shoulder, spots Noah standing at the top of the stairs, then lets out a squeal of delight.

"Will Noah read us a story?"

Cara smiles. She knew she'd be sidelined the minute they spotted Noah. To Cara's surprise, the first time Noah had met them, she'd discovered there was no accent Deakin couldn't do. No funny voice he hadn't perfected. He'd have the kids in gales of laughter, rapt as he read their latest favorite.

Tilly grabs Noah's hand, then drags him into the bedroom. Cara leaves them to it for a bit, putting the kids' discarded clothes into the laundry basket, picking a towel up and using it to mop the water on the floor. She folds the others and hangs them on the rail.

She turns as she hears soft footsteps coming up the stairs, surprised to see Lauren still there.

"Thank you for staying," she says to her.

Lauren smiles. "It's no problem, I didn't have plans."

Cara nods. The two women stand in the hallway for a moment. Lauren pushes her long blonde hair behind her ears, and Cara feels slightly awkward. She wants to tell her to go home, that she wants this time with her family alone, but thinks she might be being rude when Lauren has put herself out to help them today.

They both listen to Noah's voice coming from the bedroom, starting on the story. She smiles as he speaks in a mock cockney accent, then in deep Scottish tones. The door opens and Roo comes out.

"Rejected again?" Cara says, and Roo smiles.

"As always." He puts his arm around her and plants a kiss on her forehead. "How was your day?"

"You don't want to know."

She hugs her husband, enjoying hearing the happy giggles of her daughter, laughter from her son. She can imagine them, snuggled up next to Noah on Josh's bed, clean and warm in their pajamas.

"How's Tilly?" she asks.

"No vomiting since, eaten some toast for tea, so all looking okay. I'll go and get dinner on," he says. "Are you staying?" he asks Lauren.

Say no, say no, Cara wills silently.

"Thank you, but I should be going," Lauren says. "But I'll come and help tidy up."

Cara hears Roo's protestations as they both go downstairs, telling her she should put her feet up. I don't pay that woman enough, Cara thinks, feeling the familiar flash of guilt.

In the bedroom, Noah is sitting on Joshua's bed, her son next to him, looking at the pictures in the book as the story progresses. Tilly is sitting on the floor, and Cara joins her, sitting cross-legged and pulling her daughter into her lap.

She leans forward and puts her nose into her daughter's hair. It smells of strawberry shampoo. Tilly drinks her milk and stares at Noah, completely absorbed in the story.

Cara looks up at Noah. For the first time that day he has a smile on his face; he's enjoying reading the book, receiving undivided attention from her kids. This is an aspect to Noah that has always surprised her: this softer, paternal side. She would love Noah to find someone, to fall in love.

The second story comes to an end, and Noah stands up, giving both kids a goodnight hug, leaving Cara alone with them.

"Into bed now, please?" Cara says as the kids mess around together, eventually settling under their duvets, Tilly going next door into her own room. She hugs her son and kisses him goodnight. She stops in the doorway after she's turned the light off, just making out his shape in the darkness, feeling a swell of love.

She hears the click of the front door as Lauren leaves for the night, then Roo climbing the stairs and going to say goodnight to Tilly.

She would do anything for her family. She wonders if she should give up this job, do something more stable, more nine-to-five, then dismisses the thought. She knows she never will, then thinks: Why wouldn't it be enough?

Roo comes out of Tilly's bedroom and joins her in the hallway.

"All quiet," he whispers.

She nods and he goes in to say goodnight to Joshua, as she does the same to Tilly.

She's already half asleep.

'Mommy?" she says as Cara goes to shut the door.

"Hmm?" Cara turns back, the light from the hallway casting a glow over her daughter.

"Are you winning? Against the monsters?"

Cara sighs. "I'm trying my best," she says at last. "Get some sleep, pickle."

She closes the door behind her and stands in the hallway. Downstairs she can hear the deep laughter from her husband, then Noah joining in. Even in such domestic bliss, she feels a heaviness to her body. She knows that, at the moment, she isn't winning. She isn't winning at all.

*   *   *

In the kitchen, the table is laid and tempting smells are starting to waft from the oven. Roo stands at the kitchen counter, a knife in his hand, the blade a blur as he chops the carrots. Cara stops in the doorway.

He finishes, tipping the vegetables into the boiling water, then spots Cara watching. He throws the knife in the air. It spins once, and he expertly catches it by the handle.

"What are you? Twelve?" Deakin scoffs from where he's sitting at the table. "Showing off for your girl?"

Roo holds the knife out to Deakin. "You want to try?" he says.

"Deaks, I'm not blue-lighting you to the hospital with a macerated hand because you are trying to prove yourself to my husband," Cara says, and Noah puts his hands out in front of him.

"I know when I'm beaten," he laughs.

The oven beeps and Roo goes to it, transferring food from the oven to their plates. It's a bizarre mix: spinach and ricotta cannelloni in a

tomato sauce, perfect slices of beef Wellington, dauphinoise potatoes—
all leftovers from the restaurant. It's one advantage to having a husband
working strange hours as head chef—meals you would normally pay
twenty, thirty pounds for, served up in your own home.

They all eat. Deakin seems ravenous, and Cara wonders when he
would usually cook for himself, if ever. Roo tells them about his latest
sous chef, a delicate French girl, reduced to tears within the first hour.

"She should come to work with us for a day, then she'd have something to cry about," Noah says with his mouth full.

Roo looks at Cara. "I saw you on the news." He pauses. "It's a serial
killer?"

Cara nods slowly. She takes a sip from the glass of wine in front of
her. "It's looking that way. Nate worked out the pattern."

"How is he? I should have said hello while I was there."

"Sunshine and light, as always," Noah says sarcastically.

Cara frowns at him. "He's okay. Back with us, for the time being
anyway. I'd rather have him getting under my feet at the station than
moldering away in that basement."

Cara looks up as she hears a little voice shout from upstairs. Roo
pushes his plate to one side.

"I'll go," he says. "You're still eating."

Noah watches him leave, then glances at Cara. She catches his eye.
"What?" she asks.

Noah looks down at his dinner and has another mouthful. "Has
Lauren got a boyfriend?" he asks at last.

Cara frowns. "I don't think so, no. Why? Are you interested?" She
isn't sure what Noah is getting at.

Noah takes a swig from his beer. "She just seems a little . . ." He
pauses. "Overfamiliar with Roo."

"They've known each other a long time."

"I know, it's just . . ." He scowls. "It's nothing."

"Spit it out, Deaks."

"When they went out to the car, I saw her put her hand on his arm.
And it was there, I don't know, a bit too long. And when she saw me
watching, she removed it."

Cara shakes her head. "It's nothing, Noah. I know what you're
doing. Just because we see bad shit every day doesn't mean everyone's
at it. There's no more going on between Roo and Lauren than there is
between you and me."

Noah stops and looks at her. He holds her gaze just that little bit too
long, and she looks away.

"You're right. Forget I mentioned it," he says at last.

They finish their dinner in silence. Roo comes back downstairs and sits at the table.

"Everything okay?" he asks, looking between the two of them, puzzled.

Cara forces a smile. "Of course."

Noah takes a final swig from his bottle of beer. He picks up their plates and carries them to the sink; Cara follows him with the other dishes.

"I should go," he says. He won't meet her eye.

"No, Noah, stay," she protests, but he shakes his head.

"I'm sorry, I'm just worn out."

Roo gives him a hug and a manly clap on the back, and Cara walks him to the door. He pulls it open, picking up his jacket, then turns back.

"Cara, forget what I said—I shouldn't have mentioned it," he mutters. He pats down his pockets, pulling out the usual pack of cigarettes. He puts one in his mouth.

"Deaks, I'll give you a lift, please," Cara pleads. It's pouring down with rain, puddles forming in the road. She knows he'll get soaked in seconds, but he shakes his head again, lighting the cigarette.

"I'll be fine. I need the walk."

"At least take a raincoat."

She holds out one of Roo's and he takes it, putting it on, then striding down their road, head down, pulling the hood up against the rain. She remembers the conversation with Libby in the bar and wonders exactly what is going on between her and Noah. How exactly he feels about her.

She feels Roo put his arms around her shoulders, and she leans back into his chest.

"What was that about?" Roo asks.

Cara turns in his arms and reaches up to kiss him. "Just the investigation. Wearing us all out." She rests her face against his sweater as he closes the door. "It was good to see you at work today," she says, closing her eyes briefly.

"I always worry about disturbing you."

"No, it was nice to be reminded of the good things in life."

Her husband pulls her closer for a moment, and she feels him kiss the top of her head. Then she looks up at him.

"Bedtime?" she asks.

He smiles. She knows he's in no doubt as to what she's proposing.

"Bedtime," he agrees.

CHAPTER

30

G RIFFIN ARRIVES HOME. With a loud bang of the door, he dumps his bag on the table, then takes two pills out of a packet and throws them in his mouth.

Jess is sitting on the sofa, her feet tucked under her. She's had a boring day. Slept, got showered, dressed. Ate lunch. She hasn't dared leave, knowing people are out there looking for her.

"What happened?" she asks.

He looks up quickly, then frowns. "Nothing," he says. "Nothing at all."

"Something must have . . ."

"Nothing! Okay?" She jumps at his shout, and he sees her reaction. His jaw tightens. Then, more quietly, he says: "Just a lot of routine police stuff, Jess. No leads. We're no closer to finding this guy."

Then, without another comment, he digs in his rucksack again and pulls out a mobile phone.

"I got you this," he says, and throws it across the table to her.

She picks it up and looks at it quizzically.

"Burner phone," he says. "Untraceable. Thought you might want to call your daughter?"

A sudden excitement comes over her. She looks at the phone, pressing the screen into life. It's shit and basic, but it's a lifeline.

She stares at Griffin. "Thank you," she says, starting to cry again.

He looks uncomfortable at her display of gratitude. "Whatever," he replies. "Just don't be too long. I've blocked the number, but you never know."

She stands up, moving away and sitting on the sofa. She looks at the phone in her hand, then inputs her mother's mobile number from memory. Her breath catches in her throat as the phone rings, then cuts to voicemail. She redials.

"Hello?" On hearing her mother, anxious and uncertain, Jess starts to cry again. "Is anyone there?" her mother repeats.

'Mom?' Jess eventually manages to croak.

"Jess, is that you?"

"Yes, it's me, Mom, but be careful, please."

"Where are you? How are you?" Her mother's voice becomes a dramatic whisper. "Come home now! Enough of this messing around."

'Mom, I'm sorry, I haven't got time to argue. Can I speak to Alice, please?"

There's an audible sigh. "You always were headstrong," her mother says, as if Jess has been caught being rude to a teacher, rather than fleeing arrest for murder. "Here you go."

There is a rustle and a bit more whispering. Then a voice, high and on the edge of tears.

'Mommy?' her daughter says.

Jess feels a rush of relief. Emotion catches in her throat, but she manages to keep her voice level.

"Hi, sweetie. Are you okay?"

"Where are you, Mommy? Where's Daddy?"

"I'll . . ." Jess pauses. "I'll be home soon. I've had to go away for a while, but Grandma and Grandad will look after you."

"Okay. Can we watch *Frozen* when we get home?" Jess steels herself again. There's no home to go to, no *Frozen* DVD.

"We might not be able to go home for a while, sweetie," she says. "But Grandma will let you watch *Frozen*."

"Promise?" Alice asks.

"Promise. I love you, poppet. Can you pass the phone back to Grandma?"

"I love you too, Mommy." Then another rustle as the phone is passed back.

'Mom? You haven't told her about Patrick?' Jess asks.

"I . . ." her mother starts. "I thought that was her mother's job. That she'd need you with her when she found out."

Jess nods, swallowing. "Thanks, Mom," she manages to say before she hangs up the phone. She can't bring herself to say goodbye.

She feels tears welling up again behind her eyes, then anger building. All this emotion—all this crying, however justified—is not achieving anything. She's made a promise to her daughter now. To be back soon. And that's what she needs to focus on.

She stands up, and Griffin snaps his fingers at her, gesturing toward the phone. She passes it to him, and he opens up the back, pulling out the SIM card, then breaking it in two.

He sees her looking at it, watching her salvation being destroyed.

"Do you want them to trace you back here?" he asks, and she shakes her head.

Griffin throws the pieces in the trash, then walks over to the bed and slumps down on his back, his hands behind his head. Jess watches him.

She wonders at what brought her here. To this apartment, this man. And to this insane situation. She should leave. Nav's right: she should hand herself in. That would be the sensible thing to do—but when has that ever applied to her? And something pulls her toward the mystery, an invisible cord headed for destruction. She's always found solace in the darker things in life—those true crime documentaries, those murderers and outcasts making her feel less of an aberration. Her whole life she's been fighting for the desire to be normal. A desire to be whole, somehow, to feel what other people feel. But now everything has been stripped away and she's alone, she doesn't feel that pretense. For the first time in her life, the macabre makes a perverse kind of sense. And Griffin's a part of that.

"Are you hungry?" she asks.

"No."

"Tired?"

He shakes his head. "I feel like I'll never sleep again. All the time . . ." He flutters his hands above his face as he stares at the ceiling. "Just things going around and around. I just want to actually *do* something."

Jess doesn't speak, but slowly gets up from the sofa. She stands by his feet at the end of the bed. She feels a flush: nervousness after what happened last time. But also excitement.

"What do you want to do?" she asks.

He opens his mouth to speak, but stops as she takes her T-shirt and sweater off in one quick movement. He raises himself up off the bed on his elbows, watching as she wriggles out of her jeans until she's standing in front of him in her underwear.

"What do you want to do?" she asks again.

"Jess . . ."

"Griffin. Shut up and take your clothes off."

He hesitates for a moment, but she's aware something has shifted between them. He won't turn her down now. Sure enough, decision made, he pulls off his shirt and jeans. She takes the rest of her clothes off, then gets onto the bed, straddling him.

He reaches down, and in one quick movement, removes his boxer shorts. Then he pauses, their eyes meeting.

His hands go up to her waist, and she can feel the light touch of his fingers on her back. Neither of them moves; the room is quiet. Jess can hear rain falling outside, dripping down the gutters onto the pavement. She holds his gaze.

She moves back slightly, waiting as he reaches behind to the bedside table, swiftly opening the foil packet of a condom and putting it on. Then she raises herself up and onto him. She sees him take a deep breath in, then again, as she starts to move. His hands are still on her waist but he lets her do what she wants, moving slowly.

But then something switches in him. He can no longer hold back. He picks her up, her legs going around his waist, and he shoves her against the wall. She can feel the rough brickwork against her back— she knows it's a bad idea, but she likes it—and he pushes into her, hard.

His head is still buried in her neck, and she pulls him up to face her. She wants to kiss him. She wants to feel his lips on hers, to remember they're human, they're alive, but he pauses, as if questioning what they're doing.

"Don't stop," she says.

She kisses him, and he thrusts into her, harder this time.

She slips slightly, and their position changes. They shift, together, him resting her on the edge of the large wooden table, his fingers digging into her ass. She grips his shoulders, moving with him. She's not thinking anymore. Except about this, about the feeling of him.

She can feel the sweat on his body, the rough of his stubble on her neck. *This* is what she wants, she thinks.

* * *

Afterward they lie on the bed, passing a cigarette between them. As the room grows colder, he pulls the duvet across, and Jess watches the shadows, headlights from the cars outside flickering across the ceiling.

"You can't always use this to solve everything," he says after a while.

"Use what?"

"Sex. This." He uses the cigarette to gesture to her naked torso.

She's quiet for a second. "Are you complaining?"

"No," he says. "Fuck, no. Just at some point you're going to have to work out a way to make yourself feel better without resorting to sleeping with someone." He pauses. "Or what you were doing last night."

She doesn't like what he's saying, but his manner, the bluntness, catches her off guard.

He leans over her, stubbing the cigarette out in the ashtray on the bedside table. "It's not a criticism," he adds. He stays propped up on his elbow, watching her through the darkness. "I'm not judging. You're not so different from me. Better looking, maybe, but inside we're the same. Just trying to get through the day."

She stares up at the ceiling. "Griffin . . ." she starts slowly. She needs to tell him. She owes him that, at least. She takes a deep breath. He's going to think I'm a freak, she thinks, like most people do when they find out. But she doesn't care. For some reason, she trusts him.

"I have a condition called congenital insensitivity to pain," she says. Griffin turns in the bed to face her, and she meets his astonished stare. "I can't feel any pain," she finishes.

He pauses. "Nothing at all?" he asks.

"I can sense hot and cold. I can feel touch, and sensation. But no pain, no."

She still itches. She is ticklish. But no stinging, no agony, no hurt. At least, not the physical kind.

"So that's why . . ." he starts, gesturing toward her head, and she nods. "Sounds nice," he adds shortly.

"It's not."

She wasn't diagnosed until she was six. By that time she'd bitten off the tip of her tongue, had more fractures than she could remember, and Social Services had a file. She used to jump off the top of the stairs, tumbling carefree to the bottom. Hold her hand over candles, watching the skin blister, then burn. Her parents were driven to distraction. She was in a cast almost constantly until she was eleven.

When kids at school found out, they would punch her to test if it was true. Later, her response was to fight back: bloody disputes she always won.

As she got older, she worked out the warning signs. She's supposed to regularly check every inch of her body for cuts or bruises, any sign that something might be off. Internal bleeding is one of the biggest worries: her chest filling with blood, bursting her from the inside. She'd be dead before she realized. But she's always been too careless about it. Too reckless.

She explains all this to Griffin. He just stares at her. He seems to be thinking.

"So how do you know you haven't got a brain hemorrhage?" he asks.

"I don't. The doctors would have said."

"You might."

"I don't."

There is another long pause.

"If you keel over and die, I'm just going to dump your body in the woods somewhere," he says at last with a small smile. "Deal?"

She nods. "Deal."

He rolls over in the bed onto his front, punches the pillow a few times, then slumps down face-first onto it. "But I meant what I said," he mutters into the pillow. "You can't keep doing things to yourself."

She hears his breathing slow as he falls asleep. People have said the same things to her before, but coming from Griffin it feels different.

Her husband used to chastise her every time there was an incident with the razor. "I don't understand why you keep on doing this," Patrick said once. "Is it attention seeking? Are you trying to kill yourself?"

It was neither of those things, and it seems that Griffin tacitly recognizes that. Patrick never had. On their wedding day, Jess had overheard a conversation.

"She's too good for you," his best man had been saying. "You're batting way above your average."

Patrick had laughed. It was late in the day, and too much alcohol had made him glib.

"Never hurts the career to have a gorgeous woman on your arm," he'd replied. "And you have no idea, mate." Jess watched him do a circular movement with his finger next to the side of his head. "Mad as a hatter," he'd laughed.

She'd felt the hurt. But she'd known he was right.

She'd never mentioned it to her husband. That day she'd resolved she would get better. But it got worse. No amount of therapy worked. Nothing changed.

Until her house burned down and her husband was murdered.

Still naked under the duvet, she moves next to Griffin. She curls her leg over his, bare skin against skin, and he mutters slightly in his sleep, draping his arm around her.

Maybe, she wonders, taking in his warmth, maybe the key isn't getting rid of the crazy. Maybe it's finding someone just as broken, who understands.

31

H<small>E HOLDS A</small> knife in his hand, blade facing forward. It's large and sharp. Slowly he carves a piece of flesh out of the apple and eats it. He relishes the thought that there's traces of blood on the blade, that he might be consuming some remnant of his victims.

It's cold down here. He's strung a single light up in the corner of the room, but the bare bulb is dim, and the glow barely stretches to the bottom of the hole.

But he can see her eyes, staring up at him. Two white circles, red-rimmed, shining out of a dirty face.

Digging the pit in the basement had been hard and backbreaking, but he'd known it was necessary. It isn't big—about eight feet deep—muddy, wet. It rained last night and the bottom filled up with about a foot of water. She'd begged him again, standing there in the mud. She'd said she was cold; she'd pleaded with him to let her go. Said she'd let him have sex with her, she'd do anything.

The thought made him angry. He would have her if *he* wanted to, not when she said it was okay. He'd fucked her already, when he'd first got her here. Hands tied, she'd struggled, pleaded, kicked, but her fight had only spurred him on, his punches landing square on her face, silencing her.

And the hopeful look after? She'd thought that was it. That he was going to let her go. That look soon changed when he'd dragged her down here, shoved her into the hole.

To shut her up he'd found a long plank of wood and hit her with it. Reaching down into the pit, he'd struck her, over and over again. She'd dodged him at first, but once he'd got a good blow to her head, she'd been dazed, cowered at the bottom in the mud, and he'd been able to really go at her hard.

He can see those bruises now, the scabs dirty, bleeding, and raw. He can hear the rain again, outside. The hole's only going to get worse. He cuts another piece of the apple and puts it in his mouth.

The house is perfect. It had sat empty for years, claimed by the council after his father's death and left to rot. Much like him, in that children's home. Slowly the other houses were abandoned around it. Nobody wanted to live near the site of a double murder, let alone in the house where they took place. Nobody but him.

"It won't be long now," he says to her, and she looks at him again, eyes pleading. He throws the remainder of the apple into the pit and she goes after it, the dirty starving animal that she is, her chains rattling as she scrabbles in the water. He watches as she finds it in the mud and eats it, his lip curling in disgust.

He'll be glad to get rid of this one. She's no more than a piece of property to him right now, but the reality of facing this stinking, shit-filled, muddy pit every day isn't something he's enjoying. But maybe . . .

He looks at the electrical extension cord, its ends stripped bare. Perhaps he'll enjoy this part.

He holds the insulation on the cord, just up from the bare wires, then reaches over and plugs the other end into the wall. He moves her chains closer, and she sees him—the cable in his hand—and the metal wrapped around her wrists and torso. She looks at the water around her feet.

"Please—" she starts, but the words are snatched out of her mouth as he applies the electrical current.

She screams, her body spasms and jerks, then falls into the water.

He smiles. Yes, maybe he will enjoy this part after all.

CHAPTER

32

Day 5
Friday

FRIDAY, AND EVERYTHING moves on. Everyone is back in the incident
room, no hesitation. All the detectives know there's a job that needs
to be done.

Cara sits with Shenton, reviewing evidence collected from the
Dahmer crime scene. Fingerprints and blood work still aren't back, but
the lab have forwarded photographs of the other exhibits collected from
the apartment.

Toby slowly moves through the images on the screen, looking for
anything worth following up. Cara sees Noah arrive for the day; he
raises a hand in acknowledgment to her, slipping a Polo into his mouth
at the same time as he starts a conversation with one of the detectives.
Business as usual.

She turns her attention back to the screen. More rubbish from the
trash: a wrapper from a Mars Bar, a scrap of green paper, a parking
receipt.

She points. "Blow that up?"

Shenton zooms in. It's small, barely worth mentioning, "Pay and
Display" down one side, with a date and time and a set of six digits.

Toby points to the numbers. "Probably the location of the ticket
machine," he says. "What's the chance of finding CCTV from that
area?"

"Worth checking," Cara replies.

He makes a note and moves on to the next image—a letter, some sort of spam mail, "To the resident of apartment 214," written across the top. Then more paper, photographs of mess and rubbish.

Shenton frowns and growls quietly under his breath. Cara looks at him.

"Problem?" she asks. She knows this sort of police work is monotonous, but sometimes it's the only way to unearth a lead.

"No, it's just . . ." Shenton pauses and Cara stares at him. "Look at this mess. All this rubbish, this litter. It's not like him."

"Him?"

"The Echo Man." He looks at Cara, and she notices a red blush creep its way up from his collar. He knows he shouldn't have used the name, but she lets it go. "Look at everything else he has done," he continues. "He takes the right tools to decapitate those bodies to the Kemper scene. But how did he get home? There must have been another car. Same with Manson. Same with Dahmer. He's organized. He's planned. He's clever."

"You have a theory, Toby?" Cara asks.

"Everything he does is deliberate, right?" Cara nods her head. "So this"—he points to the mess in the photo on the screen—"is deliberate too. There's something here."

Cara looks back at the photo. There's so much *stuff*. So much rubbish. "Perhaps it's just another aspect of Dahmer's apartment. Dahmer was messy, so he has to be too?"

Toby turns back to the screen and zooms in on the photo. She sees him examining it closely.

"Shenton?" she starts, and he looks back at her. "You know about this, right? About these killers?"

"I know a bit."

"You know more than a bit. Do us a profile."

"Boss?"

"You know, a psychological profile of the killer? What makes him tick? Who is he?" Cara's not sure if this is the right move, but since Marsh won't release the budget for a proper psychologist, how can it hurt? They could ignore it, after all.

Shenton pauses. "I could . . ."

"So do it." Cara nods at him, then looks up as Griffin appears at their desk.

"She's here," he says to Cara, and Shenton looks up eagerly.

"Can I go with DS Griffin?" he gasps with the enthusiasm of a new puppy, and Cara sees Griffin roll his eyes. He doesn't want to do this interview with Shenton there, Cara knows that. But then a little bit of mentoring might be just the development her brother needs.

"Griffin, take Toby," she says.

But then Shenton seems torn. "But the profile . . ." he stutters, looking as though he might cry.

"Go," Cara smiles. "Your psychological insights can wait an hour or so."

Griffin glares at Cara, then sighs, defeated. "Come on then."

33

THE WITNESS HAS a strong Southern American accent. Returned from visiting relatives, she says, the crime scene tape gave her quite the fright. Her hands flutter at her crêpey mottled neck; she seems more excited than scared.

Griffin issues the standard warnings for the voluntary interview, and she signs the paperwork. Brassy blonde hair, makeup layered on with a trowel. Her perfume fills the small room, almost making Griffin's eyes water. He hasn't got much hope for the interview, but she's the last neighbor on the list, living in apartment 215.

"And you say you've never met the resident of 213?" Griffin asks.

Next to him Shenton is already being annoying, busy scribbling notes on a pad, seemingly trying to capture every part of their conversation despite the fact it's all being recorded.

"Knocked on the door a few times," she confirms. "To complain about the smell. But he never answered." She taps her bright blue nails against the tabletop, the noise grating on Griffin's nerves. "Good thing too—he was a depressing-looking guy."

Griffin's head snaps up.

"You said you'd never met him?"

She nods. "Not *met*. He never said hello. Just saw him the once, going into his apartment."

"And could you describe him for us?"

The woman shrugs and Griffin suppresses his impatience. "White, black? What was he wearing? You're sure he was male? Tall, short?"

She frowns. "Yes, a guy. Tall. Hard to say anything else. He was wearing all black—black trousers, black sweatshirt, sneakers. Hood pulled up over his face."

Griffin stands up; he gestures for Shenton to do the same. "How tall? As tall as me or like my colleague?"

The woman stands up in front of them. She considers them both. "Like him," she says, pointing to Shenton. "Same build as him too."

They all sit down again.

"You're a big bloke, aren't you?" she adds coyly.

Griffin ignores her flirting. "But you didn't see his face?"

She shakes her head, another gust of perfume wafting his way. "I said, 'Hi,' but he didn't turn. Just went in next door."

"I'm sorry," Shenton says tentatively. "Next door?"

"Don't be sorry, doll," she twangs with an oily smile. "Not your fault."

Griffin looks at Shenton. He's staring at his notes, running his finger across the page.

"But you live in apartment 215?" Shenton asks. "So this guy was going into . . ."

"Apartment 214. Right."

"Fuck," Griffin mutters under his breath.

"Ma'am?" Shenton says calmly. "We need to know about the resident of apartment 213."

"Oh." She sits back in her seat, crossing her arms over her chest, bangles jangling. "No. Can't help you there."

*   *   *

Griffin and Shenton walk back, downhearted. Cara meets them in the corridor.

"Anything?" she asks.

Griffin shakes his head. "Thought we did for a second—she had a bit of a description of a guy going into the apartment—but it turns out it was 214." Cara's face falls. "You been to see Marsh?"

She nods. "Usual message: Get it sorted."

"No pressure," he says sarcastically.

"None."

They walk back to the incident room together. But then Cara stops them in the doorway.

"Apartment 214?" she asks.

Griffin nods.

She drags them over to Shenton's desk. "Toby, pull up that bit of post we had earlier." She directs him, pointing to the photographs on the monitor. "There. The one they found in the trash can of 213."

"214," Griffin reads out loud. He looks at Cara. He knows that expression. "What are you thinking?"

"Toby, who lives there? Pull up council tax records."

He does as she asks, expertly navigating the system.

"DeAngelo," Shenton says excitedly, gesturing at the screen. "Joseph DeAngelo."

Griffin looks from Cara to Shenton and back again. They're smiling. Cara raises her hand and Toby slaps it with a high-five.

Griffin knows that name. Until recently, an unknown. Ex-Navy. An ex-cop. And now?

"Joseph DeAngelo," Shenton repeats. "The Golden State Killer."

Cara picks up the phone. "We've got to get into that apartment."

34

"WELL, I DON'T KNOW . . ."

Cara stands outside the block of apartments with Griffin, the same block of apartments as the day before. The white scientific services vans are still parked outside; Cara knows the SOCOs will be there for days yet, piles of evidence to log and take away. The landlord stands next to them, nervously wringing his hands.

"He's potentially killed eleven men," Cara says.

"Not Joe. Joe's a good guy."

"You've met him?"

"No, not actually met him. But . . ."

He glances upward. Cara follows his gaze. The window of apartment 214 seems to be covered with something; they can't see any blinds or curtains.

"How did you come to rent him the apartment? How does he pay?" Griffin asks.

"He put a note through my door about a year ago when I advertised. Cash every month, right on time." The landlord's gabbling now.

"And you took identification?"

"No, he . . . er . . ." He stops, looks down. "He paid me double to keep quiet. Ignore the usual paperwork." Cara and Griffin both glare at him. Chastened, the landlord holds out the spare key. "I'm sorry. How was I to know he'd be a serial killer?"

Cara takes the key and they walk toward the main door.

"How do you want to play this?" Griffin asks. "Call in armed response?"

Cara frowns. "That could take hours." She looks at Nate. "There's no way he's there, right? I mean, still staying at the apartment while the place crawls with crime scene officers and cops?"

"Seems unlikely."

"So let's just go and look around. What's the worst that could happen?"

Griffin stays silent. They walk toward the door of the block of apartments where Cara remembers vomiting in the flower bed just forty-eight hours before. She's glad Nate didn't reply. She knows the answer. More bodies. A serial killer with a gun.

But they can't waste any more time.

They pass the open door of apartment 213, blue and white tape across the entrance. Cara picks up two new white crime scene suits from the pile and hands one to Nate. They both put them on, along with the shoes and gloves. They keep their hoods down, masks in hand.

She pauses outside 214.

"Ready?" she says to Griffin. He nods. She feels reassured knowing her six-foot brother is there with her.

She knocks.

There's no answer, so she puts the key in the door. Her hand is shaking; it takes two attempts, then she turns it, pushing it open.

Inside it's dark.

The apartment feels cold, the air enclosed and stale, but she doesn't detect the same intense smell of decay as they had from the apartment next door. Even so, she puts the mask on and pulls the hood up. Next to her, Griffin does the same.

The wooden boards creak under their feet as they go into the first room. It seems to be a bedroom, although it's completely empty. No carpet, nothing on the walls except a patch of damp in the corner of the ceiling. The single window is covered by newspaper, gray light shining through. She's disappointed, then registers the absurdity of the feeling. No dead bodies are a good thing, surely.

Cara turns around to Nate, narrowing her eyes. He shrugs and points to the next door. Neither of them speaks.

A bathroom this time. Avocado-green sink and bath, white toilet. Gray grime coats every surface, curling linoleum on the floor. But nothing.

They look at the last door.

"Cara . . ." Griffin starts.

"If we've wasted our time, then so be it," she replies. "What will we have lost?"

He opens it.

And Cara knows she wasn't wrong.

Bare floorboards, the room shrouded in darkness, layers of newspaper covering the windows. But unlike the first, it's stuffed to the brim. Shelves are positioned floor to ceiling, creating a maze of books and belongings. Articles are stuck on whatever walls are visible, fluttering slightly in the new breeze from the open door.

It smells of dust and neglect. A faint odor of stale sweat and fried foods.

They walk in slowly, hands by their sides. Even with her full suit on, Cara is reluctant to touch anything. She squints at the titles on the bookshelf. *Gray's Anatomy. Simpson's Forensic Medicine. An Introduction to Crime Scene Forensics.* She leaves them, going deeper into the room.

The back wall was once wallpapered. Through the gaps in the newspaper she can see tiny red roses where some of it remains. She reads the headlines: *FIVE MURDERED IN SANDBANKS* and *PROSTITUTE FOUND DEAD.* Clippings from his previous kills.

There are spaces where the plaster has fallen away; she scuffs her feet in some of it on the floor. There's one chair—brown broken leather—positioned in front of an old bulky television. And left on the arm, reflecting in sunshine from a corner of the window, is an empty clear pint glass.

She takes a quick breath in, crouching down and peering at it in the dim light. She can see markings on the rim, the perfect semi-circle of a lip impression, and five precise fingerprints.

"You're fucking kidding me," Griffin says from behind her.

She glances backward at him. "Could it be this easy?" she mutters, and he gives her an incredulous look. "Fetch a SOCO from next door," she says. "Let's get it logged and analyzed as soon as possible."

He leaves and she continues looking around the room. She scans the shelves, pulls out one cardboard box. It doesn't have a lid: inside she can see leather straps, silver buckles, huge purple dildos. She gingerly takes something out with two fingers of her gloved hand. It's what seems to be some sort of cat-o-nine-tails, black leather, dried matter down one of the strands. She puts the box back quickly.

She continues her journey. Piles of newspapers, pornography stacked neatly. She picks up one of the magazines closest to her and immediately regrets it: the woman is wearing black leather bondage gear, a ball gag in her red-lipsticked mouth, tied to the bed on all fours, some sort of metal bar keeping her legs apart. She assumes it's been staged but, realizing with a jolt that it might not be, suppresses the bile rising in her stomach.

This guy likes it rough and nonconsensual. But they knew that, she tells herself. Why is this a surprise? Why is any of this a surprise anymore?

But then she turns a corner around one of the bookshelves, and that's when she sees them.

Small white frames, completely covering the wall on the far side. Neatly organized in rows. Cara walks closer. They're Polaroid photos, blurry images, but unmistakable. People. Bodies. Limbs. Blood.

Cara's hand goes to her mouth. She's seen death before, but this isn't it. She feels Griffin come back into the room and stop behind her. She knows he's scanning the wall, looking at the same images she's seeing.

She hears a noise, almost a groan, caught in the back of a throat, and she realizes it's coming from her.

Because these aren't Polaroids of dead bodies. These people are alive. These are eyes, looking at the camera, pleading, suffering, dying.

These are people being tortured, captured on film, for the entertainment of a killer.

And one of them is her own brother.

35

"I DON'T REMEMBER A camera," Griffin whispers next to her.

She turns to him. "Stop looking, Nate." She tries to push him backward, but he doesn't budge. "Please? This isn't something you should see."

At last, he turns. "Just tell me," he says, quietly. "Is Mia there?"

She scans the wall. She recognizes some of the victims. She remembers the girls from the Kemper Ford Galaxy, and here they are, alive. She can make out the metal of a car door; the girl is turned away, her hands in front of her. It's out of focus, but Cara can see bloody skin, the holes in the girl's chest. She can't comprehend how this guy can control someone at the same time as he's stabbing them, yet here is the evidence. She knows these are his souvenirs, the wall he goes back to, to enjoy what he's done over and over again.

But then she stops.

"Cara?"

"Yes, Nate. I'm sorry. She's here."

He turns back, sees the photo Cara's looking at. It's Mia, her hands tied, the photo taken from above. One eye is already blackened and swollen, the other looks up, full of tears. Griffin goes to take it from the wall, to hide it from plain sight, but she stops him.

"I'm sorry, Nate. It's evidence."

She knows he's strong enough to overpower her and take it anyway, but instead he turns and storms away. She runs after him, out of the apartment, past his discarded crime scene suit on the ground, catching up with him in the stairwell.

She grabs his hand, but he shakes her off.

"Leave me alone, Cara," he says. His shoulders are slumped. "Please. Just do your job. Catch this bastard."

He walks away from her, slower this time, and she lets him go.

* * *

It doesn't take long for the scene of crime officers to descend. They work fast, cataloguing evidence, taking photographs. Cara can't bear to go back to the wall, so she starts to look at what else is in the room. A tattered hardback of *James and the Giant Peach*. A whole shelf of medical textbooks. Biographies on Dahmer, Bundy, Manson, Fred West, the GSK. She pulls one down: Post-it Notes mark specific pages, and she opens it up, looking at the pencil marks highlighting passages of text. *Lift torso to drain blood,* she reads. *Head in saucepan of water eyeballs boil away flesh takes longer.* He's done his research. And he's done it well.

She moves on. Two Polaroid cameras, the sort beloved of retro-seeking millennials, smudges of something that looks like blood clear on the brightly colored plastic. Boxes of film. Notebooks of all shapes and sizes. She opens one. A piece of newspaper flutters out, and Cara leans down, picking it up from the floor. The headline: *ANIMAL KILLER STILL AT LARGE.* She replaces it back in the notebook and looks at some of the text on the page. It's childish handwriting, scribbles in capitals. She tries to read it, but she can't make out the words. They need to get some floodlights in here; she can't see a damn thing.

Cara waves to a crime scene tech. "Can we get this lot logged first?" she asks, and they nod. There are shelves and shelves of them—who knows what's written on their pages?

The pint glass has already been taken away, a rush put on the analysis.

Among all the chaos, Deakin arrives. She recognizes his posture in the white suit and watches him as he walks up to the wall of Polaroids. She leaves him to it and crouches down to the VHS player below the television. She hasn't seen one like this in years, and she picks up a video left on top. After the Polaroid photos, she has a bad feeling about the tape—and the rows of others behind.

"Cara?"

She turns toward Deakin. He points to the photographs.

"Do we know if there's anyone here we haven't found?" he asks, and she walks up to join him.

"Not that I can tell. Might help us identify the Dahmer victims."

"Hmm."

He turns back, facing the wall. She stands next to him. They look at the little white squares together. Her attention stops on one. It's a man, bare chested, smiling, willingly posing for the camera. She recognizes the kitchen in the background—it's the Dahmer apartment. She wonders how long this man lived after this photograph was taken.

"Why didn't you tell me you were coming here?"

Deakin speaks quietly. She looks at him. After a pause he turns toward her, but in the white suit and mask she can only see his eyes; she can't tell his expression.

Cara doesn't answer. Without acknowledging it, she had wanted to put distance between her and Noah. Something last night felt like it had strayed into unknown territory, but seeing his confusion now, she knew she'd been wrong. She should have brought her partner with her. She shouldn't have risked Griffin being here, and now her brother had seen the unimaginable, and he had gone God knows where.

"I'm sorry, Deaks. I wasn't thinking."

He nods, a small movement, and her transgression is forgiven. And the mood is interrupted as a voice calls for their attention from the far side of the room.

They both go over.

"Oh, fuck," Noah mutters.

It's a large chest freezer.

"I'm never going to look at white domestic appliances in the same way again," Cara says. "Go on then, open it."

They all crane forward, ready for what they're about to see. But when the SOCO pulls the lid up, it's empty. Cara breathes a sigh of relief.

Then her mobile rings, a loud break in the stillness, making her jump. She looks at the screen. It's Griffin.

"Boss," he says. And with that one word she knows it's business. "We need you. There's been another one."

36

JESS FLITS BETWEEN channels on the television. Next to her, the laptop shows the BBC News. Like the true crime programs she watched in the past, she's addicted to finding out more about this case. She watches the coverage of the press conference from the day before again, this time looking closely at DCI Cara Elliott. Griffin's sister. She can see the resemblance—the height, the confidence, the intense expression.

"The Echo Man," she repeats to herself quietly. It feels strange that the reason she's met Griffin is because of this killer. He killed Mia. He killed Patrick. A dark truth that bonds them.

She stretches, and feels the skin on her back tense, then crack. She reaches around and tentatively touches the scab, skin destroyed from being pushed up against the wall by Griffin.

He's been gone all day. They haven't spoken about last night—about what they did, about what she told him. For that, she's grateful. She's not sure what she thinks about it all—what she thinks about *him*. She knows there are things he's not telling her. And same with her. But she trusts him. More than she's trusted anyone for a long time.

She picks up Griffin's laptop, flicking around other news sites, looking for updates, but it seems they're not reporting anything new. Then her fingers hesitate over the keys. She's never been a big one for social media, but now she's apart from her daughter, she needs some connection. She needs to see her face.

She opens up Facebook. She ignores the usual banality and meaningless jabber of so-called friends, and clicks on her personal page, selecting the "Photos" tab. There's not much there, but it's enough.

Alice.

She clicks on the thumbnail of one of the most recent. It's a selfie from a walk at the beach, sun shining in the background. Jess is laughing, Alice has her face close to the camera, too close, her nose wrinkled, her deliciously chubby cheeks red and healthy. Jess remembers that day. It had just been the two of them, free to wander and do as they pleased without Patrick's watchful glare.

Jess goes back, then scrolls down to the earlier photos. Alice as a baby, just born, lying peacefully in Jess's arms. Jess seems half awake, bloated, blotchy, but Alice's gaze is fixed on her face. It's always been that way, as if through her daughter's eyes, her mother can do no wrong. Jess knows her daughter is flawless—a mother's blinkered prerogative—but unlike the rest of the world, Alice has only ever thought her mother is perfect.

Jess feels tears threaten, and she clicks away. Now here's Nav, holding baby Alice, beaming like a proud father. She remembers Nav posted this picture on Facebook himself—the comments underneath from adoring women were quite something to behold. She took the piss at the time, which Nav took with his customary good grace, but his devotion toward Alice has never changed. Jess wondered what would happen if he got married, had children of his own.

As if sensing her thoughts, the laptop pings, and a message appears at the bottom right of the screen. Navin Sharma, it says, then: *Where are you??*

With a jolt, she realizes the computer must have flagged that she's online, and she shuts the laptop lid quickly. How could she have been so stupid? If Nav saw it, what if the police had too? What if they tracked her back here?

She remembers the last time. She remembers the fear, the uncertainty. Being bundled into the back of a police car, her hands cuffed behind her back. The blood. The tears. Patrick shouting. The flashing lights of the ambulance. But there's nowhere else for her to go this time. Nowhere else to run.

She shuts off the television and the lights. She sits in the darkness in silence. And she waits.

CHAPTER

37

THE RAIN POURS in sheets, flooding the roads. The car sends up great plumes of water as Cara drives, her foot flat to the floor.

Griffin had been vague about details on the phone. Two dead. Shot. Immediately she'd put a call in to Shenton. If this is their killer, she wants to know the details straight away. About which sick fucker he's emulating. She hopes Shenton knows as much as he says he does.

He's escalating. The kills are coming faster now.

"There, there," Deakin shouts, pointing to a gap in the trees, and Cara turns quickly. The car bumps up the dirt track.

"Salterns Hill," he says. "Local beauty spot. Known to attract hikers during the day, and people wanting a bit of alone time at night."

Cara can see the vehicles now: two patrol cars and a white van. SOCO have made it there before them, but only just. Through the gaps in the wipers, she can see people hastily erecting a white tent, desperate to protect the crime scene from the torrential rain.

Deakin opens the door, and Cara follows him around to the trunk. They change out of their shoes into wellingtons, and Deakin gets out an umbrella, putting it up over them. Cara pulls the hood up on her head. She watches a crime scene officer run past them in the opposite direction, crying.

She sees Griffin standing, lit in the headlights. He doesn't have any sort of waterproof on, just the collar of his black coat pulled up over his chin, his usual black boots on his feet.

"What have we got?" Cara shouts over the din of the rain.

"Two dead: one male, one female." He points to the car on the far side. Both front doors are open, the right window smashed. "Male is halfway out of the car, shot in the head. The female"—he points down the path—"seems to have been trying to escape. Shot in the back. We have multiple sets of tire tracks at the scene, SOCO trying to get some preserved before we lose them all in this rain."

She nods pointedly to Deakin, and he hands her the umbrella, then heads over to the car.

Cara's phone rings and she answers it. "Shenton," she says. "What can you tell me?"

"I haven't had long to look at this," he starts, hesitantly. "But from what Griffin has told me . . ." He stops and Cara waits impatiently. "Couple dead, shot. You're either looking at Berkowitz or the Zodiac Killer." He pauses. "My best guess is Zodiac, because Berkowitz never actually killed both a man and a woman in a couple."

"Tell me more," she says. Griffin stands next to her, taking shelter under her umbrella, and she puts the phone on speaker.

"Zodiac Killer, active in the sixties and seventies, never found," Shenton carries on. "Estimated to have killed seven victims, but some sources say up to thirty-seven, most either shot or stabbed."

Cara's attention is diverted by raised voices over to her left. She looks across—Deakin is shouting, arguing with a crime scene tech. She hangs up the phone and goes over.

Deakin sees her from a distance and stops. He holds out his arms.

"Don't go over there, Cara," he says. The look on his face makes her freeze. He's upset, but this isn't the usual hard anger from seeing a dead body. The rain is running down his face, and he seems on the edge of tears. She looks past him, into the trees.

"What are you shouting about?"

"I wanted . . ." He pauses, looks down, gathering himself together. "I wanted to go over, make sure she's dead. I thought we could still help her. But . . ."

"But Deaks, they've already checked, they would have made sure . . ." she starts, but her voice trails off. She continues to stare over Deakin's shoulder and takes a step toward the body. He holds out his arm, stopping her from walking further. She's seen something, something that pulls at her subconscious. But—it couldn't be?

Her phone rings again and she answers it, still staring at the woman's body.

"Boss, the lab called." It's Shenton again. "The prints on the pint glass from apartment 214 came back."

He has her attention now.

"And?"

"Well . . ." He pauses. "Hit on the system to someone called Elizabeth Roberts. She works in—"

"The lab, yes, I know . . ."

Cara stops. She looks at Deakin, and she sees it confirmed in his eyes. She takes another step.

"Don't go over there, Cara," he says again, but she pushes past him, striding, almost running toward the body.

Up close, she can see for certain now. The woman lies facedown in the mud. Hands outstretched, with bright silver nail varnish. She's wearing a long black dress, a pair of Doc Martens on her feet. And her hair is bright pink.

"Oh, Libby," Cara says. Her hands go to her face, and she feels her legs go weak. She sinks to her knees, collapsing into the dirt. "Oh, Libby. I'm so sorry."

Review Report—Department of Clinical Psychology

Name of Patient: Robert Daniel Keane (DOB 03/31/1986, age 18)

Robert (preferred name: Robbie) has been seen on a monthly out-patient basis since his arrival at Northbrooke Children's Home in February 1996.

History

Robert was originally admitted following the fatal stabbing of his uncle and father. The police investigation at this time concluded that Robert had committed the murders. However, as Robert was below the age of criminal responsibility when the crimes were carried out, the judge recommended placement in Northbrooke rather than a juvenile detention facility. This has clearly benefitted Robert and has enabled him to get the increased help and support that he needed.

Current Situation

Robert has been diagnosed with depression, post-traumatic stress disorder (PTSD), obsessive-compulsive disorder (OCD), and generalized anxiety disorder, conditions resulting from the severe sexual abuse he received at an early age at the hands of his caregivers.

In addition, given the relationship between personality disorders and childhood sexual abuse, a diagnosis of antisocial personality disorder has been suggested. Concern about Robert's ability to empathize with others remains, although his scores on psychopathy have been inconclusive.

A diagnosis of dissociative identity disorder was originally given but withdrawn in 2001 after it was concluded the alternative personality states shown by the patient were voluntary role-playing, used as a tool for Robert to escape everyday life. Robert has been observed mimicking other individuals (usually well-known people in the media), but we conclude this is not an unusual coping mechanism and has no risk attached.

Following neuropsychological testing, Robert's full-scale IQ was found to fall in the very superior range (around 145). He has diligently applied himself to his studies, gaining twelve GCSEs at grades A and A*, and four A levels.

Risks
Robert has tried to commit suicide with an overdose on two separate occasions, the last instance of this occurring in 2002 (see below). We believe the suicide attempts to be related to Robert's depression: this continues to be a focus of Robert's psychotherapy, carried out with a cognitive behavioral approach.

Some incidents of arson were reported throughout 1999 and 2000, the final one resulting in the almost complete destruction of the art therapy wing. While these were strongly suggested to have been the result of Keane's actions, no concrete evidence was found, and all charges were dropped. However, Keane was closely supervised in the year following these instances: no suspicious behavior was observed.

Clinical Formulation
The extreme sexualized behavior Robert demonstrated at the time of his uncle and father's murders was unusual in a child of that age (nine), although it can be explained through learned behavior via the troubled family environment he was accustomed to.

Robert has difficulty building relationships, particularly with women. I believe this is due to Robert attributing blame for his abuse to his absent mother (she left the family home when he was three) and projecting this onto other females.

However, Robert did manage to forge one friendship during his time at Northbrooke. The departure of this boy two years ago (in 2002) did cause some initial withdrawal and a suicide attempt. Robert responded well to therapy, and no attempts have been made since.

Proposed Future Interventions
It is my belief that Robert has grown into a capable young man and, with continued therapy, will be able to make a success of his adult life.

Because of the improvement shown during Robert's rehabilitation, and the notorious circumstances of his uncle and father's murders, it is my recommendation that Robert be given a new identity and that all linked records and biological samples associated with his crimes in 1996 be expunged. This privacy is essential to ensure that he may lead a normal life without fear of prejudice or reprisals.

Dictated, not checked or signed, to avoid delay.
Dr. Mark Singleton
Consultant Clinical Neuropsychologist
08/03/04

CHAPTER

38

THE ECHO MAN wanted them to find apartment 214—Cara knows that now. The name on the lease, the fact that it was next door—right fucking next door—to the staged Dahmer scene. And he'd left that pint glass there to taunt them.

She doesn't know how he got Libby's fingerprints. He could have swiped it from a pub years ago, and in a way, it doesn't matter. What does matter is she's dead, and Cara can't help but look over to where her friend lies, under a white tent preserving the evidence on her body.

She's been through the whole range of emotions in the last hour. Pure red-hot anger, forcing her to march off down the track, tears blinding her. She'd crouched, her hands resting on her knees, out of sight of the team as the rain soaked her to the skin. She'd ignored her phone ringing until, realizing it would never stop, she'd been forced to answer it, and cold and drained, she'd walked back to the crime scene.

The show must go on.

The mood in the woods is somber. Everything is quiet. Cara watches Deakin sit in the open door of her car, smoking, staring at his feet. He's still wearing Roo's raincoat, and the cheerful bright red and blue feels out of place and wrong.

Dr. Ross calls her over to where the man's body slumps in the door well.

"Say you have something, please? Anything," Cara says, and Ross frowns. "Just give me your best guess. I won't hold you to it. But this is one of ours, Greg."

He nods. "First thoughts, this looks like a murder-suicide."

Cara stares at him. "Pardon?"

He points to the gun, lying in the mud, a small yellow triangle marking it as evidence. "Likely fell out of his hand," he says, then points to the hunched body in the driver's seat. "And the injuries he sustained to his mouth and head are consistent with a gun being fired upward." He mimes shooting, his hand in his mouth, pointing to the sky. "SOCO have confirmed gunshot residue on his right hand, with no signs of a struggle. I think he shot Libby, then turned the gun on himself."

"Do we have any ID on him?" Cara asks.

Ross reaches down, patting the dead man's pockets. He detects a lump in one and awkwardly pulls out a small black wallet. He places it into Cara's gloved hands.

She realizes she's shaking as she opens it and pulls out the driver's license. The face in the photo is sulky, pale. Dark eyebrows, dark hair. And the name on the license: Sharp, Michael.

She takes a quick intake of breath and Ross looks up.

She stares at the photo, comparing it to the dead man's face. "This is our drug dealer from Wednesday," she says.

"The guy with all the dead bodies in the fridge?" Ross asks, and Cara nods. "Then it looks like you've got a closed case, Detective," he finishes.

Cara walks away from the car, shaking her head. Griffin comes up next to her, and she holds out the driver's license, now enclosed in a plastic evidence bag. He holds it up to the light to read it, then stops, his mouth open.

"That body there?" he says.

Cara nods. "Ross says it's murder-suicide."

Griffin looks at her in disbelief. "What? He goes to all that trouble to kill man after man, woman after woman, then blows his brains out in a fit of—what? Guilt?"

"Or none of this is related after all," she mutters.

"But what about his apartment? All the dead bodies? That's not a fucking one-off, Cara. That's months, years of planning, killing, and it all looks like Dahmer purely because of coincidence? Is that what you think?"

Cara's suddenly very weary. "The only thing I do think, Nate, is I'm going home to bed."

She turns and walks toward her car. She knows she should stay, as Griffin probably will, but nothing makes sense to her. It's too late. She's cold. She's wet. The rain has started up again, edging into her clothes, freezing against her skin.

Deakin looks up as she stands next to him.

"I'm going home," she says. "You coming? You can stay in the spare room."

He shakes his head. "Drop me off at mine on the way back."

"You shouldn't be alone, Deaks."

He flicks his cigarette into the darkness and swings his legs into the car as she goes around to the driver's side, shutting the door. "This is no different from any other day. It's always someone's loved one. Someone's daughter, someone's ex-girlfriend. We catch this guy, same as we always do." He sees the look on Cara's face. "What?" he asks, and she fills him in on Ross's prediction.

She sees his eyebrows crease, the look of incomprehension. "I need some fucking sleep," he mutters.

Cara starts the engine, and they drive away from the crime scene. As she goes, she glances in her rearview mirror at the car, the lights, the pathologist's van getting ready to take the bodies away.

She remembers Libby's face, excited at the prospect of going on a date. Had it been with this guy? With Michael Sharp? And when she'd realized something was wrong, she'd tried to run. And he'd gunned her down before turning the pistol on himself.

Cara drives through the empty streets, pulling up outside Deakin's house.

"Do you want me to come in?" she asks, but he shakes his head.

"See you tomorrow, boss," he says.

She watches him put the key in the lock and walk inside. He never calls her "boss." He was putting distance between them.

His message had been clear. Leave me alone.

CHAPTER

39

J ESS IS STILL awake, sitting in bed, watching the news, when Griffin
gets back. It's the only light on in the room, casting her face in a
white glow. He looks at the TV over her shoulder—the reporters weren't
slow to get to the woods. He sees Cara, Dr. Ross, and his own bulky
silhouette next to the white marshmallowy figures of the crime scene
officers.

"I thought you'd be asleep," he says, discarding his wet clothes and
boots in a pile by the door.

She looks at him with red-rimmed eyes. "I think I fucked up, Griffin," she says, and she explains to him about the laptop and Facebook.

"It's unlikely," he replies. "But would it be so bad? You could clear
your name? See your daughter?"

She shakes her head, a quick, definite movement, over and over
again. "Not until you find something that proves it wasn't me. Have
you?" she adds, and he hears the desperation creeping into her voice.
"Have you found out anything about the fire?"

Griffin frowns. "No, I'm sorry. I've done some initial digging, but
there's nothing new."

Her face is marked with disappointment. Griffin feels the weight
of her expectation, the almost palpable despair from being apart from
her child.

He joins her on the bed, lowering himself down carefully. He's been
on his feet all day, and it does his back no favors. He sees Jess noticing
his hesitation as he leans back on the pillows.

"Are you okay?" she says, and he nods, dismissing her concern. He knows that at some point he's going to have to arrest her. He can't hide her here forever.

"I promise I'll look after you if you hand yourself in," he says, but she turns away from him, ignoring his comment. "Cara would look after you."

"Are you close, you and Cara?" she asks.

He smiles wearily at Jess. He knows she's changing the subject, but he lets it go. Pushing the point will only highlight his own failure to find something to clear her, and he could do without the guilt right now. "I guess so. We have our moments," Griffin says, "like most brothers and sisters. Growing up we'd be happily playing one minute, then screaming at each other the next. It helps now we're adults."

"More mature?"

Griffin smiles. "No. I'm bigger than her, so she doesn't dare give me a dead arm."

Jess laughs and Griffin appreciates the levity, however small, after the day he's had. Despite the protest from his back, he leans toward her, resting his head on her shoulder. After a beat, he feels her head against his.

"After I was born, I don't think my parents had much energy left, dealing with all my problems," she says. "Nav's the closest thing to a brother I've got."

"Brother, huh?" Griffin says, more to himself than to Jess. He wonders whether that's how the wonderful Nav sees it.

She moves slightly, now resting her head on his chest, and he puts his arm around her. The position feels slightly odd: a new level of intimacy despite the events of the night before.

"At university he was always the perfect gentleman. He'd never let me walk home alone from the pub. He once carried me to bed, up four flights of stairs, after too many cheap pints."

Griffin looks down at her, raising his eyebrows. She laughs. "Not like that. We've never done that." Her voice tails off and he wonders exactly why not, given Jess's seemingly open attitude to sex. Two attractive people, years of drunkenness at uni? Perfect conditions for random hook-ups.

"I never made it to university," Griffin says, slightly regretting it, especially in light of his recent thoughts about getting laid. "Cara did, so I think Mom thought I would. Until I got expelled."

"What for?"

"Do you want to guess?" Griffin's not even sure why he's telling her this.

She pauses. "Fighting?"

"Got it in one. Punched my math teacher," he adds, and Jess snorts. "But in my defense, he was a dick. I spent three months after that pissing about in front of the television and drinking in the pub, until Cara came home and gave me a good talking to."

Griffin remembers Cara appearing at the door of the Red Lion, glaring at him, then walking straight up to the bar and telling them he was seventeen. His anger at her intervention was matched only by her disappointment toward him. "You're wasting your life," she'd said, sitting him down at a table in the fast-food joint, the salt and vinegar wafting tantalizingly from the chips in front of them. "You're smart, and yet you're screwing up every chance you get. What do you want to do?"

"I want to be a cop," he'd replied without thinking. Griffin thinks the alcohol must had addled his teenage brain, because it had never been something he'd thought about before. But as soon as he'd said it, it had rung true. He'd always had a strong sense of fairness, of right and wrong. He wanted a way to punish the bullies and the assholes, but preferably one that wouldn't mean he'd end up in jail.

"I applied to the police force the next day," Griffin says.

He looks down and realizes Jess has fallen asleep. Her face is cast in shadows by the flickering light from the television, her eyes closed, long eyelashes against her cheek. He gently moves her into a more comfortable position on the bed, and she murmurs slightly, then rolls over to her side.

He covers her with the duvet and gets up, straightening out his back with a grimace, then going into the bathroom and cleaning his teeth. Done, he places his toothbrush next to her brand-new one in the mug on the sink. He looks at it for a second: one red, one blue.

He climbs into bed next to her and reaches over and switches the television off. The whole room is plunged into darkness. It's been a long day. Libby's death. Finding apartment 214. Seeing the photo of Mia, the image still etched on his brain.

His whole body feels weary, but he can't sleep. And something about Jess's continued reaction to the police doesn't sit right. A lot of people don't like the cops, but her response seems more like fear.

He remembers Taylor's comment from that first day in the hospital: *"She has a record."* His laptop is still lying next to the bed, and he picks it up and opens the lid. It throws light into the room, and he looks across nervously, but she hasn't stirred. He logs on to the system. *Jessica Ambrose,* he types, then selects the correct entry.

There it is. One line on the Police National Computer. An incident two years ago.

DV. ?GBH. w/intent? Vic: P. Ambrose. Detained 48hrs—sec 136 MHA. Released, no charge.

Shit.

He stares at it for a second, the acronyms easy for a cop to decipher. Domestic violence . . . grievous bodily harm . . . detained under section 136 of the Mental Health Act. He quickly shuts the computer, feeling a flash of guilt for the intrusion into her private life.

Griffin lies back in the bed, then turns and looks at her. Jess's hair has fallen over her face, and he reaches across and moves it, tucking it behind her ear.

He'd always thought that sleeping with someone else after Mia would feel like infidelity. A betrayal of his wife, especially when he's so comprehensively failed to find her killer. But this, with Jess, is different.

He cares for her, but it's more than that. He pauses to think, but the right word stays out of reach, too much for his addled brain. He lets the tiredness take over. And then, just on the edge of sleep, he realizes.

Redemption.

She's his salvation.

A chance to put things right.

40

Day 6
Saturday

CARA THOUGHT SHE must have got one hour's sleep, maybe two. Not wanting to disturb Roo when she got home, she lay in the spare room, staring at the ceiling. She had thought about Libby, tears rolling down her face.

She wakes to the sound of laughter in the kitchen and pulls a sweater on. She glances at the clock: it's eight AM. Some part of her brain registers it's Saturday, but not for her. This case must be put to bed, and quickly.

She goes downstairs. Lauren is there, making toast, nagging them to get ready for swimming. Roo sits at the breakfast table, a rare occurrence, meaning he won't be back until late that night. He is smiling up at Lauren, and Cara remembers Noah's words from two nights before. Lauren laughs at something he says, and hands him a mug of coffee.

Cara feels left out. A disconnection from this little scene. This is her family, yet nobody is missing her.

"Hi, sleepyhead," Roo says as she walks in. "I didn't hear you come back last night."

She sits at the table and takes the coffee Lauren gives her without a word of acknowledgment.

"He killed Libby," Cara whispers to Roo.

Roo looks up quickly, the smile vanishing from his face. He reaches over and goes to take her hand, but she pulls it away. Cara immediately feels bad for telling him, she should have handled it with more sensitivity. Roo knew Libby. She could have kept it to herself, but she'd wanted to pass on some of the misery, stop those happy little occasions of intimacy her husband was having with their nanny.

"Shouldn't the kids be leaving?" she snaps, and Lauren jumps into action, her cheeks red in response to Cara's tone. She ushers them out, up to the bathroom, to clean their teeth.

"That wasn't necessary," Roo whispers to Cara.

"She's the goddamn nanny," Cara hisses back. "She should be doing what she's paid to do, not flirt with you."

"She wasn't . . ." Roo begins, but stops, turning away and finishing his coffee.

"I'm going to have a shower," Cara mumbles, standing and walking quickly out of the room.

She shouldn't take it out on them, she knows, turning her face up to the scalding hot jets of water. It isn't their fault—it's hers, for not catching this guy sooner. She starts to cry again, sinking down onto the floor in the shower. For Libby, for letting her friend down, but also out of relief. The guy is dead. This nightmare is over. The pathologist will confirm it.

One more day at the nick, and they can draw an end to this for good.

41

CARA STANDS IN front of the team: shoulders back, the woman in charge. She knows what she has to do. She doesn't need to silence them, there is none of the usual chatter. They're all there to work.

"It's been a tough few days, and none more so than last night," she begins. "We can assume that Libby was deliberately targeted, and we owe it to her to wrap this up, and do it well." The door opens and Deakin comes into the room. He looks like she feels, black rings under his eyes. He leans against the wall on the far side, his arms crossed in front of him. She notices Griffin isn't in yet.

"Warmington, Sohal," she continues, addressing two of the new DCs on the case. "I want you to concentrate on the CCTV. Trace Sharp's movements last night, where he met Libby, where they went before they drove to Salterns Hill. And Shenton? Check everything we know against the Zodiac."

"So we're still following up the serial killer angle?" someone asks.

"Until we know otherwise, yes." She allocates more actions to the rest of the group, wanting to know what Sharp had been up to six months ago, a year ago. "Plus, chase up the lab reports from yesterday. The rest of you on the old cases, keep going."

"Do we assume that Sharp is responsible?" someone from the West Yorkshire team asks.

"He's our main suspect. But we need evidence. I want to know for sure. Keep me and your sergeants informed," Cara finishes.

The group disperses and Cara notices a uniform waiting in the doorway to her office. He looks bored, fiddling with a notebook in his hand. He looks up as Cara approaches.

"DCI Elliott?" he says, and she nods. "PC Cobb, ma'am. My skipper said you wanted to speak to anyone who knew Michael Sharp?"

"Yes," Cara replies. "What can you tell me about him?"

The cop laughs. "Guy's a dick. I mean . . ." He stops himself, looks embarrassed. "He wasn't particularly bright. I arrested him back in 2015. Domestic abuse. The guy pretty much punched his girlfriend in front of us."

"Nice bloke," Cara mutters.

"I know. But even before that we'd known him around—dealing, starting fights. A regular in custody."

He stops as Deakin joins them in the office.

"And when did you last see Sharp?" Cara asks, gesturing for him to continue.

The officer thinks for a bit. "Probably more than six months ago? Can't be sure."

Cara thanks him and he leaves. "Your average stupid lowlife, apparently," she explains to Noah, and he scowls.

"None of this makes sense," he mumbles.

Cara knows what he's referring to. A drug dealer with a record gets careful, to the point he doesn't leave a single forensic sample at any of his very violent, bloody, and calculated crime scenes? Except for the one of his next victim, deliberately left to taunt the police?

"So, what's the plan?" Deakin asks.

"SOCO have finished with some of the evidence from apartment 214 yesterday, so I'll call Griffin, get him to go over there and pick it up," she begins. "You and I are going to Libby's house." She looks at Noah: his face is gray and drawn, he looks awful, but she knows better than to ask if he's okay. "Let's find out about this date she went on. And I want her mobile phone. Ross says it wasn't on her or in the car. You know where the spare key is kept, right?" she says, and Noah nods. "Then let's go."

* * *

Cara is silent as Deakin takes the key out from the fake rock in the plant pot.

"I told her this wasn't safe," he says. "Ironic, huh? The helpless little things we try and do, when in the end someone guns you down in the mud."

Cara puts a hand on his shoulder. "You weren't to know. It wasn't your fault."

He shrugs her off, putting the key in the lock. "I was a shit when it ended between us," he mutters. "*That* was my fault."

They push open the door, then stand in the entrance, pulling on plastic overshoes and gloves. They go inside, and Cara is struck by how tidy the place is. The kitchen is clean, surfaces bare. The cushions are arranged neatly. In the bedroom, the bed is made, and there are no clothes left on the chair.

She turns back to Deakin. "Was it always like this?" she asks, and he nods.

"Always. She joked that she was a bit obsessive, but I guess that's what made her good at her job. That attention to detail, the liking for order and routine."

Cara sees her laptop on the side in the living room. She opens the top, and a password screen flashes up. She looks at Noah.

"No idea," he says.

Cara puts it in an evidence bag and labels it. "Any sign of her phone?" she asks.

Deakin pulls his own mobile out of his pocket and taps on the screen. After a pause, they hear a bright tone from the hallway.

He turns and Cara follows him, watching as he digs around in the coats hung up there. He pulls a phone from one of the pockets and shows it to her.

"Why did she leave it behind?" Cara says. "That's odd, even for Libby. Can you get in?"

"Not without the passcode. Or her fingerprint."

Cara pauses. She knows where they'll need to go to get it.

"I'll go," Deakin says, reading her mind, but Cara shakes her head.

"No. We owe it to Libby to get this sorted as soon as possible. We'll both go. We need to see where Ross has got to with the PMs, anyway." They go to leave, Cara bringing the laptop with her. "Let's get SOCO in here, just in case," she says. "I don't want anything missed. This guy might have been here before."

Cara goes out of the house, Deakin following her. She watches as he stops in the doorway.

"I really liked her," he says, looking back inside. "I just couldn't . . . I don't know . . ." He closes the front door softly. "It wasn't Libby. It was all me."

"I'm sure she knew that, Noah."

He shakes his head. "No, she didn't. And that's something I'm going to have to live with now. Something else to live with for the rest of my life."

CHAPTER

42

THE PHONE WAKES them both with its ominous trill. Jess has come to associate the noise with bad news, and sure enough, she can tell it's Griffin's sister by the tone of his voice.

He hangs up and gets back into bed, pulling her over to steal some of her warmth. He rests his cold feet on her legs.

"I've got to go to the apartment again. Pick up some evidence."

Jess nods, disappointed. Another day by herself, alone. But today she has a plan. Not a sensible one, not a logical one, but something she's been thinking about since that night in the street when she first followed Griffin.

"Could you drop me at my house?"

He looks at her, as if weighing up the options.

"I'll take you there," he says at last. He glances at the clock. "After."

They get showered and dressed. Brush their teeth side by side at the sink, an awkward domesticity they're not used to. She's almost glad when they leave, climbing into the old Land Rover.

A question flickers into her mind as they drive.

"Griffin, who's Alan?" she asks. "The guy at the Manson house?"

He glances away from the road for a second.

"He's a crime scene manager," he says.

"And why was he helping you?"

Griffin snorts. "He's not doing it willingly. He mishandled some evidence on one of the early murders. A fingerprint went missing—the actual sample and everything associated with it. He begged me not to tell anyone and I agreed. But when I got suspended, I realized it could work in my favor."

"You're blackmailing him?"

Griffin frowns. "Essentially. Yes. He lets me know about anything else of interest—and gives me access to the crime scene—and I keep quiet." He looks over his shoulder and makes a right turn in front of a block of apartments. "We're here."

The parking lot is crawling with patrol cars and white vans. Jess wonders how sensible it is for her to be here.

"Stay in the car," Griffin says. "Keep your head down."

She watches as he strides over to the door of the apartments and talks to the uniform waiting there. For a moment he chats with a crime scene tech, then goes inside.

As she waits, Jess ponders how often Griffin works at the edges of what's acceptable, how easily he lies. She's not sure what she thinks about his distinctly gray attitude to the law, but she knows it's worked in her favor so far.

She continues to watch the bustle until she sees Griffin's familiar figure emerge from the door. He has a large cardboard box in his hands and awkwardly rests it on his knee as he opens the trunk. He places it inside, shuts the trunk, then stands up and straightens his back out, scowling.

"What's in the box?" she asks as he gets in the car.

"Notebooks, videotapes."

"All belonging to him?"

"Hmm."

"And you're going to watch them?"

Griffin starts the engine. "Part of the job."

"But should it be *your* job?"

He doesn't answer, and Jess stays quiet. They drive, the Land Rover rattling its way through the busy streets. She still hasn't mentioned the photograph of his wife she'd found. She wants to ask him about it, but should she?

And then she notices where they are.

* * *

Jess can't believe it possible, but it looks worse in the daytime. There is no way to hide the devastation. The fire has ripped through the house: walls are blackened, windows smashed, the garden a swamp of mud where multiple boots have trampled through. She is expecting to see an army of fire investigators, maybe someone guarding the crime scene, but the place seems deserted.

"Where are they, Griffin?" she asks.

"I guess they found what they were looking for," he replies grimly. Evidence to incriminate her, or simply nothing at all? She can't imagine anything has survived in there.

She climbs out of the car and walks up the drive. Debris litters the tarmac: small pieces of wood, nails, pieces of glass. The front door is boarded up, but she ignores the "No Entry" sign and pushes it open. It's not locked. What is there to steal, after all?

The house is dark inside. The wall is wet where the remainder of the roof has failed to provide any sort of shelter. She reaches out with a hand and touches it. It's black with soot.

There's nothing left of the house she lived in. Everything has gone. Smashed, burned, or broken. She feels numb; her brain can't seem to catch up with what she's seeing. She goes through to what was once the kitchen. Glass crunches under her feet.

"Jess."

She turns, Griffin is standing behind her.

"Jess, there's nothing for you here."

She looks back at the room. The dining table is on its side, broken chairs stacked around it. She picks one up and stands it on its feet. But it looks worse that way, to see something the way it was, how it should have been.

She feels Griffin put his arm around her shoulders and pull her close to him. She realizes she's crying, and wraps her arms around his waist, sniffing snotty tears into his black coat. After a moment she wipes her eyes with a bit of her sleeve.

"Fucking crying again," she mutters. "Always fucking crying."

He looks down at her, his eyes serious.

"You've every right to cry. You've lost your home. Your husband."

"I'll be okay. I've been through worse," she replies. You've been through worse, she wants to say, but doesn't.

"It doesn't work like that, Jess. Ignoring grief doesn't make it go away, as much as you'd like it to."

She takes in a deep breath and slowly lets it out. "Patrick called this our forever home. But I never saw it that way." She glances up at Griffin. "I'd never lived somewhere for more than two years before here. Not since I was a baby."

"How come?"

"We moved a lot. From county to county. Because of me," Jess says. "It started when they first took me into care. Because I couldn't feel pain, I was constantly at the hospital, and doctors thought I was being abused. When I was five, they didn't tell me what was going on—they just whisked me away to a children's home." Jess looks down at her hands. "I didn't understand why. I thought I'd done something wrong. It took my parents a month to get me back."

Jess sniffs, then blows her nose on her sleeve. "And then we moved up north. Fresh start. Except I was a nightmare. Got expelled from school after school for getting into fights. I've never played well with others."

"I can't imagine what that's like."

Jess glances at Griffin. He has a slight smile on his face.

"Patrick was the exception. He said he could fix me."

There's a pause. Jess hears rain dripping through the house.

"Perhaps you don't need fixing," Griffin says quietly. "Perhaps we're all supposed to be broken, just a little."

She allows him to guide her out of the house and into the Land Rover. They climb inside, and Griffin lights a cigarette.

"Griffin," Jess says.

He looks at her, the cigarette hanging from his mouth.

"I found a photo. I know your wife was one of the victims."

He turns away from her, taking a long drag, then blowing it out the window. He starts the engine.

"I'll drop you at the garage. I need to go back to the station," he says.

"Griffin?" Jess puts a hand on his arm, but he shrugs her off. "Tell me about her?" she asks softly.

"There's nothing to tell."

He puts the car in gear and drives away from the house with a screech of tires. Jess closes her eyes, cursing herself for mentioning it. That's not the sort of relationship they have, she tells herself as they drive back to the apartment. She was stupid to think otherwise.

43

"No offense, but I'd be glad never to see you two again."
Dr. Ross looks up from the cadaver on the stainless steel table as Cara and Deakin come into the room.

"And you're early," he adds.

Cara gestures to the phone in her hand. Shenton called from the station on the way over: they have consent from next of kin. "We just need a fingerprint," she says, and Ross's gaze drifts to the row of metal doors on the far side of the room.

The three of them go over, and Ross pulls out one of the drawers. Cara can't help but gasp as he opens the black body bag and she sees Libby's face. Her skin has taken a bluish tinge from the refrigeration; her hair, stark and pink, jarring in such bleak circumstances.

Ross pulls her arm out from the bag and holds it while Cara puts on gloves and takes the phone out of the evidence bag. She gently presses Libby's finger against the sensor, and the phone opens. They wait for a few seconds while Cara disables the lock options.

"Have you done the post?" Deakin asks.

"Yes, and there weren't any surprises," Ross says. "Shot five times from a reasonable distance away—my guess, from the car, which was about ten meters. Punctured her lungs, liver, one in the spine. But the one that did the most damage hit her aorta. Bullets consistent with the gun found at the scene, a .22 high standard model, 101. Ballistics will confirm." He pauses, looking down at her face. "The only good thing is she would have bled out fairly quickly."

"Any other injuries?" Cara asks.

"No, nothing. No defensive wounds on her hands or arms. I've taken scrapings from her fingernails just in case, swabs from her nose and mouth, and a full sexual assault kit. They've gone to the lab, along with the bullets."

Cara knows what he's looking for. The site where they were parked was a well-known lovers' lane—she might have been kissing the guy, or more, before he turned the gun on her. Traces of saliva might still be present.

Deakin has turned to the corpse on the table, intently looking at his face. Ross does up the body bag, and solemnly pushes the drawer back into the wall.

"And you believe this is your killer? Michael Sharp?" Ross asks, pointing to the body.

"Looks like him," Deakin says.

"Want to stick around while I do the PM?"

They take a seat on the far side of the mortuary. Cara watches as Ross and his assistant start the postmortem, opening up the chest down the center, trying not to flinch at the high-pitched whine as the saw cuts through the breastbone. They methodically examine every part, every organ, weighing and bagging. Ross talks while he works, notes recorded for transcription later.

Deakin's phone buzzes and he looks at it.

"Car confirmed as belonging to Michael Sharp," he whispers. "Cameras show it on the M271 at twenty-two fifty-six that evening."

"Any CCTV of who was inside?" Cara asks, and Deakin shakes his head.

She turns her attention back to Libby's mobile phone. She operates the touch screen through the evidence bag, scrolling through the apps. She finds one for Tinder and clicks on it. After a few false starts, she finds the messages section.

There are a few conversations in the history, aborted chats, even a few dick pics.

"Do men really think this works?" she asks, showing one to Noah.

"Oh, please," he says, recoiling from the image. "I wouldn't know. It's not a tactic I've ever tried."

"You've been on Tinder then?" Cara asks, surprised. She couldn't imagine him trying to "date" in a traditional sense.

"Not for long," he says. "As soon as women find out what I do, they're either put off or too interested, if you see what I mean." Cara raises her eyebrows. "Want me to put them in handcuffs—you know, that sort of shit."

"Not your thing?" she asks.

"Not on a first date," he replies with a grin. "You got anything?"

Deakin looks over her shoulder as she tries to navigate the app, then takes it from her. He does a few more moves, then hands it back.

"That's the most recent conversation," he says.

He watches as she reads through the exchange. Banter at first, flirty, a bit of innuendo. A steady to and fro, going on across a few days. A few gaps: neither wanting to seem too keen, but both still definitely interested. Then, the man suggests they get together. Drinks, at the same bar she went to with Libby only days before.

She opens up her own phone, sending a text to Griffin. *Check out CCTV at the Orange Rooms. Bar in town. Libby met Sharp there.*

She carries on reading, until the last one catches her eye. *Let's go old school,* it says. *Leave your phone at home. I'll be the one with a copy of Dracula at the bar.*

Cara points to it, nudging Deakin. He frowns.

"She must have liked this guy."

"I can see why," Cara says. She flicks back to his profile. "Every aspect on here is precisely someone that would appeal to Libby. It's like someone designed a man specifically for her."

"You think she was targeted?"

"It looks that way. But how could he know so much about her?" Cara says. She scrolls through the conversation again. "The bands she likes, the TV programs she watches."

"He could have got that from Twitter," Deakin replies. "I followed her, and she wasn't discreet."

True, she thinks. Every little detail of our lives—online. It's not hard for someone determined.

Cara looks up at the buzz of metal cutting bone. Ross has moved on to the head. He's already peeled the skin down from Sharp's face and now painstakingly works his way around the crown. His assistant takes the saw, and Ross slowly pulls the top of his skull away with a slurp. Horrendous, but completely absorbing.

"Anyway," Deakin continues, pointing to his phone, pulling Cara back. "Forensics and ballistics are back on Manson. All fingerprints and bloods match to victims. Shot with a .22 caliber gun, consistent with pieces of the handle found at the scene."

"Same as the gun found here?"

He nods. "Could be. But how did he get it? This isn't America— you need to know someone who can get their hands on a gun. And specific illegal firearms at that."

Cara sighs. He's right. "And anything back from the Dahmer scene?"

"Not yet."

Hardly surprising, the lab must be swamped, samples piling up to be tested.

Her attention is diverted again as Ross moves away from the body to a microscope on the far side of the room. He's looking at a slide, then calls his assistant over to take a look. They talk animatedly, and Cara fidgets. At last they turn, and Ross goes back to the corpse on the table.

"What have you found?" Cara asks.

"Very curious," Ross starts. "He has a significant gunshot wound to the head. But you didn't need me to tell you that," he says, pointing to the slimy mess that used to be the guy's brain. "Bullet went through the roof of his mouth, completely obliterating any gray matter on the way through, before exiting at the back-top, here. No other contributing factors except maybe these." He pulls the arm away, and Cara sees a long row of track marks.

"Sampling his merchandise, no doubt," Ross adds. "Have taken blood samples, so you'll know more from that."

"So? Suicide?" Deakin prompts.

"Normally, I'd say yes. But when I started looking closer, there were some odd aspects that caught my attention. Body temp was lower than it should have been, even when you consider how cold it was last night. And much cooler in his core than his extremities."

Cara frowns.

"Fractures in large tissue masses, such as his heart and liver. Damage to some areas of skin. And this."

He beckons them over to the microscope and Cara peers down. She can make out strange shapes, but her knowledge of biology isn't what it used to be.

"Extended extracellular space and shrunken cells resulting from a freeze-thaw cycle," Ross says.

"In English?"

"This is a body that's been frozen."

"What?" Cara starts.

"And soon after death too, as none of the usual decomposition processes kicked in until he started thawing out properly in the mortuary."

Cara looks at Deakin. He seems as confused as she is.

"So when did he die?" she asks.

"Impossible to tell. Could have been days ago. Could have been months. But one thing I do know for sure," Ross finishes, turning back to the cadaver, "is there's no way Michael Sharp shot Elizabeth Roberts last night. This guy was dead, then kept on ice. You're looking for someone else."

44

D EAKIN SHAKES WITH anger. Cara's mute, almost in a daze. It had been staged. The whole goddamn thing had been staged, and the only thing going through her mind is *it's not over, it's not over*. One thing is clear: this guy is going to carry on killing until they stop him.

They drive back to the station in silence. Cara hears the noise from the incident room before she even opens the door, people talking, the electronic hiss of playback from CCTV, but none of the usual banter she expects from an investigation. Libby's death has silenced them all, eradicating the black humor she's used to.

Cara takes command of the room and tells the team about the results from the postmortem. She sees their shocked faces. There are no questions. She tells them all to go back to work.

She knows crime scene teams are still at Sharp's apartment and the one next door, plus in the woodland, working the car. Marsh pokes his head around the door, then disappears again. He looks stressed, and she knows why. He's been told to prioritize resources, but how can they? They've never known murder on this scale before. The overtime chews up the budget. They have no idea which bit of police work could turn up a lead, which piece of evidence at the lab will point them in the right direction. So many samples of blood, so many fingerprints. So many people dead.

Journalists clamor at the door. They call the PR department constantly. But what can they say? They've put out press releases warning people to be careful, that there's a dangerous killer on the loose and not to go anywhere alone, but this guy is everywhere. The only thing they can rely on is his dedication to the cause.

She feels her stomach churning. She's constantly scrabbling to keep up; he's always one step ahead of them.

She needs to think. It seems mad that someone would be carrying this all out, but she knows she'd be wrong to assume they're insane. It's clear they know what they're doing.

This man is cold and calculated and organized. He knows enough about police procedure to be forensically savvy, but anyone with access to the internet and a few episodes of *CSI* would know what to avoid nowadays. He has a plan, but to what end? Cara can't even imagine.

She sees Shenton in the incident room. Working alone, he's surrounded by the case files, putting his psychological profile together. It could give them something, she tells herself. Something, anything, she thinks with a silent prayer.

But Cara's relief is short-lived as Griffin arrives back, a box of evidence in his hand. He stands in the doorway to her office.

"That the notebooks?" she asks.

He nods. "And the tapes. You want to take a look?"

No, Cara thinks, I really don't. But she pushes her chair away from her desk and indicates her monitor. "Be my guest," she says.

Griffin has luckily had the foresight to bring the VHS player from the apartment, and he sends Shenton off for the right cables. She waits, going through the box of tapes, all bagged up individually. She pulls a few out, looking at the writing.

"What do you think this means?" she asks, holding it out so Griffin can see. It's a six-digit number, scrawled in ballpoint pen on the label.

"One of the SOCOs said it might be illegal porn." Shenton comes back into the room with the cable, and Griffin plugs it into the monitor. "The numbers are a code so the punter knows what they're ordering."

"How entrepreneurial," Cara replies with a frown.

Griffin plugs the VHS player into the wall, and at last the machine whirrs into life. Cara gestures to Deakin and he walks in to join them.

"Shut the door," she says once he's in the room. He realizes what they're doing and pulls a chair around to sit in front of the screen on the other side of Cara. She notices he's still keeping his distance from Griffin. No love lost there, she notes.

She sees Shenton hovering against the wall. "Toby, you should probably go," she says to him, and he shuffles out.

"Poor kid needs to make some friends," Cara mutters.

"He's not so young," Noah says. "I'm only two years older than him, you know."

Cara smirks. "You look more than that."

"Fuck off. Life's been hard."

"Didn't you work with him in the drug squad?"

"Only briefly." Deakin looks through the window after him. "He was the same then."

Griffin's ignoring their exchange. He takes a tape out of the box with a gloved hand. "What do you think? Start with this one?"

"As good as any."

He pulls the old tape out of its cardboard case and pushes it inside. Cara hasn't used one of these machines for years. She remembers them being scratchy and unreliable, and sure enough, the image on the screen is grainy.

Gray snow evolves into a room. The camera focuses in on a bed. A woman lies facedown, naked, on the bare mattress. Lank hair is over her face, her arms tied behind her back with tape, palms together. She's not moving. Cara's eyes scan the image, but there are no recognizable features about the room: the walls are white, no windows, no doors. The mattress is stained; the soles of her feet are black with dirt.

Next to her Griffin and Deakin are both silent. Even her own breathing seems loud.

The tape hisses. They hear a door open and a man steps inside. He's wearing what seems to be a gray tracksuit, a black balaclava covering his face. He turns and holds something out for the camera to see. It's a knife, long, clean, and sharp.

"Fuck . . ." Griffin whispers next to her.

The man turns back to the woman. With his free hand he pokes her, and she moves slightly. They hear her groan.

"Cara . . ." Griffin says slowly.

On the video the man rolls the woman over to her back. She's skinny, ribs clearly visible, hip bones jutting out. She has bruises on her knees and across her body, an angry red cut on her forehead. She seems to be awake now; Cara can see her eyes looking at the man, silver duct tape over her mouth. She sees the woman's eyes widen, tendons straining in her neck as she tries to scream. The man looks to the camera then raises the knife above his head.

Deakin and Griffin both dive for the VHS machine. They knock it sideways, the cable comes loose, and the image disappears. But Cara's still staring at the black, her mouth open. Then she turns slowly.

"That wasn't porn," she manages to say at last. She looks at the box of tapes. There must be ten, maybe twenty in there, with the same codes on the labels.

Deakin shakes his head. He tries to speak, then clears his throat.

"That was a snuff film," he says.

CHAPTER

45

J ESS CAN'T KEEP still. Back at the apartment, she makes herself a mug of strong coffee, then has a shower. She's annoyed with herself for asking Griffin about Mia; she can't imagine what he's thinking now.

She sits down at the table and logs on to Griffin's laptop again. She knows she shouldn't, but she can't help but look. She logs on to the system she has seen Griffin use a hundred times before, pulling up her own details, then the case information for her house. Griffin says he's looking into it, but he hasn't told her any more than that. And she's desperate to know. If he finds something—if he clears her—then she can see Alice.

Sure enough, the fire investigator's report has been uploaded, and she reads it, scanning the technical information for anything interesting. Verdict: fire started by deliberate ignition of liquid paraffin oil in the front hallway. One fatality. Human remains discovered on bed in first-floor front bedroom on excavation of the scene.

She clicks away, to the audio file of the 999 call. She selects the recording and it bursts into life. There's static, then the operator talking. The voice making the call is a woman, breathless and rushed. The operator tells her to slow down.

"There's a family in there, oh God, a little girl lives there . . ." The woman on the recording takes a deep breath. "There are flames coming out the front of the house—please come quickly."

"A fire engine is on its way," the operator confirms.

The recording ends. And again she wonders, Why our house? Why us? She realizes how lucky she and Alice had been to get out alive. If it weren't for her jumping out the window, knowing she'd be immune to any pain, they both would have been dead now.

She clicks the screen away, then sees another report loaded on the system. Postmortem findings: Patrick Richard Ambrose. Her finger hovers for a moment before curiosity gets the better of her.

It's a long report, and Jess scans the medical terminology, desperately trying to make sense of it all.

Soot in larynx, trachea, and bronchi, evidence of heat trauma to the mucosa. Extensive third-degree dark, leathery burns over 50% of the body, with broad, erythematous margins, intact skin appearing translucent and waxy. Skin splitting in evidence from postmortem movement rather than antemortem injury.

What does that mean? Jess wonders.

Her eyes continue to scan down the page.

Position of the body when found (prone, with hands together above head) would indicate victim had been tied to bed frame prior to the fire starting. Material found in mouth, assumed to be gag. Rope fragments evident.

What the hell? Jess recoils, her eyes wide. Someone had been in their house and had tied and gagged Patrick before setting the place alight? Why hadn't she heard anything? Why hadn't Patrick called out?

A loud bang on the door makes Jess almost jump out of her seat. She stops dead, her heart thumping. The bang comes again, then a man shouting her name.

It takes a few seconds for her to think straight, for Jess to realize it's Nav.

She jumps up and opens the door. Nav sighs when he sees her.

"Shit, Jess. I thought you were dead."

She moves out of the way, and he comes inside. "I'm fine," she replies. Jess is pleased to see him, but she's tentative, trying to gauge his mood after their argument last time they were together.

"So you say." He looks around the apartment, then back at her face. "You seem pale. How have you been feeling?"

"I'm fine," she repeats. "I . . ." Her gaze shifts to the computer, the postmortem report still on the screen.

He follows her line of sight. "What's that?"

"It's the postmortem report for Patrick."

"The . . ." He stares at it, then back at her. "Jess, what are you doing? What have you got yourself into? I saw the news, all the murders. Is this—" He points to the screen. "Is Patrick connected?"

Jess nods. "Griffin thinks so."

"Griffin . . ." Nav's voice tapers off. He reaches forward and takes her hands in his. "Jess, this is madness. You can't stay here. You can't get caught up in this."

"I already am, Nav!" Jess exclaims. She's happy he's not still furious with her; she desperately doesn't want to piss him off again. But she has to stay here and see it through. "I can't walk away from this now."

She sees his jaw clench and he shakes his head.

Jess knows Nav's already done so much for her. At university, he'd caught on fast to Jess's condition and through the years had been the voice of reason at her shoulder. Reminding her to do her daily check. Stitching her up when she needed it. She knows many people with her condition don't live to old age, or at least lose feet or hands to infection. Nav is probably the only reason she's still alive and in one piece.

She watches as he walks to the computer and looks at it, his eyes scanning the words she's already read. She wants to say something to make it better between them, but right now she has no idea what that is.

"Do you understand it, Nav?" she asks quietly.

He sits down slowly, moving the page on the screen. "Oh, Jess . . ." he whispers under his breath. His hand goes to his mouth, and he looks away momentarily, screwing his eyes shut. Then he looks up at her. "Are you sure you want to know?"

Jess nods and sits down next to him.

Nav takes in a long breath. "This basically says that Patrick was alive when the fire got to him. Someone tied him up." He closes his eyes again and pinches the top of his nose. Jess can see he's wrestling with his emotions. "They made sure he burned to death."

Nav reaches over and puts his hand on her arm. "But you know what this means, Jess? Someone targeted him—someone targeted your house. You're in danger. Please go to the police. You'll be safe there, at least. Please?"

Jess sees the desperate look in his eyes. But she shakes her head.

Nav goes to say something else, but they both turn as they hear a key in the door.

Griffin pushes it open, then stops when he sees Nav. One look at the expression on his face and she knows things aren't good.

He doesn't say anything, just takes his jacket off and throws it on the sofa. He walks to the kitchen, takes a bottle of vodka out of the cupboard, pours a generous measure into a mug, and throws it back in one.

"You're Nav," he growls.

Nav stands up slowly. He's hesitant as he goes across to Griffin. Nav's tall and lean, but his bulk is nothing compared to Griffin. Jess sees Nav stand up straighter, mentally sizing himself up to the other man.

He holds out his hand. "Dr. Nav Sharma," he says.

Griffin looks at the outstretched hand, then shakes it. "We met before at the hospital. DS Nate Griffin."

Griffin sees the laptop open and glances over.

"What are you looking at?" He sees the name on the report. "Patrick's PM?" He looks quickly at Jess. "You shouldn't be reading this."

"You knew?"

"Yes."

Jess hesitates. If he's seen this, then what else has he read? What else does he know? She's angry, she wants to have it out with Griffin, to shout at him for not telling her, but also for his continued reticence, his reluctance to open up to her. But Nav's here.

And she sees something else.

She's come to know the dark behind his eyes, the way he moves depending on what sort of pain relief he's on. The right drugs and he's looser, calmer. The wrong ones—alcohol, nicotine—and he's like this. The anger intensifies. The pain only adds fuel to the fire.

"Nav," she says, "you need to go."

Nav stares at her. She sees she's hurting him again. "I'll be in touch," she adds. "I promise. Give me your number."

Nav glances to Griffin. He's turned away, ignoring them. Nav frowns, then leans down next to her, writing his phone number on a piece of paper and handing it to her as he goes to leave. Jess follows him to the door.

She opens it and Nav steps out into the hallway.

"I don't like this, Jess. Not at all." He pauses, looking back into the apartment. "What's he on?" he adds in a whisper.

"What do you mean?"

"I know an addict when I see one. The shaking, the sweats. He's going into withdrawal. His pupils are like black holes. What's he on?"

"Painkillers," Jess whispers. "Oxycodone."

"He's no good for you, Jess."

"And you are?" she snaps back.

Nav recoils. She knows she's upset him again. "Yes," he replies. "Yes, I am."

He turns and walks quickly up the stairs. There's a flash of light as he pushes the door open at the top, then darkness as it shuts behind him.

Jess wants to cry. She doesn't deserve someone as good as Nav. She never has. It's better this way.

She closes the door behind her and goes over to Griffin.

"How much does it hurt?" she asks, and he turns quickly, glaring at her. "Take something."

"I am," he says, holding up the mug and downing another large shot of vodka.

"I mean something that will actually help."

Jess picks up his bag, digging in the pocket, holding the box out to Griffin. He looks at her, then takes it, pulling the blister pack out and showing it to her.

"Four left, that's it," he says.

"So get some more."

"I can't. My doctor wants me to go to some sort of fucking chronic pain team. To give me something else instead. I don't have time for that shit."

Griffin takes one capsule out, swallows it, then carefully lowers himself onto the bed.

She follows him, pulling his boots off his feet, then lying next to him.

"Maybe when this is all over," he mutters. "Maybe then."

They lie together in silence. The day is coming to an end, darkness closing in, but she doesn't put a light on. She thinks about Patrick, about his last moments. About the fear he must have felt, the pain. His struggle as the fire burned around him. She knows his last thoughts would have been about her and Alice, and tears silently roll down her face.

"I just want this nightmare to be over," she whispers, lying next to Griffin. "I want to see my daughter. I want to go back to my life."

"But what is that now?" she hears Griffin mutter.

She waits for the world to make sense again. And she thinks, What is my life from this point onward?

Do I stay here, in this apartment, with Griffin? Or do I leave? But go where?

She waits, as the apartment grows cold around them, as shadows form across the walls. She waits for the answer that never arrives.

46

Cara sits in her office. Everyone else has gone home, even Deakin. But she doesn't want to leave. She doesn't like to go until she has a clear idea of where to focus the investigation the next day, and right now she has no clue, let alone a clear one. There are so many routes to take. She knows she needs to make a decision.

She reads update reports from the team. So far, despite the brutal rapes, the beatings, the murders, he's left no evidence behind. Not a trace. The mood is downcast.

Earlier, she sat with one of the seconded detectives, going through the raft of evidence they'd reviewed for the cases from West Yorkshire. But there was nothing.

"And what's this?" she asked, pointing to the final document.

The DC pulled it up on the screen. "It's a report from an agricultural botanist. They had the plant matter found on the body reviewed." He shrugged. "Guess they had budget to burn because the one odd thing identified was a type of rare grass only found on peaty moorland."

Cara frowned. "And what did they do with it?"

"Nothing." He looked at Cara. "I mean, it could have been a lead—the guy could have lived in the countryside. Or"—and he listed the options on his fingers—"he could have been on holiday once; he could have brought it there deliberately to throw them off track; or it could have come from the victim."

She got him to write it on the board anyway.

And now their best leads came from apartment 214. Her gaze drops to the box of VHS tapes, still on the floor in her office. She leans down, moves them around in the box, thinking. Her stomach feels like a block of lead is inside. The tech team have already confirmed that the tapes are old, murders unconnected to their current spate of copycats, but it brings little reassurance. She can't watch them, she just can't.

But as she goes to sit up, one of them catches her eye. It's not like the others: the label is different. She picks it up. *Hampshire Children's Services, RDK (DOB 03/31/86), 1 of 2, 02/27/96.* Curiosity grabs her and she plugs the VHS machine in again, pushing the video into the slot.

To her relief, it's an office. There are toys on a table—cars, dolls, Lego bricks—and a large, hearty-looking man sitting on the right.

"Do you know why you're here, Robert?" the man asks. He has small round glasses and red cheeks. His tone is kind and encouraging. "Do you remember what happened to your father, to your uncle?"

The person he's talking to is just out of shot. Cara sees a child's hand move forward, playing with one of the toy cars.

"Can I go home?" a subdued voice says.

The man looks downcast. Cara assumes he's a social worker. "No, I'm sorry, Robert, you won't be able to go home for a while. Do you have any other family you could go to?"

The car moves back and forth. Then: "They call me Robbie."

"Who does? Your dad?"

A pause. Cara assumes the boy must be nodding. The man on the tape scratches his forehead, then flicks through his notes.

"Robbie, can you tell me more about what we were talking about yesterday? About your dad and your uncle?"

Cara watches as the car is pushed off the table.

"You said they'd play games with you?" The man swallows visibly, his Adam's apple bouncing up and down. "What sort of games?"

"Don't know."

The man points to the dolls in front of them. There's an Action Man, in full army gear, and a Ken doll. "Can you show me?"

The small hands reach out and pick up the figures. Cara's mouth is dry. On the tape the boy starts bashing the dolls together, then he puts one on the table while the other one is struck against it.

"Your father hit you?"

"Yes."

"And your uncle?"

Quieter now: "Yes."

The boy picks up one of the dolls, and with his other hand he slowly pulls down the Action Man's trousers. The man on the video has turned white. The Ken doll is faced away. Cara can't take her eyes off the small hands on the tape, child's hands, doing a thrusting motion with these two figures. She can't think about what this represents, she just can't.

"Sexual abuse."

The voice comes from behind her, making her jump. Shenton stands in the doorway of her office, watching the screen. She snaps the tape off.

"I didn't realize you were still here, Toby."

"Is this from 214?" he asks.

"Yes. You should go home . . ." she starts, but Shenton takes a step forward into her office.

He glances at the black screen, then rocks back on his heels, crossing his arms in front of him. "Child abuse is common in serial offenders. Sadly, despite what the media likes to portray, most killers are made rather than born."

"You think that's what happened here?"

"It's likely. Although it's worth adding that not all victims of sexual abuse go on to abuse others themselves. And certainly, a very low percentage actually become serial killers. But it's a common factor."

As he talks about this—something he clearly knows about—Cara sees how he grows in confidence, standing up straighter, his eyes brighter. Perhaps after this he should look into specializing, she thinks. Move out of general policing into forensic psychology.

"How's the profile coming on?" she asks him.

"Should be done by tomorrow. Can you send me the Zodiac crime scene photos? I don't seem to have access."

"I'll do it now," Cara says. Then adds: "Are you okay?"

He looks up quickly. Shenton seems paler than usual, his skin almost translucent in the harsh overhead light. He blinks at her, then looks down at his shoes again. "I'm fine."

"When this is done, we'll all get some downtime," Cara says. But her words sound insincere, even to her own ears. "Appropriate help for those who need it," she finishes.

He stares at her again, then turns wordlessly. She watches him go back to his desk. She wonders about her hollow statement. Appropriate help? Even if anyone actually knew what that was, when would they have the time to talk to a shrink? When would she?

She opens up her email and starts sending across files. She does the same as everyone else in this line of work: put all the shitty stuff in some corner of your brain, block up the wall, and walk away.

Block up the wall, she thinks as she presses "Send" to Shenton, and hope and pray that one day the horror never manages to break its way back through.

47

THE PAIN TAKES over Griffin's whole body. It's not just his back now; every muscle aches, his skin itches. He can feel his heart racing. He needs to take something, anything, but he knows it will only get worse. He needs more now for it to make a difference.

Driving back from the station, he considered taking a detour. He knows where the dealers hang out. He knows if he wants something, anything, to take the pain away, for a bit of hard cash he could get it. But he's also seen the results of such a deviation. He knows where these people end up, and he doesn't want to go there. Not yet.

Then he gets home and *he's* there. Dr. fucking Sharma with his good hair and beautiful blemish-free skin. He remembered him from before—and here he is, looking even better. Christ—even he would fuck him if he was feeling a little more on form.

But at last he leaves. And Jess stays. Griffin doesn't know why, but she lies down on the bed next to him. He waits for the one solitary capsule to work. He waits for some sort of relief.

Earlier that day, when Jess mentioned Mia, he'd felt a bolt go through him. He knew he should offer some sort of explanation, but the sudden thought of her blind-sided him.

For the best part of a year, very few had referred to her. People tiptoed around him, euphemistically talking about her "passing." But now, with all these murders, she is everywhere. Her face in photographs, her name, back in the room.

And it's good. He once thought that it would destroy him to talk about her, but it makes her feel more real. She *is* real—the person he loved, the person who loved him.

"Mia was my wife," he whispers to Jess in the darkened room. "We'd been married for exactly one year and six days when she was murdered."

And he starts to talk.

*   *   *

It must have been one or two in the morning. Griffin's confused. The flashlight shines in his eyes, waking him up. Next to him, he feels Mia jump, her body move against his back for protection. Something hard and cold is pushed against his head.

"I have a gun," a voice hisses. "Stand up."

Griffin hesitates and the man moves. The gun is taken away, but next to him he hears Mia gasp in fear.

"I have the gun to your wife's head. Don't try anything stupid." Spoken through clenched teeth, angry and hard.

Griffin slowly raises his hands. He swings his legs out of bed, looking around him. He's wearing boxer shorts, he knows Mia's in no more than a thin nightdress. In the darkness he can only see shadows, a figure in a ski mask standing next to his wife.

"Tie him up."

Mia comes over and he puts his hands in front of him.

"No, behind you."

He does as he's told, and he feels Mia wrap cord around his wrists. Her hands are cold, she's shaking. He holds them slightly apart, hoping to keep some give in the bindings, but after she's finished, he feels them being adjusted, pulled taut so they dig tightly into his skin.

"What do you want?" Griffin says. "Take anything, anything you want."

"Oh, I will," the voice says, muffled through his mask. "Now lie down on the floor."

Griffin gets to his knees on the carpet, and a hand pushes him over. He falls heavily onto his side. He's thinking: overpower him, get the gun, punch him in the face—he's probably smaller than you. But a thought goes round and round: What about the gun? What about Mia?

As if reading his mind, the man growls, "Don't move, or I'll kill her."

He feels the cord being wrapped around his ankles, then his feet are pulled up behind him.

Something is pushed into his mouth, fabric, maybe an item of clothing. A gag taut around his head to keep it in place. A blindfold next. He tries to move, but he's hog-tied—his feet securely fastened to his wrists. He pulls again, but it only seems to make the knots tighter.

He can't see, but he can still hear. Footsteps, Mia's bare feet stumbling away. He can hear whispering but can't make out what the man's saying. He guesses they're in the living room, and a door closes. He can't hear anything now; his imagination goes into overdrive.

Griffin struggles again. He curses for allowing himself to get into this position. But he'd been half asleep, he hadn't imagined—

Imagined what? He still can't hear anything. But then—Mia's voice, pleading, begging. She's saying no, don't, please, no. He tries to shout, but his voice is muffled, useless. He struggles again, the cord cutting in tighter. He pushes his head against the carpet, trying to get the blindfold off, the gag, anything.

He hears her screaming in pain. He hears furniture falling, glass breaking. Sobbing. Crying. Sounds that pull his heart into pieces. Tears soak into the blindfold. Helplessly, he thrashes in anger on the carpet, listening to his wife howling his name.

He can't feel his hands now, the cord has cut off the blood supply. But he still can't get free.

Minutes pass, then hours. He loses track of how long he's been lying on the floor. He strains to hear what's happening in the next room. Occasionally he hears cries, a few words, whispering, then silence.

Then a click. A door opening. There's someone in the room with him. He struggles again, and manages, somehow, to get upright, resting on his knees, his hands behind him. But before he can do anything else, he feels something hard strike him on the shoulders. Then in the stomach. Then across his face. He tastes blood in his mouth. Nose shattered. Pain rips through his body and he falls down, but his hands come loose. He pulls them around, numb, but the blows come fast, and all he can do is try to defend himself, putting his arms up in front of him. He feels the hit to his forearms, he hears the bones break.

It's agony. And still they come. To his back, to his head. Blood pours down his face. And then finally, he's knocked unconscious. And everything slips away.

*　*　*

His voice sounds unnaturally loud in the silence. He stops talking. He feels Jess move slightly, her eyes in the dark.

"We'd been having strange phone calls for a few weeks. Hang-ups, nothing at the end of the line. I noticed that the gate had been left open one day, but I didn't think anything of it."

He shakes his head, feeling the familiar shame of his failure. "I should never have let him tie me up. But he had the gun pressed to her head, and he said he would shoot Mia. But knowing what I know now, what he would do . . ." His voice catches, the words stick in his mouth. He clears his throat. "One shot would have been better."

One shot wouldn't have been the sadistic rape for hours. He'd read the postmortem report. He'd seen the photographs. The broken bones, the blood. The rips and tears on her beautiful skin. The beating reducing her face to an unrecognizable mush.

He feels Jess move on the bed. She rests her head on his chest, and her arms go around him. Her legs intertwine with his.

Griffin feels his hands shaking. "He hit me. Here." Griffin takes Jess's hand and guides it to the side of his head. He knows there's a scar there, a ridge where the hair hasn't grown back. He swallows. "He broke both arms, here," he says, pointing to his forearms. "Four ribs, punctured a lung, and fractured part of my L3 lumbar vertebra. I was unconscious for two days. Later, I sold the house; I couldn't go back there. I got suspended from work for being a detective who couldn't even solve his wife's murder. And now I live in a basement in return for offering security to a friend's garage, and the only way I can get through the day is with hard drugs. Pathetic, isn't it?"

Jess is still holding onto his hand, and now she winds her fingers through his. She holds his hand up to her mouth, and he feels her kiss his fingers.

"Exactly the opposite," she whispers.

CHAPTER

48

H E STANDS AT the mirror, brushing his teeth. So, they've found his apartment. He led them there, he knew it would happen, it's not a problem.

But he's lost everything. His belongings. All his treats and souvenirs. So he'll need to make some more. The thought of it gets him excited. He's bold now. He's gotten away with so much, and they know nothing. He thinks about what he'd like to do next.

Bundy, maybe. The man was a fucking pioneer. Maybe he'd do something like the Chi Omega Sorority murders: four women in one night, two of them dead, strangled, one fucked with an aerosol can. He even chewed off one of their nipples. Now there was a man who lost control. If Ted hadn't been so stupid as to bite one of their ass cheeks, maybe he'd still be around today. Maybe he'd still be killing.

He spits out the toothpaste, rinses his mouth under the tap. He smiles. He'd never be that stupid.

Only a few days to go now, and he still has so much to do.

He remembers something he read about a man who killed his victims in front of a mirror. A cord around their necks, strangling, tightening, then releasing. Letting them breathe just a little, letting them live, then repeating it. Literally watching themselves die.

He feels himself grow hard just thinking about it. What would that be like? Watching the pain and fear in a woman's eyes as he killed her over and over again. As she lost her grip on reality, then for her to regain consciousness, to find herself back where she started.

He grips himself harder, faster, as the scenario plays out. Different women's faces flicker through. This seems too good for an unknown. One face sticks in his mind, someone familiar. And as he imagines her mouth, her eyes, her torture, everything he'll do to her, he comes forcefully, ejaculating into the sink.

Oh God, yes, he thinks, shuddering and breathless. He'll save this for her.

Only her.

49

Day 7
Sunday

IM STILL WAITING IM FUCKING FED UP OF WAIT-
ING ITS AN ITCH I CANT SCRATCH NOW I KNOW
HOW IT FEELS LIKE THE BEST FEELING OF ALL
NOTHING ELSE WILL DO THE PORN DOESNT WORK
NOT EVEN THE EXPENSIVE STUFF NOT EVEN THE
REAL ONES WHERE THE BITCH DIES WHERE HE
FUCKS HER TO DEATH I WANT THAT TO BE ME
IT SHOULD BE ME NOW I KNOW HOW EASY IT IS
I WANT TO GO BACK AND DO IT AGAIN I WANT
TO STAND IN FRONT OF THEIR DEAD DESTROYED
BODIES FULL OF MY CUM AND FUCKING LAUGH
LAUGH AT THE DETECTIVES WHO CANT CATCH
ME WHO DONT HAVE A FUCKING CLUE LAUGH AS
THEY GO THIS WAY THEN THE OTHER FOLLOW-
ING THEIR LEADS THAT I PUT IN FRONT OF THEM
I WANT TO BE TED FUCKING AND BITING I WANT
TO BE RADER WITH HIS BONDAGE AND TOR-
TURE AND KILLING I WANT TO BE SHAWCROSS
AND STUFF LEAVES INTO THOSE BITCHES CUNTS
WHEN THEYRE DEAD BERKOWITZ SHOOTING
SHOOTING SHOOTING—

"Boss?" Griffin calls from across the room, and Cara holds her hand up for a second. She's been sitting in her office, one of the many note-books from apartment 214 in her gloved hand. It's a cheap A4 spiral-bound pad—lab confirmed available from any Tesco throughout the country—but every page, every line is filled. Marks made in black pen, pushed hard onto the page, sometimes going through the paper. He doesn't use punctuation, there's no marking of time or date. Just hard capitals: an incoherent diatribe of darkness and death.

She puts it back into its evidence bag, then pushes her fingertips into her eyes. Colors dance in the blackness as she rubs them. They feel scratchy and sore; she knows she's not getting enough sleep. And this stuff isn't helping.

She carries it across to Shenton's desk. He looks up as she approaches, and she hands it to him.

"Might be worth you having a read of this," she says. He nods, then goes back to the screen. She wants to ask how he's getting on, but she doesn't want to pressure him. Getting into this madman's head must be bad enough as it is.

She leaves him to it and goes to where Griffin is sitting. She's still not sure how she feels about working with her brother. So far he's been behaving himself, no warning flags. And it's been nice to see him every day, she has to admit that.

Cara pulls a chair over and sits down at the desk.

"Did you have any luck with Social Services?" she asks, referring to the line of inquiry tracking down the file connected to the video she'd been looking at last night. They find the child on the tape, this "Rob-bie," maybe they have their killer. But he shakes his head.

"It's Sunday. I spoke to the woman on call. Everyone else is still in bed. She says all records from the year 1996 were paper based, so they'd need to go to the storage facility and go through them by hand. And without a case number, that could take a while."

"Phone her back. We'll send a team down to help," she says, men-tally adding it to the list. She turns her attention to his computer, where he has CCTV on the screen. "Show me this first. From the bar?" she asks, and Griffin points to a lone figure.

It's Libby. She's sitting on a high stool. Cara recognizes the bar from the evening she spent there, but this time Libby is alone. She looks ner-vous, every now and then glancing to the door.

They scroll through the footage. A few people approach her, but they leave after a brief interaction.

"Where is he?" Cara asks.

"Never turns up," Griffin says. "She leaves after an hour, but watch."

On the screen Libby finishes her drink and gets up, and Griffin switches the footage to the outside. A car pulls up, and Libby walks around to the driver's side window, leaning down and talking to the person inside. She smiles and then gets in.

"That's Michael Sharp's car," Griffin says. "And the only view."

Cara notices Griffin seems quieter today. He's more subdued, his face is pale, with more than a few days of stubble. She makes a mental note to get him alone at some point, check that he's okay. But then the rest of the team look like shit too. The incident room is covered in discarded coffee cups and chocolate wrappers. The smell in the air echoes the cigarettes smoked, the showers missed. The lives on hold in search of this guy.

"There's no other CCTV?" Cara continues. "From any other clubs or bars?"

"Not even a cash point nearby," Griffin says grimly. "Same as with your Kemper footage. But it looks like she recognizes him."

"Shit," Cara mutters. She looks at Griffin: he's deep in thought. "You have a theory?" she asks.

He rubs his hands over his face. "So the lab results have nothing in the car, except for trace from Libby and Michael Sharp, right?" Cara nods. "And hair, blood, and water from Sharp in the trunk," he adds. "So our killer takes Sharp out of storage—"

"The chest freezer in apartment 214?"

"Probably, yes. And places him in the trunk to defrost. Arranges to meet Libby at the Orange Rooms as her date but then doesn't show. Drives there, picks her up, takes her to Salterns Hill—"

"Willingly or at gunpoint?" Cara interrupts.

"I think we have to assume willingly because it's hard to control someone and drive at the same time?"

"So she knows him well?"

"Maybe. Then when they get there, Libby discovers the danger she's in and tries to run. Once she's dead, he takes the body out of the trunk, stages his suicide, and pulls the trigger."

"So how did he get home again?" Cara asks. She misses this—playing devil's advocate with her brother. The sparring back and forth.

"Same question as with the Kemper murders," Griffin says without missing a beat. "He drove the victims out to the middle of nowhere then too. Planning in advance? Left a car there?"

"Or has an accomplice?"

"He doesn't strike me as the sort of killer who plays well with others," Griffin says. "This level of control, of planning? My guess is he wouldn't like the unpredictability that having an accomplice would bring."

"Maybe," Cara says. She looks up as Shenton comes over—he puts two pieces of paper in her hands. She starts reading; Griffin tries to look over her shoulder, curious; Shenton twitches from foot to foot. She puts the pages down and gives Shenton a smile.

"This is good, Toby. Nate, round everyone up in the conference room." Shenton gives her his usual deer-in-the-headlights stare.

Griffin looks at her quizzically. "What for?"

Cara stands.

"Shenton's going to give us the profile."

50

THE ENTIRE TEAM fills the conference room. Griffin goes to take a seat at the back, but reconsiders, wanting to give his hesitant protégé a bit of encouragement from the first few rows.

Shenton stands hunched at the front, the omnipresent notepad gripped in his fingers.

Cara holds her hands up and the room silences. Shenton clears his throat as Cara introduces the purpose of the meeting.

"I need you all to listen and give Toby your full attention," she continues. "Whatever your views on profiling," she adds with a warning look to Griffin. Griffin frowns. That's not fair. He's not entirely against the work forensic psychologists do. It's not as if they're psychics, after all.

Toby looks at the expectant faces around the room. He smiles nervously. Griffin can already see perspiration on his forehead. What's Cara thinking? he wonders. Shenton's not ready for something like this, master's degrees or not.

"I have read all the case files, looked at the photographs, and there are a few things I think I can tell you about our killer," Shenton begins.

"Self-important little fuck," the detective mutters next to Griffin, and someone else snorts with laughter.

Toby pauses amid the continual chatter in the room. Cara glares at the detectives talking, and everyone shuts up, fidgeting in their seats. Shenton carries on: "He knows about forensics; he never leaves a trace behind. He knows our procedures inside and out, so he might have spent time in the police force or a related profession. He might have even inserted himself into the investigation somehow."

"You're saying he's one of us?" someone shouts, and a burst of annoyance rings out.

"I'm not saying he's a cop," Shenton stutters. "Just someone close to law enforcement." He clears his throat and looks down at his notes. Griffin sees his trademark blush start to creep up his neck. "We know he can drive and probably owns his own car. He pays rent on at least one property, so he's holding down a steady job. He is functioning in his everyday life."

More than some of the people in the room, Griffin thinks. His gaze drifts across to Deakin, leaning against the wall on the opposite side. Griffin knows he looks like shit, but Noah takes home the award. Dark shadows under his eyes, skinnier than usual. It looks like he hasn't eaten for a week. Deakin catches his eye and glares back. Fucking Noah, Griffin thinks. Such an asshole.

Meanwhile, Shenton is still talking. "We know he keeps souvenirs of his kills. The Polaroids, and the fact he displayed them prominently, show us he is proud of what he has achieved. Some offenders show guilt or regret, using alcohol or food to cope, but this guy will not. He is actively enjoying seeing the result of his actions."

"You think it's one guy?" someone shouts to Griffin's right.

"We have no reason not to. So, yes, probably one." He is standing up straighter now, seemingly getting into his stride. Griffin feels a grudging pride for the kid, and respect for his sister. She'd obviously recognized the potential in Shenton before anyone else had. "But even if not," Toby continues, "we're looking at one dominant and one submissive. One guy calling the shots."

"And it's definitely a man?" a DC speaks up from the back.

"Yes. Definitely. And a heterosexual man, at that."

"But he's sodomized men," the DC adds, and Shenton nods.

"Yes, but the male rapes were functional. Carried out methodically as his victims were dead or dying in order to fit the MO of Jeffrey Dahmer. If you contrast them with the female rapes . . ." Toby turns and picks up one of the crime scene photos from the GSK attacks. "They were violent and brutal. None more so than in the case of Mia Griffin."

Silence descends. Griffin feels his skin prickle as faces turn his way. Fucking hell, Toby, really? he thinks. You had to choose that example? But he forces his expression to remain impassive, staring at the man at the front of the room.

"I believe he holds a woman accountable for his problems and takes his rage out on women as a result. So it's unlikely he can hold down a normal relationship. He has an emotional need to degrade and destroy. He possibly even has some sort of dysfunction, unable to maintain an erection without this sort of violence."

Shenton holds his head up high. He puts his notebook down to his side. His face is serious.

"This is a man who wants his victims to suffer," he says. "He derives sexual pleasure and satisfaction from hurting them, from the power he exerts over their lives and ultimately their deaths. He listens to their screams and gets off on their pain." Shenton pauses. The room is completely silent; he has the undivided attention of every detective there. "He is a sexual sadist, and a dangerous one. Each kill only fuels the appetite for inflicting more pain, but he'll need to do more each time to get off. He'll become more elaborate, more personal. I have no doubt that he will continue to kill, and he won't stop until we catch him."

He stops. The mood in the room has chilled. Every detective knew the severity of the man they were trying to catch, but little DC Toby Shenton has brought it home. Every word pinpointing their failures. The unspoken truth is if they don't catch him, the next murders are on them.

"So who will he kill next? Who will he echo?"

Shenton takes a deep breath. "I can't say," he says, and Griffin hears the disquiet. "But his signature is interesting in itself."

"His signature?" Cara asks.

Toby turns to her. "The MO—modus operandi—is what our offender does to kill. It's the stabbing, the strangulation, the gunshot. And as we have seen, it changes. But the signature—" He smiles. "That's the interesting part. It's what the offender does to get himself off. It's influenced by the why. And it doesn't change."

"So what about the Echo Man?"

"He's copying others. What does he get from it?" Shenton looks at the faces around the room, waiting for some sort of answer. Everyone stays quiet. "He's a sexual sadist—he could enjoy himself a lot more if he wasn't limited by the mimicry. So why do it?" he asks again.

"He can't think for himself," a detective says from the back.

Shenton shakes his head. "But we know he's clever. This guy's not lacking in originality." Still silence. "I believe he's hiding behind it. Enjoying pretending he's someone else. But it's more than that. He likes the notoriety of killers of the past, but he's enjoying beating them, exceeding their achievements. Feeling like he's better than them. And as I mentioned before, I think it's about the power. He's taking back some of the control he's lost in the past—maybe from the sexual abuse—exerting his authority over his victims. It's intoxicating to him."

"So how do we catch him?"

The question gets a wave of assent from the room. Griffin feels the energy mount.

"Um." Shenton stops. His previous confidence has faded in the face of the whole room staring. Griffin knows this is the hard part—he needs to make a decision. "He's been killing for a long time—at least a few years." He's staring at the floor, thinking out loud. "And his kills are getting more frequent. He's escalating. Where before he was patient, cleverly putting together the pieces of his puzzle—"

"His puzzle?" Griffin interrupts.

"Yes, because I think this is what this is. Take the Dahmer staging: that would have taken a long time to put together. That's a lot of bodies, a lot of killing. Plus Michael Sharp, in the freezer? He must have killed him before he took over his apartment. Yet he didn't dismember him like he did the others. He obviously had a plan. And that must have taken patience." Shenton looks around the room, at the expectant faces. "But now he's speeding up. More kills, less space between them. Something must have happened: an incident in his present day or a significant date linked to his past. And I think, by killing Libby, he's asking for attention. He wants to be seen."

"Do you think he wants to be caught?" Cara asks.

"No. At least, not yet." Shenton looks at her. "He's only leaving behind the evidence he wants us to find. Like Michael Sharp's blood in the Kemper car. And the pint glass in his apartment, with Libby's fingerprints and DNA. I think he's enjoying the mess he's creating. He's a narcissist: he feels superior, entitled. He'll be enjoying the power watching us run around after him."

Shenton's face colors, knowing he just criticized the investigation.

But Cara shrugs it off. "So what do you suggest we do?" she asks.

"I think we should hold a memorial for Libby," he says.

"Go on . . ."

"We do it somewhere public. We make a big deal out of it. Ideally it would be her funeral, but we won't have the body released for weeks yet, so let's do a memorial."

"And what would be the point in that?" Griffin asks. "Taking advantage of her death? Her relatives will never agree."

"They will if we explain why we're doing it." Shenton's hands flutter excitedly. "Because he won't be able to resist the opportunity. He'll want to see the grief; he'll get a kick out of seeing the destruction he's caused. We hold a memorial, and I guarantee, he'll show up."

"You guarantee, huh?" Cara says, and Shenton looks uncertain for a second but then nods slowly.

"Well, then." Cara stands up straight in front of the group. "Let's do this. Let's get this organized."

51

Cara watches the detectives file out, back to the incident room. Shenton's the last to go, looking back at her as he follows his colleagues.

"Well done, Toby," she says, and she forces her warmest smile. "Just shut the door on your way out."

As soon as the door clicks shut, Cara sags. She's alone in here, the blinds closed, and she slumps into a chair, putting her head into her hands. The enormity of the case is suddenly too much. Shenton's insecurities, her brother's dead wife, Noah's—

Noah's what? She can't put a label on it, but something certainly seems to be bothering him.

As if reading her thoughts, there's a light knock on the door, and Deakin pokes his head around.

"What?" she snaps, more sharply than she intended.

"We just need a few decisions about this memorial," he starts, then he tilts his head to one side, appraising her. "You okay?"

She feels his dark eyes rest on her face. She goes to answer, but her throat tightens. She can't remember the last time anyone asked if she was all right. She swallows, but before she can protest, thick tears start to fall. She brushes them away, annoyed.

"I'm sorry," Cara manages to say. "You aren't here for waterworks."

He closes the door behind him and walks over to sit next to her.

"You don't need to apologize," he says softly. "This is a fucking shitty case, and you have the unlucky job of being SIO. It's not surprising you're feeling the stress."

She clears her throat again, looking up to try to dispel the tears. She'd never cry in front of the team, show her uncertainty or weakness, but Noah is different.

"I'm just so fucking shattered. I haven't seen the kids properly for days."

"So go home. Have a nap," he says, but she's shaking her head even before he's finished talking.

"You know I can't do that." She laughs hollowly. "Look around the office." Cara gestures toward the door, where she knows her detectives are hard at work on the other side. "Nobody's had a break. Everyone's feeling the stress. I'm not quitting on them. I'm not quitting on the women, the men he's killed."

He leans forward, closer to her, and for a moment she thinks he's going to hold her hand. But he moves backward again, and a fleeting thought passes through her mind: What would she have done if he had?

Next to her, her phone starts to buzz. She doesn't recognize the number, so she lets it ring out.

She takes a deep breath, then remembers the box of evidence in her office. "And can you deal with those notebooks? Find a handwriting expert, something like that, see if they can shed any light?"

He nods. "Business as usual then?" he says with a half-hearted smile.

"Business as usual, Deaks," she finishes, and the phone goes off again. "Oh, for fuck's sake," she mutters, and answers it.

"DCI Elliott? This is Steve Gray. From the *Chronicle*."

Cara almost hangs up. She hasn't got the time for this shit. "How did you get my number? I haven't got anything to say about the case. Please speak to PR as usual."

"No, DCI Elliott, wait. We've got something you need to see."

His tone makes her pause. He sounds panicked.

"What?"

"A letter. We've been sent a letter," he splutters. "And we think it's from the killer."

CHAPTER

52

CARA AND DEAKIN stand in the newspaper editor's office. The note is in front of them on the desk, now enclosed in a see-through plastic evidence bag. Nobody speaks.

The journalist and his editor watch them. Steve Gray is short, blond, thin; his editor, the exact opposite, with a round fleshy face and button eyes. They both seem unnerved but annoyingly excited.

The letter had arrived the day before in a plain white envelope, the address written on the front in blue felt tip. *Please Rush to Editor* it says below the address, but it had been ignored until this morning, when they had opened it and a piece of black material had fluttered out.

"Gave us a shock, I can tell you," Gray had said, pointing to the fabric, still left on the desk where it had fallen. With a gloved hand Cara put it in another evidence bag.

The note inside is written on a piece of white lined paper in the same pen. Cara reads it again.

> *This is the Echo Man speaking*
> *I am the murderer of the*
> *couple over by*
> *Salterns Hill last*
> *night, to prove it here is*
> *a bloodstained piece of her*
> *dress. I am the same man*
> *who did in the people in the*
> *rest of the UK.*

I want you to print this cipher
on the front page of your
paper. In this cipher is my
identity.
If you do not print this cipher
by the afternoon of Fry. 5th of
Feb, I will go on a kill ram-
Page Fry. Night I will cruise
around all weekend killing lone
people in the night then move
on to kill again, until I end
up with a dozen people over
the weekend.

At the bottom of the page is a circle with a cross through it: the mark of the Zodiac Killer.

"What does Shenton say?" Deakin asks. The editor had already sent over a scanned copy of the message, giving their DC a head start on the analysis.

"He's confirmed the wording is almost precisely the same as notes from the Zodiac back in 1969," Cara replies. "Two merged together, just the details relevant to our case changed."

"And the . . ." The newspaper editor pauses. "The code?"

Attached to the note is another piece of paper. Across it are a number of symbols and letters. A cipher in the same style as the Zodiac Killer.

"That's different," Cara confirmed.

"So it could be a new code? Containing the identity of our guy?"

"Possibly."

They all fall silent again. Cara picks up the envelope. There are double the number of stamps needed for normal postage, all stuck on sideways. The postmark is the day before Libby's murder.

"So we'll be publishing this tomorrow," the editor says.

Cara sighs. She knows better than to hope they'd keep it quiet. It was too much of a scoop. "Can you just hold on to it for a day or two? You can still have the exclusive," she adds quickly. "But please give us a chance to solve it and catch the guy. You publish the identity of the killer, and there's a chance he'll go to ground."

The editor frowns. "You've got four days." He points to the note. "I don't want it on my conscience if we don't publish this by Friday and he goes on this rampage he's talking about. And I want confirmation on who this dress belongs to."

Cara feels a ripple of anger. That was her friend's dress. Her *friend*. Not some device to sell newspapers. But she nods; she needs to keep this guy on her side. "Thank you," she adds.

* * *

They take the original note, the code, and the piece of material with them, leaving a copy for the newspaper, and get in the car.

"Do you think this will tell us the killer's name?" Deakin asks. "It seems a bit . . . easy?"

"We haven't cracked it yet," Cara says. She still feels weary, the gravity of the case weighs on her mind.

They start to drive, and as they head back toward town, Cara wants to see Roo. She wants a hug from her husband, from someone who can tell her it's all going to be okay.

"Do you mind if we stop by the restaurant?" she asks. Deakin seems reluctant, but does as she asks, pulling the car up outside. "I'll get us some lunch while I'm here," she adds to appease him.

Cara gets out and looks through the huge plate-glass windows. Service hasn't yet begun, and she opens the door, walking through the empty tables, laid up with white napkins and shining silver cutlery. Tables she knows will soon be filled with posh clientele: ladies who lunch, businessmen making the most of steaks on expenses.

A few people working notice her and nod—they have a low staff turnover here, and most of them know her—and she goes through to the kitchen.

Tempting smells are already coming from the many ovens. A few chefs finish up last-minute prep, but she can't see Roo. Then she spots him, on the far side, standing at the open back door. He's smiling, talking to someone, and she takes a few seconds to admire him in his chef's whites.

He's good-looking: in better shape than most men his age, tall, graying, with a smile that pulls people toward him. She's seen the appreciative scrutiny from women in Waitrose. She notices his shoes—Converse sneakers. The same brand as the footwear marks found outside Griffin's bathroom window when he was attacked. Also identified by the witness on the man going into apartment 214. Seeing them on her husband's feet just confirms what she knew already: millions of men wear those sneakers. The results don't narrow their suspect pool down.

Cara goes to say hello but hesitates as she sees the person he's talking to.

He's laughing, and reaches out a hand to touch her arm. A woman with long blonde hair, parted in the middle.

It's Lauren.

Cara watches her smile back, and she frowns. But then she stops herself. Fucking Deaks and his theories, she curses, making her paranoid. She's probably just dropping something off for the kids or meeting someone for lunch. But deep down she knows this place is too expensive for Lauren. And she's never known her to come here before.

Then Roo leans forward. He puts a hand on Lauren's waist and kisses her. It's on her cheek, not her lips, or a full-blown PDA, but something about it—the slowness, the smile, something—tells Cara it's not innocent.

Cara steps away from the kitchen, then hurries through the restaurant. She feels the curious glances from the waiting staff, but she doesn't stop until she's back in the car.

"Just drive," she instructs Noah, and he gives her a puzzled look. "And give me that," she adds, referring to the cigarette hanging from his mouth.

He passes it across without a word, and she takes a long drag. It makes her feel dizzy, but she needs it. She stares resolutely out the window, letting the car fill with smoke, making her eyes water.

She feels Deakin glance across to her, but she's embarrassed and can't bring herself to say anything out loud. To acknowledge her failures. A serial killer she can't catch, mocking her day after day. And a husband cheating on her with the nanny.

53

ALL EYES ARE on Cara and Deakin as they arrive back in the office. They'd tried hard to keep the note and the cipher quiet, but news had spread rapidly around the team, and now everyone wants a piece of the action. Griffin knows it's just eagerness to latch onto a new lead, to get the case solved, but he snaps at a few of the younger DCs as their enthusiasm creeps into callousness.

Cara allocates tasks across the office, rushing the piece of material and the letter to the lab, making copies of the code, trying to find someone who might be able to crack it. A few arrogant DCs take a print themselves, keen to take the glory. Cara goes back to her office. She's been businesslike, the DCI in charge, but to Griffin she seems off. He's known her long enough to sense when she's hiding something.

He leans in the doorway of her office. He waits until she looks at him.

"What do you want?" she asks, abruptly.

"What are you not telling us?"

Cara stares at him for a moment. Then she asks: "You got any cigarettes?"

He nods and follows her to the roof.

* * *

Griffin knows they're not allowed up here, but he assumes that a DCI and a DS will get away with it. Cara props the fire door open, and they lean against a wall, sheltering away from the wind. He hands her a cigarette and she takes it, cupping her hand around the delicate flame of his lighter.

"Since when did you start smoking again?" he asks, doing the same.

"Since a maniac killer started conducting mass murder under my nose."

"Serial murder, not mass murder." Griffin smiles. "Or you'll have Shenton correcting you."

She makes a noise halfway between a laugh and a snort.

"You be nice to Shenton," she scolds. "He's trying his best."

"You always did have a soft spot for nerds." Griffin watches her as she takes another drag. "What's going on, Cara?"

She breathes in deeply and lets it out in a series of juddering sighs.

"Roo's cheating on me," she says in almost a whisper.

Griffin's hands form into fists. "I'll kill him," he growls.

"Not before I do."

But then Cara's face crumples, and she starts to cry, and Griffin pulls her close in a hug. He scowls, resting his face on the top of her head. He's always liked Roo, but this? This he can't forgive.

"How do you know?" he asks after a moment. "Who with?"

Cara pulls away from him and looks at her cigarette, burning down to the filter.

"Deaks and I went to the restaurant on the way home, and I saw them together. Him and Lauren."

"Your nanny? Oh Jesus, what a fucking cliché!"

"I know." Cara almost laughs through her tears. "I feel so stupid. What have they been doing, behind my back? At the house, when I've worked late? Some shitty detective I am." She looks up at Griffin. "Noah guessed, you know."

Griffin raises his eyebrows. Perhaps he doesn't give Deakin enough credit as a detective. And as a friend. He feels shit. He should have been there for her. He should have noticed.

"How did it get to be like this, Nate?" she asks him. Cara leans back against the concrete wall and takes another drag of her cigarette. Her hair has escaped and is frizzy around her face. In that minute, she reminds Griffin of a Cara at seventeen, smoking around the back of school, waiting for their mom to pick them up.

Cara's still talking: "You get married and you think, that's it now. Settled. And then look what happens." She stops herself. "I'm sorry, I didn't mean to compare Roo with what happened to Mia."

Griffin shakes his head. "I know what you mean. You just can't anticipate this shit." He finishes his cigarette and crushes it underfoot. "What are you going to do now?"

"With Roo?" Cara shrugs. She does the same with her butt. "Not a clue."

"You'll figure it out." Cara looks up at him and he chuckles. "Do you remember when we were about twelve or thirteen? We were on holiday, playing table tennis?"

"Remember? I still have the scar." Cara leans forward into the light, and Griffin can just make out a small pale line on her cheekbone.

"That's not it!"

"That is!" Cara laughs. "After all this time. You could have taken my eye out."

Griffin stops, stunned. He remembers the incident: normal sibling rivalry, Cara winning game after game on the uneven table-tennis table until Griffin lost his temper, throwing his bat. It took a chunk out of her face, blood everywhere, their parents furious and forcing him to apologize. Unrepentant, he stormed out, only returning hours later once it was dark.

And still he refused to say sorry. Cara stayed silent and magnanimous until the final day of the holiday, when a stomach complaint forced him into the toilet, missing the big trip to the water park.

Cara returned, skin tanned, wet and exhausted, laughing with her new friends. He was lying on his bed in the dark, miserable and jealous, when she'd come into the room.

"How are you feeling?" she'd asked.

"Awful."

"You deserve it," she'd said and he'd stared at her, disbelieving. "You should have said sorry."

Cara looks at him now in the half light of the roof. "What do you suggest I do? Put laxative in Roo's milkshake?"

Griffin laughs. "No. But you were always the calculated one, even then. I react." He points a finger at her. "You *think*. You'll figure it out," he repeats, and she smiles. Then her face turns serious.

"Nate, this woman. This murder suspect. You need to bring her in."

Griffin stays silent. He knows, he *knows* that Cara's right. He's getting himself in trouble. And Cara too.

"You haven't found anything definitive on the arson, have you?" she continues. He slowly shakes his head. "So we need to deal with it the proper way. Legally," she adds.

"Give me a bit longer," he pleads. "And if I don't find anything, I'll arrest her myself." But he knows he won't. He could never put cuffs on her wrists, see the look of betrayal on her face. He tells himself it's because she's innocent, that it would be a miscarriage of justice, leaving her to the fate of Taylor's shoddy investigation, but in his heart he knows it's something else. A part of him that doesn't want her to leave.

Cara gives him a hard stare. "Fine." She goes to say something else, but her phone buzzes and she looks at it. "That's Noah. Says he's found a cryptographer, or whatever these people are called. Let's hope they can solve this fucking code."

Griffin nods and they head back in. As they go down the stairs, he adds: "Offer's still open."

Cara stops and looks at him.

"With Roo? I don't have to break any bones, just rough him up a bit."

Cara sniggers, and Griffin smiles. At least that's one good thing, he thinks to himself. At least he can still make his big sister laugh.

CHAPTER

54

"THIS IS INTERESTING, very interesting," Professor Barnet says, his attention focused on the piece of paper on his desk. He has a look on his face usually reserved for small children at Christmas time. Deakin had already sent him a copy of the message, but they'd brought the original along in case it offered anything else in the way of clues.

"But can you work out the code?" Cara asks, impatiently.

The professor's abundant set of eyebrows dance as he chuckles. "This isn't a code—it's a cipher. Where each letter is substituted for another, or a symbol in this case. Does it translate across to the Zodiac ciphers that do have a solution?"

Cara shakes her head. They know that the first cipher received from the Zodiac Killer back in 1969 had been solved, by a teacher and his wife no less, but none of the letters match up. Same with the one cracked years later in 2020.

"Sadly not," she says. "Do you think you can do this one?"

"I'll certainly try," Professor Barnet replies. "Ciphers like this can be solved using certain rules from our day-to-day language. For example, *E* is the most common letter, followed by *T, A, O,* and *N.* Some letters often appear doubled, like *E* and *L,* and some letters often occur together. We can apply these rules to the symbols to try to work out the substitution. For example, we might be able to guess that the word *kill* appears in the text, like it did in the original."

"Seems simple enough," Deakin says, but the professor laughs.

"That all assumes your guy has done a simple substitution. But given the subject matter and what's at stake, he's probably included some random stuff in there to throw us off, and because of the way it's written, you have no idea where the words start or end. I'm also guessing it's a homophonic cipher, using multiple substitutions for a single letter." He stops and rubs his hands together. He looks happy. "We'll have some fun in the meantime. And I'll see if any of my colleagues at GCHQ want to have a go. As long as that's okay?"

Cara agrees and she and Deakin leave, taking the original letter with them.

"Well, we've made his day, at least," Deakin says. "Perhaps we should publish it in the newspaper—let the general public have a go."

"And then what? Put the solution on Twitter? What if they get it wrong and start a lynch mob, Deaks?"

As they walk through the campus of the university, Cara looks at the other people there, the students, lecturers, going about their normal lives. She envies their ignorance, their ability to carry on not knowing that someone might murder and torture them tonight. It could be the person walking at their side, and they'd never know. She sighs, and Deakin glances at her.

"What happened earlier?" he asks. "At the restaurant."

Cara can't look at him. "Let's just say you were right," she mutters.

"Ah." Deakin falls silent. "And did Griffin have anything useful to say on the subject?"

"He offered to beat him up."

"His usual way of solving problems then."

They get to the car, and Cara looks at Deakin over the roof.

"I know you two don't get along, but if one of you just made the effort, you might realize you're more alike than you know."

Deakin shakes his head as he gets into the passenger seat. "I think that's unlikely, Cara. I just can't stand the way he is. Like he thinks normal rules don't apply to him. The rest of us have to follow procedure, and that's how we get convictions. Why should he get a free pass?"

"Well, will you just please try?" she begs. "For me?"

Deakin sighs. "Anything for you, Cara—you know that."

They both sit in Cara's car. She knows neither of them wants to head to the station. Back to nagging the lab, chasing Ross for more postmortem results? To crossing their fingers and hoping they get something they can work with?

They need this time, this space. Even if it's just for a moment.

Cara reaches across Noah and opens the glovebox, finding two cookies, left for the kids one time. She's not sure how old they are, but passes one to Deakin and he opens it. She eats her own, enjoying the abrupt sweetness.

"Have you ever thought you could kill someone?"

The words come out before she's thought about them. She glances anxiously to Noah, but he's not judging. He takes another bite of his biscuit and chews thoughtfully.

"I'd like to think I couldn't. But if it came down to it, maybe. Yes. If my life was in danger, something like that."

"Is that the line for you? Someone threatening your life?"

"Or someone I loved."

Cara wonders who that is for Noah.

"Did you have to do anything like that for SO10?" she asks.

"What? Kill someone?" Deakin asks. She nods. "No. It was usually me getting beaten up. And stabbed once."

"Really?"

"Yeah, here." Noah takes his coat off, Roo's raincoat, and throws it on the back seat, then pulls up the edge of his shirt. Cara peers at the small, jagged scar down the side of his stomach, then gets distracted by the line of dark hair disappearing into the waistband of his jeans. She looks away quickly.

"Did it hurt?"

"Nah." He grins, pulling his shirt back down. "What about you? Who would you kill?"

Cara thinks about her family.

"I'd kill this guy," she says, almost whispering. "For what he did to Libby. And Mia and Griffin."

"How?"

"How?" Cara hadn't thought about it in that way. How much pain would she inflict? Would she want this guy to suffer? "Perhaps something quick," she mutters. "Gun. Poison. Plastic bag over the head. Something like that."

"Could you, though?" Deakin asks. "If someone gave you a gun? Could you pull the trigger?" He pauses. "And you trust Griffin?"

"Nate? To have my back, yes," Cara replies without hesitation. Noah shakes his head.

"That's not what I mean. In the face of the man who murdered his wife, do you trust him not to kill him? We've both seen what he did to Mia—and to him. It's a big ask—that faced with your wife's rapist and killer you won't do the same to them."

Cara chews her lip.

"Could you honestly say you'd arrest the guy if you were Griffin? Walk away? If you had the power in your very sizeable hands? You know it, Cara. He could easily kill, without breaking a sweat."

Cara goes to defend her brother, but she knows Noah's right. Griffin has a temper, and biceps to match. It wouldn't take much—a few well-aimed punches to the guy's face, and it would be game over. Griffin's life, his career, would be finished.

"I won't let that happen," she says at last.

Deakin seems to take her word for it. Or, even if he doesn't believe her, he has the good grace to let it go. He looks at the last bit of cookie in his hand. "I think these are stale, Cara." He looks at her with a small smile. "Is this your plan? To do me in with outdated baked goods?"

Her phone rings, interrupting their conversation, and she sees Marsh's number. She answers it as Deakin shrugs and eats the last piece.

"Where are you, Elliott?"

"On our way back to the station, boss."

"Come and see me when you get back. Straight away."

He hangs up without any pleasantries. Cara has a sinking feeling.

"Marsh wants to see me."

"Can't be good," Deakin comments.

"No," she replies. "Not at all."

* * *

Her hunch was confirmed as soon as Cara sees the detective chief superintendent's face.

"Sit down," he instructs. "Where are we?"

Cara doesn't need to ask what he's referring to. She gives a rundown on every lead they have followed up, every piece of evidence. It doesn't take long.

"So you have nothing, basically, except a code nobody can break, shoes marks from one of the most common brands of sneakers, a case file from 1996 that you can't find, a bit of greenery from a bog, and a queue of bodies stacking up in the mortuary?"

"We're tracking down every single piece of CCTV, testing swabs, taking fingerprints, samples. But nothing comes up. He's smart. He must be using condoms for the rapes. He knows where the cameras are, he knows how to avoid leaving anything forensics can work with."

"And don't I know it," Marsh mutters. "Have you seen my budget?" He doesn't wait for Cara to answer. "I'm getting pressure, DCI Elliott. Questions are being asked from above. About you. About the competency of my senior investigating officer to lead this case."

Cara feels her stomach drop.

"We need results. And we need them soon, before any more bodies turn up. They're talking about mentioning it at PM's question time, do you know that, Elliott? They're going to ask the fucking prime minister why the biggest case in UK history isn't being handled by the Met."

"Put anyone else as SIO, *sir*, and I assure you, they'll have the same results."

"That may be true, but we need to be seen to be doing everything we possibly can." He pauses. "You have this memorial tomorrow, right?" he asks.

Cara nods.

"You have twenty-four hours after that. Then we're handing it over."

*   *   *

Cara walks out of his office and goes quickly down the stairs, pushing open the door to the toilets. She goes into one of the cubicles, puts the seat down and sits on it, putting her head between her knees, her hands on her head.

She doesn't blame Marsh. She feels how badly the investigation is going. She knows how little they have to go on.

The memorial tomorrow is their one shot in the dark. Their Hail Mary that the guy's ego won't be able to resist and he'll show up. But then what? How will they know?

Half of her feels like she doesn't care anymore. She's barely eaten a hot meal in days, she hasn't had more than eight hours' sleep across the whole week combined. She's at home so rarely that her husband is sleeping with the nanny. It's not healthy.

She wonders whether she should just pack it in. Put everything in boxes and pass it across to the Metropolitan Police or the National Crime Agency to worry about.

Then she can go home. Have a bath. Watch the latest series of *The Crown* on Netflix.

Cara hears someone else come into the bathroom, closing the door to another cubicle. She realizes how ridiculous she's being, sitting here, listening to someone else's bodily functions.

This isn't her. This defeat. This giving up.

This man has raped eight women, killed thirteen. He has chopped up eleven men and put them in his freezer. She mentally counts up the dead. It's twenty-eight in total, not counting Taylor's arson. She can barely believe the number, it seems so ridiculous.

She leaves the cubicle and washes her hands. She stands in front of the mirror. I'm damn well going to catch him, she resolves.

Even if it destroys my entire life in the process.

CHAPTER

55

GRIFFIN'S BACK, BUT he's quiet. Jess asks if he wants something to eat but he just shakes his head, no. She assumes nothing new has happened.

But she's going crazy locked up in here.

"Griffin?" she starts quietly. She sits down next to him at the table, where he's staring mutely at his laptop. "Did you speak to your sister about my case?"

He nods. "Yes, but it's not good news. They still want to arrest you."

Jess feels her morale sink. "But you didn't tell her where I was."

"No."

Jess wants to ask why not. But she doesn't dare. She doesn't want to question what Griffin is doing, make him doubt himself. He's a cop, after all.

He's still squinting at the screen, and she remembers her thought from the day before. Does he know?

"Is it on there?" she says. He looks up sharply. And with that one expression, he answers the question. He knows. "What does it say?" she makes herself ask.

"Not much."

"It's not what they made out," Jess replies, the words falling away before she can stop them. She can't look at him and stares at the piles of newspapers still littering the table. "It was an accident."

She feels his eyes on her. She needs to tell him, now, before she changes her mind.

"He tried to stop me, with the . . . you know." She gestures toward the bathroom and Griffin nods. "It was one of those old-style cut-throat razors that I'd bought for that purpose. It was night, Alice was asleep in bed, and I didn't think I'd be disturbed. But Patrick tried to take it away from me and it slipped, gashing his hand badly. He started shouting, I was crying. The neighbors must have called the police."

She barely remembered what happened next. She'd been hysterical, screaming in the road. The police officers restraining her: arms wrenched behind her back, a knee between her shoulder blades, her face crushed into the pavement.

"They took me somewhere. I don't remember what they called it, but it was a mental hospital."

"Rapid Assessment Unit," Griffin says quietly.

"Yes, that." She stops. She takes a deep breath in. She remembers arriving at the huge brick building, the shame and indignity of being strip and cavity searched by a woman, cold plastic gloves on her hands, unfeeling and rough as Jess sobbed in the glare of the overhead lights. Nobody listened, nobody cared. The prick of the injections, then her head: fuzzy and slow. The night in the bare room, on suicide watch, the lights on, unable to sleep, listening to the shouts and wails of the other patients echoing through the corridors. "Patrick tried to have me sectioned. To keep me in there. The police agreed. If it wasn't for Nav speaking up for me, I don't know what would have happened."

They fall back into silence. Griffin's stopped what he was doing on the laptop, his fingers hovering on the keys. She waits, fearing his judgment.

He clears his throat. That'll be it now, she thinks. He'll think I'm crazy for sure.

"And you stayed with him?" Griffin says, at last. "With Patrick? After that?"

"He loved me. He only wanted what was best for me."

"Funny way of showing it," Griffin mutters.

But Jess doesn't mention how she felt at that time. That she wasn't fit to be a mother. That she knew if she left Patrick, there would be no way she'd get custody of Alice.

The crushing knowledge that she was no better than a piece of shit on her husband's shoe. Something to clean off and discard. She remembers Patrick's threats that if she didn't get better, he'd call the police again, and this time she wouldn't be leaving, no matter what Nav said. He talked of electroconvulsive therapy, of lobotomies. Drugs to dull her thoughts. She had no knowledge of what those things were, or even if they applied to her, but the fear? It was the fear that kept her in check. And that fear that now keeps her away from the police, knowing they have the power to put her there again.

"I'm sorry, Jess," Griffin says quietly, and she looks at him. He's staring down at the tabletop. "I get why you don't trust the police. I said I'd help you find who murdered Patrick, and I'm letting you down. I don't want to be another one of those people."

Jess looks at him. She shakes her head. "That's not it at all," she says. "I . . ." She pauses. "I needed to know what happened to Patrick, yes. But that feels like a long time ago now. That's not why I've stayed."

She reaches over and takes his hand. He looks at it for a few beats, then lifts his head and meets her eyes. She's never seen him look so miserable.

"You're not letting me down, Griffin," she says. "And you're not letting Mia down either."

He looks down again quickly, pulling his hand away from hers. Jess curses inside her head. She shouldn't have said that, about Mia.

She gets up from the table and goes across to the kitchen. She's not hungry, but she wants to give him some space, or as much as she can in this tiny basement. But then she hears him push his chair out and feels him standing behind her.

She turns, and he takes her face in his hands, kissing her gently.

It's not like the other times they've kissed. It's slow, soft. He moves his hands into her hair, and she does the same, then down his back, under the hem of his shirt. They move toward the bed, taking clothes off as they go, smiling when a sock refuses to come off, when her T-shirt gets stuck on her head. They fall together, him on top of her, and she enjoys the feeling of the weight of him, the warmth of skin against skin.

They're taking their time. Both of them are exploring, making the most of being with each other, in contrast to the frantic nature before. But it's not just the speed that's changed.

They're actually looking at each other. At first, the eye contact seems strange, too intimate, but then Jess realizes she can't look away. She's lost, his light brown eyes on her, his long lashes, the smile lines at the corner of his eyes. She likes it. Likes him.

The lines on his face relax. He's watching her, smiling as her expression changes, depending on what he's doing, where he's putting his hands, his fingers, his mouth.

This is different, she thinks. And then he's inside her, and she doesn't think much at all.

*   *   *

They fall asleep, their bodies entwined, but when Jess wakes, Griffin has gone. She looks at the clock, confused. It's just past midnight.

She sits up in bed, then sees his car keys lying on the table. He can't go far without the Land Rover. Something feels wrong.

She gets up, puts a light on and gets dressed. She looks around. Everything else is here—his rucksack, his laptop. But his coat has gone, his boots.

Jess hesitates. But she can't bear sitting around doing nothing. She picks up the keys and climbs the stairs, leaving the apartment.

Outside the air is cold but still. The same cars sit for sale on the lot; a taxi goes past on the road. She can't see Griffin.

She takes a few steps out of the shadow of the main building, then something catches her eye. It's a shape on the ground, clothing, what seems to be a body.

A bad feeling grips her and she runs over. But relief when she sees it's not Griffin is replaced by horror.

The woman's eyes are open, looking to the sky. Her mouth, lips raw, teeth damaged, is open in a silent scream. She's never seen a dead body like this before, not up close.

The smell snags in her nose. Decay, feces, an indescribable stench that makes her gag. Wet wounds cover the woman's body, she can see white bone poking through ripped skin.

She takes a step back, then breath catches in her throat as hands grip her arms tightly. She goes to scream, but stops as she hears his voice.

"Jess, what are you doing here? You have to go."

Griffin is behind her, guiding her back toward the apartment, but she resists. The shock of seeing the woman is making her angry, hot tears running down her face.

"Where did you go, Griffin?" she cries at him. "Who is this? Where did you go?"

He left her, to find this woman alone. He tries to quiet her, but she's still furious.

"Why is there a body here? Who is she?"

"I don't know, but I've called the police. You need to leave, or they'll arrest you." His face is frantic, pleading with her. "Please?"

She nods, tearing her eyes away from the woman on the concrete. She can hear sirens in the distance and runs back to the basement.

She closes the door behind her and gulps in deep breaths.

The serial killer. The Echo Man.

He was right outside the door.

He was here.

56

B Y THE TIME Cara arrives from the station, Deakin is already there and glaring at Griffin. Police cars surround the area, blue lights dancing on dark brickwork. Uniforms work to set up the cordon, a few passers-by show a quick interest.

She was working late. She hasn't been home. She knows Roo is there and hasn't got the energy to face him. Not yet.

"What have we got?" she asks. The two men stay silent. "Please? Someone?"

Shenton steps forward out of the darkness. Cara hadn't even noticed him. "Latest victim, female, showing clear signs of being beaten. Possibly held against her will."

While Shenton is talking, Cara crouches down and looks at the body. She can see angry marks around the woman's wrists and ankles, raw wounds across her torso and head. Her dress is dirty and torn, and she's not wearing any shoes. Or underwear, Cara realizes.

"Pathologist and crime scene are on their way."

"And do we know who this is?"

Shenton shakes his head.

"Or which serial killer it's copying?"

"Not until I know more," Shenton mutters. "Unfortunately, there are too many who have this as their MO."

Cara sighs. She's suddenly so tired. So fucking tired of this whole thing. "And we think this is a body dump? Outside where you're living, Griffin?" she adds.

"Kind of making a point, isn't he?" Griffin says. "Leaving the latest victim outside my front door."

"Unless it was you that put it there," Noah adds.

Griffin scowls at him. "Seriously? You think I'd kill someone then leave them right outside my house? How dumb do you think I am?"

Deakin pulls a face and before Cara can react, Griffin springs forward, all his weight behind his outstretched fist. She hears a wet crunch as he makes contact, Cara diving between them, shoving her brother away as Noah falls backward onto the concrete. She looks at Griffin in shock.

"Nate! Back away!" When Griffin doesn't move, she shouts again. "DS Griffin! Back. The fuck. Away!"

Deakin's being pulled to his feet by Shenton, tentatively touching his face, wincing. "Where were you tonight, Nate?" he shouts. He puts his hand over his left eye, trying to stem the bleeding. "Home? Alone? With no one to provide an alibi?"

Cara notices Griffin hesitate.

"How do we know? Seriously?" Noah turns to Cara. Blood is starting to seep through his fingers, running down his wrist. "Griffin has been here, oh so conveniently pointing stuff out every step of the way. And now this?"

"Shut up, both of you," Cara snaps. "This poor woman deserves better than this. She deserves for us to find her killer, and no," she says as Deakin goes to interrupt, "I don't think it's Griffin. Even he's not stupid enough to leave a dead body outside his own apartment.

"Noah, go and get yourself cleaned up. Griffin—this garage must have CCTV?" He nods, quieter now. "Track it down. I'll speak to you about this later."

Cara watches as Noah leaves and the group disperses. It was inevitable that the thin line of tolerance between Noah and Griffin would be crossed, and no sleep and no progress on the case meant it couldn't hold any longer. She remembers the conversation in the car. Griffin's temper frayed, and all it took was some baiting from Noah.

She glances toward the side door that she knows leads to Griffin's basement. When Cara had originally got the call she'd first thought that this was her, Jessica Ambrose, the murder suspect being concealed in Griffin's apartment. But it's clear this victim is separate, and she briefly wonders where the other woman is. Barely ten feet away, hiding, quiet? She knows Griffin is still looking into the arson, but she's done her own reading too, skimming the file, reviewing the evidence. And she agrees with him: it does fit. Another murder in the long line of serial killings, so arresting Jessica Ambrose has become less of a concern.

And she has more pressing problems to deal with now.

She looks at the dead woman lying on the concrete as she waits for SOCO to arrive. Her eyes are open and glassy, staring accusingly upward. Cara knows the body being placed here wasn't coincidence. He's closer. He knows who they are. Where they live.

The killer is taunting them.

57

Day 8
Monday

THE DAY IS cold and bright. Sun shines through gaps in the trees, lighting up the corner of the graveyard. The area is secluded from the road, with one walkway in and out. Flowers are arranged at the front, around a large photograph of Libby. It's a nice one, provided by her parents. They understood and agreed to the plan, once Cara had explained it to them. They want this guy caught. Cara is good at the people stuff, the bits Griffin has never managed.

He watches his sister now, standing at the front of the group. Her voice is steady and clear in the still air. She's talking about Libby, a eulogy worked on until the early hours, calling on input from her family and friends. Griffin knows that Cara would have wanted to get it right. As much as this is a ploy, it is still honoring Libby. Griffin had liked her. Cara said that she would have approved of this plan.

His eyes feel scratchy. He didn't get any sleep last night, as he knows nobody did. He'd tracked down the CCTV, scrolling through the footage from outside the garage, but the body had been placed in a blind spot. They couldn't see who had dumped it.

He only knew that when he left Jess, it hadn't been there. And when he got back, it had. And Jess had looked at him, questions in her eyes.

He wants to see her. He needs to explain where he went, but the shame burns too strongly. She thinks he's someone he's not. She thinks he's strong, good. Someone worthy of loving. It's a nice feeling. He doesn't want to destroy that just yet.

SOCO ran the scene all night. And as the sun came up, the remains were taken away. And he came straight here.

He's standing at the back of the group, and his gaze shifts around the crowd. One of the other DCs is taking photographs, ensuring they capture all attendees on film. Next to him, Shenton seems anxious.

"Stop fidgeting," he hisses, and Shenton stops moving, grasping one of his hands tightly in the other.

There's a lot riding on this plan, Griffin thinks—he's right to be nervous. A new corpse. Nothing back from the cryptographer about the message. No fingerprints on the note, no DNA on the envelope. And they got the lab reports back from the Dahmer apartment that morning—the only evidence belonged to Michael Sharp.

As time passes, the more Griffin's afraid. For Jess. For his sister.

Could the Echo Man be here? Could Shenton be right?

There's Libby's parents and her brother. The detectives from the investigation are scattered throughout the group. There are people Griffin doesn't recognize, their faces downcast, some of them crying. Griffin knows they must be Libby's friends, her colleagues. Something inside him assumes he'd recognize a killer, that he'd see someone and a switch would be flipped. A sudden flicker of eye contact, and he'd know it was the man from that terrible night. But he feels nothing when he looks at these people.

He feels the familiar flash of failure in himself. The self-loathing that even he, a detective, can't find the man that murdered his own wife. What point are all these years of experience if he can't recognize the one man that matters the most?

His eyes continue to take in the crowd. Deakin is on the far side with Roo. He remembers Roo knew Libby too. He wonders how much Cara has told her husband and whether he believes this memorial is real. He wonders if Cara has spoken to him about the affair.

Deakin mutters a comment to Roo, and he nods in reply. Noah's face is slightly swollen on the left side where Griffin hit him, black and green bruises starting to show in the red butterfly stitches across his eyebrow. Deakin looks miserable. But then, Griffin thinks, he doesn't think he's ever seen his sister's partner crack a smile when she's not around. He fucking hates that guy. He sees Deakin watching Cara, as she introduces someone else to speak at the front.

Not for the first time does he wonder whether Noah Deakin holds a candle for his sister, hoping one day their professional partnership will turn personal. Cara has better taste than that though, he thinks. And up until this week he would have believed that Roo, dressed today in a smart suit and tie, was a much better match for her. But even the good guys can let you down, he notes cynically.

The memorial is coming to an end, Cara thanking Libby's father for his speech. Griffin looks across to the detective with the camera and tilts his head to one side. Did you get it all? he's asking. The DC gives a small nod.

A new arrival on the edge of the group catches Griffin's eye. He's wearing a smart black coat, the collar pulled up, and he's staring at Griffin. The man raises a hand slightly and Griffin recognizes him. It's Nav.

He walks over. Nav pulls a piece of paper from his pocket and holds it out.

"What's this?" Griffin asks.

"Jess called me, she said you'd be here. She said you needed this."

Griffin takes the piece of paper and looks at it.

"This is a prescription for co-codamol."

"It's the best I can do."

"I'm on oxy, Nav. This will barely touch the sides."

"So go to your own doctor, Griffin." Nav puts his hands back in his pockets and goes to walk away. Griffin reaches out and grabs his arm; Nav pulls away from him angrily.

"Listen," Nav growls. "I'm only here for Jess. I don't know you."

Griffin catches the look on Nav's face.

"So that's it," he says slowly. "It's not that you don't like me; it's that you're jealous." Nav glares at him. "You waited years, and now the husband's finally out of the way, you're pissed you missed your chance."

Nav takes a step forward toward him. "I was Patrick's friend too," he hisses.

"Were you though?" Griffin mocks. "Really? Or were you just biding your time until Jess saw the error of her ways?"

Nav glares at him. "You're not good enough for her. She knows that."

"Maybe that's true, doctor boy. But I'm the one she's fucking."

Griffin puts the last crass word in deliberately. He's desperate for a fight. He wants Nav to punch him, to inflict a bit of deserved pain. He sees the anger cross Nav's face. He knows he's got to him, and Griffin tenses, but Nav turns on his heel and strides away without comment.

"Who was that?"

Cara's standing next to him.

"Don't worry, he's not important," Griffin mutters. "You were good today," he says, forcing his voice to sound positive.

"Yes, well, we'll see. Let's hope our man showed."

She turns and starts to walk back to the car. He follows her. As he walks, he looks at the prescription in his hand, then crumples it into a ball. He can feel his hands start to shake, the agitation in his body. He knows he only has two doses left. He knows soon he'll be in pain, his back in crippling agony. And he has no idea what he's going to do about it.

58

THEY'RE RIGHT. HE's there, watching. And he blends in among the smart suits, the black, the downcast faces.

He forces his expression to remain unhappy. Corners of his mouth turned down, head toward the grass. At one point he even manages a tear—he's proud of that. He's learned to copy emotions, to mimic the feelings of others, a necessary evil to keep plodding through the tedium of his life.

The man at the front of the group starts crying, shoulders shaking. Libby's father, he remembers from the introduction. How much more upset would he be, he wonders, if he knew how his daughter died. If he knew the look of fear that passed across Libby's face when he showed her the gun. The few seconds he allowed her to run before he started shooting. The stirring in his groin as the bullet tore through her flesh, as she fell to the ground, her hands reaching out in the mud in those last desperate moments.

How he sat in the car after, closed his eyes, and masturbated, remembering her death.

He was nine when he first realized what got him going. He'd seen the erect penises of his father and uncle. He'd seen the ecstatic looks on their faces, experienced firsthand with his small, fragile body, how they got their rocks off. And he'd wondered, how can I be normal if I don't enjoy this? He'd sneaked in and looked at their porn stash, risking a beating to flick through the pages of naked women, naked men, fucking, penetrating, bodies writhing in pleasure, and he'd felt nothing.

But then, he knew.

He'd stolen a knife from the kitchen, weighed it up in his hand, and crept upstairs. He'd waited in the hallway and peered through the open doors, bedrooms side by side. They'd been sleeping—the heavy drunken slumber of men who had satisfied themselves at his expense—and he'd gone into his uncle's room. He'd stood at the end of the bed, knife in hand, and for the first time he'd felt himself grow hard. He'd touched his penis through his powder-blue dinosaur pajamas. So this was what it was like.

He'd killed his uncle first. Thrusting the knife into his chest, over and over, blood spattering up the walls, covering him from top to toe. The man barely had a chance to wake up. He'd gone into his father's room next and done the same.

Then he'd reached down, and picked up his father's flaccid penis between two fingers. With three strokes of the knife, he'd sawed through, exerting little more effort than he'd need to cut through gristle connecting raw sausages. He'd discarded it on the floor, and as his father opened his eyes, gurgling incomprehensible noises as his chest collapsed, he knew.

He'd felt the sticky warm blood coating his chest, the metallic iron tang in his mouth, and he'd held his own penis in his hand. It didn't take long—the murders had been more than he'd needed, and with a few quick strokes he was ejaculating. Cum across the bed, across his father's dead, mutilated body.

That had been the beginning. But this? This "memorial"? This sham?

This is not the end. That will come soon. A date that's been forever lodged in his mind, that will shortly be marked by something else. Something impressive. Magnificent. Something that will haunt them all for the rest of their lives.

If they survive.

59

EVERYTHING IS A puzzle. They are studying the photographs from the memorial, painstakingly trying to identify every face in the crowd. Shenton is working on the cipher again.

"Any luck?" Cara asks him, and he frowns.

"I hate to say this," he mutters, "but I'm starting to think it's not possible to crack. After all, some of the original ciphers from the Zodiac Killer were never decoded."

Cara stares at him. A thousand swear words filter through her mind, but she somehow doesn't say any of them.

"Did you hear back about the handwriting?" Shenton asks in the face of her silence.

She nods. "The expert thinks left-handed. And distinctive enough to compare if we get any suspects."

"You know the Zodiac Killer was thought to be ambidextrous," Shenton says, off-hand. "So any handwriting analysis might not work."

Cara grits her teeth. He's just trying to be helpful, she tells herself. Don't take this nightmare situation out on him.

She moves away from Shenton before she says something she'll regret, and goes over to the whiteboard. She stares at the rows of victims, the woman found outside Griffin's apartment added to the grim lineup. Dr. Ross has given his view. Cause of death: electrocution. That, and contributory factors from starvation, dehydration, sexual assault, torture, and blunt force trauma. He guesses she was held against her will for about a week. "Gary Heidnik," Shenton had muttered, allocating a serial killer to the murder.

She picks up the lab report received that morning. Libby had a blood alcohol level in line with the few drinks they knew she'd consumed in the bar. Michael Sharp had a long list of drugs in his bloodstream, but again, nothing strange knowing the sort of pharmaceuticals he liked to imbibe.

There were no prints on the gun. No DNA. The only cells under Libby's fingernails were her own. No foreign saliva. The material sent to the newspaper with the cipher was confirmed to have traces of Libby's blood, and a matching hole was found in her dress. But nothing else.

It's been the same, all along.

"Come on," she mutters under her breath. "Make a mistake."

But she knows that might mean another murder. And how could she wish for something so evil? Even if they could catch the guy.

She looks at the names of the victims across the top of the board. Lisa Kershaw. Daria Capshaw. Sarah Jackman. Marisa Perez. Ann Lees. Elizabeth Roberts. Michael Sharp. Multiple people they haven't yet been able to identify. And Mia Griffin.

Cara resolves that once this is over, once the Echo Man is caught and behind bars, she will make sure these are the names that are remembered. These were all someone's daughter, father, brother, wife. These are the people that matter.

She taps a finger on Libby's photo, then one on Mia's. "I'll find this guy," she mutters to herself. "For you."

Then Cara wonders about Libby's phone and laptop. She takes a long breath in and out. I need a change of scene, she thinks, and leaves, walking down the five flights of stairs to the basement.

*   *   *

The digital lab requested their offices were sited down here. It was the place nobody else wanted, with the lack of natural light, the distance from the canteen. But that must be what they like about it, Cara thinks, the automatic lights flicking on as she walks down the corridor.

The room seems in darkness as she comes to the door at the end. She tries the handle, but it's locked. There's a doorbell to the right, and she presses it.

After a minute, a hiss announces someone listening.

"DCI Elliott," she says to the intercom.

A buzz indicates she's allowed inside, and she pushes the door open.

The room is dimly lit. On one side, shelves of equipment dominate, wires falling haphazardly out of their boxes, some littering the floor. There are rows of computers, a gentle glow coming from one in front of her.

"Hello?" she calls.

A face pops out from behind the monitor. The man smiles.

"How can I help?"

His appearance and friendly manner disarms her. He's good-looking, with a trendy haircut and nice eyes behind his glasses.

"DCI Cara Elliott," she repeats. "I was wondering how you were getting on with the laptop and phone."

"So you came down here?" he says.

"You don't get many visitors?"

"None." He reaches across and pulls a chair over to his computer. "Come and join me, I'll look. Charlie Mills," he says, holding out his hand.

"You're Charlie Mills?" she replies, shaking it. She can hardly reconcile this guy with the name she's seen signing off any number of completely incomprehensible reports that have passed her desk over the years. She expected someone monosyllabic, maybe balding, slightly overweight.

He laughs. "Don't worry, I'm used to it. Come back when it's not curry day in the canteen and meet my team. They'll conform to your expectations. What's the case number?"

Cara reels it off and he types it into the computer. He pulls up a report, then glances across at her.

"Says here we sent you this yesterday."

"Oh." Cara feels stupid. "Who did you send it to?"

He says the name of the mailbox and Cara frowns. It's the joint one, used for unimportant information rather than urgent reports of this kind.

"Okay, well," she mutters. It's a bit of a worry. "Can you tell me what it said? While I'm here?"

"Would love to," Charlie replies with a grin. Cara wonders if he's flirting with her, then dismisses it. He must be, what, early thirties? She's sure he's got better people to smile at than a married mother of two.

Charlie scrolls down the page, his eyes flicking over the text. "Says here the laptop didn't come up with anything useful. Didn't do much on it except social media, personal photographs, and emails."

"Anything in the emails?"

"You can take it away and check for yourself if you like, but nothing my guy seemed to think was suspicious. Oh, but this—this is more important."

Cara stares at him as he recites a long list of names that sound like gobbledygook. He laughs at her blank look.

"Illegally uploaded spyware and viruses," he clarifies. "It means that if she was using her computer, someone could see what she was doing. And monitor her keystrokes."

"So they would know her passwords?"

"Exactly." Charlie's face is suddenly serious. "Luckily, she never brought her work home, but everything else, well. This guy knew."

"Any way of working out who?"

He shakes his head. "Afraid not. Looks like my techie did a bit of digging, but they were all dead ends. Plus here." He points at the screen. "He was able to watch her through the webcam."

Cara shudders. The thought of the guy watching Libby's every move? It's terrifying. No wonder he knew how to tailor the Tinder profile to appeal to her.

"What about her mobile?" Cara asks.

She watches as he reads the next report. "Nothing of note, I'm afraid. Although we did do a bit of work on that dating profile she was connected with." He reads on. "There's even a set of geographic coordinates for one of the messages he sent."

"You have a location?" Cara's excited. This could be the lead they need.

"Wait a sec, they forgot to run it back . . ." Charlie types for a bit, then frowns. "That can't be right," he mutters, typing again.

"What?"

Charlie turns to her, a shocked expression on his face. "The location," he starts. "It comes back to here."

"What do you mean?"

"It comes back to the nick. This message was sent from within the walls of this police station."

60

CARA WALKS BACK to the incident room, her head spinning. The room is busy, detectives working behind their desks, some chatting, others silent. There's Deakin, head down, reviewing reports, Griffin with one of the DCs. She looks at them all and she wonders: Is it you?

She sits down at her computer and clicks on the group mailbox. There are a few messages in there, and she scrolls down, looking for the email from the digital team. She can't see it, so she runs a search through all the folders. Still nothing.

Has someone deleted it, wanting to hide the evidence of what they'd done? Has the killer realized he'd made a mistake?

Deakin comes over and she quickly clicks away.

"Listen, we had a thought, about the letter," he says, and she looks up at him. "Are you okay?" he adds. "You look pale?"

"I'm fine," she mutters. But she needs to tell someone. "Sit down," she whispers, and he does, his face puzzled. "I've just been with the digital lab. They said there was spyware on Libby's computer."

"Someone was watching her?" Deakin says, and she nods.

"But that's not all. They said that one of the messages on the man's profile on Tinder was sent from here."

"Here?" Deakin looks up, glancing around. "You mean, from the incident room?"

"Not necessarily. From the police station."

"What? So our guy is a cop?"

Cara sees Deakin's expression. It's astonishment, disbelief. The same feelings she knows she has on her own face.

"Could be. Like Toby said. Or a civilian—someone from Control or admin. Or any number of people working out of this building."

"But they couldn't narrow it down any more than that?"

"No. They just needed to be here when they sent that message. And this stays between us, right?" Deakin nods quickly. She sighs. "What were you going to ask me?"

"Oh. So we want to get someone to have a closer look at the paper the note is written on. There are no fingerprints, but I read that specialized machines can detect if there are tiny indentations we can't see with the naked eye. If this page came from a notebook, we might be able to make out things he had written down before."

Cara nods. "ESDA. Electrostatic detection, yes. They can find secondary impressions on the paper," she adds, annoyed she hadn't thought of it herself.

"But it's expensive. We need you to ask Marsh for the budget."

"No problem, okay," Cara replies. He'll have to say yes after yesterday's conversation, surely. "How's the face?" Deakin's hand goes up to the bruise. She reaches over and he allows her to gently push the corner of one of the bits of tape back down with the tip of her finger. He cringes slightly. "Does it hurt?"

"Not really. Just worried it's going to damage my rugged good looks," he adds with a lopsided smile.

"Will you put in a formal complaint?"

Noah sighs. "I can't be bothered, Cara. I probably deserved it. And besides, he seems to be looking worse than me."

Cara looks across the office to where Griffin is sitting. He's straight in his seat, his face tense. They all look shit right now, but Noah's right: he's not well.

"He seems ill," Deakin adds. "I think he needs to go home."

"Thanks. I'll talk to him." Deakin stands up, but she grabs his hand before he goes. He turns. "Really, Noah. Thank you."

He smiles and leaves, and she follows him out into the office, going across to Griffin. Up close he seems even worse. There is a fine sheen of sweat on his forehead, and his face is almost yellow.

"Nate, are you okay?" she asks, and he looks up suddenly.

He hesitates. "I'm fine."

"You're not fine. You're ill. Go home if you need to."

He runs his hand across his forehead. She notices he's shivering. "Yes, I think I will," he says quietly.

"Do you want me to drive you?"

He shakes his head quickly. "No, no. They need you here."

She watches as he stands, picks up his bag, and leaves. He's walking slowly, as if putting one foot in front of the other needs all his concentration. She thinks about following him, forcing someone to take him, but she knows he'll hate the intrusion. Just the fact he's agreed to leave of his own accord is enough.

She stands outside her office, at the edge of the incident room. Watching the team, all hard at work. The detectives behind the rows of computers, still examining CCTV. The analysts scrolling through data. The inquiry officers, following up on every tip from the public, however unlikely, however crazy.

Cara thinks about what the digital lab found. About the Tinder account.

She watches them all. And again, she thinks, Is it you?

Is it you?

CHAPTER

61

Now this is a nice house. He looks up at the row of windows, the bright red front door, then walks the last few feet up the gravel driveway. Her car is here, and he knows she's alone.

He's been watching her. And she's just right. This is it. He's ready. He takes a deep breath and rings the bell. The door opens.

The first blow with his fist sends her backward, blood spouting from her nose. The second on the mouth, knocks her to the floor, arms windmilling. He hears her jaw crack, he sees her eyes widen in pain. He walks into the hallway after her, and she pushes frantically away, her hands struggling to get purchase, her shoes squeaking on the tiled surface. He leans down and hits her again—knuckles breaking her eye socket, a second on the side of her head.

She looks dazed. He hears her try to say something through her mangled lips, blood and dribble running down her chin. He stands over her, savoring the moment. He knows what he's going to do.

He grabs her by the top of her arm, pulling her up and ripping her shirt open. Buttons ping off and bounce on the floor; stitches rip as he wrenches it clear of her body. Her bra is pink and lacy and delicate—he grabs it by the front and uses it to drag her further into the house, offering him little resistance as he tears it off forcefully, searing her skin.

The woman's still struggling. She has fight in her. He likes that. He places a few well-aimed kicks in her stomach, feels a crack as ribs break, and she doubles over, then vomits violently. He rolls her over onto her front, facedown, then reaches into his pocket and takes out a length of cord. He wraps it around her neck, crossing it over, then pulling, his knee on the middle of her back. She gurgles, he sees her eyes roll back in her head. But he lets go. Not too hard, he thinks. Not yet.

Skirt next, then tights. Matching underwear, nice. This bitch knows how to take care of herself. They tear into shreds as he drags them down her legs. He smells sweat and urine. Shoes have gone already in the struggle, lying on their side in a puddle of blood.

He can feel his heart beating faster. He's hard with anticipation. He stands over her prostrate naked body, fingering himself lightly through his jeans. He looks at her bare skin, bruises starting to show, at her juicy cunt, the tight ass he knows is waiting for him.

She's just looking over her shoulder, the last vestiges of consciousness still flickering.

He looks back at the open front door, to the empty street beyond. He pushes the door with his foot, and as he does so, he sees the hope ebb away from her eyes.

It closes with a click. He doesn't want to be disturbed. He wants to make this one last, remember every detail.

Because this is it.

The beginning of the end.

62

GRIFFIN ALMOST FALLS as he staggers through the door, and Jess guides him to the bed. He lies down with a thud. She can see the pain, clear on his face.

"This is ridiculous, Griffin. Take something."

"I've only got one left."

She goes to his bag and pulls out the packet. Sure enough, there's one lonely capsule. She pushes it out of the foil and gives it to him with a glass of water.

"Take it," she demands. He levers himself up slowly on one elbow and swallows the drug, then slumps back down on the bed. "Did you see Nav?"

He frowns. "He gave me a prescription for co-codamol. It's useless."

"This is ridiculous," Jess exclaims. "I'm calling him again."

"He won't help me," Griffin says.

Something in his voice makes Jess turn, his mobile in her hand. "What did you say to him?" Griffin's face clouds. "What did you say?"

"We had an exchange of views. It doesn't matter."

"Look at you! It does matter."

She turns away from him and dials Nav's number. After a few rings he answers, his voice sharp.

"What?"

"Nav, you need to help Griffin," Jess says.

"He doesn't want my help."

"Oxy, Nav. Not whatever shit you offered him."

"Oxycodone is a controlled drug, Jess. He's not my patient. Tell him to go to his doctor. Go to the emergency room. Anything."

"He says you had an argument." There's silence at the end of the phone. "What did he say, Nav?"

Another pause. "It's not important. It's not because of that."

Nav sounds upset, flustered, but Jess hasn't got time for that now. She moves away from the bed so Griffin can't hear her. "Look," she says. "I know he's an asshole. I know he can be difficult. But he's been through a lot. Please, Nav? For me?"

There's silence again, then Jess hears Nav grunt. "Fine. I'll come over when I've finished here. And Jess?"

"Yes?"

"Alice gets out of the hospital in a few hours."

The wave of emotion catches Jess by surprise.

"She's better?" she manages to croak.

"Well enough. She's going to stay with your parents. She was asking about you and Patrick."

Jess can't bring herself to talk.

"You need to end this, Jess," Nav continues. "For Alice's sake. You need to hand yourself in to the police. Then they'll let you see her. Alice needs her mom."

"Just bring the prescription for Griffin. Thank you," Jess mutters, then hangs up.

She waits for a moment, a lump in her throat, forcing it back down. Then she goes and joins Griffin on the bed, lying next to him. His eyes are closed.

"Nav's bringing a prescription over later."

"For oxy?"

"Yes."

"Thank you," he says quietly. He opens his eyes slightly and looks at her. "I'm not an asshole."

Jess smiles. "Then stop acting like one, Griffin."

He nods, then winces. She reaches over and takes his hand, winding her fingers around his.

They lie like that for a while. Jess listens to his breathing. She hears the cars on the road. Conversation coming from the garage forecourt outside.

"Alice is coming out of the hospital today," she says quietly.

Griffin doesn't reply. She wonders if he's asleep.

"I want to go and see her."

"You should," he mumbles.

"What if there are police there? I should stay with you."

"I'll be fine. You know what to look out for. Take the Land Rover. Borrow one of my credit cards in case you need money. And if you see anyone odd, just drive away." He opens his eyes, his focus hazy, then indicates toward the bedside table. "Bottom drawer."

He doesn't elaborate, and she leans down to open it. Then she stops. Inside is a gray cotton sweater, an embroidered logo of a rainbow on the front. It's soft, and smells clean and well looked after.

"You need something else to wear," Griffin mutters.

Jess looks down at her top—the same sweater Nav had bought her all those days ago. She's been washing it when she can, but Griffin's right; it's stained and dirty from nearly a week's constant use.

"I can't take this—" she begins, but he interrupts her.

"Please. She'd have wanted you to have it."

"I don't know how I'll ever be able to repay you for all of this, Nate." Jess holds the sweater tenderly, looking at him. He's closed his eyes again, lying back on the pillow. "For keeping me safe, for looking after me."

He opens one eye briefly. "Just write me an IOU," he says quietly. "Services rendered for a damsel in distress."

She reaches over and takes his hand again, squeezing it softly. He returns the gesture. Then she sits up on the bed, getting changed quickly and putting her shoes on. The sweater is slightly too big, but it's warm and clean and she takes comfort from it being a part of him. She leans over, kissing him softly on the lips.

"I'll be as quick as I can. Thank you, Nate."

She's almost out the door when she hears his voice again.

"Jess?"

"Hmm?" She turns. He's pulled himself up slightly, looking at her. "You called me Nate."

"Do you mind?"

He lies back down on the bed. "No."

She smiles, and picks up the keys to the Land Rover.

*   *   *

The truck starts without a hitch, and Jess takes it as a good sign. She drives across town and parks a few rows down from her parents' house. She knows which way they'll come from if they're driving from the hospital, but she has no idea when. Nav had said a few hours, so she settles herself down in the seat for a wait.

She scans the other cars parked in the road, but there's nobody nearby. After all this time, there's no way she's handing herself in to the police. Griffin's working on the investigation. They'll find something. They'll find this killer, and then they'll know she had nothing to do with Patrick's death.

The fire seems a distant memory. Her recollection of Patrick is hazy, like a surreal dream. It's still too much for her to come to terms with—that her husband is dead. Her life with Griffin feels, not normal, but—Jess isn't sure.

She thinks about Griffin, lying in pain back at the apartment. She can't comprehend what that's like, to suffer in that way, and for the first time she considers her condition as a blessing rather than a curse. Griffin seems like such an immovable force, to see him taken down so completely is sobering.

Sitting in the old Land Rover reminds her of him. It smells of cigarettes; there is mess strewn around. For the first time she wonders about his wife—the woman who used to wear this sweater. And what he was like as a husband.

The day is drawing to a close, and the street lights blink into life. A few cars come down the road but don't stop.

Then, at last, she sees her Mom's Nissan Note come toward her and turn into the drive. She watches as the car is parked, and the headlights turn off. Her mother gets out of the car and opens the door at the back. Then—there she is. Alice is chattering away happily; her hair is loose and cascades around her face.

Jess instantly relaxes. Her daughter is here, and she is fine. She puts her hand on the door to open it; then something makes her pause. Out of the corner of her eye, she sees a white hatchback drive slowly down the road. It stops a few cars down from Jess and turns its headlights off, but nobody gets out. She can see a woman sitting in the front.

Every muscle in Jess's body wants to get out of the car. She wants to go to her daughter, to hold her in her arms, but instinctively she knows that this car is police. She knows she can't move.

She starts to cry as she turns the ignition key to the Land Rover. She takes one last look at her daughter. The front door to her parents' house is open, and her mother is ushering Alice inside. She's safe. She's happy. She's well. That's all that matters, Jess tells herself as she pulls out of the parking space.

She drives away from the house, looking in her rearview mirror as she goes. The white hatchback isn't following her. She's alone.

She wants to get back to Griffin. The absence of her daughter is a heavy weight, but with a weird jolt, she realizes how much she needs to be back with him. That being next to Griffin will ease that sadness slightly, and she drives quickly through the dark streets.

She sees the garage ahead and pulls the Land Rover back into its parking space, then climbs out. The garage is closed now, the lights in the office turned off; she looks toward the one basement window. It's strange—it's dark there too. She wonders if Nav has been. Perhaps Griffin is asleep, lulled into slumber with the arrival of new pharmaceuticals.

She pushes open the unwieldy metal door and goes down the stairs. She puts the key in the lock and opens the door. It's dark and she stops, letting her eyes adjust. She looks toward the bed. It's empty. Griffin's not there.

She frowns, worried. He can't have gone out. She has his keys, his car. She takes a step forward, but her foot catches on something on the floor. She looks down. There's a lump in front of her, something in the dark.

She takes a quick breath in and grasps around for the light. The sudden brightness dazzles, but she knows.

She falls to her knees next to him, shouting his name.

Griffin's lying on his side, his head at an angle. It looks as if he was trying to get to the door. She shakes his body, trying to wake him, but he doesn't move. She panics, her brain racing to remember even the slightest bit of basic first aid. She shakes him again, then rolls him onto his back. She leans next to his mouth. His breathing is labored, his heart rate slow, but he's alive.

She picks up the phone on the table and dials 999.

"Ambulance," she gasps. She's put through, and a voice asks her name, where she is. She gives the address but then stops. Her name. She tells them who she is, and she'll be arrested. She's called the ambulance; she should leave, run now. But she can't leave Griffin. She can't.

"Jessica Ambrose," she says. "Please come quickly."

The operator asks her about the patient.

"Nate Griffin. He's unconscious, barely breathing."

Jess crouches next to him. Then she notices it. Written in the dust next to his hand are what look like letters. She squints. They're shaky, but she can make out a few. *S H I.* She turns her head, trying to read them the right way around. *P M.*

She takes a sudden breath. She knows. She knows what Griffin was trying to tell her.

"Diamorphine," Jess shouts down the phone. "He's had an overdose of diamorphine."

"Stay on the line," the operator says. "The ambulance is on its way."

Jess slumps back on the floor, sitting next to Griffin, the phone clutched in one shaking hand, his hand gripped in the other.

"Shipman," she whispers to herself. "Harold Shipman."

PART 3

63

THE PARAMEDICS ARRIVE, pushing through the open door, and Jess moves backward out of their way. They're a mass of movement around Griffin, relaying messages to each other, putting a mask over his face, pushing air into his lungs.

Jess is stunned to see Griffin like this: unconscious, close to death. A uniformed cop appears by her side. She's ready for the arrest, but he's oblivious, asking her questions about what happened.

"My friend Nav was supposed to come over," she gabbles. "I don't know if he did."

"Full name?" the policeman asks, notepad poised in his hand.

"Dr. Navin Sharma—he works in oncology at the General. He might still be on shift."

He makes a note, then looks up as a woman comes into the room. Her face is stern, eyes locked on Jess. She recognizes her: it's the detective from the hospital.

The woman moves forward, blocking her exit.

"Jessica Ambrose." The detective gets straight to the point. "I am arresting you on suspicion of the murder of Patrick Ambrose on Monday the twenty-fifth of January." The uniformed cop backs off, confused. The detective jerks Jess's hands away from her sides, fastening cuffs in front of her. "You do not have to say anything. But it may harm your defense if you do not mention when questioned something that you later rely on in court. Anything you do say may be given in evidence."

She pulls her away, out the door and up the metal stairs, away from Griffin, but Jess resists.

"Please," she pleads. "Just let me know that Nate's okay."

One of the paramedics goes to push past them on the stairs, and the detective gets his attention.

"How is he?" she asks.

He pauses. "We've given him an intramuscular dose of Naloxone. He's responded well, so we haven't needed to intubate," he says. "We'll take him in shortly. They'll probably follow up with an IV at the hospital."

"So he's going to be all right?" Jess asks in a rush.

The paramedic nods. "Looks that way." He looks to the detective. "He doesn't have the hallmarks of your usual intravenous drug user, although we found a needle mark on his forearm."

"He's not," Jess blurts out. "He didn't do this to himself. The floor . . ." she tries, desperate to make them listen. "He knew . . ."

The paramedic gives her an apathetic look and carries on his way to get something from the ambulance.

The detective pulls on Jess's hands, and they follow on up the stairs and out into the parking lot, where a police car awaits. As they go, Jess remembers back to where Griffin had been lying. The letters on the floor had been obliterated, scuffed out by the paramedic's shoes.

64

WHEN NOAH APPEARS in the doorway of her office, she knows from the look on his face that it's bad. But Nate? She almost can't believe that her strong, no-nonsense brother has been attacked again.

"The hospital says he's going to be fine," he adds quickly. "But I'll get your car, we'll go and see him now."

Cara grabs her coat and they rush out of the station. But before they get on the road, Cara stops him. She puts a hand on his arm, and Deakin looks at her.

"Noah," Cara says. She's forcing herself to speak slowly, her whole body in panic mode. "I need you to do me a favor. Something I only trust you to do."

He sees her expression and looks worried. "Anything."

* * *

"You're kidding me. We can't just up and leave!"

Cara stands in front of her husband at the restaurant, Deakin hovering in the background.

"Roo, listen to me. Someone tried to kill Griffin. I can't have you or the kids put at risk."

Roo gestures around the kitchen. "I have a lunch service to run. I have—"

"Screw the lunch service!" Cara shouts. "I'm not asking you, I am telling you—you need to take your car and go with Noah. Pick the kids up from school and head to the lodge. You'll be safe there."

"For how long?" he asks, stunned.

"Until this is over."

"Until . . ." His voice trails off. "This is absurd," he mutters, but Cara knows he'll do as she asks. "I'll call Lauren. I'll get her to pack the kids' things."

Cara shakes her head. "No. Not with Lauren," she adds quietly.

Roo stares at her.

"I know, Roo," Cara says. She's aware her voice is wobbling; she can't fall apart now. "I know what you've been doing. Together."

He stops. She notices his cheeks color slightly. "I haven't . . ." he starts, but she can tell by the tone of his voice that she's right. "But we can't leave her here," he manages to stutter. "If we're in danger, then so is she."

"She's not going with you."

Cara turns away.

"But Cara . . ." Roo starts.

"Do *not* fuck with me!" Cara's shaking, she's so angry. "My brother is in the hospital, there's an insane serial killer on the loose, and you want to take your mistress to our holiday lodge after having an affair under my nose for the past God knows how long?" She's shouting, knowing she's getting looks from the other chefs in the kitchen, but not caring. "Roo, get your stuff and go with Noah. Now!"

She walks out the back door of the kitchen and stands next to her husband's car. She's crying now, big snotty tears, and she angrily wipes them away with her sleeve.

Deakin appears by her side. She glances at him and he hands her a tissue.

"I'm sorry, Noah. This isn't fair on you."

"It's fine. Really. I'll take them to the lodge and get back as soon as I can. Listen, Cara?"

Noah looks uncomfortable, his hands shoved in his pockets.

"Yes?"

He goes to say something but then notices Roo coming toward them.

"It doesn't matter," Noah mumbles.

The two of them get into the car, and her husband winds down the window.

"Call me when you have the kids," she says, and Roo nods.

Once the car turns the corner, out of sight, Cara instantly feels better. Her family will be safe; that's all that matters for now. She'll deal with the shit between Roo and Lauren later.

A waiter rushes out of the kitchen, a mobile clutched in his hand. "Chef!" he calls down the deserted road. But it's too late. "He's forgotten his phone," he says.

"I'll take it," Cara replies, and he passes it across. She'll give it back to him later. There's no reception at the lodge anyway.

But as she gets back into her own car, throwing her husband's phone on the passenger seat, she remembers Deakin and wonders what he was about to say. She shakes her head. It can't have been that important.

It can wait, she tells herself. It'll have to wait.

She needs to go to the hospital, see her brother, make sure he's okay.

Then she has a serial killer to catch.

65

THE DETECTIVE SAYS nothing during the ride in the police car. They arrive at the station, and Jess is escorted to custody. The handcuffs are taken off. Jess nods at the right points, signs the pieces of paper when she's told to. She shakes her head when she's asked if she wants a lawyer.

She's shown into a cell. She sits down on the blue plastic-covered mattress. The door is closed with a metallic bang.

There's muffled shouting from the cell next door. She's aware of people coming and going in the corridor, but she doesn't move.

Now that she's here, now she's been arrested for her husband's murder, she feels numb. She doesn't feel the fear she expected. Suddenly, she's been swept along in a sea of inevitability, all decisions made for her. She thinks about Griffin, in the ambulance on the way to the hospital. She thinks about Alice.

She lies back on the crinkly plastic bed. She puts the blanket behind her head and closes her eyes, hoping that at least now she can see her daughter.

* * *

Jess is woken by the sound of the door opening. A man calls her name and beckons for her to follow him.

"It's time," he says, escorting her down a corridor and into an interview room. The detective is waiting; she points to the chair opposite. Jess sits down.

The woman detective introduces herself, then reads the caution again. DS Taylor, Jess remembers now.

"And you're turning down your right to free independent legal advice?" Taylor says.

"Yes," Jess replies. She knows it's not sensible to refuse a lawyer, but her self-destructive urge has kicked back in. Charge me with his murder, she thinks, just do something to punish me for what happens to the people I love. They end up injured or dead. First Patrick and Alice, now Griffin. "Can I see my daughter?" she asks.

"All in good time." Taylor looks at her notes. "You tell me what I need to know, and maybe we can sort something out. Now, please talk me through the events of the night of Monday, the twenty-fifth of January, when your house caught fire."

Jess opens her mouth to talk, but a knock disturbs them.

"Interview paused, seventeen forty-six." Taylor sighs and gets up to open the door.

There's a woman on the other side. She's tall, dark hair, dressed in a smart shirt and black jeans. Jess knows exactly who this is. Griffin's sister, Cara Elliott. It feels strange her being so close, like seeing a celebrity in the flesh. Elliott says something to Taylor, and Jess hears her swear.

"What do you mean, you need her?" Jess hears Taylor say.

Elliott says something else. Taylor looks furious but mutters, "Yes, boss."

Cara stares at Jess, then tilts her head toward the exit. "Come with me, please?"

Taylor watches, glum faced, as Jess leaves. Jess walks wordlessly down the corridor, into a different interview room. The DCI closes the door behind them but makes no attempt to sit down.

"Jessica, I'm Detective Chief Inspector Elliott," she says.

"How is Griffin?" Jess asks. "Please?"

DCI Elliott smiles. "He's doing fine, awake and talking in the hospital. Thank you for calling the ambulance," she says. "You saved his life."

"He saved mine," Jess replies. "Can I see him?"

"No, I'm sorry." The detective's face turns serious again. "I need you to help us. We have Dr. Sharma in custody."

"Nav? Why?" Jess stutters.

"We've arrested him for attempted murder."

"What?" Jess can't believe what she's hearing. Why would Nav want to kill Griffin? "You must have the wrong person. He's a doctor, he saves lives."

Elliott frowns. "We turned up at the hospital to interview him, and he confessed straight away. Says he's prepared to make a full statement."

"To what? What does he say he did?"

"He persuaded Griffin to let him inject him with a painkiller, then used a potentially lethal amount of diamorphine. But he wants to speak to you first. Alone."

Jess's legs feel weak. She leans against the wall.

"What does he want to say to me?" she whispers.

"That's what we'd like to know. It's against protocol, but we think he knows something. Something that might help us find the Echo Man."

Jess's head snaps up. "He's not involved with that."

"Really, Jessica?" Elliott says. "This guy tries to kill my brother in exactly the same way as Britain's most prolific serial killer, and you don't think it's connected?"

Jess shakes her head over and over again. "He's not. He can't be." Not him. Not Nav.

DCI Elliott opens the door. Jess can see determination on her face. It reminds her of Griffin.

"Let's go see, shall we?" the detective says.

66

J ESS LOOKS THROUGH the small window in the door. She can just see Nav slumped at the table. He's wearing a gray tracksuit, a light blue blanket draped around his shoulders. His hands are handcuffed in front of him, his head is bent.

She looks at DCI Elliott, standing next to her.

"What should I do?" Jess asks.

"Let him lead the conversation. He's asked to see you, so there must be something he wants to say. But there's no way I'm letting you in there without listening to your conversation—your every move will be taped, every word recorded. Understand?"

Jess nods. Elliott opens the door and Nav turns, going to stand up when he sees Jess.

"Sit down," DCI Elliott says sternly. "You have ten minutes." And she closes the door behind them.

"Jess, I'm so sorry, I'm so sorry." Nav slumps back into the chair again. He puts his hands over his face and starts to cry, shoulders heaving. Jess reaches over and takes his hand.

He looks up at her. He looks awful. His eyes are red and bloodshot, his face drawn. She grips his hands tightly; they're clammy and hot.

"Nav," Jess says softly. "What happened? They're saying you tried to kill Griffin, but that's not right, is it?"

She has to struggle to keep her emotions in check. She wants to scream at him, shout at him to stop being so stupid, but she has to stay calm. She has to help him.

He shakes his head. "I'm so sorry. He told me I had to."

Jess feels an icy shiver run through her body. "Who told you, Nav?"

Nav looks up, and his eyes fix on the black dome in the corner of the room. "They're recording us?"

"Yes."

He leans forward toward her, lowering his voice to an almost imperceptible murmur. "They can't know, Jess. He said."

"Who?"

"I don't know. I had a note left in my locker. It said he'd be back in touch soon. There was a memory stick with it." He looks down at his hands, crying again. "I plugged it into my computer. It was a video file. It was you, Jess. With a man."

Jess can hardly breathe. The room is stiflingly hot. "What man?" she whispers.

"I don't know, I didn't recognize him. It looked like you were in some restroom somewhere. You were . . ." His voice tails off and he takes a shuddering breath in and out. "You were having sex. The time stamp said it was a week ago."

Jess can't move. Restroom. Some bloke. Someone, somehow, had been filming her, the day of the fire. She feels her skin prickling, her face flushing.

"When did you get this?" Jess manages to ask.

"Today. Then as soon as I finished watching, I got a message. It said that unless I . . ." He's crying again, sniffing back snot and tears as he talks, his voice no more than a whisper. "Unless I killed Griffin, he would give this to the police. He was very specific—he talked about diamorphine. Then you called and I had the excuse I needed. I couldn't have the police having the video. It shows motive, Jess."

"I didn't kill Patrick," Jess mutters, still stunned by what he's saying.

"I know. But that wasn't all. There were . . . There were photos. Of . . . of women." He screws his eyes tightly shut. "Dead women. Murdered. He said he'd do the same to you. That he'd kill you and Alice. That he'd make you suffer. Torture you, rape you . . ."

"So why didn't you call the police? They would have protected me."

He looks at her. "The very people you hate? The people you ran away from in the hospital, leaving your daughter behind, just so they wouldn't arrest you? And he said it wouldn't make any difference. He would still get to you. I—"

"But to kill someone, Nav? To kill Griffin?" Jess cries out.

Nav can't look at her, but he squeezes her hand tightly with both of his. "I love you, Jess. I always have. I'd do anything for you."

"I . . ." There's nothing Jess can say. She did know, deep down, how he felt about her, but her shattered self-esteem never allowed her to believe it. Not really. Someone like Nav, falling for someone like her? But now—this? This is crazy.

"Where's the memory stick now?" she whispers, glancing back at the door.

"Still at work, in my locker. Why—?" Then he realizes. "You can't possibly go and fetch it? Jess, it's too dangerous, this man . . . Promise me, please?"

"I promise. But Nav, you have to tell the police. Tell them everything. Otherwise, they'll charge you with attempted murder. You'll go to jail."

The door opens and DCI Elliott comes back inside.

"Have you said all you need to say, Dr. Sharma?" she asks, her voice cold.

Nav nods. His face crumples and he starts to cry again, sobbing now, his head in his hands, fingers raking at his hair.

Jess wants to hug him, but DCI Elliott pulls her into the corridor. She hands Jess a tissue, and Jess realizes she's crying too.

"What did he say?"

"You tell me. You were listening." But they must have been speaking too quietly, and Elliott is still in the dark.

"Stop playing games, Jessica. What did he tell you?"

"Just what you said," Jess replies. "That he injected Griffin with diamorphine."

"Nothing else?"

"And that he loves me."

DCI Elliott raises an eyebrow. "That's becoming a bit of a problem around here," she mutters under her breath.

Elliott escorts her back to her cell. The door slams shut and Jess stares at it, Nav's words running around in her head. She'd promised him, but she knows there's no way she's going to leave that evidence out there. The proof that Nav was blackmailed to attack Griffin.

And a motive for killing her husband. Something she knows DS Taylor will twist and mold until she's locked away for good.

Jess needs to get to the hospital, to get that memory stick. But how can she possibly do that, locked in here?

67

THE ROAD TURNS to a gravel track. He cuts the headlights as he brings the car to a stop and climbs out. His eyes take a moment to adjust to the darkness as he stands in the clearing, his hands on his hips, looking up to the sky. A shard of moonlight cuts through the clouds; he knows it's going to rain soon.

He goes back to the car and opens the trunk. She looks up at him, her big blue eyes wide with fear. Her hands are tied in front of her, her feet bound, and she breathes hard through her nose, the tape on her mouth moving in and out in a quick rhythm. He grabs her hands and pulls her up. Her naked skin feels cold to his touch and she's shivering, but that doesn't matter to him now.

He carries her to the middle of the clearing, then drops her into the mud. She looks up, and sees the rope hanging loosely in the tree above them. Her eyes bulge; she makes a muffled scream and tries to move, but she's tied too tightly, in too much pain. He watches her, amused. He likes her spirit. Maybe once he gets going, she'll hold on longer than he thinks, and he pulls her back, rolling her over to her front and planting a quick kick in her ribs. She moans, then lies still, her chest contracting with the force of her panicked breathing.

But this woman is just the starter. His entrée, the bit you sample before the main course. He's saving the best for last—Jessica Ambrose. Beautiful, exceptional, unique. His angel. When he'd seen her at the supermarket that day, he'd recognized her from all those years ago. The woman she'd grown into wasn't so different from the kid she'd been at the children's home, and all the pieces had fallen into place. He'd seen the adoring look in her friend's eyes, the NHS lanyard around his neck, and known there and then how it would work.

He knows she's at the police station now, but he's not worried. There's nowhere he can't get access to, no obstacle he can't overcome.

The doctor had been useful; Shipman had ruined it for everyone, it was hard to get hold of controlled drugs nowadays. This guy had access to diamorphine, he knew how much and where to inject. And Dr. Sharma was perfect: honest, genuine, in love—everything he hated. He wants to destroy all that's good in this world.

He walks to the car and takes out his bag, carrying it back. He kneels next to the woman, then takes out each tool in turn, laying it down so she can see. The knives: a large hunting knife, a long, thin fillet knife, a few scalpels, all clean and sharp. A costotome—his new toy, shiny and unused, a specialist bone cutter, bought especially for today. He's looking forward to that in particular.

Time to begin.

He stands up again, picking up the biggest knife. She's been staring, as he hoped she would, and now she makes a frantic animal cry, her head shaking: no no no. But he places his knee on the bottom of her back and leans forward, his left hand on her neck, all his weight forcing her immobile.

He's enjoying the moment, feeling the weight of the knife in his hand. Then he reaches down, holding tight to her neck as he pushes the blade into the skin on her back. It goes in easily and he starts to cut, dissecting muscles, cartilage, arteries and veins.

Her fingers splay outward; her muscles tense; her feet twitch with pain. She's screaming as best as she can, her breathing labored, her face pushed into the mud.

But it doesn't stop him. He continues to work, sweating now with the exertion, until he notices she's gone still. He pauses, briefly. Her eyes are closed, and he puts two fingers to her neck. There's still a pulse, weak and thready. The last residue of life hanging on.

He stops what he's doing and moves around to her face. He picks up a small scalpel. It's only right, he thinks. When she wakes up again, she'll want to see this.

He doesn't want her to miss a single thing.

68

"YOU'RE KIDDING."

DS Taylor stands facing Cara, her hands on her hips, face like thunder.

"No. I'm not *kidding*." Cara spells it out slowly. "You have to let her go."

"She'll just run again."

"That's what I'm hoping. Dr. Sharma told her more than just declarations of love. She has something in mind. I want to follow her."

Taylor makes a loud exclamation and throws her hands in the air, turning away. Cara knows Taylor has no choice but to do what she's asked. Cara is the superior officer and has the agreement of DCS Marsh, but it doesn't stop a small part of her enjoying pissing Taylor off.

"Taylor?" she shouts down the corridor at the departing detective. "Tell me when she's released!" She receives an annoyed hand in the air in response.

Cara returns to the incident room, where the team are anxiously waiting, and stands at the front.

"Right. We know Jessica Ambrose is a flight risk, so no screw-ups please. But we need to know where she's going. Like many of you, I don't believe Dr. Sharma is the Echo Man—Warmington, follow up with the hospital for alibis, please—but I'm under no illusion that he did this under his own volition."

She assigns duties to the team, ensuring that every move Jessica Ambrose makes is covered while other detectives continue to follow up on leads at the station. She's nervous. She needs this to work.

Her phone buzzes in her pocket, and she pulls it out.

Being released from custody now, the message from Taylor says. *Called her a taxi.*

Cara leaves the incident room and goes down the stairs to the main reception, where Jess is waiting. She watches her through the glass panel in the door.

Seeing Jessica Ambrose up close has been interesting. She's seen photos, sure, but Cara's fascinated now she's there in person. The woman Griffin's been risking his career to hide in his apartment.

And she looks a mess. She's not wearing any makeup, her hair is barely brushed, tied up in a loose ponytail. She's wearing badly fitting clothes, including a sweater Cara realizes was Mia's. Seeing it makes Cara jolt. Griffin's worship of his wife was all-encompassing, and Cara realizes how much Griffin must care about Jess. Dr. Sharma too. And she wonders why.

Jessica Ambrose doesn't seem particularly distinctive. She's pretty, yes, but not astonishingly so. She doesn't smile. She's grumpy rather than charming.

But then Jess stands up. Cara's musing will have to wait. The taxi has arrived.

They're on the move.

69

RELEASED UNDER INVESTIGATION. Jess doesn't know what that means, except she's glad she doesn't have to spend any longer in that cell. She's out and in a taxi, heading for the hospital.

She arrives and uses Griffin's card to pay. She's been here a few times with Nav, so she knows where she's going. She's guessed his locker is in the men's changing room, and she heads toward it.

She knows Griffin is somewhere in this hospital, and she's desperate to see him. She needs to be with him; she feels a pull that she hasn't felt with someone for some time. With her husband, the overwhelming feeling was disappointment. That her very existence was letting him down. But Griffin takes her as she is. There's no attempt to fix her.

But she can't see him now. Finding this memory stick and the photos are more important. This is the only evidence that Nav was blackmailed. She'll give it to the police, and they'll know.

She reaches the men's changing room and, glancing around, pushes the door open tentatively. To her relief, the room is empty, and she heads to Nav's locker. She knows him well and enters his old room number into the combination on the padlock, clicking it open.

Inside she finds his laptop bag and she pulls it out, laying it down on one of the benches and scrabbling in the pockets. There are two memory sticks inside. One with the initials "NS" scrawled on in pen, the other black and bare.

And then the photographs. A bundle of five in a plain white envelope. Old fashioned, white frames around the plastic, the images blurred and hazy. But Jess is in no doubt what they are. Women: eyes wide, mouths screaming, legs apart. Bloody fingers in front of their faces, trying redundantly to protect themselves.

Her hand goes to her mouth. It's no wonder Nav felt he had no choice but to inject Griffin. With the knowledge of who this man had already killed, seeing this as evidence of what he could do. To her.

She feels cold horror trickling down her back, knowing the risk of being here. But Jess has to see it for herself first. She could have just told DCI Elliott as soon as she left the interview room, but she feels the complete humiliation of being filmed with this guy. She wants to watch it, to see what Nav was seeing. To confirm for herself what a shitty person she is.

She gathers it all up and leaves the changing room, hurrying down the corridor, looking for an empty space, anywhere where she won't be disturbed.

At last she sees a cleaner's cupboard and opens the door, turning the light on. She closes it behind her, sitting on the floor among the mops and buckets, resting the laptop on her knees. She turns it on, logs in as a guest user, and impatiently waits for it to boot up.

The home screen eventually loads, and she puts the black memory stick in. The computer hums, then the symbol for the drive appears on the desktop. She clicks on it, nerves making her hands shake. There's one file.

The video is grainy and black and white, but Jess can clearly make out the toilet she remembers from a week ago. The camera position is up high: it shows the sink and the door. There's no one in the room.

The door opens and Jess watches as she comes into the bathroom. The man follows in behind her and starts kissing the back of her neck, and she turns and they start kissing properly. Jess feels her face go red, her back sweaty. How could she have done such a thing? At the time she knew it was wrong, she knew it was reckless, but it felt in keeping with her damaged mind, her broken shell of a body. But now, watching it here? It looks awful. This random guy fucking her is horrible, she's ugly, a terrible excuse for a person. She feels as though she's suffocating. She starts crying, knowing that less than twenty-four hours after this, her husband was killed.

She turns away from the video. She can't watch it anymore. But just before she does, something catches her eye. It jars. Even more so than the rotten act itself. She wipes her eyes on her sleeve and looks back. On the video she's facing away, bent over the sink, her skirt around her waist, the man still behind her, so what was it?

She pauses the video, then winds it back a fraction. She presses "Play" again.

Then she sees it. She stops. In those few seconds she's paralyzed, her breath halted in her lungs.

The man's still there, still fucking her, but for one split second he looks up. He looks up right into the camera.

And his expression? Pure hatred.

70

WHEN GRIFFIN WAKES, his whole back is in pain. For a moment he's confused. He hears the beeps of the monitors, the sound of voices in the corridor, sees the blue curtain pulled around his bed.

Memories from just over a year ago force their way into his head. Waking up in the hospital, head pounding, barely able to open his swollen eyes, plaster casts encasing his arms. Not able to move as he was told Mia was dead.

He squeezes his eyes shut again. He remembers Jess leaving the apartment. Then the knock on the door and Nav standing there. Something about the doctor seemed odd from the word go. His shoulders were stooped, his hands shaking as he put his bag on the floor. He wouldn't meet his eyes, but Griffin was in so much pain, his body aching so badly, that he hadn't cared.

"Have you got the pills?" Griffin had asked, collapsing back down on the bed.

Nav had nodded. "But you'll need something else first. Your withdrawal is more established than I expected."

Griffin had grunted in agreement. He'd let the doctor roll up his sleeve, put a tourniquet around his arm. He felt the quick cold of the alcohol wipe, then the prick of the needle as it went into his vein.

Then the relief. The blessed all-encompassing rush of euphoria as the opioid hit his bloodstream. He'd felt Nav watching him, and opened his eyes, surprised to see the doctor crying, the syringe and needle still in his hand.

He'd shaken his head. "I'm sorry," he'd said, backing away from Griffin, then turning and rushing out the door.

Griffin knew something was wrong. He knew what these drugs were like; he'd had enough of them in his system over the past year, but this felt too much. He tried to stand up, but his brain was woozy. He wobbled to his feet. He knew he needed to find his phone, call someone, but the world was sliding sideways. The floor rushed up to his face; he felt the knock to his head as he hit the ground.

Shipman, he'd thought. How could he have been so blind? To let Sharma in to the apartment. Trust him to pump him full of drugs when there was a serial killer on the loose copying murderers from the past.

His face still pressed into the floor, he lifted his hand, and with a shaking finger, ran it in the dust. He managed five letters before he passed out.

* * *

He first woke with a jolt, still in his apartment. Unknown faces staring down at him, medical equipment in their hands. He blinked at them, his vision slowly clearing. Then again: gone.

In the ambulance, awake for longer. He asked about Jess.

"Your friend?" the paramedic replied. "Sorry, mate. She was arrested."

He swore loudly and tried to sit. The paramedic gently persuaded him back down.

"You're not out of the woods yet, mate. You've had a considerable dose of an opioid. No sooner do we pump Naloxone into you, it wears off and we're back to square one. Sit tight . . ."

The guy had been right. He hadn't been conscious for long.

* * *

And now, here he is. Alive. An IV in his arm, tubes running up to a clear bag on a stand. Oxygen tube under his nose, monitors beeping next to him. He dimly remembers Cara coming in to see him. Reassuring words that he was okay, that she would catch whoever had done this to him.

And then he remembers Jess. Arrested. Probably being interrogated by that pathetic excuse of a detective, Taylor.

"Shit!" he shouts. Then he slumps back on the pillow. "Shit," he mutters again, quieter now. But at least she's safe, he thinks. She's with Cara. She'll be okay.

At least she's safe.

CHAPTER

71

JESS IS FROZEN. The video is still playing on the screen, but she can't focus. She can't think.

He knew. Somehow that guy knew who she was. He knew what they were going to do.

She racks her brain, trying to think what happened that morning. Did she proposition him? He spoke to her first, she remembers that now. He commented on the weather, something harmless, but then what did he do? Did he smile? Casually drop an indecent remark? Why did they go into that restroom together?

She closes her eyes, tries to calm her breathing. She made the suggestion, but he mentioned the restroom. It's clear. This whole thing was planned.

This is him.

She has his face on screen. The guy she fucked. The man who set fire to her house. Who killed Patrick. Who killed Griffin's wife. And all those people.

Her gut rolls and she leans forward, the sparse contents of her stomach suddenly vomited into a bucket. She waits there for a moment, retching, her body heaving, gasping for breath.

She knows what she has to do. She needs to get this to the police.

She stands up, closing the lid of the laptop and pulling the memory stick out. She opens the door and hurries down the corridor. But as she does so she sees a pay phone on the corner. She stops a man walking past. He gives her a funny look but complies with her request, giving her a pound coin that she puts in the phone.

She dials a number, known by heart, and at last someone answers.

"St. Mary's Primary," the singsong voice says.

"Hello, yes. I'm hoping you can help me. My daughter's come home with a Transformer toy, and she says it belongs to Hayden." Jess is gabbling, saying the first thing that comes into her head. "His father's Evan . . . or Ethan. Or something. Could I have their full name so I can message them on Facebook? I'm worried it's a precious toy, and Hayden will be upset."

"Um." The voice on the other end is hesitant. "What class did you say?"

"Oh. Oak class. I think."

Jess can hear tapping at the other end of the phone. Then another pause.

"I can't help you, I'm afraid."

Jess swallows. "I know, it's a data protection thing, I'm sorry. But if you could just give me the correct first name, then I can look it up."

"It's not that," the woman says. "Well, I mean, yes, I'm not supposed to give out that sort of information. But even if I wanted to, I can't."

"What do you mean?" Jess stutters.

"There's nobody in Oak class by the name of Hayden. Nobody in that year, actually."

Jess mutters a thank-you and puts the phone down.

She knows for sure now. It was all staged.

How could she have been so stupid? He targeted her, like he had his other victims. And now Griffin is in the hospital and Nav's been arrested.

A sudden thought pops into Jess's head, and she starts to run. He knew who her daughter was. He knew where she went to school.

She sprints down the corridor, the laptop bag clutched tightly in her hand. The urgency turns her insides to liquid. She needs to protect Alice.

She pushes the doors of the hospital open, and they slam against the wall with a bang. She knows she's getting looks, but she doesn't care. She has to get to her daughter, and she frantically looks around.

But she can't see the taxi rank. The place is deserted. She runs further away from the hospital, catching a glimpse of a sign, pointing her away.

The road is dark and quiet. There is no one around, nothing in sight but an old car, parked up on the double yellows.

She pauses, desperately searching in the darkness, and a hand taps her on the shoulder.

"Excuse me?" a male voice says.

She glances for a second. He's wearing a baseball cap, his arm in a sling. The collar of his coat is pulled over the bottom half of his face.

"Could you help me carry these to my car?"

He points to a pile of books by his feet, then to his car. It's a tan VW Beetle, an old one, and the strangeness of this registers somewhere in her brain.

But she's too panicked.

"I'm sorry, I'm in a hurry," she says, and he pulls on her arm again.

She turns. She sees his face. Her mouth drops open.

It's too late.

She feels something hit her head, and her legs give way. Her body drops to the hard concrete.

Everything goes black.

CHAPTER

72

"WHAT DO YOU mean you've lost her? How have you lost her?"
Cara is aware she's shouting at the DC at her side, but she can't help it.

"I . . . We don't know. We last saw her on the pay phone down the south corridor. But then . . . She was just gone."

Cara bellows another profanity, then screams down her radio to anyone who's listening. The calls come back the same. The suspect has disappeared.

Cara's running now, heading toward main reception. She pushes the queue out of the way and shows her warrant card to the man behind the desk.

"Where's your CCTV?" she shouts. "Your security office?"

He points to a small door on the right-hand side, and Cara races toward it, opening it and addressing the guy behind the row of monitors.

"South corridor," she says to him, and he scrolls through the tape. But he's slow, painfully slow, and Cara twitches, impatient.

"There! There!" Cara points at the screen, and they follow the figure of Jess as she runs out of the hospital. The security guard switches cameras, but they've lost her again.

"Where the hell is she going?" Cara mutters. "Taxi rank. Look for the taxi rank," she says, and sure enough, they spot Jess come into view, on the edge of the screen. She's fidgeting from foot to foot, staring at the empty space where the cars should be. She turns, talking to someone out of shot.

"Can you see who that is?" she asks, but the guard shakes his head.

"No cameras on that side, I'm afraid."

Jess speaks to the person again, but then Cara sees her fall. Now only her feet are in shot and Cara watches as they're dragged away.

"Shit! Shit! Suspect has been attacked," she shouts down her radio. "Repeat. Suspect is down."

She looks at the security guard. He's scrolling through other screens, but they can't see anything. She's vanished.

Cara can't believe this is happening. Jessica Ambrose has gone.

*   *   *

Next to her, Cara can hear the DC putting calls out to Control. She phones Shenton.

"Look for CCTV—anything," she says. "We need to find her."

Cara knows this is no coincidence. The Echo Man has got her.

Dazed, she starts walking away, up the stairs, following her sudden urge to be with someone she loves, with her family. The uniform standing guard nods to her as she comes closer, and she pushes the door open.

Griffin looks up when he sees her. He doesn't look like her brother, dressed in the emasculating hospital gown, surrounded by tubes and equipment, his face gray, without the omnipresent cigarette in his hand. He smiles at first, then frowns with concern when he sees the look on her face.

"What's happened?" he says, sitting up.

"It's Jess." Cara can barely bring herself to say it. "We followed her here. But she's gone."

"He's taken her," Griffin says.

"I'm so sorry."

He starts pulling at the various wires on his body, wincing as he takes out the needle in his arm.

"Nate, stop," she says. "You can't leave."

"There's no way I'm sitting in here while Jess is out there with a serial killer. I can't—" He pauses, and Cara knows what he was about to say. *I can't let this happen again.* She knows his failure to prevent Mia's murder nearly drove him out of his mind. She knows there's no way she'll stop him.

"What about your back?" she asks, handing him his clothes from the cupboard.

"I'm whacked up on all sorts of stuff right now—I'll be fine."

She turns away as he pulls his clothes on. He's grimacing, clearly in pain, and she helps him with his boots.

"What do we know?" he asks.

"Shenton's on point; the team are scouring CCTV. She came here, then disappeared from outside by the taxi rank."

"Here," he asks. "Why here?"

She holds out her arm and he grabs it for a second as he stands up. He wobbles slightly. "She didn't come to see you?"

"No."

Cara can see Griffin starting to lose control. His scowl, the perpetual forward movement. He's acting, not thinking.

"Nate."

Her serious tone makes Griffin stop, and she takes his arm and steers him to the bed. He sits down with a thump. She crouches in front of him on the chair, resting her arms on her knees.

She takes his hands; she can feel him shaking. He's scared. Her tough take-no-shit brother is scared, and that terrifies her more than anything.

"I need you to talk this through with me," she says, her voice deliberately measured. Her brain feels scrambled; there's too much to think about, all careering around, bouncing off the sides of her skull. "Help me, please?"

He nods, slowly. He stares at the floor for a second, pulling himself together, then looks at her. "Tell me what we have," he says at last.

She shakes her head. "Very little. He's left virtually nothing behind. A footwear mark from Converse sneakers. A Tinder message sent from the police station. A few bits of rare grass found on moorlands from the Sutcliffe murders, and a cipher we can't solve."

"Anything back from Social Services?"

"It's a dead end. Too long ago, not enough to go on. They can't find the file of that boy."

"And we know he's fond of serial killers," Griffin adds. "But which one? Which one next?"

"Call Shenton," they both say together.

Cara dials his mobile, and Shenton answers immediately. She puts him on speaker.

"Toby, it's Elliott. What well-known serial killers are still outstanding? Who hasn't he used yet?"

"Er . . ." Shenton thinks for a second. "Well, there's Bundy, Son of Sam, Boston Strangler, Gein." There's a pause as Shenton mentions his name. "You know what he did, don't you. He . . ."

". . . made a suit out of women's skin, yes, thank you, Shenton." Cara meets Griffin's eyes, then looks away. "Narrow them down to murders that happened near moorlands or countryside."

"The moors murders—Brady and Hindley?"

"No, that was children. Needs to be a woman victim."

"Um. Robert Pickton? He lived on a farm. Fed dead bodies to the pigs. Ridgway? No, that was a river." Shenton's thinking out loud. Cara can see the annoyance on Griffin's face. "Hansen?"

"What about Hansen?"

"He hunted down women in the wilderness with a gun and a knife."

"Where?"

"Alaska."

"Fuck!" Griffin swears next to her, and Cara moves the phone away from him.

"Shenton," she says, "have the results come back on the ESDA test from the note?"

"Wait . . . Yes. Just this morning. They found some writing. Could be another code."

"What does it say?"

"Just a few numbers. Nine to four. Ten to twelve. I can just make out a word: *Sat.*"

Cara frowns. "Send it across to me. Anything from the CCTV?"

"No, sorry. But the lab came back on the notebooks."

Cara and Griffin both sit forward. "And?"

"Fingerprints and some DNA. But no match."

"Run it against all police profiles first," Cara barks.

"We did. Nothing. We're onto the national database now."

Cara can't believe it. She feels the disappointment cut through her. She was sure it was someone on the inside. "Call me as soon as something pops," she adds, about to hang up when Toby interrupts her.

"But boss, I had a thought."

Outside Griffin's room, two nurses start talking loudly. Cara turns the volume up on the speaker, annoyance bubbling.

"Go on."

"He'll know you're close behind," Shenton says. "He'll know you're looking. So he would have taken her somewhere where he feels safe."

"What do you mean?"

"He'll go somewhere familiar. His home. A work space. Somewhere where he can control the surroundings."

Cara feels the dread rising again. "But how do we know where, when we haven't a clue who he is?" she shouts, her voice shrill.

She looks at Griffin. She sees her helplessness, her fear, reflected in his eyes.

The Echo Man has taken Jess, to God knows where, to do God knows what. It's all her fault. And she has no idea what to do.

73

HE IS CLOSE. He can feel it.

He looks across to her, slumped in the front seat, as they rattle on in his shitty VW. A line of blood runs down her forehead where he hit her, but apart from that she is untouched. She won't be like that for long.

He's glad the end is in sight. He's tired, so weary of all this shit.

He feels as though he's two people. The one with Cara. The respected professional. And the other: the one that's killed. He is two souls, struggling for possession. Bundy knew it. Gein, Dahmer, Brady. All of them had wrestled with the evil half while going about their daily lives. Catching a bus, doing their jobs, loving their families.

Even love? Yes, even that. It was something he'd never imagined, yet here he was.

He prepares himself for what he has to do. Mentally, he pulls on the disguise; he becomes another person. He is only really himself when he is with her, and the thought claws at his insides, knowing that won't ever happen again.

But he can't think about her now.

This isn't how he thought his life would be. But it's no more than he deserves, no more than he expected, growing up in that place. He was alone at the beginning; he'll be alone at the end.

And soon. Soon it will be over.

74

THEY LEAVE THE hospital, Griffin following Cara to the car. They need to go somewhere, anywhere. Even back to the station will do, just to feel as if they're taking some decisive action.

He doesn't feel great. His head is woozy, his legs weak. He's in pain. But this is more important. He needs to keep going.

He has to find Jess. He's tense, his body on the edge of explosion. They have no idea where this madman has taken her. Or what he's going to do.

Cara blips the car unlocked and pulls the passenger side door open for him. He's annoyed at this little gesture—it makes him feel pathetic—but he slumps into the seat, sitting on something in the process.

He reaches under his bum and pulls out a phone. The screen flashes into life, showing a red alert. *Andrew! You have a new connection!* it screams, demanding attention. He recognizes the logo. The small red flame icon with a *t*. What's Roo doing on Tinder? And why is his phone here? He feels a smart of anger for his sister and shoves the phone in the glovebox to hide it.

It's cold outside the overheated hospital, and Griffin wraps his arms around himself. He's wearing only a shirt and jeans, the clothes he was brought into the hospital in. He feels grubby. Desperate for a cigarette.

He sees a coat left in the back of Cara's car and reaches behind to get it, trying to put it on.

The flood of emotion hits him like an avalanche. He feels his hands shake, his body jolted with adrenaline.

He looks down at the jacket. It doesn't fit him; it's too small, gaudy red and blue. He remembers Mia picking it out, them giving it to Roo one Christmas. And the smell . . . He puts it up to his nose and the shock of recognition burns through him, making him dizzy.

He's back there, on his old bedroom floor. Wrists blistering from the cord, muscles straining as he tries to get away. He's blind, gagged, but he hears her screaming. Thuds and bashing. Noises from Mia: primitive, desperate cries. He thrashes, turns, pulling again at his wrists, impotently raging against his bindings.

Mia cries again, then there's silence, and the quiet is worse, far worse. Then he senses someone next to him. A body, sour and hot. Sweat, coffee, unwashed skin.

Griffin smells that man now, coming from the jacket.

Cara opens the driver's door, and he reaches over, grabbing the keys out of her hand, then pushing her backward. He locks the doors and he sees her shocked face through the window as he climbs across to the driver's seat, starting the engine.

Griffin knows who it is now. He knows who it is and where they've gone.

But Cara can't know. It would destroy her. To see what Griffin's going to do.

He puts the car into gear and, wheels screaming, guns it away from the hospital.

75

CARA FALLS HEAVILY onto the pavement. She screams Griffin's name after the departing car, again and again in frustration.

He's realized something. Something he didn't want to share with her. She curses him, can't believe what he's done.

She calls in to the station, tells Control to track a blue Audi A3, repeats her license plate number. She knows he'll trigger speed cameras, but he won't care. She just wonders if it's going to be too late.

She goes to call the incident room again but sees the email notification received from Shenton. It's an image of the ESDA markings, and something about it catches her eye.

Sitting on the pavement, she brings up the image, magnifying the writing. Shenton was right: it's numbers, faint but clear. Something about it tugs on her memory, and then she realizes.

9–4. 10–12. Sat.

It's her handwriting. It's swimming times for the local pool, scrawled down in haste on their last holiday. On their last visit to the lodge.

The note for the Zodiac killings, for Libby's murder, was written on a notepad taken from their lodge. In the middle of nowhere, on moorland.

Where the killer must have taken Jess. Where Griffin is heading to now.

But why . . . But who . . .?

Her mind can barely acknowledge what she knows must be true.

She makes an urgent call, requesting a patrol car. She has to get down there. Before someone she loves dies.

CHAPTER

76

THE COLD IS sudden and shocking. Jess gasps, water running down her face.

"Wake up."

A man stands in front of her. He has a bucket in his hand, and he places it on the floor next to him. She recognizes him immediately.

She tries to move, but she's bound to a chair, her feet and hands fastened tightly with plastic cable ties. Her arms are outstretched, and she tugs at them, but the heavy wooden chair holds fast. She struggles and it rocks slightly.

"Careful, I don't want you to tip over backward," he says. He reaches over and gently moves a strand of wet hair out of her face. "How are you, Jessica?"

"Let me go," she snarls. She's wet through, and the room is cold. Her eyes dart around. It's a wooden cabin, nice pictures on the walls, throws over a comfy sofa. "Where am I?" she shouts. "Where have you taken me?"

"Somewhere we won't be disturbed." He pulls up a chair and sits in front of her. She notices he has a small penknife in his hand.

She pulls again, the ties digging into her skin. She needs to calm down, she tells herself. Think. Think. But then she catches a glimpse of a body, someone lying on the floor, his back to her. A man.

"Who's that?" she stutters.

He glances back, his half-closed eyes hardly taking notice of the prostrate figure.

"No one you need to be concerned with. He tried to defend them, you know. Those kids. What a fucking hero." He adds this last sentence bitterly, resentment creeping into his voice.

Breath catches in Jess's throat. He sees her horrified expression. "Don't worry," he says. "They're fine. Drugged and asleep in the bedroom. I love Tilly and Joshua. They were never my plan. But I needed to get back for you. So we could talk."

"What do you want to talk about?" Jess asks. She's trying to distract him. She hopes someone will find her. But how, the little voice in her head says, how? How can anyone possibly know you're here?

"You don't recognize me, do you?" he asks.

"Of course, I do. From last week. From—"

He stops her. "No. Not from our encounter in the restroom. From before."

"Before . . .?" Jess is puzzled. She looks at his face. "I don't . . ."

But then something about him makes her pause. She does know him. She sees kind eyes from years ago. His smile—nervously handing her the last bit of toast. Giving her a toy to play with. Traces of the boy he once was.

"The children's home," she whispers. "You were there."

He gives her a sad smile. "You *do* remember me! I must admit, when you didn't recognize me last week, I was upset. Because I remembered you, Jess." He looks at the penknife, pulling one of the blades out of the handle. Light shines on the silver, dancing on the sharp edge.

"But that was over twenty years ago?" she stutters.

"You were five. I was twelve," he says. "You were so scared and unsure. I heard them talking about you. They said they had to take you away from your parents. That your mom was crying as you were driven away."

"I don't remember that."

She stares at him. For the first time she realizes his manner is strange; he's quiet, reserved, his shoulders hunched. This isn't the demeanor she expected. The man Griffin had described from their police profile was a gleeful, sadistic murderer, ready and eager to kill. This man seems defeated. As beaten as she feels, even though she's the one tied to the chair.

"You were only there for a month," he continues quietly. "But I knew you were special. You showed me."

"What did I do?" Jess whispers.

"You held your hand over a flame. I watched your skin turn black and pucker. I watched the blisters form. But you didn't even flinch. You watched it and you smiled." He holds up his hand to her. On his palm is a scar, the skin tight and red. "You told me to try it. I did it for as long as I could. It was agony. But in the end I couldn't stand the pain. And you laughed at me."

Jess shakes her head. "I'm sorry. I didn't understand then. I didn't realize I was damaged."

His eye widen in surprise. "Damaged? You're not damaged." He frowns, his forehead furrowing, jaw clenched. "You have something none of us have," he says, his voice getting louder now. "Something better. I knew that then. Especially when your parents came to collect you." He laughs suddenly, slightly hysterical. "They came to collect you, Jess! Nobody's parents came to collect them from that place! Nobody's!"

"No. No. It's just a medical condition. It's nothing."

She sees his face cloud. In a quick movement he grabs her hand, turning it over, pinning her fingers flat as he reaches forward with the penknife. He jams the blade into the middle of her palm.

Jess feels it go through the flesh, hit against bone, sever tendons. It sticks in the wood of the handle of the chair, and she sees warm blood start to flow. She cries out in alarm.

"You are special, Jess," he says. "Don't ever deny it."

"You're crazy," she cries. She tries to pull her hand away, but the penknife is stuck. Blood drips from the chair, pooling on the floor. She's shaking now. From the cold, the fear, the shock.

The man smiles, but it looks forced, no more than a grimace. "Perhaps," he says. "Perhaps that's true. Because all I ever wanted was to be noticed. I wanted to be somebody." As he talks, he seems to be gaining strength. The previous weariness has faded; he sits up straighter, pulling his body taut. "I was insignificant. Everyone forgot me. My mother. Foster parents. You."

He stands in front of her, looking at her from under lowered brows. She doesn't dare move. To Jess it looks as if he's wrestling with something, an internal battle between anger and acceptance. Her eyes scan the room again. She can see trees outside the window. It's raining, dark.

Then he turns, walking to the table behind him and picking up a large knife. It's huge, with a serrated blade on one side, straight and sharp on the other, and she can't take her eyes from it.

"At least you won't suffer," he says, almost to himself. He crouches in front of her, the knife in his hand, tip pointing toward her body. "You won't experience the agony like the others. I still hear their screams, you know." He looks up, and she sees a flicker of humanity flash in his eyes. "Their pleading, their cries. But there was nothing I could do."

Jess stares at him. She won't ask, she won't. But her brain goes there, starting to imagine what he's planning, what he might do to her. She feels her heart racing, panic confusing her thoughts.

"And that other girl, what she went through before she died . . ." He screws his eyes shut tight, shaking his head slowly.

"What other girl?" Jess stutters, horrified, but he doesn't reply. "What do you want from me?" she cries. Snot and tears run down her face. "I'll do anything, please. Just let me go."

"I can't do that. I'm sorry, Jess, I just can't. You have a part to play in all of this. Otherwise, it'll never end. It'll never be over."

And then his head snaps up, as if remembering what he's there to do. He stands, goes back to the table and picks something up. It's a gun, small and black, and he puts the knife down for a moment so he can pull back the slider. It cocks with a metallic snap.

"It's time," he says.

She notices his voice has changed. He sounds resolute, certain now. The effect chills her to the bone.

"Please just let me go," she whispers.

He stays silent. Pointing the gun at her head, he pulls the penknife from the arm of the chair, out of her hand, then uses it to cut the cable ties around her ankles. She looks at the hunting knife, still left on the table. She looks at the door on the far side of the room.

He follows her gaze as he folds the penknife away, putting it in his pocket. "Try anything," he says. "And I'll shoot your kneecaps off. Pain or no pain, you won't be walking anywhere."

She doesn't move.

"Understand?" he asks.

She knows she needs to seem cooperative. If they're going outside, she'll run then. It's her best chance. It's her only chance. He's waiting for her response and she stares at him, her eyes cold. She nods.

He reaches back and picks up the hunting knife, cutting the ties on her wrists. He pulls her to her feet, then stands behind her, gun against her back, the knife at her neck. She feels the hard metal push into her flesh.

"Walk," he says, shoving her with the gun, and she stumbles on wobbly legs, reaching the door in a few steps.

"Open it."

She cradles her damaged hand. It's bleeding a lot now, the wound gaping. She fumbles with the bolts, eventually pulling them across.

The wind hits her full in the face as they step outside. It's pouring with rain. They take slow steps away from the house, and she looks out into the darkness. She can't hear any signs of civilization; she can't see any lights. She has no idea which direction to go.

She can still feel the knife on her neck, the gun on her back. But the pressure is less. It's a risk, but what choice does she have? There's no one here, no one is coming. With a sudden twist, she jerks away from him, pushing his right arm with one hand, snapping her elbow back with the other. She makes contact, but she doesn't look back.

She hears a roar of anger from behind her, making her blood run cold.

And she runs.

77

IT'S PITCH-BLACK, SHE can't see more than a foot in front of her, but she runs. Her lungs strain—she runs as fast as she can. She stumbles on a tree root, catches herself, pushing through branches and undergrowth.

Jess doesn't know how far he is behind her. She feels brambles pull at her clothes, something scratch her face. She catches an uneven piece of ground, rolling her ankle, but she pulls herself up again, running, running.

Where is this place? There are no roads, no signs of life. She claws through bushes, she's out of breath, frantic. She hears the bang of a gunshot and mentally checks herself. He must have missed, she thinks. How many bullets does he have? She thinks of the knife, she thinks of his threat, and she runs.

But then she hears another bang and something knocks her sideways. She feels the energy sap out of her body. But she pushes herself forward. She can't let him catch her. She can't.

She glances behind her, trying to see him, but then suddenly there's nothing. Her foot meets thin air and she feels herself falling, tumbling over rocks and through dirt. Her hands scrabble at the ground, trying to stop herself.

She hears the crack as her left leg hits the bottom of the slope. She feels the bone break. She comes to a stop. She can taste blood in her mouth, the crunch of mud between her teeth. She tries to move, but her leg isn't working, and she looks at it in the dim glow. White bone, a piece of her tibia, her shin, sticks out of bloody flesh, her jeans torn, leg bent at an angle.

She grabs at a tree next to her to pull herself to her feet, resting all her weight on her good leg. She tries to limp, but she can feel the grate of bone against bone, flapping flesh moving wetly around the wound. She falls to the ground again with a cry.

Jess curses her broken body. She can't feel the pain, but that can only get her so far. With her leg broken, shattered into pieces, there's no way she can outrun him.

She lies still. She tries to slow her frantic breathing. He doesn't know where she is, she tells herself. Maybe he won't be able to find her. Maybe the police are already out looking. Maybe. Maybe.

She waits ten, fifteen minutes. Her eyes dart, desperately searching. She strains her ears to listen. She can't hear anything but the wind and the rain. Maybe he's gone. Maybe.

She should move. She can't stay here all night. In the darkness she can see she's at the edge of a clearing. She imagines a path, a dirt road, anything that could lead her to help. She pulls herself forward on her elbows and her good knee, fingers gripping the mud to edge across.

And that's when she sees it.

It's unrecognizable at first. Her brain can't comprehend the shapes. It hangs above her, pale and white, in the haze of the moonlight. It turns slowly, dripping, flapping. The creak of the rope. The black hollows, the dark red, the streaks and stains.

And then she realizes what it is.

And she starts to scream.

78

S HE CAN'T LOOK away. Everything in her wants to close her eyes, wants to disappear, wants to stop looking at the horrific scene, but she's locked. Focused on the body.

It's a woman. Jess realizes that now. She hangs above her, a thick rope wrapped around her neck, her head bent toward the ground, staring directly at Jess with those unnaturally wide, open eyes. Her tongue is black and swollen in her mouth, her long blonde hair loose and limp around her shoulders, draped almost artistically over her naked breasts. A patchwork of bruises cover her pale body, mottled purple.

Her legs are streaked with red and brown. Her toes point downward; mud, rain, blood, something indescribable, dripping to the ground.

The woman is moving slightly. Rotating slowly on the rope. And when the body turns, Jess knows how she's going to die.

All of the skin on the woman's back has been removed. Calved away, parts fluttering loose, most completely gone. Out of the wound, Jess can see flesh: what she assumes to be lungs, intestines, organs, hanging down, still connected. But worst still are the ribs. Open, curving outward from her body, like stark white wings.

Jess's whole body is weak, paralyzed by the sight. She can't imagine who could do such a thing to another person. They're not human. They can't be . . . They can't be . . .

"She's an angel."

She jumps as she hears his voice next to her, then scrabbles backward in the mud. He walks slowly into the clearing from behind her. He's soaked, mud staining his clothes, his T-shirt sticking to his chest.

"I told you not to run. I told you," he says. His voice is monotone, flat and unfeeling. He points the gun at her legs, then pauses as he sees the bone and blood bubbling from the hole in her jeans.

"Please, please . . ." Jess sobs. "Please . . . What did you do?"

He glances up at the woman for a second, then back to Jess. His eyes are dark, black holes, unresponsive.

"She didn't last for long," he says quietly. "Passed out from the pain. Couldn't take it when he cut into her back. When he broke her ribs, pulled her lungs out, still breathing."

Jess's hands clamp to her mouth. She can't take it all in. What this woman must have gone through, the pain she must have experienced. She feels sick, and hot acid rises in her throat.

"Cut her eyelids off," he says, pointing backward. "She needed to watch, see what he was doing to her."

"Who?" Jess cries at him. She looks around the clearing. "We're the only people here, you sick fuck!"

He laughs, sharp and shrill, then he repeatedly thumps the heel of his hand hard into his skull, his head facing toward the ground, eyes screwed shut. She watches him, horrified. "He's everywhere," he cries. "A part of me. Always watching. Always here. And now he's going to do it to you too." He looks at her again, and points the hunting knife toward her. Suddenly she can't breathe. Her eyes flick from the sharp blade to the woman above her. "A fucking choir of angels."

But then he stops. He tilts his head and listens. Then raises the gun up again, shining, wet black in the pouring rain, the muzzle pointed at her face.

"Griffin," he shouts, the bravado back in his voice. "Nate Griffin."

Jess is confused but turns as she hears movement in the trees to her right.

The man shouts again: "Get out here right now, or I'll shoot your little girlfriend in the head."

Then she sees him. He steps out of the undergrowth. He raises his hands slowly above his head.

"Leave her alone," Griffin says.

79

GRIFFIN HAD BEEN to the lodge before. In happier times, with Mia. It was their haven, a little bit of peace and quiet. *"Where nobody can hear you scream,"* she had joked.

Griffin knows who it is. The Echo Man. He'd been at Libby's memorial. He'd been at the police station just days before; he could have sent that Tinder message, made that one mistake. And he was good with knives. He was a chef, for fuck's sake.

But the whole drive up to the cabin, he'd struggled with the comprehension. The father of his niece and nephew. Cara's husband. How could she not have realized? How could this man have killed all these people? Have killed Mia, tried to kill *him*?

But the evidence was there. It had to be true.

He'd raced through the pouring rain, knowing that as every second passed, Jess was with a killer. He'd parked, leaving the car a good distance away, not wanting anyone to hear his arrival.

He'd carefully looked through the window, but the lodge was empty. A chair stood alone in the middle of the room, with what Griffin assumed to be blood on one of the arms. The door was open, banging in the wind.

He turned and looked out into the darkened woods. He knew they were out there. But where? And then he heard her scream.

Griffin followed the noise, running through the trees. Rain poured down his face, soaking his clothes, but he hardly noticed. Stopping, listening, then running again, tracking through the woodland, adrenaline charging him forward.

But then he saw the drop, and at the last minute caught himself. Slowly, he climbed around, carefully scrabbling down the muddy walls.

Until he saw it. The—what *was* that? A woman, hanging, bloody and broken in the darkness. Griffin recoiled with shock, blood pounding in his ears. Is it—Oh God. His first thought was it was Jess, and his legs nearly gave out from under him, air rushing from his lungs with a low groan. But then he noticed the blonde hair, and his eyes followed the voices down.

There was Jess, lying on her back, her leg bent at a strange angle. But his relief was short-lived: a man stood over her, a knife in one hand, a gun in the other. And it wasn't who he was expecting.

He couldn't believe what he was seeing. But the fingerprints, the DNA on the notebook? It can't be him.

And then he heard his name.

*   *   *

"Griffin," he hears. "Nate Griffin. Get out here right now, or I'll shoot your little girlfriend in the head."

Griffin closes his eyes. He knows what this guy has done. He knows he's a cold-blooded, sadistic killer. The evidence is hanging right in front of him. He has no choice. He can't let him shoot Jess.

He steps out of the trees and raises his hands above his head. He looks at the man. The man he's worked alongside. A man he doesn't like, but whom he trusted. Because he is a police officer. A detective.

"Leave her alone," Griffin says. "Leave her alone, Deakin."

80

"NICE OF YOU to join us, Nate," Noah says. The gun moves, now pointed at Griffin's own head.

Griffin sees Jess look at him, then back to Deakin.

"You know him," she whispers. Even in the dim light Griffin can see she doesn't look good. She's pale, shivering.

Griffin smiles grimly. "He's a cop, Jess. Are you okay?"

"No, she's not okay," Deakin exclaims. "She's got a broken leg, and I fucking shot her."

Jess looks down in surprise. Griffin sees her put her hand to her side, lift it up, stare at the blood. Red shining in the moonlight.

"Do you like our little angel?"

Griffin looks up at the woman, then stares at Deakin from under lowered brows. "What have you done, Noah?"

"The endgame, Griffin! There always had to be an endgame." Deakin laughs. It's high and brittle. "This was never just about one or two murders—it's a whole fucking masterpiece. An homage, if you like, to the biggest and greatest. And this! Look at this! It's a fucking work of art! There had to be something better, more elaborate than everything that had come before."

"You're ill, Noah. Just hand yourself in. Police are on their way."

"No, they're not. I know you. You came by yourself. Fucking lone wolf. Why did you do that, Griffin? Did you have plans of your own?"

Griffin grits his teeth, shaking his head.

"Were you going to kill me—was that it? To get revenge for Mia?" Deakin waves the gun manically for a moment, then points it back at him. "How's this going to work now, Nate?"

Griffin glares through the darkness, feeling his rage build.

"How quick do you think you can be? Do you think you can get the gun off me before I shoot you? Leave you there bleeding, watching as I do that"—he points up to the woman, then back to Jess—"to her."

Griffin looks at Jess, desperate, as she begins to cry, tears dropping into the mud.

"I'll make you watch, Nate," Deakin hisses. "As I cut her open, pull out her bones, her insides. Hang her from the tree. Leave you both to die. Because that's what's going to happen."

Griffin hesitates. Can he get control before Deakin shoots? Can he bear the consequences if he takes the risk and fails? Like last time? Like with Mia?

But then he hears it. A voice, loud and clear over the wind and the rain.

"Noah, please. Put the gun down. It's over."

Griffin feels his heart beating out of his chest. Please no. Not her as well.

Cara steps out of the trees. Griffin can see she's crying, but behind the tears her face is determined. Deakin sees her and instantly his expression switches.

"No!" he shouts. "You can't be here. You have to go!"

"Please, Noah," Cara says again. "Armed police are on their way. This isn't what you want. This isn't you."

Griffin notices the abrupt difference in Noah. Cara's arrival has changed something in him. The confidence has gone; he seems more unstable, emotional, as if a mask has fallen.

"What do you know about me?" His voice is panicked, and he glances behind him into the trees. "Nothing! I killed all those people! Look what I did to her! I'm a piece of shit. I'm worthless. I deserve to die."

Deakin points to the woman, and for the first time Griffin realizes who it is. It's Lauren. And Cara knows it too.

Griffin sees her struggling. She screws her eyes shut, her body collapsing inward, resting her hands on her knees to keep herself upright. He sees her swallow, take a deep breath, and then open her eyes again. But she doesn't look up. She turns away from the mutilated corpse of her dead nanny and faces Deakin.

"I don't believe that," Cara manages, her voice shaking. "I've spent every day with you for the past three years. You're my partner, Noah. My best friend."

"Shut up!" Deakin shouts at her. The corners of his mouth are turned down. He looks as though he's about to cry. "Please. You need to leave."

"I won't leave Griffin," Cara says. "And I won't leave you, Noah."

"You have to, you have to," Deakin repeats over and over again. "Please."

And then there's a loud bang. It echoes around them, making Griffin's ears ring.

He hears screaming. He sees gray smoke rise in the darkness, curling slowly from the black muzzle in Deakin's hand.

He feels the strength ebb out of his body. He sees Jess's eyes on him, terrified, as he drops to his knees. His legs crumple. He falls onto his back into the mud.

He notices the pain. But it's different from before—to the unrelenting throbbing of his spine, to the uncompromising rage when he was beaten. He feels it in slow motion. He is calm. Accepting.

In the darkness, in the wet, Griffin lies back, watching silvery raindrops fall against the black sky.

And he thinks, This is it.

I'm dying.

CHAPTER

81

CARA HEARS HERSELF screaming, but it feels as though the sound is coming from someone else. She runs to Griffin's side and drops to her knees.

"Cara."

She looks up into Deakin's eyes. He's crying now, but the gun is still in his hand, pointing at Griffin.

"Leave, now, or I'll shoot him in the head."

"Why are you doing this?" Cara pleads. "Please, Noah. Please. Give me the gun."

She holds her hand out to him, but her whole body feels weak. Hold it together, she tells herself, for just a little longer. Backup will be here soon. Don't look at Lauren. Don't think about what he's done. Just for a bit longer.

"I can't," he sobs. "It needs to be complete. But please. You can't stay here. Or it'll be you too. You'll be one of them."

He looks up and Cara's hand flies to her mouth. She realizes what he's saying. Stay and he'll kill her. Stay and he'll do to her what he did to Lauren. But she still can't believe him. He can't be this person. Not Noah. She loves him. He's family. He wouldn't hurt her. Surely.

She looks at her brother. His eyes are closed. She can't tell if he's dead or alive, and she feels sick.

Slowly she pushes herself up from the mud. He raises the gun and points it at her. Her blood runs cold.

"Leave," he says. His voice sounds desperate. He's pleading with her.

"No."

"This has to end. These serial killers, these men, they're the best at what they did." He pauses, wiping his face with the back of his arm. "And I've beaten them all. All my life, I've been told I was nothing. That nobody loved me, that I would achieve nothing."

"I love you, Noah," Cara whispers.

"You don't!" he shouts through his tears. Cara can see his whole body is shaking. "You love Roo and your kids and Griffin. You don't love me—not like that. I have to do this. I have to. This has to end tonight." Noah's words catch in a sob; snot, rain, tears, sweat, running down his face. "Leave. Please," he begs.

"Noah . . ." Suddenly it's all too much. She's crying, her vision blurred. She knows if armed response arrives before she gets the gun from him, they'll shoot him. He'll die. She holds her hand out again. Cara can barely see through her tears. "Please," she sobs.

He raises the gun to her head, and tenses his finger against the trigger.

"No, Cara, no . . ." he whispers.

She's next to him now. The gun is against her skull; if it goes off there'll be nothing anyone will be able to do. But she doesn't look at it, and slowly she reaches out her hands and touches him on the shoulder.

She looks him right in the eyes, and she sees him. Her Noah.

"You're my best friend, Noah. I love you," she repeats. His face crumples, the gun drops, and she knows then that it's over.

She hears sirens in the distance, the armed response vehicles finally here.

He's crying harder, and she reaches forward without thinking, pulling him into her arms. It's her natural response, but as she stands, hugging her partner, her gaze drifts up to Lauren. At her unblinking eyes. She thinks about the pain she must have gone through. Excruciating, unbearable agony.

And she looks at her brother and Jess. Jess has dragged herself over to where Griffin lies, silent, his eyes closed. Jess is cradling his head in her arms, talking to him, telling him to hold on, keeping him alive.

Cara feels the repulsion, the anger. She realizes what she's doing and lets go, Deakin sinking to the ground, still sobbing. She takes a step back, as armed police barrel into the clearing. They hesitate, staring at the scene, horror contorting their faces.

She looks at Noah. He's making no effort to move, his face a mess of tears and rain and mud. She can see he's given up. He's crying, repeating the same words, but she's not listening anymore.

"Him," she says. "It was him."

Men in black with huge guns surround Deakin, wrenching his arms hard behind his back, pulling him to his feet.

"My kids . . ." she says to one of the officers. She can't bring herself to finish the sentence. "My husband . . ."

"They're fine," the policeman replies. "Being taken to the hospital now. More paramedics are just behind us."

She expects to feel relief, but it never comes. She's completely numb, and dimly acknowledges she must be in shock. She thinks of the dead women, the butchered men. The rapes, the torture. Of Libby, of Mia, of Lauren.

Her legs give way and she slumps to her knees in the mud. She looks back at Noah. He's still howling the same words as he's being taken away, his voice desperate, almost lost in the noise of the police and the wind and the rain.

But she can hear what he's saying.

"I'm sorry," he says over and over again. "I'm sorry, I'm sorry, I'm sorry."

82

Day 10, Two Days Later
Wednesday

ALICE LIES NEXT to Jess on the hospital bed, her small body gently resting against her mother's. She chatters unself-consciously, telling her about school, about what she's been doing at Grandma and Grandad's, and Jess smiles indulgently at her daughter. She's quieter than usual, grieving for the loss of her father now that Jess has told her, but for the most part she's oblivious to everything that's happened. The serial killer. The detective who murdered all those people. One day, when Alice is older, Jess will tell her the truth, but for now, Alice remains innocent to the events of the past ten days. To exactly how her father died.

Jess watches the IV slowly dripping next to her. Her leg is tightly bound in a heavy cast. She's been into surgery, gunshot sewn up, bones reset, under strict instructions not to move. Her hand's bandaged. They've done what they can, the doctors say, but she might not regain movement in some of her fingers where the knife severed the tendons. Still, she thinks, that's not bad. She's not in pain, after all.

Jess's mom and dad sit next to the bed, listening, glad to have their daughter back. Her whole family is here. She should be happy. But the only person she can think about is Griffin.

In the woods, in the dark and the rain, she'd lain at Griffin's side. She'd listened to the sirens in the distance, praying they'd arrive in time, watching as the pain on his face drained away. She'd whispered his name over and over, hoping he could hear her.

There had been voices, shouting. People had run toward them and she'd watched, desperately, as they'd tried to save Griffin. He'd come for her, and now he was dying. She'd watched as they took him away, ignoring the paramedic trying to splint her shattered leg. In the ambulance, she'd asked again and again, "Is he alive?" Until a doctor finally came to her side.

"Jess," he'd said. His face was serious, and she'd started to cry. "Nate lost a lot of blood, his heart stopped, and we had to perform CPR. But he's okay, Jess."

"He's okay?" she'd repeated.

The doctor nodded and smiled. "He's okay."

And he's here, somewhere. She knows he's awake. She desperately wants to see him, but she's not sure what to say.

What now, for her and Griffin? She doesn't know what he feels about her. But she knows she loves him. That's the one thing she knows for sure.

She hears a knock, and they all look up. DCI Elliott is standing in the doorway.

"Can I come in?" she asks, and Jess nods.

Jess looks at her family. "Can you give us a minute?" she asks, and they leave Jess and Elliott alone.

The DCI sits in a seat next to the bed. "I'm glad you're okay, Jess."

"I'm just glad your family is too, Detective."

"Cara, please," she says, with a smile. "I hear you're moving away?"

It was her mother's suggestion. The press buzzed around them like flies. They knew a headline when they saw one: the beautiful widow who couldn't feel pain.

"Let's get a fresh start," her mother had said. "Move away where nobody knows us. Alice deserves that, at least."

And Jess had agreed. Alice needs a life without the whispers.

"Is that okay?" Jess asks Cara, and she nods.

"We've dropped all charges against you. We know it wasn't you who killed Patrick. I'm just so sorry."

"Sorry?"

The detective's face is downcast, and Jess wonders if she's going to cry. "Sorry this all happened to you. Sorry we didn't see it. It was one of our own. We should have—"

"You weren't to know," Jess says. Then she asks the question she hardly dares to articulate. "What about Nav?"

"He's confessed to attempted murder. But given the threat against you and Alice, we know he was acting under duress."

"Will he go to prison?"

Cara nods. "It's likely, yes. But we'll do what we can, Jess, I promise."

Jess swallows hard. Everything about this hospital reminds her of Nav. Every tall dark doctor, every male voice in the corridor. He'll never practice medicine again. That guilt sticks with her more than anything else. Everything he worked for, gone in a second. Because of her.

"And Griffin's going to speak for him at the sentencing hearing, Jess," Cara continues. "That will help." Cara stops. She looks at Jess. "Have you been to see Nate?" she asks. Jess shakes her head. "He's been asking about you."

"I will," Jess mutters.

"Listen," Cara says, her face serious. "I know my little brother. I know he's difficult and grumpy and a pain in the ass. But underneath, it's because he thinks he's not worth it." She pauses. "But you and I both know he is, don't we?" she finishes quietly.

Jess nods again, not trusting herself to speak.

Cara pats her on the hand. "Get some rest. But go and see him, please? Burrell Ward, room six."

The detective leaves Jess alone. In the empty room, Jess starts to cry. All her life, all she'd ever felt was damaged goods. Broken, not good enough.

Griffin understood. He understood because he felt the same. He acted like a bad guy, all fists and scowls. But he wasn't. He'd loved his wife, he loved Cara, his niece and nephew. Perhaps he loved her too.

She wipes her tears away with her sleeve and sits up. She feels her stitches strain slightly; she feels the grate of the bones against each other in the cast. She should wait, ask for a wheelchair, but she knows if she hesitates, she'll back out.

She pulls the drip out from the IV in her hand, then heaves herself up, reaching for her dressing gown and the pair of crutches, left for the time when she'd be allowed to use them. But she's an old pro, and soon she's skidding along the corridor at speed, checking signs, looking for directions to his ward.

Her bare feet are cold on the tiled floor; she gets looks from nurses as she passes, but they let her go.

At last she sees the right signs and pauses. The door to the room is open, and she can see Griffin, propped up in the bed. His eyes are closed, and for a moment she watches him.

He seems all wrong, this brave, fearless man under a pale blue blanket, monitors beeping at his side.

She thinks about her plans to leave, but she can't.
He opens his eyes and turns to the doorway. He sees her and smiles.
I can't leave you, she thinks.
"Hi," he says, and she goes into the room.
Tell me to stay, she thinks, and I will.

83

"YOU LOOK LIKE shit," she says.

"So do you." But Griffin can't stop himself from smiling. She's wearing blue and white striped pajamas, one leg bunched over the top of a white cast, a navy dressing gown over the top. She's the one person—the only person—he's been desperate to see.

She sits down next to the bed.

"How are you feeling?" she asks.

"Everything hurts. I need a cigarette, but they won't let me."

"You should give up. Those things will kill you, you know."

He laughs, then flinches at the pain it causes. "Perhaps. How are you?"

She shrugs. "I'll mend."

"Jess," he says. "That night when I went out, I . . ." He stops. But he has to tell her. "I went to buy drugs. Illegally. To get something to help with the pain. I'm sorry. I shouldn't have left you—"

Jess interrupts him. "I know. It doesn't matter now. How did it go with Cara?" she asks.

"Hmm," is all he can say in reply.

When he woke, his sister was by his bedside. He'd been sedated, groggy, and at first it had taken him a while to remember. But then he had. Lauren, dead and hung from the tree. Noah Deakin, the gun in his hand. His sister's partner. The person Cara had spent practically every fucking minute with, the person who he'd often quietly wondered about, whether there was more to their relationship than just being colleagues. He had been the killer. His wife's killer.

Cara had looked up at him with red-rimmed eyes. "Oh, Nate," she'd said, then started to cry. "I didn't know, I didn't know . . ."

He'd reached across and placed one weak, shaking hand on her shoulder. "I didn't realize either," he'd said, articulating the shame and humiliation he'd felt when he'd seen Noah in the woods. He hadn't liked Deakin. But a serial killer? He hadn't had a clue.

"Do you blame me?" Cara hadn't needed to say any more. He knew what she was asking: *"Is it my fault Mia's dead?"*

"No," he'd replied.

But after she'd left, and he was alone, with only the beeping of the monitors to distract him, he'd realized he'd been lying. Yes. Yes, he did blame her. She was a detective. The senior investigating officer. A DCI. She should have known. In the same way that the guilt and failure had sat with him since Mia's death, he now shared it with Cara.

But she was his sister. Pretty much the only family he had. He would have to forgive her, he knows that. But not today.

He and Jess sit in silence for a little while. There's so much he wants to say to her, but, like with Cara, he doesn't know where to start.

Then, "I'm leaving," Jess blurts out. "I mean, we're moving away. Mom and Dad think it would be best. For Alice."

"Oh." He pauses. "And what do you think?"

"They're probably right."

"Oh," he says again. Griffin's taken aback. He thought . . . he doesn't know what he thought. That they would be together? Where? In his shitty basement apartment? It's ridiculous. She has her life back now. Her daughter, her family. She needs to organize a funeral for her husband, to grieve properly.

This past week at his apartment hasn't been real. She was stuck there, stuck with him. No more than that. It was inevitable that when this was all over that she would leave.

Griffin looks at her face, that beautiful face, and takes her in for what he knows will be the last time.

"Nate . . ." she starts, and he meets her gaze. Some part of him allows himself to be hopeful.

"Thank you," she says.

He clears his throat. "Any time," he replies gruffly.

It's okay. It's okay, he tells himself. He hasn't got time for this, anyway. Cara says they'll let him back to work when he's better. And he knows that being a detective always takes over. It was something Mia complained about. Police first, her second. Except it wasn't, was it? He never told her how much she really meant to him. Perhaps he should . . .

But Jess is standing up now. She hesitates for a moment, then awkwardly leans over, kissing him gently on the cheek. He reaches up, pushing his hand in her hair and they kiss, properly this time.

But then she pulls away. She turns, without another word, and swings her way out of his hospital room, her crutches clicking on the floor. He hears her sniff; he thinks she might be crying.

He wants to go after her, but he can't. He's stuck here: pain and tubes and wires keeping him captive in the bed.

"Jess," he calls after her.

He waits, watching the door. In the corridor he hears people talking, the buzz of a busy hospital.

But his doorway stays empty. He swallows.

She's gone.

He shakes his head. She wasn't here to stay, he reminds himself. They never are.

He leans back on his pillow and stares up at the ceiling. Clenches his jaw shut, pushing away the empty feeling in the pit of his stomach. There's a squeaking of shoes in the corridor, the efficient bustle as a nurse comes into his room.

She busies herself at his side, checking monitors, making notes, then turns to face him.

"How are you feeling?" she asks.

He doesn't look at her. Shit. Lonely. Discarded.

"Okay," he replies.

The nurse holds out her hand. "That woman, your friend, she asked me to give you this."

Griffin looks up sharply. "Who? When?"

"Just now in the corridor."

She reaches out and places something on the bed. He picks it up: barely a scrap of paper, folded in four. He opens it. Three letters, scrawled in black scratchy ballpoint.

IOU.

"She said you'd know what it means," the nurse finishes.

Griffin carefully folds it back into its small square, holds it tightly in the palm of his hand, and smiles.

84

CARA STOPS IN the hospital corridor. Her body can't go any further, and she leans against the wall, putting her head in her hands. She's spent two days holding it together for everyone else—the team back at the station, the kids, Roo, Griffin—but now there's nothing left.

Her mind flickers constantly, unable to settle on one emotion before moving to another. The guilt, the feeling of absolute betrayal, the full-on scalding rage. She doesn't sleep. He haunts her dreams, waking her with a jolt, sheets soaked with sweat, heart racing.

Tilly and Joshua are okay. They woke up in the hospital, groggy and confused, with no memory of what happened. Roo has a headache that will keep him grumpy for days, but physically he'll be fine. It's the mental side that Cara worries about.

They've spent the last few days circling each other at home. Wary, defensive cats, silently defending their territory with their claws out. And the argument, when it came yesterday, was spectacular.

She was dressed and ready for work. He was in tracksuit bottoms and a T-shirt, signed off sick, looking after the kids.

"You can't possibly be going in?" he snapped.

"I have to—"

"Why? So you can see him? That sick bastard? He doesn't deserve to live—"

"Don't, Roo . . ."

"He should be hung and quartered, same as he did to . . ." Cara noticed he couldn't bring himself to say her name. "Tortured and left to rot—"

"Roo, stop, please . . ."

"Jail's too good for him," he spat. "That perverted, fucked-up—"

"Roo! Stop!" Her husband broke off in shock as her mug had hit the tiled floor, smashing into tiny pieces around them. She stood, her hands balled into fists, coffee drips soaking into her trousers. "Shut up!" she shouted. "I need to finish this. I need to see this through."

"Your family is here. Your kids—the children that *you* put at risk—need you!"

It was a low blow, and she felt the guilt tighten in her stomach. "Fucking great you remember that now, Roo. Your family wasn't quite so important to you when you were banging the nanny."

The room hushed. Cara turned and left, out of the house and away from her husband. He'd told her about the women on Tinder. Random, unknown fucks. No more than him looking for a bit of excitement.

But she still hasn't asked him about Lauren. Was it a casual affair? Was it love? Would he have left Cara? The questions that will remain unanswered forever.

Cara had escorted Lauren's poor parents to the mortuary that morning. She had watched them cry over the battered remains of their daughter, face so badly beaten it was impossible to formally identify her that way. They hadn't asked about the details, and Cara hopes they never will.

No parent needs to know that their daughter was attacked so aggressively that her jaw was broken and her cheekbones destroyed. She had a fractured skull, massive internal bleeding. Raped repeatedly, sodomized, extensive damage to her vagina and anus. Cara knows she was alive when she was tortured: her ribs broken, body disemboweled, hung from a tree, suffocating slowly, lungs outside her body. All in the name of some sick fantasy.

She'll forgive Roo. She knows that. She has to. He's not a killer. A shitty, philandering husband, yes, but not a serial killer.

The kids need stability now. And so does she. More than anything she yearns for familiarity, for reassurance that the whole world hasn't changed, despite the feeling that she's standing on the top of a precipice and that at any second she'll get blown from the top.

Despite now knowing that her best friend was a serial killer.

Cara still can't reconcile what she saw with the man she's spent practically every day with for the past three years. Every time she tries to think about it, her mind spits it back. She wants to believe he didn't do it; her brain drifts in and out of denial. Not Deakin. Not Noah.

Cara feels like she's suffocating every time she thinks about him. He's been checked by doctors, now handcuffed in a cell in her own police station, but she can't go and see him. Her failure is absolute; she's a fool. She hadn't seen a single sign.

Marsh had been kind, the press less so. "Nobody realized," Marsh had muttered, but she knows the whispers. She was the detective chief inspector. The SIO. He'd been *her* partner.

They'd raided his house. Reports came back: it was filthy, dirty crockery filling the sink, mold, mud, who knows what else. She'd looked at the photos in disbelief; with shock she'd realized it had been over a year since she'd been there. She'd dropped him off and picked him up practically every day, but she hadn't been inside. She'd been too busy. With her own worries. Her family. Too selfish.

But even with all their searching, they didn't find any ammunition, no guns. No souvenirs of the kills, no knives—and no evidence of a pit where the dead woman had been kept. No sign of blood: even the dogs had been in. He must have another property, they said. Like apartment 214. They'd find it.

They'd searched the lodge. Found evidence of someone having lived there for the past few months. They'd found Deakin's fingerprints and DNA, unsurprising since he'd been there multiple times before. Sometimes with her and the family. Sometimes by himself, wanting a getaway for the weekend, she'd assumed with a woman in tow. Now Cara wonders what else happened there. How much pain and torture happened within those four walls.

She'll never go back, she knows. They'll sell it. Or burn the fucking place to the ground. She doesn't care.

She walks out of the hospital, back to her car. She sits in the driver's seat, but she can't bring herself to start the engine. It's worse at the police station. At every turn she subconsciously looks for him. She listens for his voice. She finds herself still wanting to ask his opinion, talk to him, feel his dark eyes watching her. She always believed they had a connection. She'd thought that maybe even it was more than that. But everything he had been doing invalidates what was between them. What was an act, and what was true? And what had he really been thinking about all these years?

She's still been going to work, despite Roo's disapproval. She has a team to run, a case to put to bed. But she's not sure how much longer she can do it. Every time she enters the police station now, she feels the doubt grow. An uncertainty, a fear: that once again she'll miss the obvious.

Cara knows her brother blames her. And he's right to, she thinks. She rakes her mind, remembering her conversations with Noah. The man that she once thought understood her better than anyone else. She scours her memory for a moment, an inkling of the killer she might have missed. But there's nothing.

I'll take some time off, she resolves. Get some counselling, see a professional. Poor guy, she thinks, and lets out a sudden inappropriate hysterical snort. She pities the therapist that has to listen to her woes.

Her phone rings and she jumps. On autopilot, she answers it.

"DCI Elliott? It's Professor Barnet."

It takes her a few seconds to place the name. The expert on ciphers, the man that had the code.

"Are you there? It's just—we've solved it."

His voice is breathless and eager. He hasn't seen the news. Someone's forgotten to update him. But she doesn't know what to say. In the space, he carries on.

"So, we did as we said. We had a look at the duplicated letters, at the words we thought he might use. We had a few wrong starts." He chuckles. "But we hit the lottery when we started looking at your names."

His levity grates. Cara wants to tell him to go away, but her curiosity overshadows her anger. It's not his fault, after all. "What do you mean?" she asks eventually.

"We looked at the double *L* and double *T* in your name, and the double *F* in DS Griffin's. And they both appear. This led us to identify the words "fuck" and "kill", and from there we could solve the whole cipher."

He pauses, obviously waiting for a round of applause that Cara isn't going to give. "Shall I email the solution across?" he adds, more subdued in the face of Cara's silence.

"Read it to me."

She hears him take a deep breath. "Um," he hesitates. "There's a lot of bad language."

Cara grits her teeth. "I won't be offended."

The professor clears his throat. "Fuck you, Elliott. Fuck you, Griffin," he reads. "You think you know me. With your profiles and your reports. But you don't know shit. I know you." He pauses. Swallows. Continues: "You're just like the other bitches. I will beat you. I will kill you. I will cut you until there's nowhere for Andrew's dick to go when he fucks you. Fuck you, Elliott. Fuck you, Griffin."

The professor stops.

"And that's it?" Cara asks.

"Um, yes." It sounds like Barnet very much regrets having solved the cipher. She feels bad for him; he's not from this world. The poor man shouldn't have been exposed to such evil.

"Thank you, Professor," she says. "I appreciate it."

She hangs up, then sees a ping as he emails it through. She reads it again. She frowns. There's something wrong about the words, she thinks, but then she shakes her head. This whole thing is wrong. Everything is so fucked-up right now, she doubts she'll ever be able to recognize right again.

She needs to go and see him. To look Noah in the eye and listen to him confess. But she's terrified. She can't predict how she'll react when faced with the man she thought she knew. Will she cry? Scream, shout? Or maybe it'll be the thing that'll tip her over the edge into an abyss she'll never leave.

Cara looks down and sees two items left in the cup holders between the seats. A pack of cigarettes and a tube of Polos. She picks up the mints, and it's as if someone has reached inside her body, taken the very core of her, and mashed it on the ground. She knows who he is, what he did, but she loved him. And she misses him. She misses her friend.

She puts both hands on the steering wheel, her body crumpling, her head resting on her arms, and she cries. With relief, with exhaustion, with pure abject misery. The mints fall out of her grasp and roll under the seat.

But it's over.

The case is closed.

The Echo Man has been found.

EPILOGUE

Day 11
Thursday

D EAKIN GLARES ACROSS the table. He's tired, hungry. Cold. Locked in that cell for days. Just waiting until they were ready.

And now it's time. He's been in the interview room for hours. Talking. In front of him, Cara's face is gray. He doesn't know why she's here. Any other detective in the nick could have taken his statement, could have listened to him go through the murders methodically, one by one. Detailing the kidnappings, the gunshots, the stabbings. Describing how he chose his victims, how he killed them, blow by horrifying blow. And yet, here she is.

He hasn't got a lawyer. He doesn't want one. What's the point? He'll plead guilty. He'll be put away for life, no chance of parole. And then it'll all be over.

Cara pauses. She looks at the pages in the file in front of her, then at DC Shenton sitting to her side.

"Noah," she says softly. Her hands grip the edge of the table, her knuckles white. "I can't imagine what you went through as a child. I know you grew up in a children's home. I hear what you're saying, about what you did, but something still doesn't add up."

He stares at her. "What the fuck are you talking about, Cara? I did it. I killed those people."

"That's just it." She sits up in her seat. "You call me Cara. You always have, even on your first day. None of this 'detective chief inspector' bullshit. And yet, in the cipher, you call me Elliott. You call my husband Andrew. You've never called him by his real name your whole life."

"So fucking what—" he starts, but she interrupts him.

"We have your biologicals on file, Noah. Your handwriting doesn't match the Echo Man notebooks. Nor do your fingerprints or DNA. And we found another contributor in the lodge. The same one." She leans forward. "So whose are they?"

He doesn't answer.

"Whose?" she says again.

"I did it," he repeats. "All of it."

"Out in the woods," she continues, "you said you were sorry." She meets his gaze, then glances across to Shenton. "And I've done a bit of reading about serial killers too. And one thing I saw over and over again is it's very unusual for a sexual sadist to express remorse."

"Perhaps I was sorry I'd been caught," he growls.

She bites her lip. He's seen her do it so many times before, trying to stop herself from crying. "Please," she says softly. "I know you. You were my friend. I can help you. There are people that can help you."

She's still looking at him. He loves her eyes. Light brown, serious. He's always liked the way she looks at him, and even today he can see an edge of empathy hovering behind the pain. But this isn't the deal. He has to stick to the deal.

"You don't know me, *DCI Elliott*," he says. "We were never friends. You and your husband played happy families in front of me. Showing off what you had when you knew I had nothing." He sees her face fall. She tries to hide it, but he knows his comments have hit home. "You pretend the actions of the Echo Man were subhuman, that we could never comprehend doing it ourselves, when inside we all know. We know who we'd like to kill. We know who we'd murder and who we'd save."

Cara turns away from him. She's remembering the conversation in their car. Back at the university. He knows how dark detectives can get.

"You were as cruel to me, Cara, as any one of those people in that children's home. I've always been alone. And there you were—parading your family in my face. You made me suffer, just as they had. You like to pretend we were friends, but you mean nothing to me. You never have."

He watches as her face crumples, and she runs from the interview room. He takes a deep breath, then turns to DC Shenton.

Toby frowns. "Interview concluded at fifteen forty-seven," he says, and switches off the video.

But he stays in front of him. He drums his fingers on the table and sighs.

"This isn't how it was supposed to go, Noah," Shenton says.

Noah scowls. "Fuck off," he mutters.

Shenton shakes his head. "She doesn't believe you. She can't accept that her beloved Noah Deakin is a sadistic serial killer. What are we going to do about that?"

Noah glares at him across the table. "I've confessed. I've done everything you asked. I kept quiet while you had your fun. I even did the first kill, Robbie."

Shenton's face goes red. "Don't call me that! Nobody calls me that anymore!" He stands up, screaming at Noah, breathing heavily, his eyes bulging. "And you didn't! You couldn't even rape the bitch. Plus you fucked up so badly you left a fingerprint behind, and I had to cover your back, finish the job." Slowly, he lowers himself down into his seat, once again a picture of restraint. "You never had the taste for this, Noah," he continues. "You're weak, pathetic. You're nothing. And yet here you are, taking all the credit. Taking all *my* glory."

"So fucking confess. You were there, in the woods. You could have walked out at any time, to revel in your *success*." Noah points to the doorway, angry. "Go on, you sadistic fuck. You tell her what happened."

Shenton shakes his head. "No, no," he says calmly, back to his usual facade. He has a small smile on his face. "That's not how it's going to go at all."

They met twenty years ago. Unlikely cohorts, bonded together out of necessity in that shitty children's home. Where they both met Jessica Ambrose. And then Noah left, and he thought he'd never see Shenton again. Until Toby showed up in the police force.

And everything went wrong.

Deakin had an aptitude for undercover work. A natural ability to blend in, to be whoever they wanted him to be. He lied with ease. He didn't make friends; he didn't fall in love. He knew he wasn't worthy of the life other people had.

He was an outsider. He drank; he took all the pharmaceuticals that came his way. He worked alongside some of the worst drug kingpins in the country: he fought, he was beaten, stabbed. But still, despite his best efforts, he survived.

And then he tried to kill himself.

Shenton stopped him. He must have followed him into the woods; he cut him down from the tree, gasping for air.

"I'm nothing," Noah wheezed, the rope falling away from his neck. "I'll always be nothing."

Toby had looked at him. "You're my friend, Noah," he'd said. "I'll look after you." And with those few words, Deakin was under his spell.

He was fascinated by the way Toby put on a show when he was at work, timid and pathetic.

"I spent nine years learning how to be weak," Shenton would say. "It's not hard to do it again."

At night, they would drive around in Shenton's car, following women, watching them through brightened windows, oblivious as they went about their lives. He was in awe of Shenton. They'd hang out together, sometimes at Noah's, sometimes at Shenton's old squalid family house, sometimes at the lodge. Toby would bring hookers, fuck them first, then pass them to Noah, ordering him what to do. While he masturbated, while he watched. Toby enjoyed exerting his will over those around him, screwing with their heads. He'd done it then, just as he had with the Echo Man murders: Mia's earring at the fire to mess with Griffin, Libby's prints on the pint glass at apartment 214.

Toby was in control, in charge. Always. Noah reveled in his attention; for the first time someone took an interest in his life. Noah would do anything he asked. Disagreement resulted in punches to his gut, black eyes. And once, when Noah had dared to refuse a prostitute, Toby pushed him to his knees in front of him. Show me you're sorry, you sulky bitch, he'd said, unzipping his fly. Apologize or I'll kill her, right here.

He'd known Toby was serious. And he'd done as he was told.

Noah took new biological samples for Toby, swapping his record on the system for an unknown. He'd complied without question, even though Noah knew Shenton had something specific in mind.

Watching those women in their homes, Toby had been excited, jittering in the passenger seat, but Noah had never asked, until one day Toby pointed to a young woman, walking home from college.

"That's her," he said. "That's your first."

Noah had looked at Toby with disbelief. "I'm not a virgin," he'd said. "You know that," and Toby had laughed at his naivety.

"First kill, you prick," he'd replied.

They'd waited until the right opportunity, then pulled the struggling girl into the car. Shenton had smiled as he'd beaten her into submission, tying her up quickly, then driving out of town. They'd stopped the car in the middle of nowhere, and Noah had watched, pressed backward against the door of the car, bile rising in his throat, as

Shenton had stripped her naked, then raped her, his white ass thrusting hard into her delicate body. Toby had no hesitation in the face of the girl's screams. No conscience. Just the same insane grin, the aroused flush of his cheeks. Blood on his hands, across his face.

And after he'd finished, he'd turned away from the woman's battered body, and he'd said to Noah: "Your turn."

Noah could only shake his head, and Toby's lip had curled. Then he'd reached over and slapped Noah hard across the face. "Don't disappoint me, you little bitch. At least kill the dirty cunt."

So he had. His face stinging, fearing Toby's rejection, he'd strangled her, pulling the ligature tight until the girl had turned blue and motionless. Then he'd thrown up in the footwell of the car.

Toby hadn't taken him with him again.

Deakin had moved to the Major Crimes team. He'd tried to get away. But Noah had known the murders were still going on. He felt the guilt. He couldn't bear their pain. He felt sick, all the time. He couldn't sleep, and when he did, the nightmares came.

And he met Cara.

She was everything. She was his boss, but more than that: his friend, the person he trusted. He was welcomed into her home, and for the first time in his life he had a family. He could almost forget about Shenton. Until one night he showed up at his house.

"Come with me," Toby said. The gun in his hand shone in the moonlight, and there was something in his voice Noah didn't dare disagree with.

They drove to a house and pulled up outside. It was way past midnight; the roads were quiet. The two of them crept around to a side window, Shenton forcing it open, and they climbed into a bathroom.

"Wait here," Shenton whispered, then pulled a ski mask down over his face.

And then he heard the screams. A male voice: shouting, angry. A woman, pleading and frantic. He put his hands over his ears, trying to block it out, to no avail. Half of him wanted to leave; the other half knew he should intervene. Stop Shenton, do anything. Something. He was a cop, for Christ's sake. *Police.* But the old fear from that first kill rooted him to the spot. He didn't want to see what Shenton was doing.

After what seemed to be hours, the bathroom door opened and Noah jumped. Shenton stood there, calmly eating a sandwich. In the other hand he held a cheap plastic Polaroid camera.

"I have a present for you," he said, as casually as if they were out for a drink at a pub. He put the sandwich in his mouth and took another bite. He chewed, watching Noah, enjoying making him wait. He swallowed. "Come with me."

The house was now quiet; Noah's heart thudded in his chest as they walked down the hallway, through an open door, into the lounge.

The lighting was dim. The television was on, muted, a towel thrown over the screen so only a dull glow lit the room. And it was a mess. Furniture had been tipped over, paper strewn around, shards of glass from a broken cabinet scattered across the floor. Pieces of something brown littered the carpet and Deakin numbly picked one up, rolling it around in his hand. Bark.

In the center of it all, a woman lay on her front, half naked, hands tied behind her, hair spilling over her face.

"I'm not . . ." Noah started, but the words came out thin and weak. Shenton just put a finger to his lips, telling him to be quiet.

He led Noah away from the woman, toward the bedroom. Then he opened the door, pointing at the man on the floor.

He was bound, breathing heavily through his nose, a gag on his mouth, blindfold on his eyes. The man heard the door opening and turned, as much as he could, struggling uselessly against the cord.

Noah inhaled sharply, and Shenton pulled him away.

"What have you done?" Noah hissed, outside the room. "That's Nate Griffin. Are you crazy?"

He frantically looked back at the closed door, then to the woman on the floor in the living room. "Is that . . . is that Mia?"

"Was," Shenton said with a brief chuckle.

"You're insane," Noah managed to say, before he felt the pain in his stomach. He doubled over, winded in response to the blow, looking up in shock. Shenton's demeanor had completely changed. His face was contorted in anger, hands in fists by his side.

"You think I haven't noticed?" Shenton jeered. "Your little crush on our very own DCI Elliott? I've watched you follow her around, moon after her like a lovesick puppy. It makes me sick, the way they treat you."

Noah had taken in a deep gasp of air, his eyes still watering from the punch.

"I hear them laughing behind your back, Elliott and Griffin. Calling you pathetic, saying how worthless you are to the team." Noah shook his head, silent. "Believe me, Noah. They think you're nothing. Nothing!" Shenton carried on talking, poisoning his mind. The same words he'd heard all his life: Insignificant. Nothing. Useless. Waste of space. Forgotten. And he felt the anger build. Tensing his muscles, blood rushing in his ears. Useless, pointless rage.

Until Shenton put the piece of wood into his hand and pushed him back into the room. And he funneled thirty-six years of helplessness and fury and loneliness into Nate Griffin, feeling the warm blood hit his face, hearing the bones break until eventually the man lay unconscious on the floor, and Noah couldn't stop sobbing, the log fallen from his hands.

He heard Shenton come into the room behind him. Noah watched him prod Griffin's lifeless body apathetically with his foot.

"She'll never love you now," Shenton said with a theatrical sigh, and Noah felt the dread, the horror of what he'd done. Toby was right. Any hope he'd had with Cara? It was gone.

He'd known, at that instant, his life was over. And he hated Toby Shenton.

*   *   *

Shenton taps his fingers on the table in the interview room. Deakin glares; he can barely stand to be in the same room with him.

"I've confessed," Noah hisses. "That was the deal."

"And it's a good confession too. Believable—that all a worthless prick like you wants is to be known for creating something brilliant. But we didn't finish, did we? It was my day." Noah can see the rage growing behind his eyes, the telltale signs of Shenton losing his normal restraint. "My mother left me when I was three," he spits. "The first of February 1990." He jabs at Deakin with each word, his long slim finger in Noah's face. "She left me with those bastards," Shenton continues, his face red. "And this should have been my masterpiece, Noah. To celebrate that bitch. One girl! One? I wanted more, that other one, hanging up there with her."

Deakin's always guessed at some strange motivation behind Shenton's plan. His specificity with the date. "You're such a cliché," he growls. "Blaming your fucked-up mind on your absent mother. At least own it. At least accept responsibility for what you've done. You enjoy it, you bastard. That's why you torture. That's why you rape."

Shenton scoffs at his words, his lip curling with disgust. "Nobody's born evil, Noah. You should know that. It took my influence to get you to kill. Me who persuaded you to fuck Jessica Ambrose in the restroom." Shenton smiles, regaining control. "You may have got a fuck out of her, but I wanted my turn." His face flushes with excitement at the thought. "I bet she would have been good too. I bet she'd have fought."

Noah remembers the hollow feeling in his stomach, propositioning that woman at the school gates, surrounded by all those kids. "I didn't want to screw her," he mutters in reply.

"But you did, Noah. You did." He reaches forward, gently tapping Deakin's cheek with the palm of his hand, condescendingly. "And consensual sex has never been my thing. We needed leverage, something to mess with her and her lovely doctor friend. Not that the threat of a nasty violent death wasn't enough." He laughs. "And besides, I needed the time to prepare. Busy night ahead. A house to set on fire, people to kill." He says this coolly, and Noah remembers the heads cut off at the Kemper scene and then the murdered woman, the baby in her tummy.

He'd done as Shenton asked: leaving his car in Cranbourne Woods on that Monday night, then walking the ten miles home. Hating himself for it, but fearing the consequences if he refused. The same on Friday, absent as Cara discovered apartment 214 with Griffin.

"I wanted to see how long she'd live," Shenton continues, his voice steadier now. "Stretch out the kill, really have some fun. See how much I could chop apart before she died. And then Elliott finds us." Toby lets out a disappointed sigh. "You lost your nerve, you dickless fuck. It could have been brilliant."

Shenton leans forward so his face is barely inches away from Noah's. Deakin can smell the sour odor of stale coffee. "She doesn't believe you."

"So? What can I do about that?" Deakin snarls.

Toby smiles, a leer of triumph. "Finish the job you started," he carries on, softly. "Kill yourself."

The words hang in the room, septic and rotten.

"They'll end it then," Shenton continues. "They'll wrap up the case. With a confession and a dead killer, they won't look for anyone else."

But Noah's not the same man he was back then. The past few years have taken their toll, but he's ready for prison. Even though he's a cop, it's going to be a fucking holiday camp compared to this. He's met Shenton. There's nobody worse behind bars.

Shenton sees Noah's reluctance and sits back in his seat, crossing his arms over his chest. "I meant what I said all those months ago. Or do you think I won't?"

Noah feels the blood rush from his face. The one bargaining chip Shenton had, used as he felt his grip on Noah weakening.

Cara.

"I'll kill her."

"Leave her alone."

Deakin feels sick. He remembers the sight of that girl hanging in the woods, how he could barely keep up the charade when he realized what Shenton had done. And when Cara had turned up? He knew what Toby would do. He knew he'd kill her.

Noah would do anything to protect her.

Shenton smiles. "It's almost touching, your love for that slut." He laughs. "You've confessed to over thirty murders, just so I won't touch a hair on her pretty little head. But what makes you think I'll uphold my end of the bargain? Especially if she still thinks you're innocent." He stops, his eyes are narrowed, staring at Noah.

"You're just a sick fucker, aren't you?" Deakin snarls.

Shenton laughs. "I guess so. But can you blame me? Not everyone has the idyllic missing dad, drug-overdosed mom that you enjoyed, Noah. I had a father and an uncle, sure, but once they'd finished using me as their own personal plaything, they'd beat the shit out of me and laugh as I cried. Is it any wonder I get my fun in a different way?" He sees Noah's glare, and his face mirrors his disgust. "Don't pretend you're any different, Deakin."

"I am," he growls. "I could never have done what you did to Lauren. I couldn't rape Mia. Or those other women."

"But you beat the shit out of Griffin! I saw you, Noah! I saw you as you hit him again and again with that bit of wood. You can't tell me you didn't enjoy that—not one little, tiny bit?"

Noah shakes his head, staring at the desk. He knows what he did was wrong. But what he'd done—killing that girl, beating Griffin—was nothing in comparison to what Shenton had done. He can't let Toby go free. He can't.

"You know what I'm capable of, Noah. You know what I'd do to Cara. You kill yourself, and the case is closed. You get your ending. I get mine."

Deakin feels the panic build, his heart starting to beat faster. He feels the walls close in.

"I even know how I'd do it." Shenton sits back in his chair. He nonchalantly picks at his nails. "Twenty-five Cromwell Street ring any bells?"

Noah's head snaps up.

"Do you know what Fred West did to Lynda Gough, *Deaks*?" Shenton sneers.

"Shut up," Noah whispers.

"He tied her up. Suspended her from wooden holes drilled in the ceiling of his cellar."

"Shut up, Shenton—"

"Almost entirely wrapped her jaw in tape to stop her from screaming—"

"Shut up." Noah closes his eyes, puts his hands over his ears. He can't help but imagine Cara. He sees her eyes, her body, her blood.

Shenton leans forward, pushing his face next to Noah's. "Cut off her fingers and toes while she was still alive. Raped her, beat her, strangled her . . ."

"Shut up shut up shut up," Noah shouts, angrily pushing Shenton away.

Toby laughs. "And I know what you're thinking," he says.

Noah glares at him. "What?"

"That you could tell your beloved Cara all about me. That she'll arrest me, and then everything'll be fine. But that won't work, Noah." He pauses, leaning back in his chair. "You know how easily I make *friends*. And there will be no shortage of new ones in prison." He idly taps his fingers on the table. "Maybe I won't stop at Cara. Maybe I'll get one of my new mates to have a go at those lovely children of hers. Not my kink, but some men get a real thrill from fucking the kids."

Noah feels sick. He knows Shenton's right. He can feel the chill as sweat slowly trickles down his spine.

"How?" Noah says quietly.

"Hang yourself with your bed sheets like Shipman; piss someone off and get stabbed like Dahmer. Pick one. I don't care, Noah. But do it. And do it fast. I'll be watching." Shenton stands up. "I own you, you pathetic piece of shit. Don't ever forget it."

Shenton leaves, closing the door behind him.

Noah's whole body starts to shake. His stomach rolls and he vomits on the floor of the interview room.

He knows how dangerous Shenton is. He saw the tortured woman, electrocuted in the bottom of the pit. Lauren, hanging from that tree. He saw Libby dead. He listened as Toby raped Mia, crying out for anyone to help her. And he did nothing.

But he won't let it happen to Cara.

Shenton was right; the power belongs to him. Ever since that day in the forest, ever since the first kill. His life was in Shenton's hands. His fate is clear.

He stands up, banging on the door of the interview room. Again and again, until his fists are raw.

"Get me out of here," he shouts. "Take me back to my cell. Take me back now."

He starts to cry, slumping down in the corner of the interview room, knees up to his chest, fists bunched, arms covering his face. Shenton comes back into the room, Cara hesitant behind him.

Shenton looks down, then crouches to his side.

"Don't worry," DC Toby Shenton says with a smile. He puts his hand on Noah's shoulder and squeezes it, tightly. "It'll be over soon, Deakin. It'll be over soon."

ACKNOWLEDGMENTS

THIS BOOK IS dedicated to Ed Wilson—agent, second to none. Ed believed in this concept from the off, encouraging me to write more—and write darker. Whether this is a dedication or attribution of blame, I don't know, but without him it wouldn't be the book it is today. Thank you also to Hélène Butler and the rest of the team at Johnson and Alcock, and to Genevieve Lowles for her early work on the manuscript.

A massive thank-you to my editor, Kathryn Cheshire at Harper-Collins UK, for taking on this insane book and loving Griffin, Deakin, and Elliott as much as I do. Thank you to Charlotte Webb for her eagle-eyed copyediting, and to the rest of the HarperCollins team.

Thank you to everyone at Crooked Lane books for taking the Echo Man across the Atlantic. It is impossibly exciting to be published in the US.

As always, thank you to Dr. Matt Evans. His commitment to ensuring I kill people in the "right" way is always spot on, and he had his work cut out with this one.

Thank you to PC Dan Roberts, my favorite copper and the person singularly responsible for my escalating bad language; impossibly patient in the face of my endless questions.

To real-life blood spatter CSI Stephanie Fox, thank you.

To the other brilliant experts—Charlie Roberts, Laura Stevenson, Susan Scarr, Meenal Gandhi, Jas Sohal, AR, GC, Sue B, Dr. SB, and KG—thank you. All mistakes, deliberate or otherwise, are mine and mine alone.

Names have been stolen from the incomparable Charlotte Griffin, Tom Deakin, Anne Roberts, and Toby Spanton. Given the nature of the book, and the unspeakable acts and final resting places of some of your namesakes, thank you for agreeing to my theft.

Last but not least, to Chris and Ben, thank you from the bottom of my heart.